PENGUIN BOOKS

The Hidden Truth

Hilary Boyd was a nurse, marriage counsellor and ran a small cancer charity before becoming an author. She has written ten books, including *Thursdays in the Park*, her debut novel, which sold over half a million copies and was an international bestseller.

The Hidden Truth

HILARY BOYD

PENGUIN BOOKS

PENGUIN BOOKS

UK | USA | Canada | Ireland | Australia
India | New Zealand | South Africa

Penguin Books is part of the Penguin Random House group of companies
whose addresses can be found at global.penguinrandomhouse.com.

First published in Penguin Books 2022
002

Set in 12.5/14.75pt Garamond MT Std
Typeset by Jouve (UK), Milton Keynes
Printed and bound in Great Britain by Clays Ltd, Elcograf S.p.A.

The authorized representative in the EEA is Penguin Random House Ireland,
Morrison Chambers, 32 Nassau Street, Dublin DO2 YH68

A CIP catalogue record for this book is available from the British Library

ISBN: 978–1–405–94392–5

www.greenpenguin.co.uk

Penguin Random House is committed to a
sustainable future for our business, our readers
and our planet. This book is made from Forest
Stewardship Council® certified paper.

Remembering Jack, my father, with love.

He wasn't around for most of my life, but that wasn't his fault.

'Nobody's perfect'

Spoken by Osgood Fielding III, in *Some Like It Hot*
(directed by Billy Wilder, 1959)

I

Sara sat on the bed, slowly pressing out a message on her phone, then deleting it, trying again: *Sorry, won't be able to make it tonight. Had a problem last minute.* Finally, she decided the text would do, but had no idea how best to sign off. Not a kiss, certainly. Not love. 'Best wishes'? 'Best'? She didn't want to upset him, but she didn't owe him anything, either. Just as she made the decision to leave nothing except her name, her mobile sprang to life.

She jumped and took a deep breath as she clicked on the call, heard Peggy, her younger daughter, say, 'Hi, Mum. You busy?'

'Umm, sort of. I was supposed to be going out in five minutes . . . on this bloody *date*.' She gave theatrical emphasis to the last word, and heard a sharp intake of breath.

'Wow! Is this the radiologist guy? Oh, my God, Mum, that's so exciting.' Then there was a pause. 'Wait, what do you mean *was*? He hasn't dumped out, has he?'

'No. But I was about to.' Sara heard Peggy give a small sigh and became immediately defensive. 'I'm just not sure I can face some random man across the table when he's no doubt expecting me to *flirt*. Not sure I know how to any more.' Which was the understatement of the decade. She not only didn't know how to flirt, the whole idea of kissing some strange male mouth filled her with horror. She had needed this shove from her two daughters to get this far.

That it would soon be six years since Pete died seemed impossible. The first two had been a fog of numbness, overlaid by the supreme effort just to survive day to day. During the next four she had felt a gradually increasing acceptance and, along with the mist of sadness that never seemed quite to disperse, the burgeoning reality that there were still pleasures to be had out in the world. But romance was in a different category: an entirely alien concept.

Her eye caught the photograph on the chest of drawers: Pete, larger than life, blond, laughing and handsome in a T-shirt and shorts, his arms around Joni and Peggy – then about fourteen and eleven respectively – squinting in the sunshine at the top of a hiking trail in the Alps. Her husband's smile did not appear reproachful. Far from it. 'Why not, Sara?' he seemed to be asking.

'Why not?' was his favourite question whenever Sara expressed doubt about a situation. He'd held all the confidence for them both.

'It's just a drink, Mum,' Peggy was urging gently. 'How bad can it be? If he's gross, do a runner. At your age you can be honest, can't you?'

Sara winced at the use of her most hated phrase, 'at your age' – she didn't consider herself old, yet, at fifty-eight – but held her peace. 'Perhaps not too honest.' She wavered. Maybe she *should* go.

'What's his name?' her daughter was asking.

'Colin.'

'Seriously? *Colin?*'

'What's wrong with that?'

Peggy began to giggle. 'Nothing, Mum, sorry. It's just Lizzie at school had a gerbil called Colin.'

'Look, do you want me to go on this date or not?' she said briskly, but was unable to stem her own laughter. She felt a little mad right now.

'I do! I do!' Peggy insisted, clearly trying to bring herself under control. 'So, what are you wearing?'

'The blue dress with the white piping. The one I wore for Granny's birthday . . . Do you think it's too smart?' Sara's wardrobe was not extensive. She had work clothes and a few summer dresses, the rest mostly jeans. She thought jeans might look as if she didn't care . . . which she didn't, really, but still.

'No, it's perfect. You look gorgeous in it. Knock 'em dead, Mum!'

Encouraged by her daughter's enthusiasm, Sara straightened her shoulders. 'Don't say that, I just might,' she joked. 'He's admitting to sixty-three, so he's probably ninety with a gammy leg and no teeth.' She heard a snort of laughter from her daughter. 'The photo's probably of his grandson! I'll blame you, obviously, if the whole thing's a disaster.'

Peggy had been the driving force in getting her mum onto an online dating site, backed up by Joni – who was a safe three thousand miles away in California and out of range of their mother's stubborn resistance. In recent years Sara had shut down her daughters' conversation about finding another partner more than once. But she knew, as she approached her sixties, that she would be cutting off her nose to spite her face if she continued hiding behind widowhood indefinitely, thereby narrowing her chances of having a companion in old age. Although she consistently failed to summon the image of sitting across the breakfast table from a man who wasn't Pete.

Her daughter's voice was suddenly serious. 'Don't go if you aren't comfortable, Mum. Me and Joni only suggested the whole thing because we were worried you might be lonely.'

I'm not lonely, Sara wanted to insist. She knew, though, that wasn't really the truth. Her own mother, Gail – a single parent after her father had left when Sara was barely two – had been dead for over twenty years now, and she had no siblings. She worked hard, she had her daughters and some good friends, as well as Pete's mum, Margaret, whom she saw most weekends. There was, though, a barely acknowledged emptiness in her life, she was well aware.

'I'm being a wimp,' she said, making the decision. 'As you say, it's just a drink.'

'Where are you meeting?'

'Pelham Arms. His choice. I hope he got there early and nabbed a table in the courtyard. It's been roasting here today.'

Sara said goodbye to her daughter and gave herself a final check in the long mirror on the cupboard door. Her light brown hair, thick and layered to just below her ears, was freshly washed. She'd also put on a smidgen of makeup: a bit of gold-brown eyeshadow Joni had given her for Christmas a few years ago – seldom used – and a lick of mascara. She'd been told her large, wide-set hazel eyes, along with her soft smile, were her best features. Pete had always called her 'beautiful', but she knew she wasn't. At a push she might agree to 'nice-looking'.

Now she settled her delicate gold chain necklace with the patterned disc – her initials SRT, for Sara Ruby Tempest, engraved on the back, a gift from Pete for her fortieth – and

4

pulled the brush one last time through her already tidy hair. 'Onwards,' she muttered to herself, as she grabbed her bag from the hall table and stepped out of the terrace house directly onto the pavement.

It was still warm and very muggy, although it was nearly seven on the June evening – the sort of weather that makes your skin feel sticky, even fresh from the shower. Sara took the short walk slowly up Lewes high street, not just because of the heat: she was aware that she was literally dragging her heels. Pathologically unable to be late for anything, she still did not want to be the first to arrive.

As she walked, she heard the beep-beep of an incoming text. *He's cancelling*, she thought, her heart lifting.

In the garden, Colin it said.

She smiled. *Good start.*

The evening light was buttery and soft, the sun still a couple of hours from setting, but the tea-lights had already been lit on the outside tables packed onto the deck, creating what might have been deemed a romantic atmosphere. Sara looked around for a single man. There was only one, the other tables full of chattering couples and groups. Grey head bent to his phone, Colin-the-radiologist sat by the wicker fence, facing her as she stepped out of the open pub door. She studied him for a moment. He was exactly as his photo suggested: slim, metal-rimmed glasses perched on a neat nose, hair trimmed short. He looked up and saw her, smiled uncertainly. *All his teeth*, she muttered silently, smiling back.

As Sara sat nursing the glass of white wine Colin had ordered for her and felt the familiar shyness she always experienced with men she didn't know, she reminded herself how used she was to meeting people – albeit mostly women – and setting them at their ease in her work as a nutritionist. Clients came through her door nervous and in need of help, and her first task was to make them feel at home. This was different, obviously, but didn't the same techniques apply? She could see Colin was anxious, his pale eyes blinking behind his glasses as he asked her a few stilted – no doubt rehearsed – conversation openers. For a while they groaned about the heat and the parking in Lewes – which was impossible and always roused strong feelings.

'You said you live in Brighton?' Sara asked, after a while and a good many topics that had died a death for want of a robust response. *Like pulling teeth*, she thought tiredly. There was a strangled quality to Colin's speech, as if he wanted to talk but the words were bunched in his throat.

'I've got a flat in Preston Park.'

'That's a great area,' she said, although she barely knew it.

He nodded, twisting his mouth as if agreeing with her pained him. He seemed to be struggling with something dark that was at odds with his mild exterior.

'Have you been dating long?' he asked into the silence.

She smiled and shook her head. 'First time. I nearly cancelled.'

To her relief, Colin's face cleared and he laughed. 'So glad you didn't. I've been at it for a couple of months now and it's really depressing when someone doesn't show up.'

The silence that followed was more relaxed, at least.

She began again. 'So, you're a radiologist. That must be interesting work.' In her head she heard Peggy giggle at her awkward efforts and had to suppress a smile. 'Just talk about *them*, Mum,' had been her exhortation.

Colin was nodding. 'It's been a good career. Stressful at times but, yes, I love it.' He stopped abruptly. Sara waited for him to go on, but when he did, his tone had changed. 'I really thought I had life sorted, Sara. A beautiful family, two wonderful kids . . .' She saw him swallowing hard, thought he might be about to cry, and held her breath. 'Then last year, Lyddie, my wife of thirty years, just upped and left me.'

Sara looked suitably horrified, although Colin wasn't looking at her, just staring fixedly into the depths of his Pinot.

'Ran off with our neighbour, Barry. The barbecue king. Every summer Saturday he worked his magic with those burgers. *Seven years* he was at it with my wife.'

Although she winced at his obvious hurt, she couldn't help feeling a strong desire to laugh at the image Colin conjured up. 'I'm so sorry,' she managed, straight-faced.

Colin's eyes – still not focusing on her – seemed to spark up. 'He had this heavy meat-press thing,' he said, 'which made these perfectly round, flat burgers.' He mimed with his two hands. 'We'd have a beer as he cooked, gas away while the girls did the salads indoors. It was a great ritual. One I really looked forward to.' A yearning sigh escaped him.

It was clear Colin was stuck so firmly in his past that even if she had found him attractive – which she certainly did not – there would have been no manoeuvring round Barry and his burger press.

On and on Colin went, detailing every ounce of the

hurt he'd endured, a litany of betrayals that was painful to hear. 'And listen to this . . .' he kept repeating, before announcing some other outrage.

For a while longer, Sara did try to listen. But as soon as she saw a gap in the diatribe, she took her chance. 'Umm, sorry, Colin. I've got an early work thing tomorrow,' she said. 'I probably should be getting home.'

Startled out of his monologue, he nodded glumly. 'I've done it again, haven't I? Sorry. Can't seem to help myself.'

Unable to refute this with any honesty, she said, 'Maybe it's too soon for you to be thinking of dating. You still seem very raw about what happened.'

He stared blankly at her for a second. 'Barry was *my* friend, you see,' he said softly. 'It's him I miss, as much as Lyddie.'

By the time she closed her front door, turned the double lock and pressed home the bolt, she was depressed and exhausted. Colin's emails had shown none of this maudlin self-pity. In fact, he'd been quite a good correspondent – intelligent and responsive – which was why she'd agreed to meet up. *How the hell am I supposed to avoid more wasted evenings like this one?* she wondered, as she trudged dispiritedly up to bed.

'Morning.' Precious Adebayo, the acupuncturist who shared treatment rooms with Sara, popped her head round the door early the following morning. She was also Sara's best friend – they'd met at Surrey University during an integrated medicine course twenty years ago and fallen into step as if they'd known each other all their lives. Precious had been a huge comfort in the weeks and months after Pete died. Now, her face broke into a mischievous grin. 'Well?'

Sara sighed. 'I'm now an expert on burger presses and how to bonk your neighbour's wife.'

Precious sucked air through her teeth. 'Ouch.'

'The dastardly Barry is worthy of comic-book status.'

Her friend laughed. She was still in the doorway, already dressed in the white tunic she wore for treatments, her hair smoothed back and glistening in a neat bun. 'Listen, I've got someone in a second. Tell me more at lunch.'

'Nothing more to tell. Nothing interesting, at least. On to the next.'

But as Sara waited for her eight o'clock, she wondered if she would try again. *What are the chances of clicking with someone, like I did with Pete?* It just didn't seem remotely possible – even given Colin was only her first try.

A small involuntary sigh escaped her as she remembered the summer after college when she and her friend Nem had been paddling their kayak down the Fal river in Cornwall. Rounding a bend, they found Pete in the water, hanging on to his two-man canoe convulsed with laughter, his friend Vic wobbling perilously in his wetsuit on the rocky, wooded bank, nursing a bleeding hand. They didn't need help, but the girls stopped anyway and offered. Sara thought they were a couple of prats, but Vic insisted they meet up down-river at Turnaware Bar where their friends were waiting with copious supplies of Beck's. Nem declared she had the hots for any man in a wetsuit – so they did. By sundown, Pete had convinced Sara that he wasn't an idiot, just not yet very accomplished in a boat.

That won't happen again, she told herself now. *We were*

young, our lives so uncomplicated. Last night had served to remind her that people 'of her age' came with a whole heap of baggage. She certainly did. *How can I not compare another man with Pete and find him wanting?* The thought of kissing Colin was preposterous. And Pete was conveniently lost in the mists of nostalgia now. She'd forgotten his faults, if he ever had any. Plus she would have to deal with all the problems that came with another person's romantic involvement. *It's probably too much hassle*, she thought, as she heard the ping of the bell and rose to greet her client.

When Peggy rang later to find out how the date had gone, Sara could tell that, although her daughter was sympathetic, she was avoiding being too much so, in case it gave Sara the wriggle room to quit.

2

Heather Crocker, tidy in loose tunic and slacks, opened the door to the garden flat in the thirties block where Sara's mother-in-law lived, just behind the station. As usual, she had a cheerful smile on her round face. Calm and very kind, she'd been Margaret's live-in housekeeper/carer for more than three years now and was the best thing that had ever happened to Margaret *and* Sara. Sara gave her a hug.

'How is she?'

'Good timing,' Heather said, ushering Sara inside. 'She's just getting bored.'

They laughed. Margaret was a force to be reckoned with. With her tiny frame and pretty, birdlike quality, it seemed as if even a small shove could break her in two. But she was as tough as old boots at ninety-one. If it weren't for severe, crippling arthritis and a weak heart, she'd still be hurrying up and down the town's hills, chatting to everyone and taking people to task for dropped litter, unruly dogs or cluttering the narrow pavements with café chairs.

But today Sara was nervous. She hadn't mentioned, the last time she'd visited, that she'd joined a dating app, or that she was going on her first date because, she told herself, she wasn't even sure she would. As her mother-in-law got older and weaker, she seemed to want to reminisce more and more about her only and beloved son. *Will she think I'm betraying Pete?* she wondered now, as Heather set some slices of Madeira cake on the coffee-table, alongside a pot of tea. *Do I feel as if I am?*

When they were both settled and Sara had admired the roses poking round the open French windows to the little patio garden, then commented on the warmth of the afternoon, she took a deep breath. 'I thought I ought to tell you . . .' she hesitated, not knowing the best way to put it '. . . I've started dating. I've even been on an actual date.' Margaret looked confused for a second, so Sara blundered on. 'The girls insisted I join an online site and the other night I met this man for a drink.' She watched the old lady's face, normally so inquisitive, and saw, with horror, tears in her eyes.

Margaret being Margaret, she quickly blinked them away, taking a strategic bite of her cake before replying softly, without looking at Sara, 'Was he nice?'

'No, he was grim . . . I've upset you, Margaret, I'm so sorry.'

Her mother-in-law shook her head. 'I'm being silly. I knew you'd meet someone else one day, a lovely girl like you. But, well, it doesn't seem so long since you and Pete and the girls were sitting round the table in the old house eating my roast chicken and apple crumble.'

Sara bit her lip. She didn't want to remind her it was nearly six years, knowing that time was slipping in Margaret's world, these days. 'To be honest, I can't even imagine being with someone else. But I suppose I'm also scared of staying on my own for the rest of my life.'

Margaret nodded. 'I must have been about your age

when dear Arthur shuffled off. And I'd say I've had a pretty good life since . . . all things considered.' She didn't have to mention the trauma of losing her only son. 'I'm sure it would be nice for you to find someone.' She paused. 'Although I've discovered, over the years, that you don't necessarily need a man to be content.'

Sara knew she was right. 'I'm probably thinking of a companion sort of person. Someone I could do things with, like holidays and stuff . . . not love like I had with Pete.'

She noticed a twinkle forming in her mother-in-law's eye. 'Probably a few frogs out there, dear. Be careful who you kiss.'

Sara laughed. 'If the other night was anything to go by, there certainly won't be any of that sort of thing going on,' she said primly.

Margaret seemed suddenly to be miles away. 'It's a strange thing, love. I knew the instant I set eyes on Arthur. He was showing off with his mates, down on the beach at Saltdean, racing around with a ball like a silly fool. He wasn't looking where he was going and he crashed into me and my friend Moira, nearly knocked me over . . .' She laughed almost girlishly. 'He actually did knock me over, in the other sense, of course.'

'I thought Pete was a bit of an idiot when I first saw him, too.'

Margaret smiled. 'But you know, don't you? Part of you always knows.'

Sara nodded, although the thought made her sad. Could she ever 'know' again?

'I never thought to find someone else, after Arthur

died. But then our generation didn't so much, not like they do today.' She gave a slight frown. 'Just make sure you don't fall for a wrong 'un, dear. Older women are very easily flattered, in my experience.'

Sara was pretty sure her radar wasn't functioning properly, or even at all, when it came to romantic engagement. 'If there ever is anyone, Margaret, I'll bring him round so you can give him the once-over.' They laughed, but Sara was finding it almost impossible to imagine the encounter.

Gareth-the-engineer gazed at her across the table, a flirtatious smile playing around his mouth. He was an attractive man in a robust, confident way – broad-shouldered and tall, with a pink monogrammed shirt, his short brown hair peppered with grey, amusement in his brown eyes. Right from the start he'd made it clear he found her attractive. It was more than two weeks since the challenging evening with Colin, during which time Sara had made no effort to meet up with anyone else on the dating site. It was only because Gareth had been persistent, saying he was off to Denmark for three weeks on a project and he'd love to get together before he left, that Sara had reluctantly agreed to the date.

They were at Bill's this time, another short walk from her house, but indoors, as it was raining hard. The restaurant was crowded and lively. Gareth had ordered a bottle of Italian white, some olives and a bowl of spicy tortillas with avocado and red pepper dips. When the wooden table wobbled alarmingly, he was quickly on his knees with a folded napkin, sorting it out.

Could I kiss him? Sara wondered, as the bottle emptied

and she experienced a pleasant loosening of the usually tight grip she kept on herself. He was good company, an easy conversationalist on a wide range of subjects. She was surprised to find the answer was 'maybe' – and that she was enjoying herself.

'What's an attractive woman like you doing on your own?' Gareth was asking.

She winced theatrically. 'Seriously?'

He threw his head back and laughed loudly. 'I've got lots more where that came from . . . But I make no apologies. The sentiment is real.'

The look he gave her made Sara blush and bend her head to her glass.

'I've been on this lark a while now,' he went on. 'You can take it really seriously, or you can have a bit of fun. I know there's a lot of bullshit about the horrors of online dating but meeting a pretty woman for a drink is never a chore, not in my book.'

'Depends on the woman, no?'

He grinned and tapped his nose. 'Ah, but I'm a careful picker.' He waved the empty bottle in the air, his eyes searching around for the waitress. 'Another one?'

Sara was about to shake her head: she'd had way too much already. But she didn't want the evening to end quite yet.

'And an order of the triple chocolate brownie for pud, I think.' He pulled a face. 'Not something you approve of, as a nutritionist, I imagine.'

'Actually, I love them,' she said – and it was Peggy's favourite dessert.

*

15

By the time they stepped out into the wet night it was past eleven and Sara's head was swimming. Gareth took her arm. 'You live nearby, you say? I'll see you to your door.'

'No, I'm fine,' she insisted, pointing to the opposite side of the road and down the hill. 'It's right there, the one with the red front door.'

He steered her across the road, nevertheless, and along the pavement to her house. Sara fumbled with her keys, managing, somehow, to insert the right one in the lock and open the door. She turned to Gareth. 'That was lovely. Thank you.'

He raised his eyebrows. 'Aren't you going to invite me in?'

She stared at him, surprised. 'Umm, better not. It's a work day tomorrow . . . and you've got a plane to catch.'

But before she knew what was happening, Gareth had his arms around her. His bulk crushed her as he pushed her towards the open doorway, his mouth pressing first to her neck, then, swiftly up to her cheek, her lips – which his thick tongue attempted to prise open. Struggling to free herself, twisting her face away and pushing hard on his chest with her hands, she heard him groan. 'Stop, Gareth, please . . . *Let me go.*'

She felt his arms drop and he stepped away. In the glow from the street-lamp she could see he looked befuddled and knew he was way more drunk than she'd realized.

'I thought . . .' he said, frowning at her. 'Get the wrong message, did I?'

She wasn't sure if he was angry, but she didn't wait to find out. 'Sorry,' she said, and stepped quickly into her house, shutting the door firmly behind her. A shudder shot through her as she stood in the dark hallway. The combination of more wine than she'd consumed in months, the heavy, sugary brownie and Gareth's sudden assault produced a wave of nausea that made her almost retch. She ran to the downstairs loo and turned on the cold tap, splashing her mouth, gulping water from her cupped palm until she'd got rid of the taste of him. The mirror showed her face pale with shock.

Did I ask for that? she wondered, as she leant tiredly against the sink. *Did I lead him on?* She knew she'd flirted mildly in response to his more vigorous attempts, but no more than that. Certainly, she felt she'd neither said nor done anything that would give him the idea she might ask him into her home. *That's it*, she told herself, as she climbed the stairs to her bedroom. *I'm never going on another date, ever again.*

'I don't think he meant any harm,' Sara told Precious, over an early cup of green tea in Sara's consulting room the following morning. 'He was pretty drunk . . . I suppose he thought I was up for it.'

Her friend frowned. 'You say he lunged, Sas. Didn't ask. Not good enough to use booze as an excuse.'

Sara shrugged. 'Maybe not. I'm just such a bloody novice, I don't have a clue about the etiquette these days. I reckoned *at our age* . . . but perhaps he thought I led him on . . .'

Precious held up her hand. 'Stop right there. Having a drink with a man you've just met does not give him the right to expect anything but a polite thank-you, unless you give your *explicit* consent.'

'Yeah, I know.' Precious was reassuringly militant about

women's rights. 'But it's never as black and white in the moment, is it?' She cringed at the memory. 'Anyway, that's it. I'm not getting back on the horse. If it means I spend the rest of my life alone, then so be it.'

Her friend laughed at her melodramatic pique. 'Come on, girl, you can't give up yet. You've only just started.'

'All very well for you to say, with gorgeous Sammi waiting at home.' Precious, who was younger than Sara by ten years – now in her late forties – had been living with her Spanish partner for almost fifteen years. He was a successful businessman who imported foodstuffs such as olive oil and sardines from Spain. They had no children, by mutual agreement.

'I know I'm lucky. And I sympathize, I really do . . .' She started to say something else, stopped and took a sip of tea.

'What?'

'Look, I know you're fine, Sas,' she said gently. 'You jog along with your life, you've got your lovely girls, your work, but . . . perhaps you're missing out on something more?'

Sara felt tears welling. Precious was right, of course, but, stubbornly, she knew what agreeing with her friend would mean: *more dates*. Much easier to just 'jog along', as Precious put it. Stay in her narrow comfort zone where she and Pete were still a couple.

'Give it another try,' Precious was saying, 'and if the next one's a creep, we'll have a rethink.' She raised her eyebrows at Sara, waiting for her to reply.

Reluctantly, Sara said, 'But this one will be a single cup of tea in the middle of a sunny afternoon in a crowded café for precisely forty-five minutes. And Sammi can station himself at the next table with a Stetson and a shotgun.' This made them laugh. Precious's partner was slight, mild-mannered and charming. Hardly threatening, even rigged out as an armed vigilante.

Julian Cameron, her first client of the day, was a pale, neatly dressed music teacher in his early sixties, whom Sara had immediately identified as anxious. He was too thin and blinked rapidly with red-rimmed eyes whenever she spoke to him. The vast majority of her clients were women, and she was ashamed to say she preferred it that way. Brought up without a father or any close male relatives, educated in all-girls schools, she was aware of a certain diffidence around men. She never felt quite the same confidence with them that she did around women.

Julian looked twitchy today, crossing and uncrossing his legs and shifting in the padded wooden armchair Sara provided for her clients, fiddling with a hangnail on his right thumb and chewing the inside of his cheek as he waited for her to read through the food diary she'd asked him to keep for the previous three weeks. This was his second appointment.

'I've done what you said,' he began, his tone defensive and slightly arrogant, as if he expected to be challenged. 'I've written down everything that's passed my lips religiously. And I know what it is. I told you last time.'

Sara nodded patiently.

'My stomach swells like a balloon every time I touch anything with wheat. I've always got indigestion and I'm always tired. I'm allergic to wheat. It's coeliac.'

Julian's diet, as seen from his food diary, consisted mainly of scary quantities of black coffee and raw food. Sara was certain his symptoms mainly stemmed from caffeine overload, lack of protein and all the indigestible raw vegetables he was consuming at his age. 'It doesn't look as if you've eaten any wheat at all since I saw you last.'

'Well, no. Why would I?'

'And have you noticed your symptoms improving at all?'

Julian shook his head impatiently. 'Not yet, obviously. I imagine my body has to expel all those wheat toxins before I can feel better.'

'I think, after three weeks, you'd begin to see a slight change, if you did have gluten intolerance.'

'But you'll get me tested, won't you?'

'I will arrange a test – which you can get via your GP – if it'll reassure you. But, since you've been gluten-free for a while, you'll need to eat gluten in more than one meal, every day for six weeks before testing. Otherwise, you risk a false negative.'

'Six weeks? That's ridiculous.' Julian's mouth twitched in outrage. 'So I have to make myself more ill to get a test to make myself less ill?' He blinked angrily. 'I don't believe you.'

Sara took a slow breath. 'If you want to go ahead with the test, we can try some modifications to your diet in other areas while you wait. I really believe you'll see a marked difference.'

'I won't if I have a wheat allergy,' he retorted stubbornly.

Sara, undeterred, began to outline a regime. This client was tricky, but she loved the challenge. Like a detective solving a case, the thrill of finding the culprit – or culprits – in someone's diet and restoring them to good health never palled.

Julian settled down a bit as she talked, but she could sense frustration simmering beneath the surface. As she well knew, clients often came to her as someone they could talk to, with whom they could share their general anxieties as well as their food worries. She tried to make the sessions a dialogue about their lives, not just their eating habits. Food was not just fuel: a whole psychology was attached to how people ate. But Julian didn't want to talk about his life. He seemed fixated on having an actual, definable disease. As she saw her client out, she had a hunch that, despite his polite smiles, he was not happy with her advice. He had agreed reluctantly – as well as reintroducing gluten – to cut down on the caffeine, steam some of the vegetables, eat small amounts of chicken or fish, but she wasn't very confident he would follow her advice.

The session over, her next appointment due to arrive in less than ten minutes, Sara found herself staring into space, her thoughts returning to the previous night. She felt stupid for letting one lunge – which had lasted barely a minute – get to her like this. She'd liked Gareth, enjoyed the evening, after all – even considered she might be willing to kiss him at some future stage. But it was the lack of control that had frightened her. Pinned in his drunken embrace, she'd felt physically helpless and afraid for what she realized was the first time in her life. *If I'd asked him in . . . If he'd forced his way through the door . . .*

She mentally shook herself and, after a few brief jottings in Julian's file, clicked on the details of her nine o'clock. *Stop being such a drama queen*, she told herself. But by opening the door to the possibility of another relationship, she knew she was making herself vulnerable on a number of fronts. Not just to a tiresome evening or to frightening, inappropriate behaviour, but also, potentially, to the effort involved in forming another attachment . . . even to heartbreak. Maybe she was too old for this caper. Maybe it was just too difficult, unlocking her heart to someone new. *There's nothing wrong with my life*, she insisted silently, as she updated herself on her next client – a woman who'd had her gall bladder removed the previous year and was having ongoing digestive problems. *Precious and the girls might want more for me, but I'm fine as I am.*

3

Sara got out of the car in the little tearoom car park at exactly a minute to four-fifteen, two weeks since her date with Gareth. She was wearing jeans and a navy cotton top as she didn't hold out much hope for this encounter. Randall-the-dentist had made one too many jokes in their email exchanges, which Sara, generously, had put down to nervousness, but might be because he was just a bit silly. The tearoom was in a village a few miles east of Lewes. *Her* choice: she'd reckoned that the white and green spotted oilcloths on the tables, the cosy cloth bunting hanging from the beams and large quantities of Victoria sponge would scupper any unnerving ambush Randall might have in mind.

She was only here because Precious wouldn't let her off the hook. They'd almost fallen out over it. Sara, seldom one to lose her temper, let alone sound off, felt as if she were struggling against her own stubbornness as much as her friend's wish to see her find some nebulous happiness in a man's arms. But it was easier to get annoyed with Precious than with herself.

'Don't take it so seriously,' Precious had urged, when Sara showed no sign of responding to any more potential dates. 'Think of it as a chance to meet interesting people, rather than the love of your life. It takes the pressure off.'

'That's sort of what Gareth said, minutes before he pounced.'

Precious's expression became deliberately patient. 'You can't let one idiot hold you back forever, Sas. That's dumb.'

Sara bridled. 'Thanks. Good to know you think I'm "dumb".' She'd risen abruptly, picking up her cup from the desk in a marked manner. But her friend, leaning against the therapy-room wall, arms crossed, just grinned.

'OK, OK, got the message.'

Which left Sara with the problem sitting square in her own lap. She'd gone home that night and steeled herself to open the app and find another connection.

As she walked across the gravel of the car park now, she breathed in the fresh summer air. *It would be lovely to sit outside in the sunshine*, she thought, but the tables on the terrace were empty, the breeze gusty and cool today, up there on the Downs. This was a place she often brought Margaret to when her mother-in-law fancied a day out. It was run by a young couple: Liam baked, Jessie managed, with help from a rotation of waitresses barely out of school.

Sara hovered in the doorway as her eyes adjusted to the dim interior, winding herself up to be bright and forthcoming with the dentist. The low-ceilinged room was crammed, the buzz of chatter and chinking crockery filling the warm, sugar-laden air. She tried to recall the photo Randall had posted – but she'd flicked through so many recently they'd all begun to blur. *Grey hair, bland features, nice smile*, she decided. And he'd be sitting alone. *Shouldn't be hard to find*, she thought nervously, surveying the mostly female clientele.

'Hi, there, Sara,' Jessie greeted her from behind the till. Sara went over to say hello. 'I'm meeting someone,' she said, after they'd caught up, anxious to get this whole thing over with, but suddenly self-conscious, as if she were up to something shady.

She turned back to the room. And noticed *two* grey-haired men. Both alone, neither with tea, the first by the French windows onto the garden at the back, the other near the till. The one by the windows was staring at his mobile. The other was sitting quietly, gazing off into space, hands clasped on the table, where a black notebook and pen lay. Sara hesitated.

The man near the till, perhaps sensing her stare, looked up. *Oh, hello*, Sara thought. *He looks nice – although not like his photo at all.* She smiled. He smiled back. She moved towards him. 'Randall?'

He looked confused. 'Umm, no, sorry . . . wrong guy.'

Sara was instantly embarrassed. 'Sorry . . . I thought . . .' she said, finding herself a little disappointed.

His light-grey eyes creased with amusement.

They eyed each other for another second. Then Sara pulled herself together. 'Sorry,' she said again, turning back to check the table near the window.

'Looks like my date is a no-show,' the man went on. 'If this Randall guy doesn't materialize either, why don't you join me for a cuppa? Saves us both a wasted journey.'

She pulled a face, lowering her voice. 'I think that might be him over there,' she said discreetly swishing her eyes across the room. Randall – for it must be him, although it was hard to tell as she could see only the top of his head – was still absorbed in something on his phone screen.

The man followed her glance and shook his head from side to side in a considering way. 'Seems pretty intent on what he's doing. Maybe he won't notice your absence,' he said. 'Please, have a seat, if you like? You can text to say the cat's sick and you have to take it to the vet.'

Sara grinned. 'I don't have a cat.' But, without thinking, she pulled out the chair opposite and sat down. 'This is so rude,' she whispered, although there was no chance of Randall hearing across the hum of voices. 'What if he recognizes me when he gets up?'

The man pondered this for another couple of seconds. 'He hasn't ordered yet. If that were me, and I got your text about the cat, I'd just curse and walk straight out of the French windows. If you hurry, he won't bother to look for you.'

Feeling like the naughty schoolgirl she'd never been, Sara, her face firmly turned away from where Randall was sitting, rooted about in her bag for her phone. She felt guilty about him, but not guilty enough to have tea with him. Not when this charming man was offering.

Sorry, she typed hastily, *last-minute work thing. Won't be able to make it. Sara.* Unlike her dithering over that first text she'd never sent to Colin-the-radiologist, this time she barely bothered to read it before pressing the 'send' arrow. 'Done,' she said nervously.

He seemed amused as he turned his gaze to the dentist, Sara guiltily burying her head.

'Has he got it?' she asked, when he said nothing.

'Umm, must have . . . Hold on, he's . . . Yes, he's shaking his head . . . Getting up . . . oops, looking around . . .' The man's eyes widened in mock panic. 'No, it's OK, just grabbing his jacket. He's frowning, seems a bit put out . . . but . . .' long pause '. . . off he goes.'

Sara felt a bubble of laughter in her chest. She looked up, gave a quick glance around, then breathed a huge sigh of relief. She turned back to him. 'That was really rubbish behaviour,' she said, suddenly ashamed by how rudely she'd treated someone who was probably a perfectly decent person.

'He might be pissed off momentarily, but it won't be terminal. Look, I've just been dumped by a Ruth and I'm fine.' He stretched out his arms, as if to prove his point.

Sara cocked an eyebrow. 'Maybe she's bonding with Randall in the car park as we speak, relieved she's been saved by some random stranger from having to endure tea with you.'

He grinned, holding out his hand across the table. 'Bernard Lockmore.'

She shook it. 'Sara – without an *h* – Tempest.' As she said it, she had a flash of the first time she'd told her mother about Pete. 'Isn't Pete Tempest such a wonderful name?' she'd said dreamily. Her mother had just laughed and given her a knowing look. Sara had been happy to dump 'Colquhoun' when she married . . . not just because it was impossible for anyone to spell.

She felt a sudden pang of the usual shyness. The joke had carried them through the introductions, but now Randall had been summarily dispatched, she was alone with this complete stranger.

'Shall we order?' he was asking. 'I don't know if you've been here before, but the coffee cake is delicious.'

A pot of tea and two slices of cake sat on the table between them.

'So was Ruth a first date?' Sara asked, as Bernard poured tea for them both.

'No, much worse. We had a drink last week.' He gave a rueful grin. 'This is a humiliating rejection of me personally, not just my online profile.'

'You liked her, then.'

'She was nice enough. But my friend Joe – who's never online-dated in his life, while insisting he's a world expert – says the first date should be considered ground zero and you have to give it one more go.' He shrugged. 'Clearly Ruth didn't get the memo.' Smiling, he added, 'Which, I have to say, seems like a bonus right now.'

Seems like one to me, too, she thought, surprising herself, amazed by how quickly she was starting to feel at ease with a man who, half an hour ago, she'd never set eyes on before. 'Everyone's been on my case about dating,' she said.

Bernard seemed to hesitate before asking the next question. 'Divorced?'

'Widowed. Pete, my husband, died six years ago.'

Sympathy was immediately apparent in his eyes. 'Five years and four months since Ilsa died.'

Sara thought this was oddly precise. Silence fell between them. She didn't know whether it was all right to ask what had happened or wait for him to tell her: she never volunteered details about Pete's death unless required. But Bernard seemed to invite confidences, and although she didn't have one single fact about him, apart from his name and his wife's demise – she knew way more about Randall-the-dentist, whom she'd never even met – she found herself beginning to speak.

'Pete had a cerebral aneurysm,' she said. 'He got this

blinding headache, out of the blue . . . As if he'd been clubbed on the head, was how he described it.' She took a breath. 'Then half an hour later he just fell down right there, in the street, walking home with me from lunch at a friend's house.' She stopped again. It never got any easier, taking herself back to that moment. 'Everything's gone blurred,' was the last thing Pete had said to her as he slumped to the pavement, clutching his head. 'He never regained consciousness . . . died that night.'

Bernard was watching her quietly as she talked. He had a strong, intelligent face, with a slightly crooked nose and dark brows, although his hair was almost white, in a long-ish crewcut. His tanned, weather-beaten skin made his light-grey eyes stand out and implied, as did his lean frame, a fair amount of time outdoors. *By any standards, he's an attractive man*, Sara thought.

'So sudden. That must have been terrible. I can't imagine.'

His eyes were full of compassion. So much so that she felt her own well up. It still surprised her, after all this time, that memories of her husband's death had the power instantly to reduce her to tears.

Sometimes the moment of his death seemed almost more real than the rest of his life. Not saying goodbye to Pete had been the most painful. 'One second he was there, walking along, completely normal. The next he was just gone.' And telling the girls, of course. It had happened in June: Joni just finishing her finals at Loughborough, Peggy away in Indonesia on her gap year. Neither had answered her first call. She would never forget the horrified, stuttering quiet her words evoked when her daughters eventually got through.

A shadow passed over Bernard's face. 'So cruel, that moment when everything changes, when life is never the same again,' he said.

The silence that followed did not feel awkward. Here she was, divulging her innermost feelings and Bernard had absorbed them, made her feel heard. So many people, she'd discovered, shied away from anything more than platitudes when confronted with death. 'I know exactly how you're feeling,' they would say, with all the best intentions. 'My brother died last year.' But nobody knew how she was feeling: it was different for everyone.

He didn't reciprocate with details of Ilsa's death, and Sara didn't ask. The atmosphere had become sombre and she wanted to lighten it. 'Right,' she said. 'You'll have to tell me something about yourself. I've got no online profile to refer to.'

Bernard cleared his throat. 'OK . . . where to start? I'm sixty-two, an architect. I share a practice in Eastbourne with Joe Fane – the friend I mentioned. We do mostly eco-stuff. My twins, Adam and Carrie, are now in their twenties, both off doing their own thing.' He paused. 'What else? Grew up in Broadstairs. Dad was an industrial designer for rehab equipment – splints, supports, that kind of thing. Mum stayed at home. Both long dead. One older brother, who died more recently.' He paused again. 'Oh, and I live up on the cliffs just past Hastings.' He grinned. 'Your turn.'

Still trying to take in the information he'd given her, she stumbled through a similarly brief outline of her daughters and her job, her dead mother. She didn't mention her father or that he had not been in touch – made no attempt whatsoever to communicate with her throughout her childhood – until the day of her mother's funeral, when Sara was thirty-six. That now she had contact with him once a year, for Thanksgiving, at his North Wales bungalow – his third wife, Lois, to whom he'd been married for fifteen years, hailing originally from Kentucky. It was all a source of embarrassment to her and endless fascination to anyone she told. But Bernard either didn't appear to notice the omission or chose not to ask.

'A nutritionist, eh?' He pointed to the remains of the coffee cake with a raised eyebrow, and she laughed, although it was such a tired old joke.

'Not you as well,' she said. 'It's always assumed us nutritionists are prim spoilsports who frown on anyone who doesn't eat kale and spirulina for breakfast, lunch and supper. I *truly believe* good food – a nutritious diet – is one of the principal secrets to a happy life. The difference it makes is *huge* . . . but it doesn't mean you can't enjoy the odd piece of cake.' She heard her voice rising and couldn't help blushing at her zeal in front of this stranger.

Bernard was looking at her appraisingly. 'It's great to feel so passionately about something,' he said.

Still embarrassed, she hurried on: 'I reckon Liam's cakes are good for the soul. It's just people always get self-conscious when I tell them my job. Like smiling at a dentist.' She cringed guiltily at the thought of dentists.

He chuckled. 'Don't worry about old Randall. He'll get over it.' His phone suddenly pinged with a text as he spoke and he picked it up, glancing briefly at the screen. A fleeting look, which Sara interpreted as worry, crossed his face, then he put the phone down, without answering the text, and gave her a smile. 'Sorry,' he said.

Sara had her back to the room, but she saw Bernard glancing over her shoulder. He seemed distracted now, his mood quite changed. 'Think they're closing up . . . We're the last men standing.'

She was surprised – she'd been completely unaware of what was going on around her. Then she remembered she'd deliberately made the appointment with Randall to last, at the most, forty-five minutes.

Outside, they stopped before heading for their cars, parked in opposite corners of the almost empty car park. Hers was a much-loved duck-egg blue Mini, Bernard's an old, stately silver Mercedes. There was a fleeting moment of awkwardness. It seemed to Sara as if his mind were elsewhere now and he was in a hurry to get away. He held out his hand, but barely met her eye. 'That was a pleasure, Sara. Thanks for choosing me.' He imbued his last words with a terrible American accent.

She laughed, although the joke fell a bit flat now the magic between them had ebbed away. 'It was rude, but I'm glad I did.'

Again, there was a self-conscious silence.

'Bye, then,' Bernard said eventually.

Oh, she thought. *Is that it?* 'Bye,' she echoed, and quickly turned away so he wouldn't notice her disappointment.

When Sara was safely on the road again, heading in the opposite direction to her tea companion along the coast, she felt thoroughly despondent. Bernard obviously had no intention of seeing her again. The atmosphere had changed after the text and she wondered who it was from.

Another woman? He'd enjoyed her company, she was pretty sure of that. She sighed. This was obviously how it went. But there had been something about the man. From the first moment she saw him, she'd felt it. *You always know . . .* She remembered Margaret's words but quickly pushed them away. There was no point 'knowing' if the other person didn't.

4

Wow, Bernard thought, as he drove away from the tea-room. *She was like a breath of fresh air.* However unwelcome, he was perversely grateful for the timely text from Adam, reminding him – if, indeed, he needed a reminder – of all that stood in the way of him sailing into the sunset with any woman. Plus, the message itself had worried him. Instead of the usual *Talk soon*, which was pretty much standard for his son's fitful communication these days, Adam had written, *Everything's pretty rubbish, Dad, since you ask x.* He vowed to try to actually talk to his son as soon as he got home – these cryptic texts were hopeless.

As his mind reverted to the tea, he felt bad about not suggesting they meet again. He'd seen the flash of puzzlement as Sara said goodbye – and he couldn't deny how well they'd got on. But real involvement with someone wasn't the plan. Not that he'd known exactly what the plan was when he'd begun dating in the spring – significantly, just after the fifth anniversary of Ilsa's death. Diversion, he supposed. Being alone in the house often felt so suffocating and sad.

So, today faced him with a new problem. The woman he'd just had tea with was different. He'd immediately felt a connection. She seemed gentle, really grounded . . . someone with whom he could relax, laugh, be himself. He shook his head. He hadn't anticipated that. Casual dates were one thing – there'd been a few of those, none lead-ing to anything. Something more serious was out of the question. *When would you tell her?* the voice in his head taunted him. What *would you tell her?*

He sighed now, wondering if this feeling of isolation, of being set apart from the rest of the human race, would ever soften into something he could live with. It seemed to have been made even harder by meeting Sara, however fleetingly. She'd provided a tiny glimpse of something he thought of as normal – although not his normal – and he forced himself to sweep away the afternoon, like so much dust. *I should have left her to the dentist*, he thought resentfully, as he drew up outside his empty, echoing house on the cliff.

Once inside, for a second it was as if he were arriving home from the Eastbourne office and Ilsa was upstairs. He almost called out to her – his wife's presence was so strong in the silent kitchen. He shivered, turning on the lights in an almost reflex action, because sunshine was still pouring through the windows.

At the five-year marker for Ilsa's death in March, he'd gone to the cupboard in his office and reached up for the box pushed to the back of the top shelf, behind packets of printer paper. The rectangular, pale-oak urn was wrapped in a Sainsbury's bag. Taking it out and placing it on his desk, he'd sat and stared at it for a while. He always spoke to her like this on the yearly anniversaries. Told her how much he loved her, missed her . . . how sorry he was.

But that day his mind refused to settle into the groove. None of the usual phrases formed in his head, only flickering images of Ilsa: her flying white-blonde hair, her soft laugh, her light, frightened eyes, which were capable, on the turn of a penny, of switching to solid steel. And instead of the sadness that usually engulfed him, he'd sensed a small renegade spike of rebellion. One that made him instantly glance around, as if the walls could hear.

Nonetheless, he'd found himself whispering to the remains of his wife, 'I love you, Ilsa, always will. But it's five years, now. I need to start again.' It seemed, however, as if she and the house – always more hers than his – had chosen to ignore his plea. Ilsa was still there, in every corner of every room . . . in the very air Bernard breathed.

5

'I liked him,' Sara told Precious, as they sat across from each other at Sara's desk, eating lunch. 'Clearly more than he liked me.' She had the usual salad, brought from home in a Tupperware box, Precious was munching a tuna-mayonnaise sandwich she'd picked up from the deli next door.

'Maybe he has someone else up his sleeve,' Precious suggested, through a mouthful.

'Maybe. He did get a text at the end of tea, which seemed to distract him.'

'Hard to tell what someone's really like after one cuppa, especially with no social context. Have you googled him?'

She had, of course. 'All I found was his architect's practice: Lockmore, Fane, that he shares with Joe Fane, his partner and friend. Didn't find anything else, although I'm not much good at digging.'

'Familiar name, Fane ... Well, if he doesn't come through, perhaps you can resuscitate the dentist.'

Sara pulled a face.

Precious folded the remains of her sandwich into the greaseproof paper and scrunched it up, reaching for her glass of water. 'It's encouraging there are men like Bernard doing online dating, eh?'

'Not if he doesn't want to see me again!'

Precious laughed. 'He stole you off your proper date, for goodness' sake.'

'Obviously I didn't live up to his expectations.'

Her friend got up. 'Nonsense. You have no idea what's going on in his life. You should believe in yourself more, Sas. You're gorgeous.'

She shook her head, brushing aside her friend's compliment. 'It's just disappointing, when you can't imagine even liking any man romantically again . . . and then you sort of can . . . and he isn't interested.'

'More fool him,' Precious commented robustly.

She remembered her mum often exhorting her to 'believe in yourself'. Which she felt she did in most areas these days, except the crucial one of men. Gail, a hard-working pharmacist employed by the same Woking chemist for the whole of Sara's childhood, had seemed happy for Sara to be her only focus. She had led a quiet, enclosed, loving childhood, punctuated only by the occasional visits from and to her dear grandparents in Croydon. Frank, her father, was never mentioned. Gail had airbrushed him from her daughter's life, deflecting any questions with vague, unsatisfactory replies, as if the man wasn't worth the breath she'd need to expend in the telling.

Pete, bless him, was the one who'd slipped under the wire. She'd always felt at ease with him, right from that first evening on the beach at Turnaware Bar. And unquestioningly loved and respected by him.

I did feel comfortable with Bernard, she thought now, in surprise. *Even on such short acquaintance.*

During the days that followed, Sara often thought of the man in the tearoom. But their contact had been too brief for her focus to be sustained. Late morning on Saturday, a fortnight later, she was walking home from the supermarket with the weekend groceries. Peggy, on summer break from the South London primary school where she taught, was coming for the night to pick up some camping equipment, en route to Iceland with her friend Natasha. As Sara walked, she was thinking of what they might do this afternoon. It was a beautiful early August day: cool and sunny. Maybe they could go over to Charleston and walk up on the Downs. Although Peggy would have to pack. *Just lunch in the garden*, she eventually decided.

She shifted her straw shopping basket to the other hand as she approached the house, so she could retrieve her keys from her shoulder bag. A loud bang made her start and look up – only scaffolding coming down across the road. But her eye caught a distinctive figure walking up the hill towards her, on the other side of the narrow high street: *Bernard Lockmore*. His hands thrust into his jacket pockets, he was gazing straight ahead. Her heart thumped. *Shall I say hello?* She hesitated: he seemed deep in thought. But as he drew level, his head turned and for a second his eyes seemed to rest on her. She thought she detected a moment of recognition, but he instantly turned back and – was it her imagination? – quickened his pace.

Surprised and unable to suppress an instant pang of humiliation and hurt, Sara bent her head and hurried the remaining yards to her door. *Did he recognize me?* she wondered, as she dumped the basket on the kitchen worktop. He'd seen her, she was pretty certain. *If I had any illusions, that's really told me*, she thought despondently.

6

'Shit, shit, shit,' Bernard muttered to himself, as he hurried up the street. 'That was her.' He was sure she'd recognized him, but did she realize he'd spotted her, too? He cringed at the thought of snubbing such a decent woman in that way, and for a split second considered running back and apologizing. He resisted, however, until he reached the crown of the hill, when he found himself slowing and looking back. But she'd vanished and he felt a heavy stab of disappointment. *She looked so pretty in that green dress.*

Banging on Joe Fane's door, he continued to think of *Sara without an* h *Tempest* and couldn't help but smile. Then his smile fell. His position hadn't changed.

Joe, a thick-set, dark-haired man of Bernard's age, with an open, mischievous smile, greeted his friend and almost immediately pressed an opened bottle of cold beer into his hand. They wandered out into the small, untidy garden behind his house, where two rickety striped deckchairs wobbled on the weed-strewn, uneven paving.

'I've just seen the woman I had tea with a couple of weeks ago,' Bernard said, relaxing back in the sunshine and taking a mouthful of his drink.

'Oh, yeah. The one you can't see again because you actually like her?'

Bernard winced. 'All very well for you to mock. But just say – and obviously it's not going to happen with this one – but just say I do meet someone in the future I want to be with and who wants to be with me . . .' he sighed and looked Joe in the eye '. . . I'd have to be honest, right? I can't be serious about someone and not tell them the truth. But if I do . . .'

It was Joe's turn to sigh. But his was one of frustration. 'Come on, mate, get a grip. Isn't it time to move on? You can't put your life on hold indefinitely, just because you're worried about how someone will react to your past. You've done the penance.' He nudged Bernard's shoe with his trainer. 'Step one: find the right woman.'

Bernard thought again of Sara and quickly dismissed her. He'd blown that already, by not calling, blanking her in the street. 'Then what?'

'You pick your moment. You'll know when it is. And if she's the right one, she'll understand, won't she?' He shot Bernard an encouraging smile. 'I would . . . I *do*.'

Bernard wanted to believe Joe. But his secret seemed to define him now. Telling someone, however understanding they might be, wouldn't alter that.

'Go on, get in touch with this tearoom damsel, for God's sake, Bernie, and see if you do like her.'

7

Peggy spent most of the afternoon rootling around in the attic, finding all the things she needed for her camping trip. The family had often camped when the girls were younger, and the attic was crammed with moth-eaten sleeping-bags, water bottles, sleeping-mats and backpacks. Without Pete, Sara hadn't had the energy or the inclination for any such trips.

'I'm jealous,' she said lightly, as she watched Peggy – tall, blonde and athletic like her dad – rinsing out a couple of water bottles at the sink. 'I'd love to get away.' She hadn't meant it too seriously, although her life, since she'd had to acknowledge there might be something missing, did seem rather humdrum. Her daughter turned, though, her expression instantly concerned. 'Aren't you going to Spain with Precious and Sammi? You always do.'

'Not this year. They have asked me. It's just so bloody hot there, now. And although they're incredibly kind and include me in everything, my Spanish is terrible, and they talk so fast I only catch the odd thing, or they have to stop to translate, which is even worse.' She laughed. 'Stop looking so worried, Peggy. I'm fine. I've got a few clients during August, anyway. I'll do something later in the year.'

Peggy stopped packing and they went outside with a cup of tea and cake to sit in the pretty, paved garden at the back: a Japanese acer, a blue French hydrangea and some bamboo lined the bottom wall, large pots containing a variety of plants, herbs and flowers dotted the flagstones, smaller ones sat on shelves built into the right-hand brick wall. A wooden bench and a rectangular oak dining-table that Pete had sanded down and sealed, years ago, stood against the opposite wall – which was west-facing and caught the sun for most of the afternoon. It had the atmosphere of a small, secret haven, away from the rest of the world. Sara loved it.

'So, Mum, any new Colins on the horizon?' Peggy gave her a cheeky grin as she munched her brownie. 'Or shouldn't I ask?'

Sara shook her head. 'Nope, nothing doing.' She spoke firmly, closing down the conversation, unwilling to engage about her recent rejection. She suspected her daughter might be outraged at the slight. And the way Bernard had blanked her on the street still rankled somewhat. *He could have said a friendly hello without compromising himself*, she thought. *Or did he worry I'd leap on him and drag him into a relationship against his will – in broad daylight?* The notion made her smile to herself, at least.

'I've been thinking about Dad a lot recently,' Peggy said, after a brief silence.

'Because I'm . . .' Sara didn't finish. 'Dating' seemed such a juvenile, inappropriate word for someone her age.

Her daughter gave her a rueful grin. 'Now it's a possibility I suppose I'm finding it hard to imagine you with anyone but him.'

Sara smiled gently. 'You and me both, sweetheart. No one will ever replace him, you know that.'

Neither spoke for a moment.

'Don't get me wrong, Mum. There's no way I want you to be by yourself for the rest of your life, obviously. I hate the thought that you're lonely.' Sara saw the incipient tears, quickly blinked away. 'There's still the odd morning I wake up and forget he's gone, you know, even after all this time . . . And when I realize, I can't bear it all over again.' She rubbed her fingertips under both eyes, sniffed. 'He was my hero.'

The tears came now, blurring her daughter's blue eyes without constraint. Sara reached for Peggy's hand, her heart breaking. She had no real idea what her daughter was feeling, or what it was like to have a father to miss. Her own grief was as familiar to her as her face in the mirror. But Peggy had always – even in the months immediately following Pete's death – wrapped her sadness in layers of concern for her mum.

'Oh, Peggs, I'm so sorry.' Sara rubbed her daughter's hand. 'I know what you mean. Those moments are so cruel.' *Waking, sliding her hand across the mattress and finding only cold sheet. That split second of forgetting.* She knew it well.

Peggy took a deep breath. 'Anyway, Mum, let's not get gloomy. We should be looking forwards, not back.' She pulled a face. 'Joni would kill me if she thought I was putting you off finding a lovely man.'

Sara laughed. 'Oh, no worries on that front, sweetheart. The men are doing a splendid job of that all by themselves.' Before Peggy could ask any questions, she added quickly, 'I thought we'd drop in on Granny later, if you're up for it. I know she'd love to see you before you go.'

*

44

Sara got up at four on Sunday morning to drive Peggy and a mountainous, clanking backpack to the airport. Coming back to the empty house – it was still barely eight o'clock – she felt a wave of self-pity. *What's wrong with me these days?* Sunday stretched ahead and she thought of all the couples waking to each other, to a day spent lazing around with croissants and coffee, chatting and exchanging views on the papers, maybe meeting friends for lunch. Sara had friends, of course, but she was heartily sick of being the sad single at these gatherings, always having to enter a room alone, often being set up with another sad single – kindly meant, but embarrassing.

The buck always stopped with her. No one else would ring the insurance company to complain about a hike in renewal payments, or the service centre when the washing machine leaked all over the kitchen floor – as it had only the previous week. There was no one at whom to shout her frustration when her laptop crashed, a client played up, or even just relay day-to-day anecdotes to – about an amusing exchange she'd heard in the supermarket queue, for instance, or something she'd read somewhere. She'd just been plodding along in her own private lane since Pete, not really considering her situation that closely. But now this version of the world was beginning to seem less appealing. Fortified by a cup of coffee and some summer berries with yoghurt and local honey, she reached for her phone and opened the dating app.

Monday morning dawned. Sara had spent a long Sunday doing some gardening, trying to concentrate on a novel Joni had said she *must read*, and chatting aimlessly with

Mike-the-market-gardener online – not a good fit, pretty much his only topic of conversation being this year's tomato crop. Unlocking the main door of her work building – a ten-minute walk downhill from her house, set on the ground floor of a newish brick-and-brown-window-frame behind the District Council office – she bumped into Becky, the podiatrist upstairs, nipping out on a coffee run. Precious wasn't in on Monday mornings, so the place was empty and silent without her friend's cheerful presence to fill the space. Julian Cameron was her first appointment: she was hoping her suggestions had made a difference and lessened some of his health anxieties.

She sat down at her desk and opened her website to check for appointment requests. Some people still used the landline to leave messages, some used the online form, but increasingly she was employing her work mobile to send and receive booking texts. There was nothing online this morning, so she moved on to the landline where there was one cancellation for later in the week, and another message she was about to listen to when her mobile beeped with a WhatsApp from Peggy, attaching a photo of an amazing Icelandic sunrise. Typing a response, she had no time to listen to the landline message before she heard the ping of the practice bell.

'So, how's it been going, Julian?' she asked, although she could tell from his demeanour that it wouldn't be good news. He seemed extremely tense from the outset, barely looking her in the eye as he perched on the edge of the chair, his thin, long-fingered hands twisting in his lap.

'Not well, is the answer,' he said, his voice pinched. 'In fact, nothing's really changed since I last saw you, Sara.'

She frowned. 'I'm sorry to hear that. Did you manage any of the adjustments we discussed?'

'Not really.' Julian gave a small sigh. 'If I'm being honest, I don't see the point in improving my diet when I'm being forced to eat gluten. No wonder I'm not feeling well.'

'You're not being "forced", Julian. It's only that if you want a gluten intolerance test you have to eat a certain amount.'

He frowned at her. 'Which I do, so I am, wouldn't you say?'

Sara was taken aback by the scorn in his tone and inhaled slowly. 'Tell me what you've been eating.'

Julian shrugged. 'I tried to cut down on coffee, as you suggested, but it just made me even more tired. And I take the probiotics, when I remember.' He sighed. 'Otherwise, it's the same as before. And bread, of course.' He pulled a face as if even the thought disgusted him.

Sara smiled encouragingly, glancing down to check his notes. 'Well, you can be tested now. Maybe you'll feel more confident to move forward when you have the results.'

Julian suddenly got to his feet, although he'd been there barely five minutes. 'You make the assumption it'll be negative, of course.' His tone was rude, although that was not what she had said. 'I'm wasting my time . . . and my money. You're just not listening.'

Sara rose too. 'I can understand you're anxious, Julian. But the changes to your diet I've outlined could really help. Will you at least give it a go?' She gave him her most winning smile. 'You have nothing to lose while you wait.'

The smile, though, fell on stony ground. Not answering her question, Julian shook his head impatiently, his expression closed.

'Please,' she said gently. 'Sit down. Let's talk this through.'

But her client swung angrily towards the door, as if he hadn't heard her, leaving the room without even saying goodbye.

Precious popped her head round the door just as Sara was finishing her lunchtime soup. Sara told her about Julian. 'I've never had a client walk out on me before.'

'So rude,' Precious commented.

Sara shook her head. 'He was upset with me. But he had no reason to be. I'd agreed to the gluten test, even though I don't think he needs it, and we could have run other sensitivity tests, if he hadn't legged it. He just wants me to agree he *is* coeliac, and I'm pretty sure he isn't.'

'So what are you going to do?'

'Oh, I'll call him in a couple of days when he's had time to cool off, wrangle him back onboard.' She grinned. 'I'm determined to help him, whether he likes it or not.'

Precious laughed. 'My crusading friend. You know you can't save everyone, Sas.' She came into the room and sat down on Sara's client chair. 'So what else? Did you have a good time with Peggy? Is the dear girl safely off on her travels?'

They chatted for a few minutes before Precious went next door to prepare for her afternoon sessions. It was only when Sara lifted her landline receiver to make a quick call to a client for an appointment change that she noticed the other voicemail still flashing on the machine. In a hurry, because her two o'clock was just about to arrive, she pressed the button. Silence. She was reaching to delete it, when a long intake of breath stayed her hand.

'Hello, this is Bernard calling to speak to Sara Tempest,' said the polite male voice. 'I don't know if you remember . . . coffee cake at the tearoom?' There was a pause. 'I'd love to chat . . . if you fancy it. Here's my number.' She listened as he enunciated the eleven digits twice, said goodbye, then clicked off. *Oh*, she thought, taken aback. She wanted to play it again, but the double ting of the bell prevented her.

She was puzzled as she replayed the message at the end of the day. Hearing Precious saying goodbye to her last client, she went out into the hall. 'Hey, come in here a sec, will you?'

Her friend followed her. 'Listen.' Sara pressed the voicemail button again.

Precious raised an eyebrow when Bernard had finished. 'Tearoom man?'

Sara nodded. 'I saw him on Saturday, on the high street. I was pretty sure he recognized me but he didn't even say hello. Just blanked me and walked on.'

'You must have reminded him that he liked you, though.' She frowned. 'It does feels like there's a bit of resistance going on here . . .'

'Only a bit?' Sara asked, with a wry grin.

'The wife is properly dead, isn't she?'

Sara grimaced. 'You think he made that up?'

Her friend laughed and gave Sara's arm a friendly punch. 'Hey, only teasing. Anyway, if Mrs Bernard is cavorting in the attic, you'll find out soon enough.' She turned to go, then swung back. 'You are going to phone him, aren't you?'

Sara baked a potato for supper, filled it with leftover ratatouille she'd made for Peggy on Saturday night and crumbled feta cheese over the top. She poured a small glass of white wine – for fortification – and drank it all perched on a rush stool at the wooden island in the middle of her small kitchen. It was her favourite room in the house, these days: she had recently painted it Tiffany blue, taken away all the cupboards and put up open shelves for all her crockery and glassware – which wasn't much for just her. She'd also replaced the black marble worktops Pete had installed with pale oak, hung all her pots, pans and ladles, whisks, spoons and spatulas on a mesh of metal hooks on the wall beside the stove. The faded Italian quarry tiles had been there when they'd bought the house the year before Pete died, after selling their rambling, impossible-to-heat home in South Malling on the north side of town.

Now, as she ate, she was aware of fluttering in the pit of her stomach. *Should I call him?* she kept asking herself. Her head told her not to. He'd bothered to track her down, but why hadn't he taken her number at the time . . . called sooner? She didn't buy Precious's sinister, albeit jokey, premise. Still, she wondered why he'd waited two weeks.

If Sara had been a game player, she might have waited a similar length of time before calling back. But she wasn't that sort of woman. She couldn't help remembering how comfortable she'd been with him, how much she'd enjoyed his company. *Better the devil you sort of know?* she thought, imagining all the other 'frogs' – as Margaret liked to call them – she would have to wade through to find someone she liked better.

Suppose I get his voicemail? she worried, as she continued to dither. *Should I leave a message?* And, if so, what should that message be? It all seemed way too complicated.

Sara went on with her meal, but she was distracted, barely noticing what she ate, her phone lying accusingly on the worktop by her side. It was realizing that if she *didn't* call she would continue to wonder if she *should* that in the end made her grab her mobile and press the number she'd stored in her contacts earlier – on Precious's insistence – before she had a chance to change her mind.

It rang twice, then a male voice – deeper than she'd remembered – said, 'Hello?' He sounded wary, but then he wouldn't recognize her private number.

'Bernard?'

'Yes.'

'It's Sara. Sara Tempest.'

'Oh . . . hello.' His voice softened: he sounded pleased. 'You got my message then.'

Sara felt a stab of panic at the ensuing silence, even though it was barely a couple of seconds. 'How are you?' she blurted out, then kicked herself. It was the sort of thing you asked someone you actually knew, with whom you had a reasonable amount of shared context. If Bernard said he was OK, that would mean nothing to her.

'I'm OK,' he said. 'I thought I saw you the other day, in Lewes. But you were across the road and I didn't have my glasses on, so I couldn't be sure.'

'Might have been me,' she said, noncommittally. 'I do live there.'

'Yes, I remember you saying.'

They both sounded so formal with each other, it almost made her laugh.

'I was visiting a friend, my business partner, actually, Joe Fane. Do you know him? He always says it's a very small town, Lewes.'

She laughed. 'I don't, but he's not wrong. I sort of like that. Although Pete, my husband, used to find it pretty claustrophobic at times, but then he was never particularly sociable.' She stopped, worried she was babbling.

'I'm not either,' Bernard said.

'Nor me. In fact, I hate parties, I always think people would rather be talking to someone else. But I like the cosy community side of the town, it makes me feel safe, ridiculously.' She winced, thinking she was putting out a weedy, socially insecure image of herself that was no longer right.

'Since I've been on my own . . .' He paused. 'I never noticed it before, when Ilsa was alive, the heavy, clockticking silence in the house. Sometimes I like it – when I'm working, for instance – but often I feel so lonely out here on the cliffs that it almost hurts.'

Sara was touched at the sadness in his voice and taken aback by his honesty. 'Even in noisy Lewes I get that – the silence of living alone,' she said. 'I listen to a lot of radio.'

Bernard laughed. 'Me too.' He fell silent for a moment. 'I don't want you to get the wrong impression of me. I'm not often lonely,' he added, clearly worried that he, too, wasn't sending out the right signal.

'I knew what you meant,' she said.

'So, what are you doing right now?'

'I'm sitting at the island in my kitchen, eating a baked potato and ratatouille.'

Sara heard him chuckle. 'You're making me jealous.'

'What about you?' she asked.

'Glass of red and a bowl of Twiglets,' he said.

'*Twiglets?*'

'I know, so last century. An old bloke's snack, like meat paste and Ovaltine,' Bernard joked, and they both began to laugh.

'Listen,' he said, 'do you fancy meeting up for a drink . . . maybe supper one night?'

Sara smiled, and was glad he couldn't see it.

When their call ended, she pushed the half-finished plate away and gave out a long breath. *OK*, she thought. Restless suddenly, she got down off the stool and went to stand outside in the garden. It was after nine and the light was almost gone, but the sky still glowed a faint wash of primrose. She wrapped her cardigan round herself, although there was still a lingering warmth from the day, inhaling the soft scent of roses on the night air and the more pungent waft of honeysuckle poking over the wall from her neighbour's garden. For the first time in a long while, she was aware of a small fizz of excitement in her gut. *His voice is lovely*, she thought, smiling again at the Twiglet comment.

'I know this place that has the most delicious fish soup,' he'd suggested, after she'd agreed to meet up. 'It's less than half an hour from you. Do you like fish?'

'Sounds perfect,' Sara had replied.

'If it's a nice evening, we can sit outside,' Bernard had said.

She was already nervous at the prospect.

Joni's face appeared on FaceTime a few minutes after Bernard's call.

'Who were you just talking to?' Sara's daughter – all blonde and tanned and smiling in the Californian sun – demanded, sounding restive. 'I've tried you a couple of times.'

Sara laughed. Joni had always been impatient, eager for the next experience, keen not to let the grass grow under her feet. It had been a family joke when she was young: 'Watch out, Joni's looking bored.' Luckily, her current occupation – starting a fitness centre in Los Angeles with her Californian husband, Mason, also a sport and fitness instructor – used every ounce of her energy and resources, and then some. 'Just a friend,' she said, hoping Joni wouldn't ask which one. But her daughter was already swirling her phone around.

'Look where I am, Mum . . . Our new gaff!'

Sara saw the outside of a small, adobe-style house, with pink-washed walls and a terracotta-tiled roof, arched windows with pretty sky-blue shutters.

'And here's the pool . . .' The image wobbled round some spiky brush and hillside to show an oval turquoise swimming-pool. 'It's the size of a pea but, God, you really need it here. It got to nearly ninety-eight degrees the other day.' She laughed. 'They still use old money for the temperature here. I've had to adjust.'

'It's gorgeous, sweetheart. Wish I was there with you right now.'

'Oh, I totally wish you were too, Mum. Wouldn't that be brilliant? When we've got sorted you have to come out. There's three bedrooms, so Peggy can come too.'

They chatted on and it was late before Sara began to clear away her supper things. She was still smiling. Seeing her daughter so happy and involved in her life warmed her heart. There had been a time after Pete died when she'd worried Joni was coming off the rails. She'd turned down the job she'd lined up – post sports-science degree – in a primary school in Buckingham and returned home to Lewes, where she'd taken to her bed in silent despair. So unlike Joni. Sara, distraught herself, and unable to focus on pretty much anything more than getting through the day, was at a loss as to what to do. It had been Precious stepping up, cajoling Joni into volunteering with the kids at the Shoreham sailing club, that had finally rescued her daughter, brought her back to life. And it was at the club that she'd met Mason – who was crewing on a large yacht owned by friends of his parents.

As she poured herself a glass of water from the filter jug and made her way up to bed, her thoughts returned to Bernard. She hadn't asked why he didn't call earlier, of course. But she wasn't investing too much in the supper with him. If he had stuff going on in his life that was making him reluctant on some level, she didn't want to get involved.

8

Sara's hair was playing up. Usually, she just turned upside down and blow-dried it without any product, but this evening, of all evenings, she'd rashly introduced some mousse to give it more body, resulting in a set of uneven bulges she couldn't brush out without wetting her hair. Now it looked like she'd had a row with her hairdresser and walked out mid-styling. Sighing, she shook her head vigorously from side to side and left it at that. *If my hair's a deal breaker, then so be it*, she thought, managing a small smile through her fluster.

It was another hot, muggy evening as Sara made her way to her car, which was up the hill in the council car park behind the church – there was no parking on the high street in front of her house. She set the satnav, although she didn't really need it, then pulled out onto the main road, her stomach hollow with nerves, as it had been all day.

'Don't have too many expectations,' Precious had warned.

Sara didn't think 'expectations' were the problem. She told herself she didn't have any at this stage, beyond managing to get through the evening without making a fool of herself. But the step change from a chance forty-five minutes over a piece of cake and a cuppa to dinner seemed daunting.

*

She was led through the other seated diners, out to the pretty courtyard garden. She saw Bernard at once, seated beneath a fig tree, arms leaning on the white tablecloth as he perused the menu. As she approached, he rose, laying his glasses on the table, and held out both hands, taking her own – cold from nerves, despite the hot night – in his and squeezing them in greeting. He was dressed in a white shirt and blue linen jacket, with faded black jeans, and looked different, somehow, from how she'd remembered him. Just as attractive, certainly, but also tense, almost wary, she thought. Seeing him, instead of calming her nerves, made her heart up its rhythm.

'You found it OK, then?' he asked, when she was seated and a bottle of wine had been ordered from the proprietor, who appeared to know Bernard.

She smiled. 'No excuses, these days.' Looking around, she added, 'This is lovely.'

He hesitated, then seemed to come to a decision. 'I came here sometimes with my wife.' He shrugged. 'I wasn't going to mention it, but we might as well be upfront, don't you think? Seeing as we're in the same boat.'

A bit startled by his directness, she nodded. 'I'll mention mine if you mention yours sort of thing?'

Bernard laughed and she saw his face suddenly open up.

'OK,' Sara said. 'Well, in the spirit of confession, Pete and I used to get takeaway fish and chips from the place next door in the summer and eat them on the beach.' She hadn't realized until she arrived that her destination that evening would be so close to the chip shop, and had felt a wave of nostalgia so powerful it had brought tears to her eyes. Pete, a perennially fussy eater, said the smell of fish made him retch, so she'd always done the ordering: haddock for her, a minced beef and onion pie for him, plenty of chips for them both.

'Sounds like fun.' Bernard suddenly looked worried. 'Would you have preferred the beach tonight?'

'No, no, this is perfect,' she assured him, then panicked that 'perfect' was too strong.

They smiled at each other, as Sara scrabbled for a follow-up.

'It was so much easier dating when we were young, wasn't it? Our lives were simple by comparison,' she commented.

'Ooh, not sure about that,' Bernard replied. 'My world seemed endlessly complex and gripping back then – to me at least.'

After their laughter, silence descended.

She took a breath. 'I was nervous as hell coming here tonight.'

A fleeting frown of sympathy was followed by a grin. '*You* were nervous.'

Sara couldn't meet his eye. Luckily, at that moment the wine arrived with a basket of freshly baked rolls and butter. They both ordered the fish soup.

'Is that why you left it so long before ringing me?' she found herself asking, when they were alone again. Her tone was teasing but she immediately froze, wanting to swallow her words. *Could I sound more uncool?*

Bernard wasn't looking at her, wasn't replying, wasn't laughing. His lack of reaction alarmed her. Then his gaze met hers. His expression was steady, strangely challenging, his voice so quiet as to be almost inaudible above the hum of the surrounding tables. 'I . . . I suppose I don't want to let you down.'

Let me down? Sara wondered if she'd heard him right.

Before she had a chance to speak, he'd composed his face and was smiling. 'You know that feeling? That you won't measure up?'

She did, of course, but he seemed overly concerned, so soon after meeting, and his response didn't entirely ring true.

'Tell me about your house,' she said, keen to dispel the intensity that seemed, inadvertently, to have built up between them, move on to more general ground. 'Did you design it yourself?'

It was a safe subject, surely, but she thought she detected a shadow pass across his tanned features. When he spoke, however, it was with apparent enthusiasm.

'It's sustainable, an eco-house, right on the clifftop. Ilsa and I built it together. She was an architect too. It'll be twenty-five years old next January.' He paused. 'I'd show you photos, but they don't do it justice.'

'Look forward to seeing it in the flesh,' she said, without thinking, then quickly backtracked. 'I didn't mean . . .' She stopped, blushing. The hole she'd dug was already deep enough.

Bernard roared with laughter. 'What are we like?' He levelled his gaze at her. 'I really hope you will see the house, Sara.'

To say she wasn't flirting would have been wrong – there were frequent flashes when she met his keen grey eyes, when they laughed together, which made her feel as if she were being prodded alive after many years of deep slumber. But her feelings were not so much sexual as quiet pleasure in his company, the lack of constraint he seemed to engender in her.

Sara loved being outside on summer evenings, watching the sky turn through the colours of the rainbow as light slowly faded, the quiet intimacy of darkness. In the courtyard, candles were lit on tables, cooking smells mixed with the sweet fragrance from a clump of white snowdrift in a pot close to where she and Bernard sat. Supper had gone in a flash, the early awkwardness dissipating with more general chat about their lives, their families, the state of the world. He told her that his son Adam was at Nottingham, in his fifth year of medicine; Carrie, his daughter, was doing a design apprenticeship in Liverpool, for Matalan. A million more questions buzzed in her mind that she wanted to ask the man sitting opposite, but she felt there was no hurry, they had time.

Over coffee Bernard asked, 'I know I left it a long time after Ilsa died before dating . . . but why did you?'

He was not the sort to fob off with a glib reply. That was becoming increasingly clear. Unlike so many people, Bernard seemed able to talk about anything and everything, to confront his feelings in a way more familiar with her female friends, such as Precious.

'I really loved Pete,' she said, as she considered her answer. 'Our marriage wasn't perfect – although since he died, I've made it so.' She gave a quick laugh. 'It's taken me a long time to get over, I suppose. I think I persuaded myself I'd never find a relationship that worked so well . . . That and being terrified of the whole dating palaver.'

She wondered if she'd said too much, set the bar too high.

Bernard was regarding her thoughtfully. 'You were lucky,' he said.

'You and Ilsa . . .'

'Yes, I loved her very much, too,' he said, then stopped. She waited, but he didn't go on, his head bent to unwrapping the foil of a mint chocolate the waitress had brought with the coffee. Then he looked up and met her gaze. To Sara, the expression in his eyes seemed filled with regret, rather than the more obvious sadness of loss. 'Marriage is a complex business, in my experience,' he added.

'You can say that again.' She smiled brightly in an attempt to dispel his sombre mood. 'I've just folded mine in gold tissue and tied it firmly with a bow.'

'Sensible plan,' Bernard said, almost as if he envied her.

They left the restaurant, Sara feeling a quiet pleasure in the way the evening had gone – there had been laughter and good conversation, real moments of connection about a lot of things, including their marriages.

Stopping on the pavement, Sara said, 'Mine's this way,' indicating to the right. Her Mini was parked around the corner.

'I'm that way.' Bernard pointed left. 'I'll walk you.'

Sara did not protest. They were close on the narrow pavement – she could feel his jacket brushing her bare arm and enjoyed his proximity. As they turned the corner, she slowed down. Three figures were lounging against her car: lads in their late teens, she assessed, beer cans in hand, drunkenly shoving each other and laughing raucously. 'That's my car,' she said softly.

Bernard followed her gaze. She heard him take a deeper breath. 'Stay here,' he said, straightening his shoulders and advancing towards the group. Despite his advice, Sara followed him.

'OK, lads,' Bernard said politely, when he reached them. 'Off the car, please.'

The tallest and loudest – clearly the ringleader – scowled, pressing his face close to Bernard's, but did not shift from his seat on the bonnet of Sara's car. 'Yeah?'

In a second, the atmosphere changed. The other two crowded threateningly round Bernard, in solidarity with their leader. Sara stopped, held her breath. *Don't do anything stupid*, she pleaded silently, knowing real violence could stem from just such an innocuous beginning. But to her astonishment, she heard Bernard laugh. He seemed genuinely amused. 'What's that you're drinking?' he asked.

Taken aback, the lad stared at him, then at his beer can, as if seeing it for the first time.

'Me, I like a Bud,' Bernard said.

The youths began shifting about, clearly nonplussed by the turn the encounter had taken.

'Carling's the best,' one of the acolytes commented sulkily, waving his can – which was not Carling – in the air.

'Haven't had one in years,' Bernard said. As he spoke, he firmly, but without any aggression, waved them aside. 'Have a good evening, lads,' he said, as they began silently sliding away from the car. For a moment, Sara thought they might kick off again – the leader's expression as he eyed Bernard was still sullen and resentful. But after a moment, he turned and sloped off down the street, his two friends in tow. She heard them muttering, then a loud laugh.

'Phew!' she said, giving Bernard a grateful pat on his shoulder.

'They didn't mean any harm. Just too little to do and too much to drink.'

'It could have turned nasty.'

He nodded. 'I used to do a lot of judo. I hope I can still handle myself.'

She was impressed.

'"Never waste your energy on things that don't achieve your goal," judo philosophy says. Being aggressive would have got me nowhere.'

Sara pressed her key fob to unlock the door. She looked up at Bernard. 'That was such a lovely evening. Thank you . . . And thanks for rescuing me.'

He laughed. 'You are so worth it, Sara. I've had a wonderful time.'

Will he kiss me? Will he suggest another date? The questions flashed across Sara's mind.

But Bernard just pulled her into his arms and gave her a friendly hug. Then he stepped back.

'We should maybe, I don't know, do something again . . .' he began, opening the door for her and seeing her inside. But he hesitated, seemingly undecided about how to go on. In the end, all he said was 'Safe journey', accompanied by a final wave. Then he turned towards the corner.

Sara started the engine. She would have liked to sit for a while in the quiet of the car and contemplate the evening. But she worried the teenagers might return. And she didn't want Bernard driving past and seeing her still there: he might think something was wrong. By the time she got home, though, she'd begun to lose confidence in how he felt about her. *He started to suggest another meeting,* she thought. *Then, for some reason, changed his mind.*

9

Why the hell didn't you make a proper plan to see her again, you numpty? Bernard berated himself, as he walked slowly back to his car, pausing in his stride and almost turning back to do so. The evening had gone so well – from his point of view, at least. *Was she waiting for me to kiss her?* The notion had definitely crossed his mind, but he'd lost his nerve, hugging her instead, like a friendly godfather after the yearly ice-cream treat.

He groaned quietly as he sat in the car, watching Sara's blue Mini emerge at the corner and speed away westwards. *I really like this woman,* he thought, recalling the way her hair had flopped over her gorgeous hazel eyes at supper, how she'd flick it away with her fingers almost apologetically. How she'd cradled her glass as she listened to him banging on, as if she were genuinely interested. He loved her wit, and how easy it seemed to make her laugh.

Sighing, he realized he wanted to freeze the clock, to contain the supper, Sara, his feelings, in a padded box where nothing and no one could hurt them. *It's lucky I didn't kiss her,* he told himself, knowing, with someone as straightforward as Sara, it would be crossing a line, mean committing to more than he was ready for. He was beginning to regret following Joe's advice.

'You can't avoid meaningful relationships forever,' his friend had said, when urging him to contact Sara.

'Why not? You do,' had been Bernard's retort. But he realized as he said it that in fact, unlike Joe, he yearned to be with someone, to share his life again. There just seemed one too many hurdles to get over before that was possible: the obvious one, of course, then the twins . . . Ilsa.

He checked his mobile again before starting the car. Just a short, noncommittal text from Adam in response to the three voicemails he'd left. It drove him nuts, that impersonal, automated 'Please leave a message after the tone' each time. Neither of his children seemed interested in actually talking to him, which really upset him. Adam used to call for the occasional chat, although recently even that had been reduced to a series of infrequent one-line texts. Carrie, never. How would he explain this to Sara, who talked about her two girls so easily, and obviously had such a close relationship with them both?

The following morning Sara made herself a cup of coffee and put a slice of wholemeal bread into the toaster. She pulled the Saturday newspaper towards her as she ate, but she couldn't concentrate. Memories of the charming evening played through her mind, slightly marred by Bernard's vague suggestion, in parting, that they 'do something', while not making a plan. Like in the car park of the tearoom, he'd seemed constrained by something that went against his better instincts. Because it was clear to her, unless Bernard was a truly brilliant actor, that he had enjoyed the supper as much as she.

Plus, she'd sent him a text before she went to bed, saying, *Thanks again, Bernard. I had such a lovely time tonight.* And so far – she accepted it was not yet nine – he hadn't responded. She reminded herself that he had said, at the time, that he'd had a 'wonderful' evening. So, maybe he was just indecisive, not given to hasty commitments. After all, he'd walked away from her at the tearoom and phoned eventually. She shook herself, wanting to clear her head. *Nobody mentioned how confusing dating can be*, she thought.

Her phone signalled an incoming text.

Pop round for a coffee? Precious's message suggested.

Precious and Sammi's house – a ten-minute walk down a steep, cobbled cut-through off the high street – was, like many of the Lewes houses, on a slope. So, while the front of the house was on street level, what might have been a dingy basement was in fact a light, spacious kitchen at the back, the garden sloping down to the road below.

The kitchen smelt of baking, and Sara grinned as she saw Sammi carrying a wooden board of his legendary *bollos* to the long table that ran the length of the glass doors – now open onto the garden. The summer sunshine was bright, the breeze pleasantly cool as the three of them sat in a row, looking out over the little park below towards the nearby hills. Precious had made coffee and handed Sara a large stoneware cup, beautifully decorated with hand-painted floral motifs. She indicated the golden-brown rolls, the buttercream poking out where they had been split.

'My favourite.' Sara smiled her thanks as she helped herself, closing her eyes as she savoured the crunch, then the warm, pillowy sweetness on her tongue. 'Heaven,' she said to Sammi, who was watching her anxiously with his dark eyes, just to check his offering was up to scratch.

'OK . . . So, last night?' Precious enquired through a mouthful of bun.

Sara filled them in. 'He did say we should get together again when we said goodbye, but it seemed a bit vague, not exactly wholehearted. And he hasn't replied to my thank-you text.' She felt suddenly upset. 'We had such a great time.'

Precious frowned. 'Hmm. What do you think, Sammi? Male perspective? Why is he dragging his feet?'

Her husband considered this. 'The old-fashioned type, maybe? His age . . . Doesn't want to rush into anything?'

Sammi had lived in England now for over thirty years, and although he spoke perfect English, his accent was still recognizably Spanish.

'The man should at least have texted you by now,' Precious commented, glancing at the kitchen clock, which read ten thirty. 'That's rude.'

Sara nodded. 'He said this odd thing when I asked – having an uncool moment – why he didn't ring sooner. Said he was worried he might let me down.'

'Oh, my God!' Precious threw her hands theatrically in the air. 'Maybe instead of the mad wife in the attic he's got a serious problem . . . Like he's an addict or something? Drugs, gambling . . . *sex*?'

Sara laughed. 'Thanks, Precious. Very reassuring to think I'm dating a junkie . . . Well, clearly *not* dating yet.' Trying to remember, she said, 'There was something a bit dark, or sad, about him sometimes.' Then she pulled a face. 'Think I prefer the mad-wife scenario.'

The three of them sat in silence, watching Precious's black cat, Chinko, slink elegantly past and out into the garden, as if he were a model in a runway show.

'Have you heard from your disgruntled client, by the way?' Precious asked.

'I rang him and left a message offering another appointment, but he didn't pick up. Then I got this strange email saying, and I quote, "Thank you for your message. Please don't contact me again. You will be hearing from me in due course."'

'Whoa, is that a bit threatening?' Precious asked.

Sara sighed. 'I know. I thought so, too. I've checked through my notes and I've played it totally by the book with him. But I wonder if he thinks I've put him in danger or something, made him ill by saying he needs to eat gluten prior to a test.'

'He's probably angry about something else and taking it out on you,' Precious observed.

She nodded. 'I hope he doesn't get nasty, though, and report me to the HCPC ... Or take to social media. Although he doesn't seem the type to have a Twitter or Facebook account.'

'I'm sure you haven't done anything wrong, Sas.'

No one spoke for a moment, then Sara said, 'Men, eh?' rolling her eyes and silently including Bernard in the incomprehensibility of the species.

To which Sammi held up his hands, eyes wide with mock hurt. '*Un momento, por favor!*' he said, making them all laugh.

Walking back up the steep hill towards home, Sara straightened her shoulders and took a long breath, letting it out slowly, enjoying the summer sunshine on her face. When her mobile buzzed with an incoming message, she automatically dragged it from her pocket, her thoughts still on Julian as she pondered how to respond to his cold email. But he'd specifically asked her not to contact him, so she had little choice, really, but to wait and see what transpired. She'd had one client, some years back – not long after Pete died – who had reported Sara to her regulatory body, the Health and Care Professions Council. The client had suffered from quite severe mental-health issues, and nothing had come of it. But it upset her a great deal at the time, and she didn't want to have to go through the arduous procedure of proving that proper standards had been met, not again. With her mind elsewhere, she was almost surprised to see the text was from Bernard.

Sorry, Sara, just got your message. Stupidly left my phone in the restaurant last night. ☹ Had such a great evening too x

She'd stopped at the entrance to the cut-through. An anoraked man, clearly in a hurry, pushed past her and she stood to the side. Reading Bernard's text again, her heart twitched slightly. She put her phone back into her pocket, and her steps were noticeably lighter as she climbed the rest of the hill to her front door.

Nightmare, Sara typed into the text box. *Glad you got it back x.*

Not, she conceded, the most scintillating of replies. On the verge of sending it, she wondered if she should suggest another meeting herself. Was it OK, in the modern world, for women to be bold and not wait for men to make all the running? Her confidence deserted her, though, and she left the text as it was. She wasn't sure if she would hear from him again. But she *was* determined she wasn't going to waste any more emotional energy hoping she would.

She spent the afternoon cutting back the burgeoning castor-oil plant in the far corner of the garden, then made some blueberry muffins to take round to Margaret and Heather on Sunday. It took a full hour to compose a conciliatory email to Julian, asking if he would at least speak to her, so she could allay any fears he might have, but she decided, on balance, not to send it yet.

Bernard didn't respond to her text and by Saturday night she had reluctantly consigned him to the bin of experience. They were obviously just not on the same page.

Heather greeted Sara with a hug and a worried smile, pulling her into the kitchen. Her voice lowered, she said, 'Margaret's not been so well. She seems confused, been wheezing a bit.' Sara frowned. 'She doesn't like the hot weather,' Heather continued, 'but it feels like more than that.' She sighed. 'And her ankles have been quite swollen for a few days now, before it got really warm.'

'Do you think I should call Dr Withy?'

'It might be good to get her checked out. She hasn't seen anyone in a while, or had her medication reviewed. I'm worried it's her heart again.'

'I'll give the surgery a call first thing.'

Heather looked relieved and smiled. 'So, how's things?'

'Oh, you know,' Sara said wearily. 'Touch of the same old, same old.'

Heather smiled sympathetically. 'Yup. The world keeps turning, nothing changes . . . and we aren't getting any younger.'

Heather's remark made her feel inexplicably tearful. She nodded and turned away, hurrying out of the kitchen and along the short corridor to the sitting room.

Immediately, she saw what Heather had been talking about. Margaret was fidgety, her breath definitely more wheezy than usual.

'Did you bring him?' she asked, as soon as Sara sat down on the sofa next to Margaret's chair.

'Who?'

The old lady waved a bony hand, a confused frown on her face. 'He said he was coming today.'

Taking her mother-in-law's hand, Sara asked gently, 'Is it Pete you're expecting, Margaret?'

She gave a tiny sigh and her face cleared as she peered at Sara, as if seeing her for the first time. 'Hello, dear . . . how nice.'

The room was quiet and very warm, although the French windows were open. Heather served tea and the muffins Sara had baked, but the old lady only picked at hers.

'Peggy had a bit of a wobble about Pete before we came to see you the other day,' Sara said. 'It's hard for me to know what it's like, losing her dad at her age, and in the way she did. I'm not sure how best to help.'

Margaret nodded slowly, raising an eyebrow. 'Speaking of which – although I don't even like putting your sad excuse for a father in the same sentence as dear Pete – have you heard from the man?'

Sara shook her head. 'No, but I never do, not until the annual Thanksgiving invitation from Lois, which always arrives on September the first, on the dot.'

Her mother-in-law chuckled. 'I know it wasn't funny for you, dear, but Pete used to make me laugh so much about those ghastly Thanksgiving trips.'

'Oh, God, yes. The rotten-egg smell of Frank's home-made wine. Those yappy dogs weeing all over the carpet . . . and Lois's marshmallow pumpkin pie – just a whiff of all that sugar made our teeth splinter.' She grimaced. 'Not forgetting the delights of Prestatyn in November. Me and Pete used to get quite hysterical in the car on the way home. The girls never really understood what we were laughing at.'

'Why do you still bother?' Margaret asked. 'I've never met the fellow, but he sounds like a thoroughly bad lot to me.'

Sara wasn't sure why. 'I suppose I keep hoping he'll come through for me in some way.' She gave a wry grin.

'You know, throw his arms around me and say how truly sorry he is for walking out of my life and not giving a toss about me or my family. Explain it was some life-threatening event over which he had no control.'

Margaret smiled sympathetically. 'Well ... perhaps don't hold your breath on that one, dear.'

Sara squeezed her mother-in-law's hand. 'I'm lucky. I've got you, Margaret. You've loved me and looked after me so brilliantly. I don't need Frank in my life.'

Her mother-in-law looked a little abashed at Sara's words – they seldom expressed their feelings for each other. Nevertheless, she smiled her appreciation.

Sara had repeatedly told herself over the years that she wasn't bitter about Frank's absence in her life. But when the children were at the age she had been when her father had left, and she saw Pete holding each of them tenderly to his broad chest, his face lighting up with such love, it was hard to understand how her father could have walked away so comprehensively.

Margaret had nodded off, her head lolling uncomfortably on her chest. Sara did not get up. She continued to sit, regarding the woman in front of her. Pete's mum. The only other person who'd known and loved her husband so intimately. It had been one of her greatest pleasures, talking about him endlessly with Margaret, often repeating the same old stories, over and over, both of them imbuing their memories with a consolingly rosy glow. There was no one else with whom she could do it so openly, not even the girls – she didn't want to overburden them.

Feeling sleepy, she laid her head against the sofa back.

Heather had gone to the shops and wouldn't be back for a while. She closed her eyes, but was jerked awake a few moments later by her mobile vibrating in her pocket. Grabbing it and clicking on the call, in her haste to avoid waking Margaret, she got up and hurried out into the garden.

'Hello?' she said, in a fierce whisper.

'Is this a bad time?' Bernard's voice sounded apologetic.

'I'm with my mother-in-law and she's sleeping.' Surprised to hear his voice, she found she was also mildly irritated. No reply to her message, then he rings at the most inconvenient moment.

'Sorry. I'll call back later.'

'No, go ahead.' *Bird in the hand*, she thought.

'Short notice, but I wondered if you fancied a film this evening? I still haven't been over to check out the Depot – although I know one of the architects quite well – and they're showing *Rear Window* . . . I thought it might be fun.'

When she didn't immediately reply, taken aback by the sudden invitation, Bernard went on, 'You do like the cinema?'

The question felt vaguely patronizing. 'Doesn't everyone?' She, Precious and Sammi went every couple of weeks to whatever was showing. The new three-screen cinema, built around an old warehouse complex, was a big boon for the locals.

'Ilsa didn't. Too many people crushed together. Germs.'

'Oh . . .' *Odd*, she thought. She'd been about to add that in fact Pete hadn't liked the cinema either, reasoning that it was a waste of his day when he could be out climbing something, biking somewhere or taking his dinghy for a sail.

But Bernard was speaking. 'Sorry . . . nervous tic, can't seem to stop mentioning my wife.'

She laughed, no longer offended.

'So, are you up for the movie?'

After thinking she might never hear from Bernard again – or at least not in the immediate future – Sara was suddenly faced with two dates in one weekend. It took her breath away. *He is interested in me, after all*, she thought, with a smile.

Sitting next to Bernard on the plush new cinema seats in the semi-darkness, Sara found that she was pleasantly aware of his closeness as their shoulders touched. The glass of wine they'd drunk at one of the outside tables before the film had loosened her inhibitions and she was tempted to lean into his warmth. But she resisted, and soon she was lost in the suspense on the screen. By the time Jimmy Stewart was sitting in his wheelchair with yet another broken leg, she'd almost forgotten she was there with Bernard. When the lights came up and they rose to their feet, neither immediately spoke.

Outside it was dusk, the August air only just beginning to cool.

'Are you hungry?' Bernard asked.

She had been amused and fascinated by his animated appraisal of the building, his talk of design, the cinema complex, and discussion of Hitchcock before the show, but she hadn't thought about what might happen after-wards. Standing there now, watching his brows rise in question above his grey eyes, she felt suddenly bold, on a bit of a high after her enjoyment of the film. 'Come back to mine? I could rustle up an omelette and salad – and there are blueberry muffins . . .'

Later, they sat opposite each other at the kitchen island, eggs and salad dispatched. Outwardly, she'd prepared the meal with her usual quiet efficiency, while inwardly rattling like a tree in a storm. A plate of muffins lay on the table between them. She had a moment of bewilderment, seeing Bernard sitting there in her kitchen. It wasn't to do with Pete, she thought. It felt very much like her place, now, rather than the old marital home. But she rarely had guests, let alone an attractive single man.

Bernard looked up at her and asked, 'What do you want from your life, Sara . . . at this stage in the game?'

Caught off-guard by the sudden shift in tone – they had been laughing a minute ago about how ridiculously perfect Grace Kelly was in *High Society* – she wondered what he was really asking.

'Generally, do you mean?'

He nodded. 'We've both got our kids. We've recovered as much as we're going to from our spouses dying. We're both involved in our work . . .' He trailed off.

Taking a deep breath, Sara hesitated. 'OK . . . Well, aside from all that . . . I suppose I would like to be with someone . . . not be alone forever.'

Bernard's eyes widened. It wasn't surprise, she thought, more recognition she saw there. 'Me too,' he said softly. 'Me too. I wasn't sure. These dating apps skew your sense of what's real, what people are after. I've never been good at sexual politics, anyway.' He gave a small shrug. 'But I don't want to hook up with someone just for sex.'

He must have seen her mouth twitch in amusement, because he hurried on: 'I didn't mean . . . Obviously I'd love to have sex with you . . . Oh, God, now what have I said?' Then he added, 'But if that's all you want . . .'

Sara could not help blushing, at the same time delighting in his outburst.

Bernard groaned. 'Sorry, I'm famous for coming out with stuff inappropriately, along with losing things and wandering about the cliffs at night. You should hear my kids on the subject.'

She frowned, then took the less contentious conversational option. 'You have trouble sleeping?'

'Persistent. For years. So I like to walk at night, that's all. But the neighbours – and particularly their dogs – freak out, thinking I'm some evil home-invader. I suppose I can see their point.'

'That must be so horrible,' she said simply, and saw Bernard's eyes cloud. *Precious might be able to help with acupuncture*, she thought, but did not articulate her notion. People, she knew, weren't always looking for solutions. They just wanted to be heard.

'It really is. If you don't suffer from it, it's hard to understand just how bad it feels.'

He looked so lost, she was tempted to reach out and take his hand. But he beat her to it. At his touch, Sara felt a deep, buried yearning . . . to be held, just held tight, to rest in a man's embrace. Those moments when Pete had gathered her to him and wrapped her close, she missed them so much.

Letting go of her hand, Bernard got up. Coming round to where she sat, he waited as she too stood. Very slowly, he opened his arms. The touch of his body against hers, the rough warmth of his cheek, the feel of his shirt beneath her fingers as her hands encircled his back, and his clean, masculine smell of soap and fresh laundry was so achingly enticing – surprising, but also familiar in an atavistic sense – that she heard herself give a soft gasp. She paused a minute to savour the sensation, wanting this not to end. The frisson between them as he met her gaze was palpable and, again, she wanted to cherish it, to experience every inch of it, make it last. He seemed in no hurry either, his previous awkwardness replaced by a certainty she had not anticipated.

The moment stretched out, every second they didn't kiss making her breath shorter and shorter in her chest, until it was fluttering high in her throat. Then his mouth was seeking hers, his lips warm, charged as they touched her own. She tasted salt and wine and the sweetness of blueberries on her tongue.

Finally pulling back, dazed, she heard him let out a long, slow breath as her own heart began to ease off from its frantic syncopation.

Bernard was smiling as if in slow motion.

Trembling slightly, she leant back against the island. 'I didn't expect that,' she murmured.

'You didn't?'

'I wasn't sure you fancied me.'

Bernard let out a soft laugh. 'Oh, you can be very sure I do.'

She blinked, suddenly exhausted and overwhelmed, not only by what had just happened, but by how she felt about it. 'Would you like a cup of tea?' she asked, and they both began to laugh.

They sat in the darkness on the garden bench. The lights of the town rendered the sky pale, and the summer night air was chilly, but there was a lovely intimacy as he threaded his arm across her shoulders and pulled her close. Neither spoke. Neither tried to kiss the other again. It was as if they were delicately holding the secret of what had just happened between them, like a precious thing.

When they'd finished their tea, Bernard said, 'I suppose I'd better get going.'

She could have asked him to stay. It was late, he had an hour's drive ahead of him, and his car was down by the cinema still as they'd walked to her house after the film. But she didn't and he didn't seem to expect her to. She wanted more than anything to be alone, now, to go over the evening in minute detail in her head, to relive the joy of his kiss, her delight in his embrace.

'Shall I call you?' Bernard asked, as he shrugged on his jacket. 'Or you could call me . . . Might be more reliable.'

She laughed. 'I'm saying nothing.'

He grinned, then bent to kiss her. Just a single soft one, plumb on her lips. 'Goodnight,' he whispered.

I 2

Driving home through the summer darkness, Bernard accompanied one of his favourite Dylan songs on the radio at the top of his lungs . . . until he realized what he was singing about. 'It Ain't Me Babe' chronicled a man pulling relentlessly away from commitment, from love. A man who knew he couldn't give the girl what she wanted. But while Dylan cheerily – almost smugly – wriggles free of his responsibilities, it was already too late for Bernard. He knew he was in too deep now. *That kiss.* It was like nothing he'd ever experienced before. *Not even*, he thought guiltily, *with Ilsa*, who'd seemed perpetually to slip through his fingers, even when he actually held her in his arms. Sara had been so giving, so open, so – words failed him – so *there*.

For the first time in years, Bernard felt a tiny spark of optimism. He was not a terrible person, he knew that. And he was sick of being consumed by the past, constantly on the back foot, feeling bad about himself because of the decision he'd made. Perhaps Joe was right. When the time came, maybe Sara would understand.

As he unlocked his front door, he took a deep breath, steeling himself to face the house. Tonight he'd crossed the Rubicon. Not just because of their spectacular kiss. For Bernard that had been the icing on the cake. The bigger betrayal was the way Sara's company was making his mind, almost imperceptibly, begin to slide away from Ilsa – the woman who had taken centre stage in his psyche for such a long, long time.

The house seemed to watch him silently. He felt the air heavy with imagined reproof. It was ridiculous, he knew, the foolish obsession he'd developed about four solid walls of wood and glass. It had begun even before Ilsa died, this sense, each time he entered the place, that it was somehow measuring his worthiness like a judgemental gatekeeper – a paid-up agent for his wife. He remembered his sheer relief on the times when Ilsa greeted him with a smile and a soft kiss of welcome – rather than the more familiar punishing stare, denoting some wrongdoing on his part, of which he was unaware. Since her death, the feeling of reproof – tinged, he knew, by the various strands of guilt from which he continued to suffer – had only intensified.

Turning on the lights in the open-plan kitchen-living room, he glanced around. The usual brooding silence greeted him. But this time he squared his shoulders, inhaled the warm air until his lungs were full and ready.

'I met a woman tonight, Ilsa.' He spoke loudly to the empty room, surprised by the confidence he detected in his voice. 'She's called Sara. We went to the movies . . . and then I kissed her.' He waited, breath held, expecting, ridiculously, some kind of reaction, a sign that Ilsa had heard him. When there was nothing, the room as hushed and still as ever, he was unnerved . . . almost disappointed.

13

Walking to work the following morning, the memory of Bernard's kiss still feathering her lips, the sound of his laugh in her ears, Sara found she was smiling to herself. This thing they seemed to have with each other . . . In all her vague imaginings about a relationship at this time in her life, the timbre of the connection had been sedate, companionable, what she'd thought of as 'older' love. But the surge of longing Bernard had evoked in her last night was just as intense – if not more so, for the sheer unexpectedness of it – as what she remembered feeling for Pete in those heady early days.

Back then, though, it had been almost a given. You were young, you fell passionately in love – everyone did. Now, at her age, surely this was exceptional, feeling so – she flailed around in an attempt to find the correct word – just so *right* with him. Her heart seized at the thought it might not be real.

Opening her email, she was disappointed that there was no further communication from Julian Cameron. It felt like unfinished business, and it niggled at her. She turned her attention to Martha, her next appointment. The charming middle-aged woman was keen to accept Sara's advice, although her digestive issues, post gall-bladder removal, were proving slow to respond to the dietary changes and she was having frequent bouts of irritable bowel syndrome. Sara intended to start her on a digestive enzyme today, see if that might help.

All in all, it had been a tiring day: client after client, notes to write up, appointments to confirm, arranging for Helen Withy, Margaret's GP, to visit her mother-in-law. By the time she'd had supper and was sitting outside at the table in the garden – it was a beautiful, still, warm summer night – a cup of fennel tea and a square of dark chocolate in front of her, she should have been worn out. But the thought of perhaps speaking to Bernard hovered over her tiredness, creating a fluttering excitement in her gut. *Does it seem over-keen to call so soon?* she asked herself. But she knew it would be playing games to wait three days when she fancied speaking to him tonight. *He doesn't have to answer if he doesn't want to.*

'So, tell me more about your twins?' she asked, when they'd been chatting for a while. They'd sketched out their families in previous meetings, but only briefly.

'They both work really hard. And they're so far away . . .' His reply sounded flat and a little bleak. She waited for him to go on, to supply the sort of personal things she'd divulged – facets of their personality, like Joni always needing to be in the middle of the action, for example, and Peggy being a very private person, seldom disclosing anything about her social life – but he went so silent Sara thought briefly they'd lost connection.

'I suppose that means you don't see them much?' she prodded, treading carefully.

'Hardly ever.' Bernard's reply was blunt, almost angry.

Sara felt a sudden frisson, which she didn't understand. For a second, she let the silence lie, then found herself

85

trying to reassure Bernard. 'It's the stage they're at, trying to establish their careers. It's so competitive out there. I really miss my two.'

He didn't immediately answer. Then he said softly, 'I miss mine, too.'

His words were so full of sadness and seemed oddly final. Sara felt his resistance, like the pull of the tide, dragging her away from the subject with a quiet relentlessness. She hesitated, wondering what was behind his unwillingness to engage about his children. But she felt she didn't know him well enough, yet, to ask.

Bernard was talking, deftly changing the tenor of the conversation. 'OK, so I've visited your place. Time for you to visit mine.' Before she had a chance to agree, he added, 'Are you free on Saturday? There's this Thai café in Hastings, in an old bookshop. You sit and eat in these little nooks, surrounded by floor-to-ceiling books. Great food, too. All home-cooked. Maybe you could come and see the house, then we'll go there for an early supper?'

'Sounds wonderful,' she replied, thoughts of his children forgotten in her pleasure at the prospect of the weekend. The brief silence that followed felt almost alive with possibility. 'Look forward to it,' she said softly.

14

The part of the phone conversation about the twins left Bernard feeling very uneasy. It was the beginning of all that he'd dreaded when he'd taken the plunge with Sara – made the call last Sunday that had ended in probably the best kiss of his entire life. Like the first tiny crack in an eggshell. Checking the time on his mobile – it was only just after nine – he pressed his daughter's number, knowing as he did so that the chances of Carrie picking up were beyond slim. He was right. The call went straight to voicemail.

'Hi, sweetheart,' Bernard said, unable to keep the weary frustration from his voice. 'Please . . . can you call me? We really need to talk. It's been ages.' He paused. 'Hope you're OK,' he added, in a more conciliatory tone.

Sighing, he clicked off and immediately pressed Adam's number, with the same vain hope that his son would pick up. He almost jumped when an actual voice said, 'Hey, Dad.'

'Just rang for a chat,' Bernard said, almost adding, as he had in his message to Carrie, 'It's been a while,' but thinking better of it. He didn't want to sound peevish, now he finally had his son on the line.

Silence.

'How's things?'

A tired sigh, then Adam replied, 'Yeah, you know . . .'

'Keeping on top of it?'

'Just about . . . on the work front, at least.'

Bernard thought he knew what Adam meant, and didn't like the sound of it. 'You seem exhausted. It's the summer. Aren't you due a break? You should come home, get some good sea air, recharge your batteries.'

He heard a harsh snort and his son snapped, 'Fat chance. I've got a major assessment coming up next month, Dad.'

Adam sounded annoyed that he didn't know – although how could he, when his son never called? – and Bernard had to take a breath to prevent himself snapping back. 'What sort of assessment?'

'Clinical skills. I'm shitting myself.'

'Oh, you'll be fine.'

Adam laughed. 'Like your confidence, Dad. I could be a really crap doctor, for all you know.'

'I'm sure you're a brilliant one. Mamma would be so proud.'

There was a long silence. 'Adam?'

'Mamma never really thought about whether I'd be suited to medicine, though, did she?'

Bernard was shaken by the bitterness in his son's tone. 'What are you saying, Adam?'

'I'm saying . . . I'm saying . . . Fuck knows.' He stopped abruptly. 'Can't do this now, Dad. Got to go.'

'No, wait, son. You sound –'

'I'm fine,' Adam interrupted, his tone closing down further enquiry.

'Have you heard from Carrie?' Bernard asked quickly, before he lost him.

'Umm ... She's OK, I think,' Adam replied vaguely. 'Anyway ...'

Desperate not to let his son go, Bernard said, 'Listen, maybe I could come up for a weekend after your assessment thing? I'd love to see you. Catch up properly.' He winced at the pleading note in his voice.

'Yeah ... See how things go, eh, Dad?'

Which means no, Bernard thought sadly.

Heavens, he reminds me of his mother, he realized, as they said goodbye, the thought making him uneasy. The same veiled listlessness, the same plaintive tone, implying that things were harder for him than for others. *It's just the rigours of the course*, he assured himself, blocking the notion that his son was buckling under a more serious pressure, never spoken of between them.

But Adam had never been robust like his sister. Bernard had always put this down to Ilsa's determined mollycoddling. She called Adam her 'little faun' and regularly used to sleep in the boy's bed because – after a mild attack of croup when he was two – she said she worried about his breathing. Adam became like her shadow, always knowing more about what his mum needed – what ailments currently plagued her, how best to remedy them – than Bernard.

He knew it wasn't healthy for Adam, or for Carrie, who'd got only a fraction of her mother's attention, but he'd felt powerless in the face of his wife's stubborn willpower. He knew he'd let both the twins down, of course, in more ways than one. But he had no idea how to remedy the problem in the here and now, how to relate to the adults his children had become, how to find the closeness he remembered from the past, when they'd seemed so happy to see him, hugged him with such clear love. These days he felt as if he was a mere irritant, an unwelcome interruption in their day.

15

Sara knew where his village was, perched high on the cliffs to the east of Hastings, but she'd never been there. Bernard had given her specific directions, because the satnav lost the will to live round the tiny single-track lanes that wound, like a rabbit warren, around the houses lining the cliff edge.

She'd had a stressful week. Giving in to the tension of not hearing from Julian, she had emailed him again, asking how he was and whether he would consider having a phone conversation to smooth things out. But she'd sent it on Monday and so far there had been no response. With back-to-back clients and a nutrition workshop in the village hall at Ditchling, there was little time to think about Bernard. Also, it seemed Heather had been right, and her mother-in-law was now in heart failure, although so far only to a moderate degree. So, there'd been tests and Dr Withy had prescribed more medication. But the general feeling was that, at her age, any aggressive treatment would be unkind. It had upset Sara. 'Heart failure' sounded so final. The strings that bound her to her dead husband, although stretched by Bernard's kiss, were still the foundation of her life, Margaret her surrogate mother, ever since her own had died from breast-cancer complications when Sara was in her thirties.

She bumped the Mini along the pitted lane, the grass

hump between the tyres swishing against the undercarriage. Slowing almost to a stop, she saw the wooden gate – propped open – and the house name, *Kittiwake*, on a worn slate plaque, almost hidden in the hedge. It was another hot, sultry night, the air thundery with summer rain. Her stomach was in knots and she took a moment to breathe and calm her pounding heart as she pulled around the final bend and out into a large rectangle of limestone gravel.

The house was ahead, silhouetted against the sky, the clumps of sea pinks and the silvery fronds of buckthorn bushes planted either side dancing in the breeze. As Sara stared, she felt a tiny stab of disappointment. Without much information to go on, she'd imagined a modern, architectural structure with clean lines and lots of glass – the sort of house you'd picture on a clifftop, with stunning views to be had. But what she saw was a low, boxy, timber-framed house with a single sloping roof positioned towards the sea. The wood, in vertical planks, was faded to a pleasing driftwood grey, but the windows – on the landward side of the house, anyway – were small.

Her thoughts were interrupted by the heavy wooden front door being thrown open. Bernard emerged, in a white T-shirt and shorts, onto the slate-flagged surround, a welcoming smile on his face as he came towards her.

Sara parked and took a final deep breath. *Here we go*, she thought, more nervous than she could ever remember being.

'Hey.' Bernard opened the car door for her. 'No problems getting here?'

She grabbed her bag and climbed out. 'Lucky you told

me. The satnav would probably have driven me over the cliff.'

He banged the car door shut and there was a moment when they might have embraced, but instead he held out his hand, ushering her towards the house.

Bernard's tanned face was tense with expectation, she noticed, as she took in the space, fronting the sea, that constituted the living room and open-plan kitchen.

'This is great,' she said dutifully. But the windows on this side were not much bigger than the ones at the back, the spectacular sea view broken into a row of square panes that lined the wall. Nor was the ceiling particularly high. *Maybe the view is upstairs in the bedrooms*, she thought, as she looked around, conscious of Bernard's eyes on her. The furniture was modern but comfortable: two large sofas in neutral colours, lined with beautiful tapestry cushions in geometric patterns and muted hues, flanked the woodburning stove in the sitting area, a long slate coffee-table between. Abstract art in blues, yellows and greys hung on the walls, a rectangular, glass-framed mirror above the stove. The simplicity of the furnishings and the atmosphere of insulated quiet should have been restful, but for Sara it felt too quiet, almost claustrophobic. She quickly brushed off her first impressions. 'These are lovely,' she said, with genuine enthusiasm, picking up one of the cushions and smoothing her hand over the surface of the exquisite needlepoint.

'Ilsa did them. It was her passion,' Bernard said, almost dismissing her remark as he asked quickly, 'Is the house what you expected?'

She smiled. 'You didn't tell me anything about it except

it was an eco-house, so I had no expectations,' she said. 'Explain what makes it so sustainable.'

'OK, but first, can I get you a drink? Cup of tea? Glass of wine? Shall we go outside? It's so hot in here . . . although I can feel a storm brewing.'

He moved towards the kitchen area, which, puzzlingly, was not cluttered, like her own, with bottles and jars and pepper grinders, bowls of lemons and tomatoes, coffee machine and pods and a basil plant, but had polished granite work surfaces on which there stood nothing but a kettle, a toaster and a barrel cactus, its pale spikes lined up as neatly as the rest of the space. As if he'd just moved in and hadn't yet unpacked. *Must be an architect thing*, she thought. 'Tea would be good.'

'Builder's, Earl Grey, Lapsang, herbal?'

She opted for builder's because her brain was so over-excited she couldn't process the rest of the list. Mugs in hand, he ushered her outside onto the terrace, where he'd already laid cushions on the wooden bench-seat and chairs. She felt her lungs fill with the fresh clifftop air, and was relieved to be in the cool breeze – Lewes had been stifling all day. The view over the sea as the sun went down to the west in a haze of hot gold was breathtaking and she took a moment just to stare. 'It's amazing up here,' she said, as Bernard indicated the bench for her and took one of the chairs for himself. The house stood perhaps two hundred yards from the cliff edge across an area of patchy windswept grass – dry and yellowing from the heat. Stony, chalky soil, a bramble hedge and a rackety line of barbed wire was the only barrier between it and the sea.

On the terrace, the atmosphere felt instantly lighter

between them. Conversation had seemed to flounder in the dense quiet of the house – a quiet that she remembered Bernard mentioning as a 'heavy, clock-ticking silence' in one of their early phone conversations. Now she knew what he meant.

But she was still nervous and found herself almost holding her breath, her tea going untouched on the garden table.

'So, the house,' Bernard began. 'We used recycled wood for the structure, and there's a ground-source heat pump, smart thermostat, big emphasis on insulation – walls, windows and doors – solar panels on the roof and rainwater/grey water conservation.' He stopped, grinned. 'The old girl's a bit long in the tooth now, nearly twenty-five years old. But it really is cheap to run. Expensive to set up, but my energy bill is tiny.' He eyed her keenly across the table. 'Do you like it?'

'I think it's great,' she said, with as much enthusiasm as she could muster. 'What a location. It felt quite insulated inside . . . I suppose you have to keep the weather out, up here.' Glancing at the horizon, she noticed heavy clouds beginning to mask the sun, the wind suddenly much fresher. 'Speaking of which, it looks a bit threatening over there right now.'

'I'd have more light, more view, if I was building it now,' Bernard said, also glancing across at the impending storm but making no comment. He seemed keen to get his point across. 'But Ilsa . . .' He cleared his throat. 'She was Finnish, and she loved the old-style wooden houses back home. Plus, she suffered from terrible migraines all her life. Light hurt her eyes. She insisted on the windows

95

being smaller and designed to be shaded, if necessary. You can't do that easily with a wide expanse of glass, of course.'

Sara didn't know how to react. She didn't want to agree with Bernard – although she did – and so denigrate the design of the house. 'You two worked together?' she asked carefully.

'At the beginning,' he replied. 'But when the twins were born, she made the decision to be a full-time mum.' He shrugged, and Sara wasn't sure if he was questioning his wife's decision.

'I didn't go back to work till mine were at school. I don't know how women do both with small kids, especially twins. That must have been exhausting.'

'Ilsa had poor health, too . . . crippling asthma. It was what killed her, in fact.'

'Oh, God . . . how awful. I'm so sorry.' The air went still for a second. It was clear that the words had been wrenched reluctantly from Bernard's mouth.

Then he was talking again, his speech hurried, as if he were running away from the revelation of his wife's death. 'She would never have managed work as well . . . But she was a good mother, absolutely devoted to Adam and Carrie.'

'I admire her, sticking with it. I'm afraid I couldn't wait to get back to work when Peggy started nursery.'

Bernard didn't reply immediately. He was making her nervous. His face seemed to have settled into vexed lines as he gazed out to sea and at the darkening sky, the air now heavy, thick with tiny thunder flies. She wondered what on earth was going through his mind.

He got up, stood there in the dying light, arms folded defensively. Looking down at her, a frown between his brows, he said, 'I've been so looking forward to seeing you. Seeing you and showing you the house.' She opened her mouth to reply, but he was in full flow. 'But all I've done since you got here is bang on about Ilsa.' He stopped. 'It's just having you here, in her space . . .' For a moment he looked lost.

She hesitated. 'I can imagine.' Although, interestingly, she hadn't found having Bernard in her home a problem. Odd, but not a problem.

Bernard took a long breath, his arms still clutched tight to his body. She thought she saw a shudder pass through him. He gave her an anxious smile, his eyes softening. 'I don't want to keep thinking of her, not when you're here.'

She laughed. 'I struggle with that too. When I'm with Pete's mum, Margaret who's old and not well – I feel like I'm betraying his memory, just thinking about you. It's natural, I suppose.'

Before Bernard had time to reply, there was a long, low roll of thunder, which seemed to be barrelling towards them over the sea at high speed. They looked at each other in alarm. 'Better get inside,' he said, grabbing the cushions as she collected the mugs. They were just in time. A bolt of lightning silently lit up the clifftop scene, like a black-and-white movie, followed by a deafening crack of thunder directly overhead. Sara felt large fat raindrops cooling her hot cheeks – she loved summer storms.

Inside, she was immediately aware of the claustrophobic warmth of the room, which wrapped around her like a sticky blanket.

Bernard rinsed the mugs at the sink. Speaking with his back to her, almost as if he were talking to himself, he muttered, 'Being haunted by the past can be hard, though.'

'Do you feel "haunted"?' she asked, surprised by his choice of words, surprised even more to feel a faint shiver run up the back of her neck as she spoke. She glanced around, reacting involuntarily to the sensation that she was being watched. *Did you expect some headless phantom levitating in the corner?* she chided herself, feeling instantly foolish. There was, nonetheless, a strange atmosphere in the room.

Bernard seemed to shake himself. His voice was firm as he stood the mugs upside down on the draining board and turned to her, 'No . . . no, of course not.' He lifted his hands in a gesture of apparent apology. 'Listen, can we start again? Pretend you've just arrived?' The smile he gave her was brighter. 'Would you like a glass of wine or something, before we go down to the bookshop? We can take my car. You won't be driving till later.'

'Thanks, wine would be nice.' Sara hoped a hit of alcohol might dissolve some of her own tension. She wished they could relax with each other in the way they had previously. *Is this a terrible mistake?* she asked herself. In his own home, where she might have assumed he'd feel the most at ease, Bernard seemed so on edge. Not at all the man she'd had tea and dinner with. *I should go, put him out of his misery.* At the thought she might have to drive home, she hesitated before sipping her wine. She'd been right: there was something dark beneath the ever-changing landscape of confidence, humour and painful vulnerability on his handsome face. Something odd about the house, too. But she knew she wouldn't leave precipitously: she liked him too much.

As they sat at the oak kitchen table, he with a glass of elderflower, she with her wine, both jumped as another thunderclap drowned what Bernard had begun to say. The rain was beating on the windows with fury now, the maelstrom outside unrecognizable from the gorgeous summer evening of an hour ago.

'Bloody hell,' Bernard said, laughing – the first genuine laugh she'd heard since she arrived. 'We're used to the full Monty up here, but they're really putting on a show for you tonight.'

Sara nodded, eyes wide. She might like storms, but this elemental force outside – the house so exposed and precarious – was unsettling. She knew the whole area of cliff was potentially crumbling, and tonight it felt like another bite was being taken out.

Bernard was eyeing her. 'Umm . . . it's so nasty out there . . . What do you say to giving the Thai a miss? We can go another time. I'll cook?' It was as if the storm had released a pent-up tension in Bernard. He looked almost relieved.

'OK,' she said cautiously. She had no desire to drive in this weather, although she still wasn't sure how much Bernard wanted her there. Or, indeed, how much she wanted to stay.

He got up immediately, found another glass and poured himself some wine. Holding it up to Sara, he said, 'Sorry.'

Sara couldn't tell exactly what he was apologizing for.

*

The storm had abated, but rain still poured down. Bernard hooked a ladle of steaming spaghetti out of the copper pan and piled it into the two bowls he'd placed on the pristine worktop. 'Cream in a carbonara is tourist-inspired sacrilege, according to my Italian friend, Alessandra,' he said, handing Sara her bowl. He had lighted a couple of fat beeswax candles and placed them in the centre of the kitchen table, tossed a green salad and grated some pecorino.

Sara laughed. 'I don't put cream in mine, but I'm not being smug. My recipe was obviously written by an Italian.'

When they were both seated – on either side at the corner of the table – she looked at him and grinned. 'I think you're affected by barometric pressure, you know, this muggy air. You've been much happier since it began to rain.' Much happier, and the connection between them had revived suddenly, like power being restored after a blackout, as she'd sat with her wine and watched him cook.

He gave a sceptical laugh. 'That's a thing?'

'According to my friend Precious, it affects blood pressure, joint pain, headaches. Before a storm it usually drops very low.'

'Hmm, I think it's more to do with being here with you. Being able to tell you how I'm feeling . . . and you understanding.' He stopped eating, his fork poised over his bowl. 'You don't think the things I say are weird?'

Not 'weird' exactly, she thought, with a private smile.

'I told you the other night. I'm bad at filtering stuff.'

'You're just being honest. Nothing wrong with that.'

For a moment his face went still. He began to speak,

then stopped. It was a habit of his, despite his insistence that he didn't filter his words. 'Not sure it's honesty,' he said.

She stared at him. He stared back. The breath she exhaled was light as air, floating from her body like a wraith. She put her fork down in the silent kitchen and was surprised by the sharp ting it made as it grazed the china bowl. Bernard was still watching her. She blushed but did not break his gaze.

After what seemed like an eternity, Bernard spoke, his tone almost regretful. 'You're able to be so . . . so relaxed, when you talk about your Pete. You must have had a really good marriage.' When she didn't immediately reply, he went on, 'I suppose if it was that good, I'm worried you'll compare me to him and find me wanting.' He gave her a sheepish grin. 'Not that it's a competition, of course.'

Sara considered her reply. 'You and Pete are so different, it would be impossible to compare you,' she began. 'He was uncomplicated, loved the outdoors, worked to live rather than the other way round. He made me laugh . . . and he was a great father.' She stopped, catching a sudden vivid image of Pete's open smile, aware of incipient tears. But, with Bernard so close, the memory didn't seem to touch her as forcefully as usual. Pete's face was like a small thumbnail image in the corner of a big screen containing Bernard's. Still significant, but no longer present.

Bernard was eyeing her, a hint of amusement in his grey eyes. 'You think I'm complicated?'

She smiled as she nodded. 'Maybe "complex" is a better word. But, yes, I'd say so.'

'Is that a bad thing?' He reached for her hand. 'God, Sara, it's so good talking to you. I feel as if there's this open channel between us . . . like I can be who I really am – complex or not. You . . .' He stopped as if he were suddenly aware of the strength of his words.

The touch of his warm hand was the utmost pleasure to Sara. She swallowed nervously, waited. The air was humming. Food forgotten, both pushed back their chairs and rose simultaneously. Without another word, they moved into each other's arms. Not kissing at first, they just held each other close. He smelt of pine and the sea, as if he'd become part of the natural world around him. She breathed him in, wanting to kiss him, but also just wanting to hold him, to feel him, to know him this way.

When she looked up, her eyes met his. Both hesitated, drawing the moment out, every second increasing the rate of her heart, the vibrations coursing through her body. She saw the faintest twitch of a muscle in his cheek, the flutter of his dark lashes, the small scar that broke his right eyebrow in two. She reached up as he leant down and their mouths touched. Hot, charged, yet soft and infinitely sensual, his kiss aroused her just as much as it had the first time.

Breathless, she pulled back, having an odd moment of realization: *Me, in this room, kissing this man . . . wanting this man.* Bernard was looking at her, his hands on her upper arms, holding her gently. She could tell from his eyes, dark with arousal, that he was as fired up as she.

'Come,' he said, taking her hand and leading her over to the sofa.

As her head fell back against the cushions, she felt her

body letting go, taking over her thoughts and blocking all previous uncertainty. This was elemental. His mouth found hers again and she closed her eyes.

A while later, the time incalculable, irrelevant, they lay breathless in each other's arms.

Bernard, stroking the back of her hand very gently with his thumb, gave her a questioning look. 'You're not thinking of going home tonight, are you?'

His question, even through the haze of sensuality they had created, caused Sara to hold her breath.

Bernard's bedroom was warm, dimly lit, rain pattering on the skylight, the bed large and high, covered with soft white linen, a faded turquoise quilt folded tidily across the foot. She sat down; he sat beside her. And suddenly she felt self-conscious, the spell from earlier broken.

Turning to him, she swallowed nervously. 'I haven't done this.'

'Nor have I, if it helps.'

He got up and eased her to her feet. Holding her face gently between his palms as he cast a long, searching look into her eyes, he pressed another kiss on her mouth. Then, tossing the duvet back, he held out his hand. Kicking off their shoes, they sank onto the mattress fully dressed and pulled the duvet over them. She laughed as he drew her close. 'Better?' he asked.

It took them a while to relax, to retrieve the same desire that had ignited their earlier kisses. Fumbling with each other's clothes made them laugh. The bed was hot, but she needed the shelter of the duvet, suddenly aware of her age and her less-than-perfect nakedness. The sex, halting at first, gradually whispered to life, like a long-neglected motor. As with the kisses, neither was in a hurry. It felt fragile, almost tentative: the beginning of something, not an end goal. It had been so long. Just being in a man's arms, feeling how much he wanted her, meant she came almost as soon as he pressed up inside her.

Both were smiling as they lay close, their bodies hot and sweating. Bernard turned to her, his finger drifting gently down her cheek. 'The way you are, Sara . . . so real . . .'

The strength of feeling she heard in his words embarrassed her. She took his hand and kissed his fingers, holding them briefly against her lips. 'You don't know me,' she said.

'Ah, but I think I do.' He turned on his side, propping himself up on his elbow. His almost white hair was sticking out at all angles, his tanned face still flushed, his eyes bright. 'I think you're someone who's at ease with herself. You don't posture or pretend. As I said before, that's rare.'

'You don't posture or pretend either, as far as I can tell.'

But he moved his arm and fell onto his back again, not answering. He let out a careful breath. 'It's not as simple as that with me.'

She frowned. 'Meaning?'

Again, he didn't immediately reply. Then he laughed and rolled over, pulling her into his arms. 'Nothing! Just being my usual crazy self.' He dropped a kiss on her hair. 'Do you want tea, more wine?' He glanced past her at the bedside clock. 'It's late, nearly twelve. You will stay, won't you?'

Sara hesitated. The rain had finally stopped, but the

thought of driving over an hour back home in the damp, clammy summer night was not appealing. Still reeling, her body tingling gently from the unaccustomed sex, she didn't feel she had the energy to move. But sleeping beside someone, she'd always thought, was almost more intimate than sex, especially here, in what must have been the bed Bernard shared with Ilsa. *Will it be awkward in the morning?*

When she did wake, disoriented for a moment until she remembered where she was, the space beside her was empty. She sat up and looked around. It was getting light outside, the fine August dawn creating a soft haze through the uncurtained windows.

'Bernard?' she called.

She got out of bed, glancing at the clock: 05:06. Needing to pee, she pushed open the door to the en-suite bathroom, flush with the wall to the right of the bed. A navy towelling dressing-gown hung from the hook behind the door, and she wrapped it round herself – her clothes were still scattered over the bedroom floor where they'd been kicked from under the duvet during their lovemaking.

The bathroom was like the kitchen. No shaving paraphernalia, no toothbrush or paste, only a thick, square bar of soap, studded with dark specks she found to be lavender when she lathered her hands.

Everything, as she noticed when she opened the mirrored cupboard above the basin, was stacked neatly on the shelves. *Strange.* She widened her eyes at herself in the mirror.

Downstairs, it was quiet and still. She went over to one of the windows. It was a gorgeous day, sparkling fresh from the dousing it had received last night, the early sun already hot on her face through the windowpane. As she stood watching the morning light gather strength, she saw a figure walking slowly towards the house from the east. Bernard had on a white T-shirt and navy shorts, but he hugged his arms to his chest as if he were cold. He seemed deep in thought and she wondered what was going through his mind.

Anxious not to be caught staring, she turned from the window and was aware again of the solid, watchful atmosphere of the room that greeted her. The quiet unsettled her, and she didn't know what to do with herself as she waited for Bernard to return.

16

Bernard started when he saw her curled on the sofa and gave a small groan. 'Oh, God, I disturbed you. I'm sorry, I tried to be so quiet.'

'You didn't. I just woke with the light and came to find you,' she said. 'I saw you outside.'

He came over and stood looking down at her. He'd brought with him the salty smell of the sea, the freshness of the morning air. The smile he gave her seemed relaxed, a far cry from the tense man who'd greeted her the previous evening.

'Coffee?'

She nodded and stood, suddenly conscious of her nakedness beneath his dressing-gown, her bare feet.

'Hmm, looks better on you,' he said.

She laughed as he pulled her close.

When they made it back downstairs for the coffee Bernard had proposed earlier, it was nearly ten o'clock. They had slept after they made love, the sex like a gentle echo of the night before, reinforcing the pleasure they felt in each other's arms.

After a shower and putting on yesterday's rumpled summer dress, Sara sat at the table while Bernard made the coffee, put some croissants to warm in the oven, and set the table with jams and a bowl of blueberries. She felt lost in a haze of sensuality. Sex had been so absent from her life that it was almost like the first time, this recognition of herself as a sexual being, a woman who is desired. A gratified smile played around her mouth that she made no attempt to control. *He looks so handsome in his clean blue shirt*, she thought, and every time he came close, she caught a waft of his soapy freshness and wanted to make him stop so she could breathe him in.

'Well,' he said, as he put the pastries on the table and sat down, 'I have to say . . . you're something else.' He sounded so serious it made her laugh through her blushes.

'Don't look so tragic,' she said.

'I just mean, being with you . . . it's really blown me away.'

She nodded a silent agreement.

'When I was walking on the cliffs this morning, I couldn't stop smiling.' He looked apologetic, as if he'd caught himself out in an embarrassing confession. There was silence as he took a gulp of coffee. 'Is it our age, do you think?' he asked. 'Have we reached a time in our life when we're more open, more aware of ourselves . . . less of the grab-and-go of our youth?'

It was impossible not to compare what she felt for Bernard with what she remembered feeling for Pete in those heady early days of falling in love for the first time. Back then, they'd slipped into their love affair with a naïve certainty she no longer felt about anything in her life. 'I don't think you can explain it,' she said.

His face relaxed. 'And better not, eh?'

*

Sara left Bernard late morning. She was due at Margaret's for a sandwich lunch at one. Driving home, she wanted to sing. She set the radio to Gold at full volume, the windows wide, and accompanied Debbie Harry for the chorus of 'One Way Or Another' as she hit the A27, her lungs feeling as if they could project her voice all the way over the clifftops to France.

Heather's eyes widened slightly in amusement as she greeted Sara, but she didn't comment. Sara wondered if she had jam around her mouth, or toothpaste in her hair.

'She's a bit away with the fairies today,' Heather said, in response to Sara's query about her mother-in-law. 'She'll be glad to see you.'

Sara checked the hall mirror before she went in to see Margaret. She instantly understood what Heather had spotted. The face that looked back at her was lit up like a chandelier, eyes glittering, the dark circles beneath offset by a glow on her skin she had never seen before. She pulled a face, tried, unsuccessfully, to make herself look respectable, vaguely normal. Then gave in to her joy and laughed at her reflection, sweeping her hair back and shaking it out, running her finger over her lips in imitation of Bernard's earlier.

Margaret was dozing when she went in. But when she woke to Sara's presence, her face broke into a gentle smile. Sara bent to kiss her cheek. Her kiss was especially tender today, her love for this woman magnified by the fear that she might not be with them much longer.

'Shall we get the albums out?' Sara asked, when both had helped themselves to a couple of Heather's unique tomato sandwiches – bread cut wafer thin, just the right amount of butter and salt, crusts off for Margaret's teeth and cut into titchy squares. Sara adored them.

The old lady stared at her for a moment. 'Do we need to? He's right here.'

Sara didn't need to ask who Margaret was talking about this time.

Margaret nodded slowly, as if she were listening to someone Sara couldn't see. When she spoke, her voice was oddly mechanical. 'He says not to worry, dear.' She smiled to herself. 'He says . . . he says you don't need to wait any more. Everything's fine.'

A shiver went down Sara's spine. She reached out and laid her hand over her mother-in-law's. 'Is Pete . . .' she began, tears springing to her eyes.

Margaret stared blankly at her. Then she focused again and gave Sara a radiant smile. 'Oh, yes. He's here. My son's always here with me now.' Then she closed her eyes, the hand that had held the sandwich dropping gently to her lap.

Sara took it from her and removed her plate. She wanted to cry. All the emotions of the past few days flooded in. Bernard had overwhelmed her. It was he who, every minute, filled her thoughts, these days. Not Pete any more. But the loosening of that solid, comforting, uncomplicated bond with her dead husband was like another bereavement. *Is Margaret telling me this is OK? Does she know, without being told?* she asked herself. Or was she really talking to Pete somehow, somewhere in the ether? *Is he the one who's telling me it's all right?*

Sara tiptoed out of the room. Heather was sitting at the kitchen table, reading the local paper. 'She's asleep.'

'Fancy another cuppa?' Heather enquired, closing the paper.

'No . . . thanks. The sandwiches were lovely, as usual.' She hovered as Heather eyed her closely.

'You OK?'

Sara sighed and crossed her arms, feeling a tremor run through her and realizing she was incredibly tired. 'She seems to feel she's with Pete,' she said quietly. 'Talking to him, even.'

Heather raised her eyebrows. 'It's easy to say it's just in her head but . . .' she gave a small shrug '. . . who knows? Maybe she can hear him.'

Sara frowned. She was not given to fanciful notions about other worlds – although she found the idea comforting, in principle, and had especially after Pete's death. 'Margaret's never shown any signs she believes in anything but a robust Christian afterlife,' she said.

Heather hesitated. Then she said, 'I've seen it before. Sometimes when people get very frail, it's like the veil gets thinner between them and whatever's going on out there.' She gave a self-deprecating laugh. 'I'm not saying there is anything, just that I've seen people affected by it.'

'If it comforts her,' Sara said, still touched by her mother-in-law's pronouncement. 'I get the feeling she's slipping away, Heather.'

Bernard phoned around six that evening. Sara was making minestrone, the soothing task of slicing the onions and garlic, of chopping the carrots, celery and potato into small cubes, like a meditation. It was pretty much all she could manage. She'd spent the rest of the afternoon clearing weeds from the garden paving, putting a wash on, napping for half an hour in the navy velvet Edwardian armchair in the kitchen, wrapped in her large cardigan. She looked at his name on her phone screen for a second and smiled.

'Hello,' she said, putting the knife down and wiping her free hand on the teacloth hanging from her black joggers' pocket.

'Hello,' Bernard said. She could almost hear him smiling. 'What are you doing?'

'Making soup. You?'

'I tried to work. Then I went for a walk. Then I listened to some stirring Beethoven and read for a couple of paragraphs.' He chuckled. 'Nothing very useful. I can't seem to concentrate.'

She laughed, knowing what he meant.

'How was your mother-in-law?'

Sara wasn't sure if she could share her experience, but she found herself telling him, anyway. 'She was in quite a strange mood, actually. Hearing voices . . . Pete's, specifically.' She thought he would laugh, pooh-pooh the very suggestion, but he didn't.

'Lovely for her.'

She asked, 'Do you think she *can* hear him?'

'Just because we don't know how doesn't mean it can't happen.' He added, his voice pensive, 'I can sometimes feel things . . . people.'

Sara frowned. *Does he mean Ilsa?* It was on the tip of her tongue to ask, but something in his tone stopped her. It seemed like a private moment, not one he would want to be quizzed about.

'Makes sense,' he went on. 'We spend our whole life

keeping our defences up in order to survive. It must be nice to let go and allow the voices in.'

Sara thought she agreed. There was always that layer of holding herself together, functioning, doing the proper thing. She'd often wondered what it would feel like to stop. 'Pete . . .' She was about to tell him the words Margaret had heard from her son. Bernard didn't interrupt, and she took a breath. 'Pete apparently told her he was OK,' she went on, almost embarrassed.

'That must be good to hear . . . for anyone who's lost someone.'

He's talking as if he believes Pete actually spoke, she thought. 'Margaret . . . she said he told her I shouldn't wait, that everything was all right,' she finished reluctantly.

There was silence.

'How do you feel about that?'

She swallowed, trying to clear the lump in her throat. Then she found herself crying. 'Sorry, I'm so sorry,' she mumbled, trying desperately to get herself under control. 'I think I'm just tired.'

'Sara . . .' His voice was so tender, it only made her cry the more.

'It's just . . .' She didn't know what it was 'just': her thoughts were swirling around in such a crazy hotchpotch of past and present that it made her feel almost dizzy.

'Hey, it's OK,' he said. 'Must have been pretty disturbing, being given a message from your dead husband.'

'I don't know if I even believe it. But Margaret certainly did.'

There was a long silence, while Sara found a tissue and blew her nose.

'You know, if we're going too quickly,' Bernard said, 'I'll quite understand if you want to take things slower.'

'No,' she said firmly. 'No. Pete is my past. I've stayed there way too long.' She took a shaky breath.

After another silence, Bernard said, 'What sort of soup?'

She told him, and he asked, 'Do you put pasta in?'

'No. Just beans. I know I should, traditionally, but it gets too starchy, with potatoes as well.'

'Save some for me?' he said.

'I'd ask you over,' she replied, thinking how lovely it would be to see him right now, 'but I'm so tired, I can hardly speak. You've worn me out.'

She heard his warm laugh. 'Me too. Fun, though, eh?'

After they'd said goodbye, Sara went back to dicing and frying and stirring, her hands on autopilot. *This thing with Bernard*, she thought. It was as if she'd jumped from a plane without a parachute: both thrilling and utterly terrifying at the same time.

17

This thing with Sara . . . Bernard thought, as he sprawled on the sofa, phone still in his hand after their call. Images, sensations from the previous night floated back to him, sending a delightful tremor through his body. *It's serious*.

But on top of these visions, crowding out the current pleasure, came older memories, triggered by their conversation about the dead. He realized he was envious of Pete's words – so kind, so sanguine – whether they were real or not. Setting Sara free, if that was what she wanted. *If only,* he thought.

These memories seemed not to be in the past, though. They were not even distanced, like watching a movie. This was immediate. Real life playing out, right there in his living room, himself one of the main protagonists.

Ilsa's call had summoned him back from a site visit nearly an hour from home that March day. He was irritated, to say the least. This was the third time in as many weeks that she'd interrupted him to say her breathing was bad and she was frightened. But each time, when he arrived back, he found her pale and exhausted, but not at all breathless.

The asthma attacks did seem to be getting more frequent, he'd noticed, but Ilsa, with her recent unexplained aversion to hospitals and mainstream medicine, refused to be checked out, to get her medication reviewed. She relied instead on Fran, her holistic practitioner, who bombarded her with foul-tasting herbal infusions that made her retch, acupuncture and breathing exercises, none of which seemed to make the slightest difference – not least, perhaps, because Ilsa was flaky, dilettante in her compliance.

This time seemed no different. It was bitterly cold – spring seemingly still a long way off. When he got back, after a panicky drive across the frozen Downs, she was lying quietly on the sofa, her head on one of her tapestry cushions, blinds down. The room was very still. Bernard remembered forcing himself to be calm, to be patient when he saw, yet again, that she was not struggling for breath. He *was* sympathetic, obviously. Not being able to breathe must be hell.

'How are you?' he asked, looking down at his wife.

Ilsa opened her eyes. She had beautiful eyes, the palest Nordic blue, clear like an early spring sky. She reached up for his hand and smiled. A smile that always melted his heart. He sat down on the sofa beside her. 'Are you feeling better?'

She nodded. 'Sorry, Bernie,' she said weakly. 'I'm such a nuisance, aren't I? But I was frightened it was serious this time. I hate the cold – it always sets me off.'

He'd fetched her a blanket, made her a cup of green tea, checked that she'd got her inhaler by her side, then shut himself into his office to catch up on some work calls. He remembered being restless, resentful, wondering when he could decently take off again. He hadn't heard her. At least, he heard her coughing, but then she often did. By the time he emerged, nearly an hour later, she was turning blue and gasping, almost unconscious.

The doctors saved her. It was touch and go for a while, though. She hadn't been taking her medication, apparently, and her lungs were on fire. By the time they removed the tube – early the following morning – and Ilsa was able to breathe again, weakly, but unaided, Bernard was a complete wreck. He hadn't slept all night, his whole body crooked and aching from the slippery blue hospital chair. He'd even contemplated summoning the twins: Carrie, au-pairing in Ireland for a rich Dublin family – which she loathed; Adam, in Rabat, volunteering with kids, preparing to start his medical training in September. But the doctors assured him there was no need.

The first words Ilsa said, when she opened her eyes were 'I haven't died?'

Bernard smiled as he held her long, cool fingers. 'No, thank goodness. You're going to be fine.' Now the danger had passed he felt so angry with her for not taking her asthma drugs properly that he thought he might scream. But he wasn't going to have that conversation now.

His wife, impossibly beautiful in her wan, huge-eyed infirmity, had almost imperceptibly shaken her head on the pillow. 'I'm not, Bernie. I'm not going to make it.'

Bernard was very familiar with Ilsa's dramatic pronouncements about her health. He squeezed her hand. 'The attack was a bad one, sweetheart, but you pulled through. Look, you're breathing normally. You can go home tomorrow, the nurse said.'

Her eyebrows rose a little as she stared at him. Then her eyes filled with tears. 'Look after my babies for me. Please make sure they're safe, Bernie. Be a proper father.'

She took her hand from his and wiped away the tears. 'You haven't always been there for them, you know.'

Bernard bridled, but held his peace. 'Stop it, for God's sake, Ilsa. This is nonsense. *You are not going to die.*' He spoke the last words slowly, as if to a frightened child.

Nonsense. The word had snagged in his brain for months afterwards.

'Just promise me,' Ilsa begged quietly.

So Bernard did. He realized his wife must be discombobulated after the near-death experience of the previous night and decided to indulge her.

'I'm going to grab a coffee,' he told her, dropping a kiss on her forehead.

Ilsa closed her eyes.

By the time he got back – he'd been idling, half asleep, on a bench outside the hospital in the chilly sunshine – she was dead. A heart attack, probably brought on, they said, by the strain on her organs from the asthma attack. This time they couldn't save her.

If I'd paid attention to her coughing and got her to hospital sooner? If I'd realized she wasn't taking her drugs? If I'd believed her when she said she would die? If I hadn't gone for a coffee . . . These were the questions that plagued Bernard on a continuous loop in the early weeks after Ilsa's death – not least when he'd had to explain what had happened to his devastated children. There was no satisfactory answer to any of them at the time . . . or since.

On Monday morning Bernard drove to his office in Eastbourne, arriving just after seven thirty. Joe was in before him, as usual – Bernard often wondered if he slept there.

'Coffee? Beach?' Joe asked, as soon as Bernard walked in, leaning his large frame back in his chair and stretching his arms above his head, the sound he made somewhere between a yawn and a groan, his chair creaking loudly in sympathy.

'You look your usual knackered self, mate,' he said, once they were sitting nursing coffees in the sunshine on a bench along the promenade near the office. There was a tidy rectangle of colourful municipal blooms behind them, the lazy blue sea in front of them – still, as far as the horizon. Joe wiggled his eyebrows up and down and smirked.

Bernard sighed. 'Sara spent Saturday night with me . . . She's magic, Joe.'

His friend looked amused.

They sat in companionable silence, the early-morning stream of runners and dog-walkers flowing round their bench swelling with each passing minute.

'Listen, I'm sure she'll understand when you decide it's time to tell her,' Joe said, reading his thoughts. 'Or,' he added, as if the idea had just occurred to him, 'I suppose you could just not bring it up for the time being.'

'Basically keep on lying?' Bernard snorted derisively. 'You know where that's got me.'

Joe turned on the bench, his expression more serious than usual. 'Yeah, but the five years are nearly up, mate. You'll be off the hook. She's unlikely to find out unless you tell her.' He shrugged. 'I'm just saying, perhaps you don't need to mention it until you're much further down the line.'

He had thought about that. But his friend never seemed

to understand. What had happened was like an all-encompassing miasma from which he was unable to escape. The facts themselves no longer seemed relevant. It was the consequences – the twins, for instance – that haunted him and would continue to do so whether he told Sara or not. But entering this relationship with her seemed to have focused the miasma. Where previously it had swirled uncomfortably above his head, now it was twisting and narrowing, gathering force, like an oncoming tornado across the plain. He could feel it.

'If she sticks around, she'll meet the twins. They'll end up letting something slip, even if I don't . . . I can't lie to her, Joe. She's not that sort of woman.'

Now it was his friend's turn to snort. 'Tell Sara your secret and you'll have to kill her, you realize.'

Bernard tried to laugh at his friend's jest. The issue wasn't whether he trusted Sara or not – he knew he did. But it wasn't just *his* secret.

18

Sara and Precious sat with the usual cup of tea before their Monday-afternoon clients arrived. Sara had been regaling her friend with the events of the weekend. 'The house is sort of strange . . .' she added, after they'd discussed the storm, the supper, the significant fact she'd stayed the night.

'In what way?'

'It wasn't what I'd expected, I suppose. It's very closed up, almost muffled . . .' She stopped, not knowing how to articulate the atmosphere in the cliff house.

'Muffled?'

'Wrong word. I can't explain. It's a perfectly nice house. You probably wouldn't notice anything odd . . . Although it's really tidy, everything in cupboards, nothing on the kitchen surfaces. Even his toothbrush is put away. I assume it must be an architect thing.'

Her friend looked puzzled.

'And no photos. I've just realized. I didn't see a single photo.'

'Do you think he put them away before you arrived? Thinking you'd feel awkward or something, seeing pictures of his wife?'

'I wouldn't have felt awkward, although I suppose he couldn't have known that.' Bernard had even shown her his office, its desk covered with the paraphernalia of design, including a large computer and a separate tilted draughting desk, rolls of what she assumed were plans, a black saddle chair on castors. But there was nothing personal on show, unless you counted the exercise mat propped in the corner. 'It sounds really stupid, I know, but at one point I had this peculiar sensation . . . as if there was something behind me. Like I was being watched.'

Precious's eyes widened. 'Oh, my God, darling. You think the place is haunted?'

'No, no, of course not,' she said briskly, managing a laugh. 'It was just a peculiar feeling . . . I'm being ridiculous.'

Precious did not look convinced.

Sara sighed. 'I so wanted to like the house. I thought it would be open and modern, with huge windows, lots of light and views, but there's this unusual heaviness . . .'

'Hmm . . . Is the place putting you off, Sas?'

'Not at all,' she insisted. But she felt disconcerted nonetheless. In the telling of her night with Bernard, thoughts had coalesced. Thoughts to which she had no intention of giving credence.

Precious blew out her cheeks, checked her watch. 'Look, everyone's got stuff, Sas. You'll work it out. Sounds like he might be worth it.'

'Oh, he so is, Precious. It's how I feel about *him* that counts, isn't it?' She drained the remains of her tea. Apart from the house, the only lingering niggle she had was the curious absence of his children in his conversation . . . in his life.

'So what news of Adam and Carrie?' she'd asked over Sunday breakfast, having again banged on about the girls:

Peggy had sent her more extraordinary images of her Icelandic adventure, which she'd shared with Bernard.

Bernard had taken a moment to reply. 'Nothing, really. They're both a bit of a mystery to me as adults,' he'd eventually told her. 'I've seen so little of them in the last few years, since they left home.'

His reply was so toneless that Sara wasn't sure how to react. All she was asking for was a sense of them as people, as Bernard's children. But he wasn't giving her much to work with. *It's almost as if he's embarrassed by them*, she'd thought at the time.

'So enjoy every minute! It's about bloody time.' Precious was holding up her palm to Sara's in a celebratory high-five across the desk.

Sara sat for a moment after her friend had gone. She and Bernard had made a plan to meet the following Friday night, spend the bank-holiday weekend together at his house – the weather was forecast to be very hot and they could swim. The thought made her twitch with nervous excitement. She couldn't wait.

Sara took Thursday afternoon off to be home when Peggy, grubby and exhausted, arrived back from Iceland.

'Oh, my God, if I don't get a hot shower right this minute, I'll literally expire,' her daughter exclaimed, as her monstrous backpack thudded to the kitchen floor, the tin cup dangling from the strap clanging on the tiles. 'Tell you everything in a sec, Mum,' she added, scooting upstairs two at a time. Sara was delighted to see her, but she also felt apprehensive. It was going to be impossible to hide how strongly she felt about Bernard. Would her daughter be shocked at the speed with which things had taken off? Peggy had left on holiday before Bernard had even contacted her.

It was warm and bright again, but not as hot as it had been, so they had lunch outside. Sara thought her garden looked so pretty today. The blush-white shrub rose she'd planted a few years back was in full bloom, its sweet scent filling the small space; French marigolds sat in a large planter near the table, their orange and yellow flowers reflecting the sunshine; the neighbours' clematis flopped elegantly over her side of the wall, like a pretty young girl. She'd made a big salad and added some crusty rye bread and soft goat's cheese. Peggy was scrubbed and glowing – although her blue eyes had the jazzy look of the unslept – as she enthusiastically regaled Sara with her trip.

'It's a totally extraordinary country, Mum. You wouldn't believe,' she said. 'Beautiful and so empty, compared to ours. A lot of brown and green and grey in the landscape. But then you have this amazing light, which washes everything in these gorgeous colours and just blows your mind. It never really got properly dark.'

'I loved all your photos.'

Peggy swallowed a bit of bread. 'We stayed mostly in the south, did the whole hot-springs thing and the beach, checked out the unpronounceable volcano that caused all that trouble with the ash cloud. But the wildness, the feeling of freedom, really got to me.' She waved a hand in the air. 'England suddenly seems so crowded and tame.'

She talked on, Sara listening with real pleasure, enjoying watching her daughter's animated face.

'Did you and Natasha get on all right?'

'Yeah, you know . . . just a few minor irritations. Tash never wants to eat, and I always do. And she hates getting up early, even when it's stunning out there. Stuff like that. But we got on great most of the time.' She grinned. 'There were a couple of days of grim weather – no joke in a tent. But it was a fantastic trip, Mum.'

Sara made tea and brought out chocolate chip cookies. Still she hadn't managed to find a gap in the conversation into which she could drop Bernard. And remembering Peggy's anguish before she'd gone to Iceland about missing her dad, Sara wondered if she should say anything at this stage. But as they sat chatting with their drinks, she noticed Peggy eyeing her.

'Have you lost weight or something, Mum?'

'No . . .'

'You look great . . . sort of really healthy?'

Sara laughed, self-conscious under her daughter's forensic stare. Because she knew exactly why she was looking good, if that were the case.

'So, what's been going on? How's work?' Peggy gave her a sly grin. 'Been batting off any more pensioners?'

'Bloody cheek!' Sara swallowed, allowing herself a small smile. Given any more leeway, her face would crack open and she would be just one gigantic beam. 'Now you come to mention it, I have been spending time with someone . . .'

Her daughter was checking her phone, not really listening.

'We met in a tearoom before you went away. And, well, we've seen each other a bit since.' *That's enough for starters*, she thought, the breath fast in her chest even at this anodyne beginning.

Peggy, obviously half dead with tiredness, didn't appear to have taken in what she'd said. Then the penny dropped. She stared at her mother, mouth open. 'You've been . . .' She was lost for words.

'It's very early days,' Sara said, feeling hot with embarrassment.

Peggy continued to gape. 'Blimey, Mum . . . Who is this guy?'

She briefly filled in her daughter.

'Wow,' Peggy said. 'Does Joni know? Have you spoken to her?' The question was slightly anxious. She always looked to her big sister for the line to take with her mother. Now she seemed uncertain as to whether she should be pleased or not.

'Not yet.' Sara shifted in her seat. 'Is this a bit freaky for you?'

After a big intake of breath, Peggy gave her an apologetic grin. 'It sort of is . . . But it's great, Mum.'

There was silence, neither looking at the other. Sara gazed off down the garden towards the bamboo, trying to calm her breathing. For almost the first time ever, she wasn't sure what to say to her daughter. 'I know Dad's left a big hole . . .' she began, then faltered.

Peggy straightened. Ignoring her words, she said, 'So this Bernard, will I like him?'

It was a good question. Sara had always used her girls as a yardstick when considering her reaction to someone or something in life. 'I think you will . . . I hope you will.' She knew her smile was probably too revealing as a sudden image of Bernard making love to her sprang to mind. But she couldn't help it.

Peggy laughed self-consciously. 'Is that a blush I spy, staining your fair cheek, Mum?' Then her eyes took on a wistful look. 'God, I wish Joni was here. She *should* be here. It's horrible, her being so far away . . . forever.'

'I know. It's rubbish, isn't it?' Sara reached over for her daughter's hand and gave it a squeeze.

'Listen,' Peggy said, her tanned face clearing, 'me and Joni just want you to be happy.'

Sara gave a tentative smile of relief as she brushed her hair back from her face, realizing she was sweating. *This is every inch as hard as I imagined*, she thought. 'Thanks, sweetheart. It's all really strange for me, too.'

'As long as he doesn't mess you about, Mum.'

'If he does, Precious has already warned she's first in line.'

Peggy pulled a mock-terrified face and they both began to laugh.

'Need a hug,' Peggy said, and they both rose, Sara relishing the love she felt as she embraced her daughter tightly in her arms.

After a long moment, Peggy drew back. 'So, when are you going to introduce me?'

19

Sara and Bernard met at the so-called Thai bookshop on Friday night. It was, as Bernard had promised, a wonderfully eccentric environment. Their table was surrounded on three sides with packed shelves. Tonight, their chosen subject was biography.

He poured her a glass of the white wine he'd brought with him – none was served in the café. 'Cheers!' He smiled as they clinked glasses, his handsome face glowing in the candlelight.

Sara took a long sip to calm her nerves. Spending the whole weekend together felt huge.

'What do you think?' he asked, waving a hand round the room.

'It's brilliant,' she said. 'What a lovely idea, combining two of the greatest pleasures in life in one place.'

'So, what do you read?' he asked.

She considered his question. 'Endless books on nutrition, of course. Otherwise mostly fiction, I suppose, and anything about social history . . . What the poor ate – or didn't eat – in Victorian times, for instance. You?'

'Work stuff, like you. And I love books about how the world works. Sort of popular science about things like genes, space, evolution . . . survival.' He laughed. 'I'm gripped by how people cope, faced with life-threatening situations.'

For a moment they cast their eyes across the books on the shelves in the alcove. Pulling one out, Bernard said, 'Good example. This is about a couple of climbers in the Andes, and one is forced to cut the rope, leaving his friend to die.'

'Oh, my God!'

'Yeah, but his friend doesn't die. It's really about friendship and having to make agonizing, split-second decisions . . . the fallout from them.' His eyes had taken on an almost feverish aspect that seemed out of proportion to the book clutched in his hand. 'Consequences. It's about consequences.'

There was silence. Bernard slowly replaced the book on the shelf just as June, the Thai owner and cook, appeared with two bowls of fragrant *tom kha gai* – coconut soup – and some vegetable spring rolls.

'Nice to see you, Bernard,' she said, as she laid the food on the patterned cotton cloth.

'And you, June. Been a while.'

'You cancel before, the night of the storm,' June went on. 'I worry about you up there on the cliffs.'

'As you see, I haven't been swept away yet.'

After June had gone back into the kitchen, Sara said, 'Is the house in danger? I thought they'd put up sea defences.'

'They did. But at certain points it's made things worse. They stuck these two berms – concrete barriers – at the base of the cliffs, but in the gap between them, the sea funnels in furiously at high tide and scrapes out even more cliff than before. I used to be on the committee of the preservation trust, but after Ilsa died I lost the will to listen to the endless wrangling.'

Sara frowned. 'Doesn't it worry you?'

Bernard gave a shrug. 'One of the roads to the west is the most severely affected – the residents there are living a nightmare.' He grinned. 'But it's OK at the moment where we are. I plan to outlive the cliff.'

'Life's hard enough without waiting for your house to fall into the sea.' As she spoke, she felt a small spike of trepidation, recalling her feelings about the place. She would be staying for two days this time and hoped the house would be kind.

'There are worse things,' Bernard said, after a moment's silence. And she knew what he meant.

As they drove up separately to the cliff house after the delicious meal, Sara's feelings about the oppressive atmosphere inside took away some of her pleasurable anticipation about the weekend ahead. Had she imagined it last time? Was she just affected by Bernard's odd mood that night, the violent storm? By the time she'd parked her car alongside his Mercedes, she had spoken to herself severely. *Just enjoy yourself*, she insisted, silently.

And the night was so hot, Bernard immediately threw open the doors onto the terrace. They sat close together on the wooden bench, sipping the remains of the bottle of wine he'd taken to the restaurant and chatting quietly, bathed in the soft light from three candles he'd placed in the centre of the garden table. No foolish imaginings were going to ruin such a flawless moment for Sara. Things seemed so right, sitting beside him out in the summer darkness. If the house felt strange, she hadn't noticed tonight.

*

She and Bernard spent most of Saturday outside. In the open air of the clifftop, she'd been freed from any negative energy contained within the four walls. They went down to the beach early in the morning – to miss the crowds – and after a swim, the water blissfully cool after a sweaty night, sat on the beach wall with a cup of coffee and a cream-cheese bagel from the pop-up food truck in the parking area. They didn't talk much, just made the odd amused comment about the goings-on along the stretch of shore. Sara loved the fact that already they felt comfortable enough not to have to make conversation all the time. Then, after a light lunch of fresh prawns, home-made mayonnaise – one of Sara's specialities – French bread and a good deal of rosé, they spent most of the afternoon in bed.

Their lovemaking was, to Sara's mind, the ultimate in decadence, with the duvet stripped off in the sultry air, all the time in the world to touch and taste and gaze and brush hot skin to skin. It was a far cry from the sex she'd enjoyed with Pete – most often, in later years, a hurried, under-the-covers, muted release after a tiring day: married love. But Bernard's confidence, his lack of inhibition, carried Sara up in a swirl of sensuality, successfully blocking out thoughts of the other woman who had once lain in this very bed.

At first, she felt self-conscious as he slowly viewed every inch of her nakedness in the sunlight, feathering his fingers across her nipples, running his hand down across her belly, dropping tingly kisses up and down her thighs. She liked her body, it wasn't perfect by any stretch, but it had stood by her stalwartly for nearly six decades now, through thick and thin, with very little trouble. Revealing it to an almost stranger, though, was something else. But he refused to let her cover herself or pull away. And gradually she let go, began to allow herself to receive his caresses without shyness. Her body felt as if it barely belonged to her.

Saturday night found them outside again, watching the sea darkening in the twilight. It had been burning hot all day, the air muggy and heavy. Gone nine, now, the night was still stifling. Bernard barbecued sardines for supper, she roasted rosemary potatoes and sliced beef tomatoes, which she drizzled with olive oil and salt. A bottle of Gavi stood almost empty on the table in front of them, among the debris of the meal: she was definitely a little tipsy.

A delightful breeze got up and Sara gave a grateful sigh, leaning back against the cushions in the garden chair and brushing her hair off her face with both hands. She wore a slip dress with spaghetti straps in faded coral, Bernard was in shorts – showing off his lean, tanned legs – and a grey T-shirt. It had been the most perfect day. One Sara could not even have imagined only a month ago. There were no heavy conversations – no dead spouses or distant children interrupting their exchanges.

She watched lazily as Bernard adjusted the ivory pillar candles on the table, pushing them with his finger until they were perfectly aligned in the centre. 'You're very tidy,' she observed. 'All the surfaces are scarily pristine.'

He laughed. 'I know. Looks as if I've just moved in. It's the way we always lived, me and Ilsa. She was a self-confessed neat freak, but I can't blame her. I find the clean, clear spaces soothing.'

He must have seen the doubt in her eyes because he added hastily, 'You can make as much mess as you like, Sara. I won't mind.'

'And no photos either?' she ventured, made bold by the wine.

He hesitated, then said, 'Oh, that's just a throwback from Ilsa. She had this superstition about displaying images of the family.' There was a pause. 'Her parents belonged to this incredibly pious sect in Finland, which didn't allow mirrors or any images in the house. I know in my head, of course, there's nothing on earth wrong with a photograph, but then I remember her anxiety and it stops me putting any up. I've got them all in albums, if you want to have a look tomorrow.'

'Quite unusual,' she said cautiously, wary of questioning his dead wife's habits.

'Ilsa was definitely "unusual", and she wouldn't mind me saying that. I suppose you are, if you're brought up in one of those exclusive, hard-line communities.'

There were a million things Sara wanted to ask, but she held off, realizing she might have pushed him enough on the way he lived, his family, for now – it was clearly not an easy subject for him, for reasons she had yet to fathom.

Bernard gave a contented sigh, his hand reaching out to take hers. 'I've loved today,' he said, looking across the table at her in the fading light. 'Loved the last few weeks, in fact, since that mad moment in the tearoom . . .'

Laughing, she said, 'Imagine if I'd done what I usually do, which is the right and proper thing, and chosen Randall.'

'Why didn't you?' His question was teasing, flirtatious.

'Umm . . . it was packed in there and you were closer?'

He burst out laughing. 'Serves me right for fishing.' He stretched his hands up into the night sky and she heard his knuckles crack. Then he leapt to his feet. 'Time for another swim!'

Sara was cosy right there, and felt lazy, pleasantly tired from the day. But Bernard's hand was pulling her upright.

'No need for costumes at midnight,' he said, his eyes alight.

As they drove the five minutes from his house to the beach, Sara's excitement mounted. When they climbed the bank, the beach was deserted, an almost-full moon shining on the glassy sea and banks of pebbles to create an unreal, almost photographic effect. Bernard had his arm around her shoulders as they stood and stared.

'So beautiful,' he whispered, as if somehow noise would spoil it.

She felt him squeeze her closer. 'Ready?' he asked.

She grinned up at him and, simultaneously, they began to strip. Neither was wearing much in the warm night, and within seconds they were naked. 'Let's go,' he said, grabbing her hand and beginning to hop across the pebbles to the cool sand beyond and the surf lazily flopping on the shore. The tide was midway, the ancient petrified forest – visible at low tide – hidden beneath the dark water.

The night breeze felt like balm to her hot skin, but the contrast of her own body heat and the cold of the water was a shock. As they splashed through the waves and the water crept up her thighs, she gasped and shrieked, clinging more firmly to Bernard's hand.

He looked across at her, his face bursting with joy. 'Isn't this perfect?' he shouted.

They tumbled into the sea and began to swim, the glorious cold washing over her nakedness so sensual and exhilarating that she cried out. Bernard turned towards her, his freestyle smooth and practised. His arms encircled her as their bodies pressed together, his legs entwined with hers. The water made his skin feel silky. She kissed his salty mouth, the dark waves brushing their chins. Throwing her head back and staring at the moon, she thought, *I'm in Heaven.*

A minute later they fell apart, both floating on their backs in the water, faces to the starry night, hands still clasped. She lifted her toes out of the water – bright pink nails from a recent pedicure – and he laughed and followed suit, the swell rocking gently beneath them as they lay there in silence.

Later, cuddled up in bed, Sara said, 'That was a first for me. I've never skinny-dipped before.'

'You're kidding . . . You really have led a sheltered life.'

'As I told you, it was just Mum and me. She was always working . . . and wasn't the adventurous type, anyway. Her idea of relaxation was the cinema or a Chinese meal. If we went on holiday it was to stay with my grandparents. Which was lovely, but Croydon isn't exactly famous for its beaches.'

Bernard laughed. 'What about with Pete?'

Sara cast her mind back to the holidays they'd taken together. 'He was all about action – Joni's the same. It was full-on hiking, kayaking, windsurfing. He wasn't like you . . .' She stopped, feeling the betrayal like a soft punch in her gut. Pete hadn't been romantic, though. He wasn't afraid to say he loved her occasionally, but even at the start of their relationship, he'd just got on with it, his heart never displayed on his sleeve. Which had been fine with her. Although she couldn't help loving the romance Bernard brought to her life. She felt a shiver of pleasure as she remembered the smooth wetness of his body as they'd dipped beneath the night-time surf, his face ghostly in the light filtering through the water from the moon as he set a bubbling kiss on her mouth. 'What about your family holidays?'

The room was dimly lit, only one bedside light on, but she turned her head to look at him. He shook his head slightly. 'Ilsa needed a lot of looking after, Sara. She wasn't strong. Well, she was strong-willed, but physically not so much. She didn't like travelling and didn't like me taking the twins off without her . . . it worried her.'

She felt him shift slightly away. He interlocked his fingers tightly together on the duvet and she could see the tautness in the muscles of his tanned arm. 'I probably should have done more with them in the holidays. But you know how it is. Me and Joe were always so busy.'

'I suppose you do live by the sea . . .' she said, wanting to dispel the note of self-blame that always entered his voice as soon as he spoke about his family, while at the same time trying to picture the unusual life Bernard seemed to have led with them. *He claims to have no filter*, she thought, *but when it comes to his wife and children, he filters everything*. She shivered. The air above the bed suddenly seemed oddly dense and chilled, and she found herself looking into the corners of the semi-dark bedroom. If Bernard felt it, he gave no sign. His arm went round her, pulling her into his embrace beneath the covers.

*

'OK,' Sara said, on Sunday morning, beginning to rise from her chair on the sunny terrace, 'it's album time.' They'd finished their fruit and buttered toast and the day was already as hot as yesterday – even so early – although a faint breeze was freshening the air on the clifftop. She was looking forward to getting a handle, finally, on his family. She hoped he wouldn't stall, make some excuse.

But he jumped up purposefully. 'Sit. I'll make more coffee and bring them out.'

Two of the three he laid on the garden table were traditional albums with photographs stuck behind clear plastic, the third a photo book full of uploaded snaps.

'You don't have to look through them all,' Bernard joked. 'Just giving you a flavour of the Lockmore tribe.'

Ilsa's strange beauty stared out from the first page of the album he opened. Her wispy white-blonde hair hung nearly to her waist from a middle parting, her blue eyes clear and fierce, almost challenging the photographer as she sat on a mossy wooden deck beside a lake, long legs bare and stretched out in front of her, her slim figure wrapped in an oversized light-green jumper.

'She's so beautiful,' Sara said, suddenly daunted by her predecessor. *So this is the woman with such a firm hold on Bernard . . . the woman who hasn't entirely gone away*, she thought. Ilsa was much more frail-looking than her fevered brain had invented. Younger in the photograph, of course, but she imagined she'd retained that girlishness even into middle age.

'She was . . . almost ethereal,' Bernard said. 'Never really of this world.' He looked up from the album and she saw residual bewilderment in his eyes. 'I found her fascinating, but she was also elusive . . . I'm not sure I ever . . .' He stopped, gave a small shrug.

Into the silence she asked, 'How did you meet?'

'On an Istanbul ferry. I'd finished studying. Ilsa had taken a year out and was just bumming around the world. We sipped little glasses of black tea and watched the sun set behind the Blue Mosque . . . Like something out of a romantic travel brochure.'

He turned the pages, and Sara was greeted by baby photos of the twins, progressing through snapshots of their childhood and teens. Carrie was very fair like her mother, but looked solid and robust, whereas Adam was dark and slim and shy, often standing back while his sister fronted the camera. Bernard turned the next pages quickly, offering the odd remark as he flicked through. The photo book, more recent, was of his children in their teens. Mostly summertime, English beach shots, mostly just the two of them. Ilsa only appeared in a few, her youthful beauty, as Sara had predicted, barely changed by the years.

'That's Joe, my business partner.' Bernard pointed to a burly, dark-haired man standing beside him on a river-bank, arms round Carrie and a girl of about the same age, 'and Ariel, his daughter. Joe and her mum, Marisa, divorced when she was in her teens.'

Sara glanced at the date on the front of the book and saw it was from seven years ago. 'No more?' she asked.

'Got stuff on my phone. It's always something I mean to do, make another book, but I never get around to it.' He didn't offer, though, to show her. In fact, as he tidied the books away, she sensed he was relieved to have got it over with. Sara, who'd worried there might be some dark secret lurking in the family albums, was also relieved. The twins' smiles were charming and genuine, the hugs with their parents seemed close . . . They looked like the most normal of families. *Just like mine*. Which was intriguing. She wasn't sure what she'd expected from the albums, but the photos gave no clue to the obvious distance that currently existed between Bernard and his children.

She followed him inside, needing to get ready to leave for Margaret's. Bernard was standing beside the worktop in the kitchen, clutching the tall wooden pepper mill in his hand, but not moving. He spun round as he heard her and she saw he was smiling to himself.

'What's so funny?'

'Oh, just having a mad moment . . . I was about to put the pepper back in the cupboard and I stopped myself. *Live dangerously*, I told myself. *Leave the pepper out.*'

He was really laughing now, as he carefully, and with exaggerated precision, placed the heavy grinder on the worktop. Then held out his hands to her in a gesture of triumph.

Sara laughed along with him. 'Impressive,' she said.

He came over to her and swept her into a powerful embrace. Arms still round her waist, he said, his expression confused, 'You've taken me by surprise . . . I never expected to feel this way about anyone again.'

They both jumped as a loud clunk rang out behind them. The pepper mill had fallen over and was rolling from side to side on the worktop. Startled, Sara raised an eyebrow at Bernard.

20

After Sara had left, Bernard flopped onto the sofa. The exuberance he'd felt in Sara's company – the lift of hope in a possible future with her – deserted him, old doubts crowding back in. 'Nice try, Ilsa,' he muttered, to the empty room, his tone sarcastic.

The more I like her, the harder it gets, he thought. It was like holding a precious object in his hand and worrying he might drop it. She was the exact opposite to him: an open book. He'd seen it clearly written on her face on her first visit: she didn't like the house much. He'd seen it and had felt almost pleased – although he'd never have dared say so – because he didn't like it much, either. He never had. It was a well-made, functioning, comfortable house, but the design embarrassed him. Ilsa and he had fought about it for weeks, until he'd given in, knowing he would never win.

But in recent years it had come to represent all the claustrophobia of the past: his marriage, and the frustrations of two very different personalities; even the wrong decision he'd made that terrible day soon after she died seemed tied up in how he saw himself through the prism of his marriage. And now he felt inextricably tied to it, unable to escape Ilsa's domain.

For a moment, he recalled better times – the spectacular birthday cake she'd made him one year, for instance, in the image of the house: an intricate, detailed affair that had taken his breath away and brought tears to his eyes at the time, every tiny line in the icing a perfect depiction. He'd glimpsed the photo of the cake in the album earlier, but Sara hadn't noticed and somehow he had been reluctant to draw her attention to it.

His wife had used the house like a snail uses her shell. She rarely went out, creating a cocoon for the children as they grew. He didn't blame her. She had this strange hypersensitivity to her body, where even the slightest itch or ache, which most people would hardly notice, or ignore if they did, became a new focus of anxiety. So she never felt really well. Her genuine health issues were also made worse by her inability to move past them, to distract herself and engage in the world outside the cliff house and the children.

He had driven himself mad trying to help her – right to the bitter end. He loved her so much. She had such a loving heart when she allowed herself to reach out of her fearful self-absorption. For instance, she used to wait up for him, whatever the hour, when he was out or working late. 'I hate you coming back to a dark, silent house,' she would insist. But he felt he'd failed her on all counts – including keeping her alive – and the house was like a symbol of it. Sara's reaction only validated something he found hard to admit, even to himself.

Does she sense Ilsa's presence in the house? he wondered now. *Does she notice that I'm hiding something from her?* He tried so hard to be normal with her, to suppress the secret that hovered over him day and night. It wasn't easy, but he hoped that as every strand of connection between them strengthened, his chance of being understood became greater. Meanwhile, he vowed to enjoy time with Sara to the full . . . basically to bury his head in the sand until such time as he was forced to lift it.

I want to spend the rest of my life with this woman, he thought. But although his heart allowed for this decision, his brain, apparently, did not. Suddenly, in the vivid colours of guilt, the crystal-clear image of another woman's face sprang before his eyes. Not Sara. Not Ilsa, this time. So young, so painfully vulnerable, large brown eyes staring up at him . . . The stuff of nightmares.

21

Sara's life took on an aura of quiet excitement – tinged with disbelief at what was happening to her – as the weeks moved through September and the leaves began to fall. Everything about her world appeared enhanced in the light of her burgeoning relationship with Bernard. She even attacked her work with renewed vigour, realizing just how dull and plodding her existence had been – how jaded she'd become. It wasn't all midnight skinny dips and rosé and making love in the afternoon, but their increasing closeness, day to day – the way Bernard seemed to understand her – felt like a small miracle.

'You drive,' he began to say, whenever they went anywhere together. 'I hate driving and I can see you love it.'

Sara had not told him this, but he was so right, she did love it. Her Mini was secretly her pride and joy, considered almost a member of the family. When she took to the road, she always felt confident and free. And, unlike Pete, Bernard didn't stamp on the floor every few seconds or clutch the door handle, shouting, 'Watch out!' or 'Slow down!' at every turn. He appeared entirely relaxed in her hands.

They spent as much time together as their work schedules allowed. Sara would get to Friday and feel her heart rate rise in eager expectation as she drove towards Hastings and a weekend with Bernard. If the cliff house sometimes seemed to object to her presence, like a toddler having a strop, and she felt the air thickening or the temperature dropping for a brief period, she tried, and mostly succeeded, in ignoring it.

'Shall I stay at yours on Wednesday?' Bernard might ask as she left his house on Sunday for her visit to Margaret and to prepare for the working week.

'Or Tuesday?' she teased. 'Wednesday seems ages away.' Although the intensity of her time with Bernard meant she also relished the quiet in her own space, too.

Neither had confirmed in so many words how strongly they felt about each other – in Sara's case, the word 'love' was the final hurdle: she had only ever applied it, in a romantic sense, to Pete. But she knew she was in love with, and beginning to love, Bernard. She knew because, for example, she might catch sight of his trainers by the front door. Just shoes, obviously, although somehow, knowing they were his, totally rent her heart.

But this particular early October morning, Sara woke in Bernard's bed with a jolt, fighting off the duvet and sitting bolt upright, trying to fill her lungs with air. Something had frightened her: a feeling of heaviness, something pressing down on her, almost suffocating her. It still lingered, now she was awake, and seemed too real to be a dream.

'Bernard?' she called, her voice high with panic. Through the skylight she caught the eerie half-light of dawn. *He must be out walking*, she thought, brushing the sweat from her forehead in the hot room as her pulse began to return to something like normal. She looked around. The place was empty, of course.

Then, a second later, the sun emerged from behind a cloud, flooding the room with brightness and she breathed a shaky sigh of relief. *Just a dream*, she told herself, climbing out of bed.

Sara didn't tell Bernard about the dream until they were cuddled up on the sofa, with a cup of tea, after supper. She felt stupid mentioning it, despite memories of the panic haunting her, at times, throughout the day. He looked uneasy for a moment, then squeezed her hand. 'That must have been scary,' he said. 'Probably just a trick of the mind when you're half asleep.'

Sara would have liked to discuss it further, to make sense of what she'd experienced, but Bernard seemed preoccupied, as if his mind was on something else.

Which, as it turned out a moment later, it was. She heard his lungs expand, as he took in a deep breath.

'Not sure at our age there's any point in hanging around, is there?' he began, his tone outwardly nonchalant. But Sara picked up on the edge in his voice as he unwound his arm from her shoulders and moved away a little.

'Hanging around?'

He leant forward, forearms on his thighs, hands clasped, not looking at her as he went on, 'Well, we've known each other more than a couple of months now . . . and I'm wondering . . . maybe it's not something you want to do yet, or ever, even . . .' He inhaled deeply again and turned to face her. 'OK, I'll come right out and say it. Do you think we should move in together, Sara? Pick a house, yours or mine, stop having to go back and forth all the time, things always in the wrong place?' He smiled nervously. 'I suppose what I'm asking is, would you like to live with me?'

His suggestion made her gasp. She was aware, of course, that it was the next step, but hearing it out loud was almost shocking: both sudden and precipitous. 'Goodness . . .' she said, feeling an immediate palpitation around her heart. The silence was like a vibrating gong and she hurried to fill it. 'Umm . . .' But his face had fallen at her clear equivocation.

So many reasons crowded her mind as to why it wasn't a good idea. If they chose his house – which was the obvious one, given hers was much smaller and there wouldn't be room for his office, plus the parking problem, the noise of the high street – it would mean digging herself, once and for all, out of her controlled existence, learning to share her space again. There was also Margaret, in the last stages of her life. And her work: it would take an hour to commute. But the thought of committing to living full time in the house on the cliff was the most daunting – an uncomfortable flashback of waking this morning, and how she'd struggled to breathe, coming back to her now.

'You think it's too soon?' Bernard was asking.

Sara still hesitated. 'I agree it's a hassle, living in two places. And I want to be with you, Bernard, very much.' She stopped, not knowing how to go on. 'I'm not sure my house is a practical option, though – it's just not big enough . . . And I'm thinking about Margaret, my work . . .'

He gave a soft sigh. 'I understand.'

She frowned, puzzled by his resigned expression.

'It's the cliff house, isn't it?'

Sara felt her heart jump in her chest. The way he said it,

part accusation, part defensiveness . . . She didn't want to fight.

The silence that followed felt dangerous to her, as if her response might fatally impact the strained and delicate undercurrent that had sprung up. 'Maybe we should think about selling both houses in the future . . . buy something that's ours?'

She saw Bernard twitch. 'Sell the house?' The barked response seemed propelled from his mouth before he had a chance to stop it. He looked immediately embarrassed by his outburst and attempted a laugh.

'Would that be a problem for you?'

He got up, paced off across the room, hands crammed into his jeans pockets. When he turned, he seemed tense. 'Listen, if you don't want to move in together, that's fine with me. We should just keep things as they are.'

Sara held her breath at the terseness in his voice. She didn't understand what was going on in his head. 'Bernard . . .'

For a second, his stare was almost unfriendly. Then his face collapsed and he hurried to her side, pulling her into a fierce embrace. 'God, sorry, sorry . . .' When he drew back he added, 'The house . . . I . . . I'm just not sure I'm ready to sell it yet.'

It must be a big thing, she thought, *when you've designed and built it yourself, brought your kids up in it, buried your wife from it . . .*

'Is that OK with you?' Bernard was asking.

'Look, why don't we wait,' she replied steadily, 'think about it again in a month or so? See how things are going?'

Bernard was silent, but he appeared almost relieved that she had put a temporary brake on his proposal.

As they made their way up to bed, she sensed a very slight distance between them, both adopting a careful politeness that was new. They had survived their first skirmish, it was true, but Sara was left with a small uneasiness. *He looked at me as if I'd suggested killing his grandmother when I mentioned selling the house.*

'It's not fair! Peggy gets to meet him and I don't,' Joni wailed, when she rang the following day. Sara was in Lewes tonight and she was almost relieved to have a couple of days apart, after the conversation the previous night. Bernard had been partly right when he blamed the cliff house for her reluctance to move in with him. There were other considerations too, of course, but the house had certainly been a factor. She was sure she'd get used to it – or it would get used to her – but she wasn't there yet.

'You'll have to bring him over, Mum,' Joni was saying. 'Come in February, when things have settled a bit workwise after the New Year rush, and it's not too hot. We could plan and get some dates in the diary, so at least we've something to look forward to.'

Sara was about to protest that it was too early to make that sort of plan with Bernard. But February was a long way off. 'I'd love that, sweetheart.' Then she added nervously, 'Oh, God, suppose Peggy doesn't like Bernard?'

'Well, it's you who's got to live with him eventually, Mum,' Joni replied, ever the pragmatist. 'Us liking him is only the icing on the cake, isn't it?'

'So you'd be fine if I shacked up with some creep you both loathe?'

Joni laughed. 'You're saying Bernard's a creep?'

'Very funny.'

'As long as he makes you happy, Mum, and he's treating you well, then I reckon it's up to you.'

'Precious and Sammi are coming as ballast,' she said. 'I want them to meet Bernard, obviously, and I thought it might be too full-on to have just Peggy there the first time. Precious will carry the day. She doesn't know what an awkward silence is.'

'Unless *she* thinks he's dodgy. In which case, I fear for the poor guy's life!'

Sara felt a swell of happiness around her heart as she said to goodbye to her daughter. It was so lovely to be able to talk to her girls about Bernard, to have them on her side, wishing her well. She was a lucky woman. There had been no reciprocal invitation to meet Adam and Carrie, although she told herself the time would come. The twins now knew she was on the scene, apparently, and had not objected. 'Next time they're down, we'll all get together,' Bernard had assured her.

Margaret peered at Sara's screen. 'He's rather handsome,' she said, giving Sara a mischievous smile. 'Not as handsome as our Pete, of course, but I like his face, dear.'

Sara had been in two minds about whether to tell her mother-in-law about Bernard but had felt she must, now that it was serious between them.

'I hope you'll bring him round to meet me, one day,' Margaret was saying. She seemed very bright this afternoon, but

Heather said she came and went, sometimes barely saying a word all day.

'Would you like that?'

After a short pause, Margaret said, 'I expect you'll be moving in together . . . Does he live in Lewes?'

Sara heard a frisson of apprehension in the old lady's question. 'Hastings. On the cliff . . . He's asked me, but we're taking it slowly.' She didn't want to explain her feelings about Bernard's house: Margaret might think her daft.

Her mother-in-law eyed her, then took her hand. 'I want to see you settled, Sara. I fear I've been a bit selfish, held you back all these years.'

'You haven't –' Sara began.

But Margaret squeezed her hand to silence her and went on, 'You should be out there enjoying life, not tied to an old lady and her memories.' She blinked her pale eyes tiredly. 'You mustn't put things off on my account. Hastings is no distance.'

Sara held Margaret's fragile, bony hand more tightly between her own, her throat so choked with tears, she couldn't reply.

'Don't waste time, dear, if you love him,' Margaret went on. 'Life's too short. Arthur and I were married three months after we met.' Her eyes twinkled. 'And that wasn't because there'd been any hanky-panky, I'll have you know.'

Sara swallowed, managed a laugh.

'If you're not sure, of course . . .'

'I'm absolutely sure.' Sara heard the solid conviction in her voice, and so did Margaret.

She gave her a loving smile. 'Well, then . . .'

It was as if her mother-in-law were placing a full stop on their joint grieving for Pete, setting Sara free to be with Bernard, although Margaret hugged her son ever closer as her own life faded. Sara felt a wave of sadness, but she was also grateful. The last vestiges of guilt about moving on from her husband fell away with Margaret's words and she felt a surge of exhilaration.

22

It was a gradual thing, Sara's incorporation into the cliff house, accomplished without much discussion between her and Bernard, as if both were fearful of having another tricky conversation like the one when he'd first brought up moving in together.

She'd had time, in the weeks since then – Margaret's exhortation that life was 'too short' ringing in her ears – to consider his suggestion more carefully. And she'd come to accept that it was senseless to go on in the way they were: her shuffling back and forth to Hastings at weekends, Bernard shuffling back and forth to Lewes during the week. So, she'd begun gradually to shift her client appointments, pack them into the three midweek days. Now, she planned to stay only Tuesday and Wednesday nights in Lewes, the cliff house becoming her official home.

Her concerns about the house had not gone away, but she told herself they would learn to rub along, given time. Days would pass when she didn't feel anything odd, although the other morning it had put on a bit of a display. She'd been thinking of other things, her arms full of supermarket bags for the weekend, but when she opened the front door she'd been greeted by what seemed almost like a physical barrier, a solid wall of cold air – as if she were walking headfirst into a gale, although the air was dense and static. It brought her up short. For a split second, she couldn't seem to move forward. Then it was gone. She thought one of them must have left the door onto the terrace open – there was often a tearing wind up on the headland. But when she checked, it was closed and firmly locked. She clicked on Radio 2, turned the volume up as she unpacked the shopping. *It was nothing*, she told herself, deciding her disquiet about the house was creating situations in her mind that didn't exist.

But this particular Saturday, Sara was back in Lewes, her anxiety building as the hour approached when she would introduce Bernard to her daughter and friends. She imagined the three faces round the table, watching the man she loved. Watching and genuinely wanting to like him, she was certain about that, but also hugely protective of her, alert to anything that seemed a bit off. Being in love skewed your reason, she was well aware. But she also knew that if – unthinkably, ridiculously – they highlighted some niggle, there was not a chance that she would give him up.

Surveying the wooden kitchen island – the extension raised – that served as a table in her small kitchen, she straightened a knife, moved a water glass a little to the left, and smoothed the cloth napkins she rarely used because of the hassle of laundering them afterwards. It looked welcoming, a small posy of freesias in the centre, flanked by two blue and gold glass tea-light holders. She took a shaky breath and another deeper one in an attempt to calm herself. Peggy's train would be getting in shortly, so she would have half an hour with her daughter before Bernard arrived. The others would follow an hour later – probably more, as Sammi was always famously late, despite Precious's nagging. It was like a military operation.

Sara hugged her daughter tight. 'You look lovely,' she told her. Peggy, blonde hair loose for once, was dressed in a green floral dress with a wavy hem that brushed her calves, light tweed jacket and ankle boots.

'Where is he, then?' Peggy's stage whisper echoed through the house and made Sara laugh.

'He'll be here in a minute. Just wanted to see you on your own first. Come into the kitchen. I'm finishing off cooking.'

Peggy dumped her small backpack with her overnight things in the hall and followed her mother through. 'This looks nice,' she said, eyeing the table as she pulled herself up onto one of the stools. 'Can I do anything?'

Sara, who'd been frying breadcrumbs and grating cheese to sprinkle over the fish pie, turned to her. 'No, all under control.' Then she pulled a face. 'All except me. I'm very far from under control.'

Sliding off the stool and going over to her mother, Peggy gave her another long hug. 'It'll be fine, Mum. Chill. I'm sure I'll love him.'

'I really think you will, sweetheart. It's just it means a lot, obviously, you liking him.'

Peggy grinned. 'No pressure, then.'

Her daughter chatted as Sara made the final touches to supper, filling her in about her new class – she taught year three, seven- to eight-year olds – gossip about her fellow teachers and the problem she was having with the landlord fixing the locks on the front door. Sara listened with half an ear, the other half expectant, like a horse in the starting gate, for the sound of Bernard's knock.

When it finally came, she nearly jumped out of her skin, making Peggy whisper as she shot past to open the door, 'Breathe.'

He looks perfect, she thought, as she ushered Bernard into the kitchen. He had on his trademark black jeans and a pale-blue pinstripe shirt, with darker buttons and trim, off-setting his tanned face, although the October weather had been dire. The shirt looked new, and she wondered if he'd bought it especially for tonight . . . wondered if he was as nervous as she.

He had kissed her quickly on the lips in the dark of the hall, but once in the kitchen, he did not put his arm round her or make any proprietorial gestures. The wine he'd brought he handed to Sara, rather than put it into the fridge himself, as he would have done if they'd been alone. And he did not sit down, but hovered like a guest, accepting the glass of South African white she handed him.

Peggy had got up to greet him, and the two of them stood there, glasses in hand, exchanging bright pleasantries while Sara gratefully turned back to the task of mixing the salad dressing, holding her breath for the conversation to get under way.

'Mum says your partner's name is Fane?'

'Yes, Joe. We have an architect's practice in Eastbourne, as Sara probably also told you, which we started nearly thirty years ago. He lives here, in Lewes.'

'So is Ariel Fane his daughter?'

'*Yes*. She's my goddaughter. How do you know Ariel?'

Peggy said, 'We were at Priory together. Ariel was in the class above, so she won't remember me. But she was the toast of the school – she was so beautiful and popular with everyone.'

Bernard laughed. 'Sounds a bit sickening. She's a great girl, though, I love her to bits. She's working in New York now, a dogsbody at *Vanity Fair*.'

'Exciting. I can so imagine her in the magazine world.'

Sara, listening, noticed her heartrate calming as two of the most important people in her life began to laugh and chat with apparent ease.

By the time her friends arrived and they were settled at the table – Sara doling out the pie, Peggy offering round the buttered broccoli – she was beginning to enjoy herself. She knew she could rely on Precious to fill any lapse in conversation. But tonight there were no awkward silences. And from the look on her friend's face, Sara gleaned she was liking Bernard.

'This is a bit like one of Peggy's Ofsted inspections,' Precious declared, as Sara cleared the salad plates from the table. 'Even though you knew we were coming, there's only so much you can do last minute to make sure we like what we see.'

Sara twitched inwardly, eyeing Bernard to see how he was taking the joke. But he was clearly amused.

'So how am I doing?'

Precious sucked her teeth. 'Ooh, we couldn't possibly tell you that now. You'll get a written report in due course.'

Bernard pulled a face, showing mock alarm. 'You

realize my whole future depends on getting "Outstanding"? I hope you'll be kind.'

They were all laughing now, but Sara saw the fleeting uncertainty in his eyes as he looked over at her. It made her heart swell and she gave him an encouraging smile in return.

Precious was shaking her head solemnly. '"Kind" doesn't come into it, I'm afraid. But we'll always be fair, I promise you that.'

Sammi got up to retrieve the little clay ramekins of *crema catalana* he'd brought over in a cardboard box. As he placed one in front of Bernard, he winked at him. 'No need to worry. If Precious didn't like you, you would know by now.'

The following morning, Sara and Bernard did a post-mortem about the night before and agreed it had gone even better than they'd hoped. It was still very early, but Bernard was already sitting on the edge of the bed, pulling on his socks, having insisted he get off and leave Sara to gossip about him behind his back with Peggy. Sara had felt a little uneasy about Bernard staying the night, with her daughter in the room next door. But when she'd asked Peggy if it was all right, her daughter had just replied, 'Of course, Mum.' She didn't seem to understand what the problem was.

'OK . . . Well, first round completed successfully,' she said now, as Bernard got off the bed. 'Next, the twins . . .'

He didn't turn as he said, 'Yes . . .' His tone was full of uncertainty, and he said no more.

'Could we make a plan, then?' she urged, despite his unenthusiastic response. 'Maybe a weekend in November?'

Bernard's head was smothered in his jumper, his back still to her. She heard a muffled 'Yeah, must do that,' that held the same degree of half-heartedness.

Wanting to lighten the sudden tension in the room and not ruin the atmosphere after such a triumph of an evening, she changed the subject to something she considered less contentious. 'I told you Joni's dying to meet you? Well, she suggested we go over next year . . . end of February. She's not so busy, then, and the fares will be cheaper.' When Bernard didn't reply, she went on, 'Would you be up for it? Could you take the time off work?'

Now, he spun round. 'You want me to come with you to LA?' His question seemed to hold an edge of panic.

Surprised, Sara said, 'Well, yes . . . if you'd like to. Obviously I want you to meet Joni and Mason, and I can't imagine they'll make it over here any time soon.'

Bernard was standing very still, hands thrust into his jeans pockets. He was looking at her, but his gaze appeared far away, not seeing her.

'It'd be fun, don't you think? You must be due a break . . .' she added, wavering in the face of his silence.

He smoothed his hair back with both hands, inhaling slowly. 'It would be great fun. Talk about it later?'

Sara frowned. 'Are you OK?' His expression, far from mirroring the enthusiasm his words suggested, appeared oddly bleak.

With a smile that seemed to cost him dear, he assured her, 'I'm fine. Just got work stuff on my mind.'

'Say, if you don't want to come with me this time, Bernard. It's not a problem.'

He shook his head with exaggerated conviction. 'Of course I want to come.' He bent to kiss her. 'Have a lovely time with Peggy. I'll see you later.'

Sara lay down again, pulling the duvet close. *What was all that about?* she wondered.

23

Bernard left Sara's house almost unable to breathe. As he got into his car and began the journey to Eastbourne, he found he was actually shaking and cold. It was a dreary day and drizzle sheened the windscreen of the Mercedes, the wipers screeching as they cleared it. *This is it . . . This is it*, he kept repeating silently: the moment he'd been talking about hypothetically with Joe, all these years. Every conversation had included the rider 'When' or 'If', and always at some non-specific time in the future. Concomitant, too, on him actually finding someone with whom he might need to share his secret. There was no longer anything hypothetical, though, about Sara's invitation to go with her to California. Which he could not do. It wasn't that he didn't want to. It just *couldn't happen*.

Now he realized the moment had come. His back was well and truly against the wall, his ninth life hanging by a thread. He would need to respond, imminently, to her plan to visit Joni. *Sara*, he told himself, as he pulled into the parking space behind his office, *will have to be told. Or I will have to invent yet another blasted lie.* Both options made him feel so physically sick, he was quite unable to work out what was best to do, or how best to do it.

24

'I thought I'd bring more stuff over when I come back next Thursday,' Sara said, as they lay in bed one morning, a couple of weeks after the dinner with Peggy and her friends. 'Could you make room in the cupboard, please?'

Bernard did not reply, he seemed miles away.

'You do want me here?' she asked, half joking but offended by his silence.

He started, then dragged his eyes to her face. But in the split second before he pulled her into his arms and began to drop hungry kisses on her mouth, she'd seen what she thought was a look of bleak despair in his eyes. She gently pulled away from his embrace.

'What was bothering you just now?' she asked, not for the first time. He'd been displaying some strange moods in previous days. One minute he'd be hugging her and saying how much he loved her. The next, although physically present, he would disappear for seconds at a time – like just now. *Does he even hear what I'm saying?* Sara wondered.

She traced the change in him to the morning after the family dinner, when she'd invited him to come with her to LA and nagged him about the twins. He'd stood beside the bed and stared down at her as if she'd suggested he cut off his right hand. She wasn't even sure if it was the proposed Joni trip or meeting with Carrie and Adam that had upset him most. *Or something else entirely?* Any attempt to get him to open up, though, had so far been met with a gentle rebuff – and there had been no progress in either case.

The morning sun was lighting Bernard's face, now, his eyes soft and full of love. 'Nothing. I'm fine. Sorry. I'll clear out the cupboard today,' he said, laying his warm hand to her cheek in a tender caress. 'Oh, and Joe's picking me up this morning. We're going over to Rye for a planning meeting. I asked him to have breakfast with us first, so you two can finally meet . . . if that's OK?'

At the prospect of being introduced to Joe, Sara pushed her worries about Bernard's mood temporarily to the back of her mind. So far, apart from the odd neighbour they'd bumped into on their cliff walks, she had met no one from Bernard's life. He seemed to have few friends, except his business partner. Which she found strange, although she put it down to his work obsession and Ilsa's death. Many of her own friends – couples with whom Pete and she had socialized – had gradually fallen away in the years after his death. She saw that as more her fault than theirs.

Joe, larger than life, even at eight in the morning, greeted her warmly, his voice booming across the quiet room. 'So, at last I get to meet the woman Bernard's been banging on about all this time,' he said, squeezing her hand in both of his and eyeing her shrewdly.

Sara took to him immediately. His dark eyes, in a broad, open face, were kind and full of mischief; he seemed very much at ease with himself as he plonked his bulky frame down at the table. She'd rustled up bacon and fried eggs, grilled tomatoes and piles of wholewheat toast and marmalade – Bernard had told her Joe was a man who loved his food, as long as he didn't have to cook it.

Bernard poured coffee for them all, then sat down, glancing from Sara to Joe and back again, with a cautious grin.

'So how are you finding life at Lockmore Towers?' Joe asked her, eagerly picking up his knife and fork and setting to with his breakfast.

'Not so bad,' she replied. 'I get to leave stuff on the worktop occasionally and my toothbrush on the washbasin . . . put up the odd photograph, even,' she joked, pointing across the room to the image of her daughters hugging each other, taken when the girls were in their teens, and the four of them had spent a week at Sammi's mother's large Valencia house. Dripping from the pool, they sported huge, toothy grins on their young faces. This got a laugh from both men.

'Crikey . . . Very bold,' Joe teased. 'But the old fella doesn't seem to be complaining. Things must be going well.' As he spoke, Sara caught a look passing between them that she couldn't interpret. *Almost like a warning*, she thought.

Joe was amusing company. Sara and he chatted on, about Lewes, their children, the upcoming fireworks – a huge event in Lewes, famous worldwide. She realized later that she'd found out more about Ariel in the hour with Joe than she knew about either of the twins after three and a half months. It made her sad for Bernard, who seemed to retreat from the conversation, eating mostly in silence unless his friend prompted him for his opinion.

'Join us for the fireworks at mine,' Sara suggested to Joe, as the men got ready to leave. 'I'm bang on the high street, so it's front-row seats for the parade.'

Joe raised his eyebrows, considering. 'I'm afraid I'm already taken . . . but I'd love to drop by for half an hour. I'm not due at my friends' till later.'

After they'd gone and Sara was clearing up, Bernard's unresponsiveness during the meal brought her worries rushing back. She wondered, as she closed the dishwasher, if he would tell his friend what was bothering him, because he certainly wasn't telling her.

'Have you thought any more about California?' Sara waited till after supper the next day to tackle Bernard, hoping her question would prod him, finally, to explain the cause of his recent unease.

They were sitting together on the sofa, the woodburner giving out almost too much warmth on the relatively mild autumn evening, with two cups of mint tea and a bar of lime and sea salt chocolate on the coffee-table in front of them.

'Yeah, sorry,' Bernard said, after a moment's hesitation. 'I'm just not sure I can get the time off. It's this one client who can't make up his mind on the project schedule. If he wants his house when he's implying, there's no way I can be away then. It's a big job, I can't land Joe with it. And I can't afford to turn him down.'

Sara felt a stab of disappointment. 'OK . . . When do you think you'll know?'

Bernard shrugged, but Sara thought he seemed more tense than ever, his shrug struggling to be nonchalant. 'I'll speak to him again tomorrow, but I might have to cry off this time . . . which is a real shame.'

After a moment's silence, she asked, 'Are you sure this isn't because you don't actually want to come?'

Bernard looked stricken and grabbed her hand, dropping a kiss on the palm. 'Of course I do. I can't wait to meet Joni.'

Sara tried to smile. But she sensed his prevarication. It frustrated her, the darkness that lurked behind his eyes these days, a darkness she couldn't reach, however hard she tried.

He pulled her gently into his arms.

'It's Bonfire Night tomorrow. I hope you're prepared,' she said, giving in to his embrace. *Come over about five*, she'd told Precious. They'd do what they always did: hang out of the upstairs windows of Sara's house and watch the parade with a bowl of macaroni cheese, then follow the crowd down the hill to the bonfire and fireworks by the river at the end of the evening. There were other bonfire sites – each of the Lewes bonfire societies had their own – but Railway Lane was the closest. 'This'll be the first year Margaret won't be well enough to make it,' she added sadly.

Her mother-in-law relished the occasion, even when she could no longer manage the crowds. She would watch the parade from Sara's window and throw out caustic comments about the quality of the fancy dress and the floats passing below. Pete had loved it too, dragging the girls into the smoky, noisy thick of it, shouting and waving torches with the best of them.

'I'm amazed you've never been,' she said, when Bernard remained solidly silent.

He seemed to shake himself. 'Me too. I'm really looking forward to it. As you know, any whiff of religion turned Ilsa's stomach, so I gave it a wide berth, in solidarity.'

The event had the reputation of being anti-Catholic, because it commemorated some sixteenth-century Protestant martyrs burnt at the stake, as well as Guy Fawkes. But, these days, it was a secular festival, the mocking effigies mostly of the current crop of politicians. Only Paul V, the pope at the time of the Gunpowder Plot, came in for regular stick.

It was the perfect night for fireworks. The temperature had dropped and it was cold, but not freezing, a clear sky and almost no wind. Supper had been a great success. Precious and Sammi were delighted to meet Joe, and everyone seemed almost more interested in chatting and laughing with each other than watching the drumming, thumping, whistling, shouting, raucous parade weaving down the hill below Sara's window. She was thrilled they were getting on so well. Peggy, it being a weekday, could not get away from school, and she missed her, as she did Margaret's sharp observations.

As usual, the parade consisted of pirates in striped jumpers and red beanies, patches over their eyes; Native Americans with totems and feathered headdresses; groups of men and women in seventeenth-century bonnets and tricorn hats; ghouls in monks' cowls; and a variety of purple-clad popes. Most were carrying flaming torches – some blazing crosses for the martyrs – that choked the night air, along with firecrackers and the dangerously red-hot barrels being rolled down the slope. Everything was accompanied by the thrum of marching bands and drums and the proud brandishing of grotesque contemporary effigies, Guy Fawkes getting barely a look in.

Bernard seemed to be loving it. 'Can't believe what I've been missing,' he told her.

Later, Joe having gone off to meet his other friends, they piled into their coats, hats and scarves and set off in the wake of the parade. Families and groups of friends, many quite drunk by this time, wove through the narrow streets in the smoky chill – the air tinged with the smell of scorched onions and sausages from the stalls along the way – towards the bonfire site. There was an atmosphere of celebration and community, despite the many visitors to the town for the event, and people chatted with strangers in a wonderfully un-British way. Bernard and Sara held hands. She had a moment of deep contentment as they strolled along, neither speaking. *I love you*, she whispered silently, glancing up at him.

The massive, toppling bonfire on the wetlands beside the river, the burning effigies and astonishing fireworks setting the sky aflame felt pagan, cleansing and wild to Sara, as if she were experiencing a catharsis, her old life going up in flames to clear space for the miraculous new one. She whooped and sang with the rest of them as she gazed into the hotness of the fire, sparks cracking and hissing into the darkness, cheeks scorching, her back chilled by the night air.

She nudged Bernard, leaning in close. 'This is pretty insane, eh?'

Either he didn't hear, or he was too absorbed in what was happening, because he didn't answer. As she caught the fire's reflection in his eyes, he appeared detached from the proceedings. 'Are you OK? Not enjoying it much?'

After a second, he seemed to come to. But his smile was less than convincing. 'Beats a few sparklers in the back garden,' he said, although his words were barely audible above the racket.

Sara squeezed his hand. 'All these flames and smoke, I always find it quite unnerving. But somehow it feels good tonight – unless you're the prime minister, of course,' she joked, staring at the bulbous melting head as it blackened and began to fall apart. Bernard didn't laugh, just managed a distracted smile. She wondered what had converted his previous enthusiasm into another of his unaccountable moods.

When they got home, both of them were tired and cold. 'Glass of wine?' she offered. 'Cuppa? Hot chocolate?'

Bernard nodded but didn't say which. His mood seemed to have dipped even further after they'd waved goodnight to Precious and Sammi at the cut-through. Trudging up towards her house, he hadn't said a word, only clutched her hand firmly as if he couldn't bear to let her go. Now, he sat himself down on one of the stools at the kitchen island and watched her fill the kettle. But his expression was blank, as if he were not seeing her at all.

'Tea, then?' she prompted.

His gaze flicked to hers and she felt her heart jump in her chest. His eyes were filled with such bleakness, almost desperation. But still he didn't speak. She held her breath as she poured boiling water onto teabags, lifted milk from the fridge door. Handing him his mug she, too, sat down.

It had been a wonderful evening – she'd felt so exhilarated at the bonfire – but now she had the grim sense that Bernard was about to tell her something she didn't want to hear.

He inhaled deeply, then fixed his grey eyes on her face. 'Sara, there's something you need to know.'

There was a heart-thumping silence.

Another breath. No words. Eyes steely now, determined. 'OK . . .' But he seemed unable to go on. Then he squared his shoulders and took a deep breath. 'It's so hard to say this . . .' He stopped, tried again. 'I've been imagining this moment ever since the day I met you and realized you were special.' His eyes met hers, dark with anguish. 'I can't come to Los Angeles with you.'

She frowned, baffled by what he was saying and the intensity with which he said it. Speaking slowly, aware she wasn't really grasping what was going on, she replied, 'It's no big deal. There'll be another time.'

His voice was trembling slightly as he went on. 'No, you don't understand, Sara. The reason I can't come to LA with you is because of something that happened five years ago. Something terrible. An absolute nightmare, in fact.'

She stared at him, both of them frozen by his hesitation.

'I did something . . . It was an accident, but . . .'

She nodded. *Say it*, she urged silently. *Whatever it is, just bloody say it.*

Another deep breath, his nostrils flaring with the effort. Then the words were blurted out as if he were vomiting. 'I killed someone. A cyclist. A young woman.'

Sara gave a gasp of horror.

'I lost control . . . took the bend too fast . . . and . . . well . . .'

He looked as if he were barely breathing, his face pale in the dim kitchen light. 'Oh, my God,' she whispered. Flashes of understanding – and a million questions – pierced her shock. *So this is what's behind his sleepless nights. Did he go to prison? Is that why he can't come to California? Are the twins still angry with him?* 'You hadn't been drinking,' she said, more as a statement than a question.

He shook his head firmly. 'It wasn't long after Ilsa died and I wasn't sleeping. I was a bit of a wreck, to be honest. Not that that's any excuse.'

Sara was too stunned to speak. *He's been carrying this huge secret around with him all this time and I didn't know?* She was shocked that this was even possible, that she had so little insight into his psyche when she loved him so much.

As if reading her mind, Bernard went on, 'I wanted to tell you, Sara. Wanted to and didn't want to, obviously.' He lifted his hands in despair. 'I knew you'd have to know eventually. But how do you tell such an awful thing to someone you've only just met?' He blinked back tears. 'When I look at your face now, it says it all.'

'It was an accident,' she said softly. 'But just so awful . . . I'm so sorry.'

He slumped, clutching his mug with both hands.

In the stunned silence, Sara tried to piece together what that moment must have been like.

He sighed resignedly. 'It's all such a haze in my mind. The airbag activated and nearly knocked me out. I know I was going too fast, swerved on the corner, it was a smallish road with no central markings, but not narrow enough to excuse me. She must have been riding towards me, but she'd stopped. I don't know why. I've always wondered about timing . . . if she'd been moving, whether we'd have missed each other. But I was on the wrong side of the road when I hit her, I doubt it would have made any difference.'

'So you called an ambulance . . . the police?' she probed gently. 'Was she killed instantly?'

'Yes. I tried CPR, of course, but I could see . . .' he gulped '. . . I could see her neck was broken . . . She had no pulse.'

'Oh, Bernard. That's just horrible.'

'I had to go to the police station and make a statement.' He gave a shaky sigh. 'The woman was wearing this bright neon pink biking jacket . . . She was so young.'

Sara reached across the table and put her hand over his. The air was thick with his distress and she had no idea how to comfort him.

'I was convicted of causing death by careless or inconsiderate driving.' He gave a terse laugh. 'Sounds so insignificant, doesn't it? "Careless", "inconsiderate" – like I'd been a bit rude to her. When, in fact, I'd fucking killed her.' He shook his head. 'It was so ghastly, the whole thing. And so avoidable.'

Sara shuddered at his devastation, the dull rage edging his words. 'I'm so, so sorry,' she repeated softly.

There was silence, neither able to look at the other.

Then he said, 'I showed remorse – plenty of it. I was considered a man of good character . . . and I'd just lost my wife. All they gave me was two hundred hours' community service, a two-year ban and a small fine. Not that I wanted to go to jail.'

'Could you have done?'

'Oh, yes. If I'd had other convictions. Or, I don't know, been drunk or cocky or insufficiently remorseful. If I'd run away from the scene, of course.'

Another silence, this one dull and heavy, as Sara searched for some response. 'Who was she? Did she have a family?'

'A husband and small daughter. I saw him in court. He looked . . .' Bernard sighed. 'Well, you can imagine how he looked.'

'Is this why you can't come to California, because of the conviction?'

He nodded miserably. 'You don't need a visa as a well-behaved tourist, but with a criminal record I would have to jump through hoops – fill in countless forms, provide police and court paperwork, be interviewed at the embassy, then wait months for a decision . . . with no guarantee that it would be successful.'

Sara got up and went round to where Bernard was sitting. She was aware of drunken singing, loud and immediately outside the front door – the tail end of the party – and thought how far away the fireworks and the fun seemed now. She hugged his sagging shoulders, kissed the side of his head. He was cold and smelt of smoke. 'It was an accident,' she repeated, feeling an odd sense of relief that she now understood why he'd been so strange with her.

She wondered if the accident were in some way at the root of his problems with Adam and Carrie, although she couldn't fathom how it could be, after all this time. Surely they would sympathize. Her heart ached with compassion and sadness – both for Bernard and for the woman's family. 'It could happen to anyone.'

He pressed her hand, his own icy. 'Maybe, but it happened to me, Sara. It was entirely my fault,' he said, in a small voice.

Drawing back, she said, 'You could have told me sooner, you know. I would have understood.'

He looked up. 'I almost did, so many times. But I didn't know how . . . and I didn't want to ruin things.' He added, 'Then you told me about Joni's invitation.'

'So will it always be a problem for you to go to America?'

'My conviction is "spent", so-called, after five years – which is next June. I'll probably still have to declare it, though, when I apply for an ESTA.'

Sadness ran through Sara, like a slow-flowing river. She pulled him up and guided him to the sofa. He seemed almost frail, all his confidence evaporated in the telling.

They sat in silence for a while, Sara horrified at the level of guilt Bernard had been carrying all these years in secret.

'What did you have to do, for community service?'

'I helped out at a homeless charity in Hastings. Did stuff like clearing up after meals, cleaning the place, chatting to the guests over a cup of tea. They were kind to me, didn't seem to judge – I met some wonderful people. It didn't feel like much of a hardship, though.'

'Would you've rather it had?'

Bernard looked round at her sharply. 'I took someone's life, Sara. That's no small thing.' He shook his head despairingly. 'I used to have this agonizing sensation – haunted me for months, still does, sometimes – the feeling of *if only*, going over and over what had happened, desperate to turn the clock back and rewrite history. Of wanting things to be totally different.' He glanced at her. 'I'm sure you understand.'

She did, the moment Pete fell to the ground and never spoke again suddenly foremost in her mind. 'So, how did the twins react?'

She noticed the muscle in his cheek twitch violently, his mouth contort. 'I . . . I perhaps didn't . . .'

'They don't still blame you, do they?'

He hesitated for a long moment. 'It was all mixed up with the way I handled Ilsa's death. Coming so soon after . . .'

Puzzled, she asked, 'How do you mean?' *What has this got to do with Ilsa?* she wondered, although she was coming to the realization that everything in Bernard's life had something to do with his dead wife.

'It's hard to explain.' Shifting slightly away from her, Bernard looked as if he didn't want to say any more. 'I'm really sorry not to have told you earlier, Sara.'

She kissed his cheek softly but had no words with which to comfort him.

They trailed up to bed in silence. Although she was thankful he'd been able to unburden himself at last, she was aware of an ongoing distance between them as they lay in bed, waiting for sleep. As if telling her had not brought him the relief she might have expected. He didn't seem to have taken in her sympathetic reaction and reassurance at all. Apparently it hadn't touched him. Which made her very sad. She was also sorry, on a selfish level, that he wouldn't be travelling with her to visit Joni.

There'll be another time, she told herself, as she closed her eyes.

Next morning, the conversation of the night before hovered over them. Sara felt tired and sluggish, as if his secret were somehow inflaming her body, like pollen would a hay-fever sufferer. *Five years of punishing himself is enough, isn't it?* she thought, when she pondered Adam and Carrie's behaviour – although Bernard had said no more by way of explanation.

As they ate breakfast in silence, he glanced at her, then said, 'No one outside the family – and Joe, of course – knows about what happened. Not even Ariel. There was a tiny paragraph in the local paper, but no one has ever brought it up, if they saw it.'

'You don't want me to tell Joni and Peggy?' The thought of keeping the secret from them made her feel uneasy.

Bernard, on the other side of the table, dropped his gaze. She heard a low groan. 'God, what will they think of me? It's hardly the best introduction to your mum's new partner, is it?'

'I imagine they'll be incredibly sympathetic. There but for the grace of God, et cetera.'

As she watched his face, the sadness in his eyes turned slowly to resolve. 'There's been too much silence.' He nodded, as if to himself. 'You can tell them, if you like.'

Joni gave a low whistle when she heard why Bernard would not be joining her mother on the trip. 'God, poor guy. The very worst. And that poor family.'

'I know.' Sara wanted to change the subject. She felt

bogged down by Bernard's confession. Nothing much more had been said – what else was there to say? – but it was there, like a sorrowful shade, in the corner of every room. She told herself that at least she now knew what was behind his strange moods. But a secret, selfish part of her wished she hadn't had to.

'Anyway, I'll go ahead and book my own flights for February. I'm so longing to see you, sweetheart.' In fact, she had the strongest urge to be with both of her daughters right that second. To hug them and sit with them, relax as they chatted and laughed together, like in the days when they were still close by. Dispel the sadness that had almost imperceptibly built up around her – as a backdrop to knowing Bernard – from so many aspects of his life.

25

In the days that followed his confession, Bernard kept kicking himself. He honestly wanted to scream. Ostensibly, he'd come clean, finally admitted to Sara the horrible secret he'd been harbouring – the secret that was at the root of his occasional dark moods, and that she now assumed was behind his problems with his children. She'd been so incredibly sympathetic, so kind. Not that he'd have expected her to be anything else. Sara wasn't judgemental – it was one of the things he loved about her. *It was an accident.* Her words echoed in his head, mocking him.

So why the hell had he mangled his confession with another bloody lie? *Why didn't I tell her the whole truth, when I had the chance?* Although he knew the answer to that, of course. But now things felt worse between them, rather than better. His heart ached, remembering the hurt look on her face, that he hadn't trusted her to understand. What drove his despair was the knowledge that, sometime in the future, he would disappoint her much, much more comprehensively.

That evening he watched as she carefully took the dish of kedgeree out of the oven for supper and laid it on the worktop, lifting the foil lid so she could press the tip of a knife into the centre to check that it was done. Her movements were calm and practised, but he knew that her expression, if he could have seen it, would be one of bewilderment at his current mood. He had tried so hard to appear relieved to have got the secret off his chest, but it wasn't happening . . . for obvious reasons.

And however sympathetic Sara might be right now, when she finally discovered that his so-called truth was just another version of a much bigger lie, that he still didn't trust her enough to reveal his real crime . . . He swallowed hard, choked by his own cowardice.

Since exposing the accident, he had found himself increasingly unable to function and push the bigger problem of that day – even now unresolved – to the back of his mind. He knew he must come across as sulky and self-pitying, but he couldn't seem to do anything about it.

They ate in silence. 'I'll come to Wales,' Bernard offered after a while. He knew how wound up Sara was about the Thanksgiving visit to her father, but she had not once suggested she wanted his company.

Sara smiled gratefully. 'Thanks, but Lois mentioned Frank's heart is bad when I tried to get out of coming this year. If he's ill, it's probably better I go alone.'

She never called him 'Dad', Bernard noticed, as he said, 'I could support you, call him out if he's mean to you.'

'My father invents his own truth. He's vain and selfish, but he's not specifically mean to me,' she said. 'Just completely uninterested in anyone but himself.' She grabbed his plate and stacked it on her own. 'I'll be fine. Lois is sweet and it's just for one night.'

He felt embarrassed suddenly. At least one of the characteristics she applied so scathingly to her father could equally well apply – *did* apply, indeed – to himself. *She doesn't deserve to be let down by me as well.*

26

It was sunny and dry on the Thursday Sara drove north – unusually good weather after days of rain and a biting wind. She stopped at a shop in town to buy Lois some flowers and a box of chocolates, a bottle of wine for Frank, planning to arrive by four o'clock – they always ate on the dot of six. She would stay the night, have a quick breakfast – Lois used to serve pancakes with bacon and maple syrup when the girls were younger, but it was now a piece of sliced white toast and cheap strawberry jam, unless Frank was up – and be on her way by nine.

As she drove up the various motorways to her destination, the November morning sparkling, she felt the spell of the cliff house fall away and her spirits lift. She realized just how much Bernard's low mood was affecting her, especially as she couldn't fully understand the root cause.

Her own mood was further enhanced because she had finally heard from Julian Cameron. A letter, beautifully hand-written in black flourishes on good paper, had arrived at her consulting rooms yesterday. It was at least two months since he would have had his test and the results, but it had obviously taken him a while to be able to admit to her that it was negative and seek her advice again. 'I'm sorry I disrespected you, walking out like that and being so rude when you were only trying to help,' he finished, before signing off. She was pleased, both to hear from him again and to get his apology. She knew she could help him and felt quite excited about the challenge. The one thing in her day-to-day life that felt clear and straightforward at the moment was her work.

By the time Sara neared the dreary conurbation of Prestatyn, the clouds had rolled in off the sea and it had begun to rain. Her previous optimism had deserted her and she was tired from nearly six hours on the road, her gut churning not only from the slimy, refrigerated egg sandwich she'd eaten on the way, but in grim anticipation of what lay ahead. *Is Frank dying?*

Her stepmother – although Sara had never thought of her as such – and the corgi's excitable yapping welcomed her at the door of the neat, pebbledash bungalow, which sat in a row of almost identical houses, two blocks back from the sea. Sara could sense the eyes of all the other bored resident-retirees trained on her behind the nets in the quiet street, storing up information about her car, her clothes, the flowers she carried, the length of time she stayed, for gossiping about later.

Lois was dithery, plump and powdery, her dyed blonde hair piled on her head in a frizzy topknot, pink lipstick from the sixties garish against her old skin. She had a tinkly laugh, which she used instead of speech when she felt self-conscious – which seemed to be a lot of the time.

'My, those are just gorgeous,' she said, in her wavering American accent, when Sara handed her the flowers. 'You're so kind, sweetie. Frankie loves dahlias.'

'You should put them in water right now, Lois. I'm afraid they've suffered a bit from the journey.' The house smelt of roasting turkey, but she couldn't detect the usual rotten-egg pong of Frank's homemade wine and hoped this meant they would drink the bottle she had brought at dinner.

'I'll do that right away. Go ahead and say hi to your daddy,' Lois said, waving towards the sitting room. 'Stop it, Shula. Leave poor Sara alone, will you?' She shooed the dog away from Sara's feet, where it continued to yap insistently.

'Where's Jill?' Sara asked after the other corgi, and wished she hadn't, because Lois's eyes clouded with tears. 'Oh, I'm afraid she passed a while back. It was her kidneys.'

'Sara?' came a weak call from the sitting room.

'You'd better go in,' Lois said nervously.

The room was boiling, the gas fire – a glowing rectangle surrounded by shiny metal and brown wood – was on full blast, the double-glazed windows firmly shut. Frank was sitting in a beige flock La-Z-Boy in the centre of the room. The side table to his left held an impressive array of pill bottles and packets, water jug and tissues. The one to his right was piled with car magazines, the local newspaper, a small radio and two pairs of spectacles.

Frank was now slight, bald and thin – much thinner, as Lois had warned, than when Sara had last seen him, his skin bearing the bluish tinge of someone with a compromised heart. She had seen photos of him – found among her mother's things after she died – in which his then lustrous dark hair and sharp blue eyes, his jaunty, flirtatious air, might have been attractive. But since then he seemed to have sunk into weaselly bitterness, a frequent twitch around his right eye disconcerting, almost piratical.

He had once said to Sara, his voice whiny with disappointment, 'Life never treats you the way you deserve, Sara.' To which Sara had responded silently, *Your problem is that life has treated you in exactly the way you deserve.*

He held out his hand to her, producing a charming smile with obvious effort. 'You made it all right?' His voice was still surprisingly strong and held the faint flat echo of the Midlands, where he was born. 'I heard on the radio that the M6 was blocked around Stoke.'

Sara, after clasping her father's hand for a brief second, had retreated to the blue chintz sofa. 'It wasn't too bad by the time I got there.' She felt strange, sitting there trying to think of what to say to this man who had hovered so invisibly, but still powerfully, over her life. Whose features she searched for familiarity, and found none, whose gaze she plumbed for signs of affection, and also found none. But each time she still hoped for a breakthrough, some indication – she didn't know what – that might finally redeem their relationship.

'I should go and see if Lois needs my help,' she said, after a few more minutes' chat about the weather and the roads.

'She's fine,' Frank said tersely. 'Tell me how you are. It's been such a long time since I saw you.'

Sara didn't rise to the dig. 'I'm OK. Busy, work's going well.'

'The girls?' He always referred to them this way, as he seemed never to remember their names.

She filled him in, drawing out the detail to occupy the time, although she could see he wasn't really taking it in, his gaze wandering, waiting till she'd finished.

'You know I'm not well,' he finally interrupted her. 'It's my heart.'

'Oh . . . I'm sorry.'

'I could go any time.'

'Have the doctors said that?'

'Pretty much.'

Sara didn't know whether to believe him or not.

'Lois is getting worked up about it. But there's nothing to be done.' He spoke nonchalantly, but Sara could hear the anger beneath his words.

'That must be scary for you both.'

Frank was eyeing her. Ignoring her comment, he said, 'I wanted to tell you . . . I've seen you right, Sara. You should know that.'

Not quite understanding what he meant, Sara nodded. *Is he talking about his will?*

There was a sudden loud clank from the kitchen and she got up. 'I'd better go and give Lois a hand.'

Lois was flustered and red-faced, her frilly apron spotted with gravy. When she saw Sara she laughed self-consciously. 'Nearly there,' she said, as she spooned roast potatoes into a white china serving dish.

The meal seemed to go on forever. Sara was exhausted, the wine and the overheated air making her head ache. Conversation jogged along effortlessly, though, Lois wittering, in a steady stream, about local dramas, the dog's sleeping habits – it had taken to lying on her pillow at night, since Jill had died, much to Frank's distaste – the terrible storm a week ago. Sara had only to nod and smile. Her father contributed pompous tales of his genius in controlling the idiots on the parish council and occasionally berating Lois for some detail she got wrong, when he didn't have his head bent over his plate, shovelling in the turkey and gravy and potatoes.

Sara helped Lois clear up afterwards. 'It was a lovely meal,' she said, not completely untruthfully, although the pie had been the usual challenge.

Lois pulled a face. 'The pumpkin was out of a tin this year, I'm afraid, potatoes and gravy M and S. I haven't the energy to cook any more.' She paused in her drying of a stemmed wine glass and glanced towards the door. 'I need to speak to you privately, Sara, before you go,' she muttered anxiously.

Frank shuffled slowly off to bed with the pained martyrdom of a man who feels nobody fully appreciates his suffering. Sara was longing to do the same, even though the single bed was narrow and pressed against the wall, the fitted sheet slippery nylon, the pillow microfibre. But Lois was giving her meaningful glances. As soon as they heard the bedroom door shut, she hurried over to the sofa and sat down next to Sara. She could smell stale lily of the valley as Lois moved closer. Shula leapt onto her lap and Lois petted her, her hand movements jerky with tension.

Staring hard at Sara, she began to whisper: 'This is so embarrassing. I'm just going to come right out with it.' There was a split-second pause. 'Frankie has left you the house. When he dies, you . . . will . . . own . . . this house.' The last words were enunciated slowly, as if she were worried Sara wouldn't understand.

Sara wasn't sure she did. 'But . . . but . . . as his wife . . .'

Tears were forming in Lois's pale eyes. 'Frankie never married me. He said two was enough.'

Sara was shocked – but not surprised – by her father's selfishness towards a woman who had cared for him devotedly for fifteen years, and was of the generation to whom marriage was a necessary social requirement. 'I didn't realize, Lois.'

The old lady shrugged. 'I don't mind too much. I know he's a difficult old cuss, but I love your father.' She hesitated. 'You two aren't close, but he does love you, sweetie. I understand why he's done it. But I'll have nowhere to go if you sell the house.' At this, Lois began to cry softly, digging a tissue from her sleeve to hold to her nose.

Boiling with fury, Sara took Lois's hand. '*I don't want the house*, Lois. If Frank has left it to me, I'll give it to you.'

Lois blinked through her tears. She didn't appear to hear Sara. 'It's worth a bit. I've kept it nicely and it's only a short walk to the sea. You have the girls to think about.'

Shaking her head, Sara said, 'Listen, I would never make you homeless in a million years, Lois. As far as I'm concerned, this house is yours.'

Lois, almost shaking with relief, clutched Sara's hand ever tighter. 'You should talk to your father. He won't be pleased you don't want it. He'll think I've been manipulating you.'

Inhaling what was supposed to be a calming breath so she didn't immediately go and drag her father out of bed by the scruff of the neck and give him what for, she put her arm round the old lady by her side. 'I don't give a toss what my father thinks. What he's done is beyond cruel.'

Lois looked horrified. 'Don't speak like that, Sara. He's your father.'

Sara shook her head. 'I share his DNA. That's the sum total of his involvement in my life. I know you've tried . . . but honestly? I'm very fond of you, Lois, but he means nothing to me.'

Eyes wide with shock, Lois must have sensed Sara's rage because she said, 'What are you going to do? Don't say I said anything, *please*. It'll only upset him, me going behind his back like this.'

'I will speak to him. But I won't involve you, I promise.'

Tired as she was, Sara found it hard to fall asleep. Adrenalin, triggered by the conversation with Lois, rendered her wide awake and twitchy as if she'd downed five cups of full-strength espresso. She wanted to ring Bernard and offload, but the walls of the bungalow were thin, and she was so livid, she might end up shouting. She lay there, instead, nursing her fury, constructing and refining what she would say to Frank in the morning.

Lois made herself scarce after she'd set the breakfast on the table. She looked washed out and fragile and Sara's heart went out to her. Frank, on the other hand, seemed rested, tucking into his fried egg and bacon with his usual absorption.

'You said last night you've "seen me right",' Sara began. 'What did you mean?'

Her father's expression took on a knowing look. 'Aha, so you're interested, eh?'

Trying to keep her temper, she nodded.

Frank waved his knife around the room. 'This is all yours when I go.' He smiled magnanimously, a teasing glint in his eye, waiting for her gratitude.

'Oh?' she said, as if this were news. 'And what about Lois?'

He frowned. 'You're my daughter, Sara. I want to leave you what I have. I know I've not always been around for you.'

A little late to work that out, Sara retorted silently. 'So what would Lois do, if I sell the house?'

'She has a sister in Louisville. She's always saying she misses Kentucky . . .'

Unable to believe what she was hearing, Sara took a minute to reply. Then, almost without thinking, she said, 'Please change your will, Frank. Leave the house to Lois . . . Or marry her, for God's sake. You know it's the right thing to do. I don't feel I can see you again, unless you do.' It seemed like a very feeble threat to Sara, the withdrawal of her once-yearly visits, but her father's eyes widened in consternation.

'Has she been saying things?'

'Why do you ask? Is it because you know she's probably worried sick?'

Frank had the grace to look shamefaced for a second. Then his confidence was back. 'I can't understand why you don't want my house, Sara. I thought you'd be grateful.'

Sara stood up fast, nearly toppling the kitchen chair in the process. Her heart was exploding with rage. She was on the verge of spewing out a lifetime of resentment towards a man who had abandoned her and her mother, never paid a penny towards her childhood upkeep, never even sent her a birthday card, then turned up unannounced at her mother's funeral in a shabby brown suit and declared he was Frank Colquhoun, clearly expecting Sara to fall at his feet. When she'd asked him why he'd come, he replied, *Because I'm your father*, as if the notion had suddenly come to him in a vision.

But she knew there was no point. He was a man who had never taken responsibility for his actions, everything always and exclusively revolving around *him* and what *he* wanted. He was leaving her the house not because he cared for her but because it made him feel better about his transgressions. 'I should get going before the traffic builds up,' she said flatly.

Hugging Lois – who clung to her for a long moment – Sara wondered if she'd ever see her or Frank again, whatever he decided about the house. When Pete and the girls had come with her to Thanksgiving, it had felt like a nod to their history, a duty call. Now it just seemed a pointless waste of her time.

27

'I know it's only two days, but I've missed you.' Bernard was lying beside her in bed on Sunday night, regarding her in the half-light of the bedside lamp. 'I didn't like you driving all that way alone, especially on such a grim mission.'

'It was OK, in fact . . .' She didn't explain. She wasn't sure she could articulate it yet. But Sara knew that something had changed for her during this visit to North Wales. In the past, she would come away on a high, relieved to have got the visit over with for another year, but also feeling sad that there had been no progress in her relationship with Frank. This weekend had been different: she had finally stopped hoping. Her father's pathetic attempt to salve his conscience, his cruel treatment of Lois, had shone a light so bright that Sara saw all the cracks in painful relief. There was no equivocation. This was a man from whom she could expect nothing. She was someone who'd always believed people could change if they put their mind to it, that bad eggs didn't always have to remain so. *But perhaps*, she thought, *Frank Colquhoun is the exception that proves the rule.*

'I thought maybe you'd have second thoughts about us while you were away,' Bernard said, his voice low and tentative. 'Come to the conclusion it wasn't worth the hassle. I've been a bit of a pain recently . . .' He stopped, waiting for her to respond.

His skin was cool, the night damp and wet, wind howling beyond the skylight. She was exhausted, her thoughts swimming in and out of coherence as she listened to him.

She understood his fears: the ground they stood on seemed shaky for the first time. They had no historic foundation to their relationship. Nothing to fall back on. And neither seemed to know what to do with Bernard's revelation. Or how to move past it. At the moment, it seemed to be in the very air they breathed, closed up in the insulated house, stifling the love they felt for each other.

'You're right,' she began carefully. 'I have been thinking.' In fact, on the long journey back, she'd found herself thinking more about Bernard than about her father. Standing up to Frank had been cathartic, and she wasn't about to let things slide with Bernard. He was the twins' father. She wouldn't let him risk a moment like the one she had just experienced with her own. 'The accident isn't the issue here,' she went on. 'The issue is the fallout. Whatever is ruining your relationship with Carrie and Adam, you have to sort it out, Bernard. Or you're forfeiting any possible chance of a happy life . . . for yourself *and* for the twins.'

He looked shocked and turned onto his back without responding. She wanted immediately to retreat from her words – which had sounded preachy, almost dictatorial – but she knew she wouldn't chicken out, as she had done in the past.

He closed his eyes for a long moment. When he opened them again, his gaze was more focused. 'I hear what you're saying, Sara. And it's all true.' He reached for her hand.

'Please, give me a chance to sort things out. I don't know what I'd do if you left me.'

'I wasn't threatening you,' she said. 'But this is really serious. You absolutely cannot go on like this, sweeping things under the carpet.' She reached over and kissed his cheek. 'You have to do something about your relationship with the twins. *Now*, not in five years' time, when it might be too late.'

She saw his face twitch at her insistence.

'I'll help, if you'd like me to,' she added, 'as long as you don't keep fobbing me off, pretending you'll sort things, then doing nothing.'

He was staring at her intently, as if he were about to say something important. She felt an odd blip in the air around them, as if everything paused. But the moment passed and his mouth clamped shut as if to stop the words he'd been about to utter before they escaped.

'Bernard?'

'I'll ring them both tomorrow, I absolutely promise,' he said softly.

There was a short silence, during which Sara tried to believe him.

'Why don't you ask them for Christmas?' Her spur-of-the-moment suggestion felt dangerous as soon as it left her mouth, and she held her breath as she waited for him to respond.

He nodded slowly. 'Nice idea. But I already did, months ago, and neither responded. I'll try again, but I very much doubt they'll come. They always seem to have other plans.'

She was shocked. No family Christmases? *How sad*, she

thought, as she brushed her fingers lightly down his arm, took his hand in hers and brought it to her lips. He tasted of the lavender soap in the bathroom, and of his essence, the thing she loved. A thought struck her. 'I know this isn't about me, but if you think my presence will be an added incentive for them not to come, I can leave you to it. Peggy told me yesterday she's off to Berlin with the mysterious Beng this year, but I can go to Margaret's.'

'You're not the problem.' He gave her an anxious smile. 'If, by some miracle, they do change their minds and come, I'd love you to be here, if you're OK with that.'

'I hope they do,' she said, forcing aside his resistance and her own apprehension. The thought of meeting his children – when she'd be resident on their turf – was making her more and more nervous.

Bernard shot her a worried glance. 'Me too . . .'

They laughed, picking up on each other's anxiety.

Both fell silent, the twins casting a long shadow, before Bernard added, 'By the way, Joe's just back from Germany. He's offering to take us out for supper in Lewes tomorrow night. His house is a tip, so he suggested we get together for a curry at this little place at the top of the high street. We've been there a few times, and the food's not bad.'

'Great,' she said. 'Maybe we could ask Precious to come along. Sammi's in Spain and won't be back till Friday.'

'Come to mine? *Please*,' Precious begged when Sara rang later and told her of the plan. 'Sammi's left this mound of food a mile high, terrified I might starve to death in his absence. I'll never get through it on my own.'

*

Precious and Sara were deep in conversation as they negotiated the narrow pavement on their way to Precious's house from work the following evening. They were discussing an article Sara had read online about the merits of intermittent fasting as a weight-loss tool, in which a few of her clients were interested. They'd almost reached the steep cut that led down to the house when Sara heard someone call her name. Spinning round, she saw Joe on the other side of the road, waving over the lights of the rush-hour traffic grinding down the high street. She grinned and waved back as he hopped across the road, dodging the slow-moving cars with ease.

'Hey, thought it was you,' he said, hugging her against his heavy tweed coat, damp with drizzle.

Turning to Precious, he said, 'Good to see you again,' as they shook hands. 'Appreciate you having me over, by the way.'

'Where's Bernard?' Sara asked.

Joe looked puzzled. 'He was over near Robertsbridge this afternoon, taking a client through the plans for his house. Told me he'd come straight to yours when we spoke earlier.'

Sara pulled out her phone, where she found a message she'd missed from earlier. *Pls call x.*

'Where are you?' she asked, when Bernard picked up.

'Excuse me a minute . . . got to take this,' he muttered to someone. After a pause, during which Sara heard the background hum of voices and the chink of glasses, he went on, 'Sorry . . . it's going on a bit here. Just having a drink.' His voice dropped even lower: 'Doesn't look like I'll be able to get away soon enough for supper. You'd better go ahead without me.'

'Shame. OK, then. But we'll miss you. Just bumped into Joe on the high street. We're heading over to Precious's now.'

'Say hi to the others,' Bernard said, obviously in a hurry to get back to his client.

'Oh, well,' said Precious when Sara relayed the news. 'We'll have even more food to get through, then.'

Joe, seemingly undeterred that his friend couldn't make it, grinned. '"Lead on, Macduff!"' he exclaimed, raising his arm in the air as if he were a tour guide. 'Always ready to sacrifice myself for the greater good.'

Sammi's *pollo en pepitoria* – chicken with saffron, almonds, spices and sherry, which Precious heated up and served with rice and hardboiled eggs, a sprinkling of parsley – was as good as any curry. Joe made steady work of it.

'Can't be bothered to cook for myself,' he said, thanking Precious for the millionth time. 'Marisa was a great cook, but since she left, I mostly eat sardines and frankfurters, baked beans, peaches . . . wine. Anything in a tin or a bottle, although I aim to cover all food groups. My kitchen cupboard looks like I'm preparing for the apocalypse.'

'What went wrong between you and your wife?' Precious asked.

Sara winced, both at Joe's shocking diet and Precious's familiarity. But her friends had established a teasingly forthright, no-bullshit rapport right from the moment they'd met on Bonfire Night. It made her laugh and wish Bernard was there to enjoy it too.

'Oh, she found someone slimmer, younger and more compliant than me. Not very difficult.'

Precious frowned. 'I loathe him, whoever he is.'

'Yeah, me too. But it was a while ago now and I've got over it. Quite like the old scumbag, these days.'

As they laughed, Sara asked, 'Would I have liked Ilsa, do you think?'

She wasn't sure what answer to expect as Joe considered her question for an almost embarrassing length of time.

'Ilsa was strange,' he finally pronounced, after a couple of false starts. 'Ethereally beautiful – she had the sort of beauty that made you want to stare – but odd and often ill, as Bernie has probably told you. I never really got a handle on her, if I'm honest, although we knew each other for decades. Not sure she approved of me . . . or of poor old Bernie, come to that.' He hurried on, 'Don't get me wrong. They loved each other, no question. Almost too much, perhaps. But mostly she wasn't a bundle of laughs.' His broad shoulders rose in a shrug. 'May have been a translation thing, I suppose.'

Sara was not entirely surprised by Joe's assessment of Ilsa. It tallied with the snippets Bernard had let drop. She would have liked to find out more about the Lockmore family, but she didn't think it was appropriate to question Joe further. She felt almost guilty for having asked about Ilsa behind Bernard's back.

'Such a lovely evening, Precious,' she said, into the silence that followed, realizing it was after eleven. 'Thanks . . . I should probably get home.'

Joe stretched. 'Yeah, me too. I'm going your way.'

For a while they walked through the dark streets without speaking, both tired. But as they began to climb the steep cobbled alley – still slick and slippery from the earlier rain – Sara found herself saying, 'Bernard told me about the accident.'

Joe, huffing at the gradient, shot her a quick glance. 'He knew he had to, eventually. He was just waiting for the right moment. Then the visa problem came up . . .'

Sara digested this. 'He needn't have worried about how I'd react.'

'I'm sure you can understand, though.' He put a friendly arm around her shoulders. 'You mean a great deal to him, Sara, you know that.'

'And him to me.' She paused, picking her words carefully. 'I just worry about the twins. I don't know them, so perhaps I shouldn't comment, but they're being a bit unfair to Bernard, aren't they, five years on?' When he didn't immediately reply, she added, 'Isn't there anything you and I can do to improve things? Bernard's asked them for Christmas, but he seems to think they won't come.'

Joe dropped his arm and stopped, hands on hips, to catch his breath as they reached the high street. 'It's so fucking complex, isn't it? Not sure how well either of the twins are coping. Adam and Bernie were close at first, and for a while after it happened, although Carrie was furious. Now they both seem to be giving him a hard time.'

Sara sighed. 'Their behaviour feels really extreme to me. And not very kind. From what I can make out, it was a terrible accident.'

'Well, yes . . .' Joe's words hung in the air.

'I don't understand what they're still so angry about,' Sara said. 'I mean, Bernard's taken his punishment – even if he does think he got off too lightly.'

Joe's open features sharpened suddenly and seemed almost wary as he eyed her, a slight frown twitching his brow. The atmosphere between them had changed to something altogether more charged.

'What?'

'Bernie explained what happened, right?'

She nodded, puzzled. 'Careless driving, the cyclist killed, yes.'

He took her elbow and began to walk again, quickening his pace, in complete silence. She felt tension coming off him in waves.

'What is it? What are you not telling me, Joe?'

Joe stopped as they drew level with her red front door. Biting his bottom lip, he gazed at her without seeing her, and seemed, after a few seconds, to come to a decision. 'It's Bernie you should talk to.'

Grabbing his sleeve, she protested, 'Please, Joe. You know what he's like, he just brushes aside stuff he doesn't want to deal with . . . like the problem with the twins. If you don't tell me – whatever this is about – I might never find out. And I really should know.'

Joe took a deep breath. 'I can't. I'm sorry.' He patted her arm as he repeated yet again, '*Talk to Bernie.*' Then he waved a hand in farewell and was gone.

Sara watched his bulky figure trudge up the hill in the light from the streetlamps. Unlocking her front door on autopilot, her mind was whirring, going over and over the cryptic conversation she'd just had. *What did Joe actually say?* she asked herself. But it wasn't what he'd said so much as what he *hadn't* said . . . how he'd looked.

Sara paced the small kitchen. It was after midnight, but

she knew she wouldn't sleep. *Something about the accident . . .* Had Bernard been drinking? Was there something wrong with the car – the brakes, for instance – that he had been aware of and ignored? How could the twins be involved? Had he made them lie about something?

There was a text from Bernard, sent an hour ago, saying he loved her and wishing her goodnight, to which she hadn't yet replied. At sixes and sevens, she didn't know what to do with herself. Calling him when he was probably asleep, then demanding an explanation over the phone, didn't feel right. Clutching her arms round her body, she swayed on her toes for a moment, then grabbed her bag and keys, lifted her coat from the hooks in the hall and made for the front door.

28

The roads were almost deserted so late, and her journey was quick. The house sat there in isolated darkness, the usual wind swirling up from the sea like a malign spirit, the security light bathing her in its cruel beam.

She let herself in quietly, still uncertain as to what she would say, words batting round in her head in unedited chaos. *What hasn't he told me?* she kept asking herself, over and over. *What did he do? Why can't he be honest?* But the predominant question in her mind was *Who is this man I've fallen in love with?*

Bernard was asleep, although the bedside light was still on. When she tiptoed into the room, he jerked awake, pushing himself up with a loud 'Who's there?', his sleep-washed eyes wild. She hurried over to the bed. 'It's OK, only me.'

'I thought you were staying in Lewes.' He rubbed his face with one hand, smiling sleepily. 'How was supper?'

She took a steadying breath, plonked herself down on the edge of the mattress, one knee drawn up under her. Now she was here, she wasn't sure where to start. *No point in beating round the bush.*

'Tell me what really happened the day of the accident, Bernard.'

His eyes narrowed. 'What do you mean?'

'I mentioned to Joe that you'd told me about it.' She

took a breath, realized she was trembling. 'And he implied by his reaction . . . He didn't say as much, but there's clearly stuff I don't know . . .' She trailed off. 'He said I had to talk to you.'

The following silence burnt the air and made her shudder. Bernard was breathing in short gasps. When his grey eyes finally met hers, she saw only an overwhelming despair. He swallowed. 'I've been such an idiot.'

'Tell me,' she whispered, feeling anger begin to take over from bewilderment. She just couldn't comprehend why this man would bring her into his life, tell her he loved her, but continue to hide so much that was so vitally important.

Bernard sat up straighter, crossing his legs beneath the duvet, clasping his hands tightly together in his lap. His blue T-shirt had a small tear just below the neck and she couldn't help staring at it. She thought his silence would last forever, but she was not going to speak again until he did.

'OK, I'll tell you . . . But I must warn you, Sara, it'll shock you.' He took a large gulp of air and looked away. 'God, this is so hard to say out loud. I've kept the secret for so bloody long.' Another pause, during which Sara thought her heart would burst through her chest. 'The truth is, Adam was driving the car.'

Absolutely stunned, Sara stared at him. 'Oh, my God . . .' As it began to sink in, she repeated more softly, 'Oh, my God.' Then added, 'And you . . . you took the rap?'

He nodded miserably.

She thought for a second. 'Adam went along with it?'

'He didn't have much choice. He was in shock and I took charge . . . made probably the worst decision of my life.'

It was hard, immediately, to comprehend the ramifications of what he'd just said. The knowledge that he'd continued to lie to her, however, was clear as day. 'You described it all to me in such vivid detail . . . The bend, the car swerving, the girl on the road . . . as if it were totally real . . . As if you'd done it.'

'All that *was* real.'

She shook her head at his dissembling. 'Real, but not the truth. Why did you do that? Why couldn't you tell me what really happened, for God's sake?' Her voice had risen, her words echoing sharply around the dimly lit room.

She saw the muscles around his mouth tense at her onslaught. It was a moment before he spoke. 'The reason I lied . . . why I didn't feel able to tell you . . . tell anyone . . . is that both Adam and I perjured ourselves. We lied to the police. For that alone, we could face prison. The courts take a dim view of people who pervert the course of justice.' The calmness with which he spoke belied his wretched expression.

'Fine, I get that. But you didn't trust *me*?'

'It's Adam's life we're talking about, Sara,' he said patiently. 'In the heat of the moment, both of us were so stunned and horrified by what happened . . . I reacted almost without thinking. My instinct was to protect my son at all costs . . . I thought I was saving him.' He stopped and added softly, 'But I fucked up.'

Sara tried to take in what Bernard was telling her.

He was speaking again. 'I realized I'd done the wrong thing as soon as I got the chance to calm down and gauge the situation. But by then it was too late. And now, how can I tell even one other person and keep him safe? I tell you, for instance. You tell your girls or Precious . . . she tells Sammi, he tells I don't know who. And suddenly it's not a secret and my son's whole future is in jeopardy. All those years of study, the hard work he's put in, gone for nothing. I just didn't dare.'

Sara considered what he'd said. She saw that he had a point. The whole thing was so complex. But acknowledging the complexity didn't soothe away her hurt.

'I'm so sorry,' he was saying. 'It's not that I don't trust you, Sara. I absolutely do. One hundred per cent.'

'I wouldn't have told anyone, if you'd asked me not to.'

Bernard sighed. 'I'm sure you believe that. But these things have a habit of coming out in the end. An unguarded moment . . . like tonight with Joe.'

A tense silence fell between them.

'Were you really intending to just carry on with me never knowing?' she asked.

Bernard bowed his head for a second. When he looked up again, his expression had hardened. 'It's not *your* child, or Joe's for that matter. It's impossible for you to understand, Sara, to put yourself into my position.'

She turned away, biting her lip. 'So what's happened with the twins? Why are they so angry with you?'

He looked as if the effort to explain was almost too much, throwing his hands into the air in apparent frustration. 'Carrie was never on board with it. She thought, right from the start, that Adam should stand up and be counted.'

Bernard flopped back on the pillows, eyes shut. 'But Adam went along with it back then. He was abject . . . and so grateful.' He lifted his eyebrows in resignation. 'But he was only nineteen. How could he have predicted the after-effects, the mental toll of such a terrible event . . . or the path I persuaded him to take? How could I?' He gave a rueful shrug. 'I'm honestly not sure what Adam is thinking now or how best to help him.'

Another silence, this one weary rather than tense. Sara pulled off her clothes and got into bed beside him. They lay stiffly apart for a few seconds, then turned to hold each other.

'Isn't it better, in the end, to come clean, go to the police?' Sara asked gently. 'Won't it poison all your lives until you do?' The notion of a nightmare of this proportion prising her own family apart, of her losing touch with Joni and Peggy, made her shudder.

Bernard stiffened. 'With all due respect, Sara, you have absolutely no idea what that means,' he said coldly.

Absorbing his rebuff as best she could, she asked, 'OK, so, tell me. What does it mean?'

'Well, in the last resort, we could both go to prison. Adam would have a criminal record – with all that implies for his future. It would be the end of everything for him.' He fixed his gaze on Sara. 'You think it's as simple as "coming clean"? Believe me, I've lived with this nightmare for five long years. There is nothing simple about it.' Taking a deep, fierce breath, he finished, 'I am not going to let that happen to my son, if I can help it . . . whatever you think.'

Sara heard his dismissal but was too tired to argue any

more. She closed her eyes, but sleep wouldn't come. Uppermost in her mind was the thought that, if nothing changed, she wasn't sure what she would do. Living with this impasse, with the secret Bernard seemed determined to hold close, would, she knew, eventually break something.

The following morning she was in a daze, arriving at work scratchy-eyed and tense, still so stunned by Bernard's revelation – and lack of sleep – that she could hardly think straight. When she'd surfaced from a short, heavy doze earlier, after a fitful night, Bernard had already got up without waking her and left for work. The note on the kitchen table said he had an early appointment, although she wasn't sure she believed him. *He's avoiding me*, she thought. It made her angry. And, of all people, Julian Cameron was her first appointment. She could have done with a less tricky start to the day, although she was pleased he was giving her another chance to help him.

Julian smiled sheepishly at her, however, as she welcomed him into her consulting room. 'Apologies again for last time, Sara. I'm afraid I can be a stubborn old sod sometimes.'

She laughed. *There's plenty more stubborn than you out there*, she thought, remembering the intransigent look in Bernard's eyes the night before.

Waiting while Julian made himself comfortable, she was heartened to detect a definite shift in his appearance. Although he was still pale, the hollowness around the eyes was gone, and he seemed less gaunt. She thought he'd even put on a little weight. But she wasn't going to make any assumptions and upset him again. 'So, how have you been?'

'Well,' he said, cautiously, 'I do feel a bit better . . . on your regime.' He shot her a shy grin. 'So, I'm back for more advice.'

Sara was gratified. But she responded to what he was telling her almost on autopilot. She tried to shake herself internally, get a grip on the session. She didn't want Julian to feel let down again. But it was so hard to concentrate. *What just happened with Bernard?* she kept asking herself.

29

Bernard was heading home around nine, after what seemed like a very long day. He was tired from the previous sleepless night and still smarting from the row with Sara, trying to decide the extent of the damage to her feelings for him. The thought of losing her made him feel sick, although she had every right to question his cowardly behaviour in lying to her.

He knew, of course, that the key to everyone's happiness – Sara's, Adam's, Carrie's, his own – lay in sorting out his relationship with his children. But how the hell was he to do that? He felt paralysed, all at sea, the same old fears – arguments and counter-arguments – swirling around his brain until he was ready to go mad.

His phone rang, Bluetooth kicking in. Adam's voice was suddenly loud in the dark car – as if he'd channelled his father's thoughts. Bernard's last communication had been the latest messages he'd left inviting his son for Christmas, which both Adam and Carrie had so far ignored.

'How's it going, Adam? Get my message about Christmas?'

Bernard, instead of turning right towards the narrow lanes that led to the cliff house, kept driving until he got to the beach, knowing there was a spot where he regularly lost signal close to his house. He couldn't risk it, not when he finally had his son on the line. He pulled into one of the vacant parking bays behind the shingle bank that served the summer tourists, and turned the volume down a little on the call.

Adam, it was clear, had not rung to talk about Christmas. Ignoring his father's query, he launched into a quiet, despairing monologue – almost as if he was talking to himself. 'It's not going well, Dad. I'm really struggling . . . It's the pretence that's killing me. I can't ever be myself, not for a single second. Everyone sees this guy they think is me . . . and underneath is the *real* me – this totally other person – and they don't have a fucking clue.' There was a long sigh. 'I thought it would get easier. You promised it would, back at the beginning . . . but it's the total fucking opposite . . . and I don't know what to do.'

Bernard, hearing the hopelessness in his son's voice, felt his heart seize. But before he'd had a chance to work out how best to respond, Adam was speaking again.

'We never talk about it, Dad. *Never*. There's this . . . I don't know . . . hole, and all the shit's in there, but it's like we stroll around the edge and totally ignore the stink.' He stopped and Bernard heard him inhale sharply. 'It isn't that I don't appreciate what you did. You know I do.' Another audible breath. 'But you never ask me what *I*'m feeling about it, how it's affecting *me*.'

Bernard gulped. Still reeling in the face of Sara's anger and bewilderment, it felt now as if, by telling her the truth, the catch on a dangerous portal had been loosed, letting out all the foetid feelings he'd gone to such pains to contain. 'I'm sorry, son. I – I suppose I hoped you'd forget . . . Not forget, that's stupid, of course, but put it to the back of your mind, get on with your life, your training.'

There was a frustrated snort. 'Like I give a fuck about my bloody training. I just want to find a tiny bit of peace . . . Stop this endless, horrible churning in my mind,' he finished softly.

His son's words cut him to the quick.

'You know that's why me and Carrie don't want to see you, right?' Adam went on, relentless. 'Because you keep pretending nothing ever happened, that life goes on, tra-la. That we're all just *fine*. It's fucking mental.' His voice was vibrating like a taut wire. 'What sort of family does that?'

The car had gone chilly now the engine was no longer blasting hot air. Bernard felt his heart pounding uncomfortably in his chest. 'We can talk,' he said eventually, remembering Sara's words. 'Come home in the holidays and we'll deal with this then, face to face. It's hopeless over the phone.'

He heard Adam sigh. 'Talking's not enough, Dad. We passed that point long ago. We need to actually *do* something.'

Bernard waited for him to go on, hugging his arms across his chest, his fingers pushed into his sleeves and freezing against his skin. 'What do you mean?' His voice echoed, reedy and uncertain, within the confines of the Mercedes. Although he knew what his son meant, of course. He just didn't want to acknowledge it.

The silence was absolute from his son. Then a small sound escaped him. Bernard realized he was crying. 'Adam? Adam, please, son . . . don't get upset. I know how hard it must have been for you. And I haven't handled it well, I admit, because I just didn't know what was best for any of us. But we'll find a way. I promise we'll sort this out. Come home, Adam. Please . . .'

There was a soft sigh at the other end, then the line went dead. Bernard, distraught, pressed redial on the media system, listened to the burr of the ring tone blaring round the car, heard the click to Adam's voicemail. Did it again, and again. He picked up his phone, tried from there, as if it would make the slightest difference.

Finally, he slung his mobile onto the passenger seat and hurled himself out of the car. Slamming the door, which reverberated loudly in the still night, he ran up the steps onto the dark, deserted beach. As his shoes crunched on the pebbles, his legs weak, his body shivering, he felt like the most useless specimen of fatherhood on the planet. Adam had reached out to him and he'd let him down yet again. And, worse, Adam was implying he'd got to the point where he might take charge and do what Sara was also advocating: go to the police. It was as if a huge truck was careering towards him and he couldn't move out of its way.

But what his son was suggesting was completely out of the question. He would not allow him to go there. He *would not*. He felt the warm wash of tears sting his cold cheeks and began to run towards the water. As pebbles gave way to sand, he told himself firmly, *We just need to talk. Everything will be OK if we can sit down and talk.*

Joe had suggested, way back after Ilsa died, that the twins might benefit from some sort of grief counselling. But the accident had fouled up any chance of that. He wasn't going to risk someone else finding out what had really happened that day. He didn't know if a therapist would feel obliged to tell the authorities, but they might encourage Adam to do so.

He walked on, barely aware of the freezing wind coming off the sea, the mechanical tears it wrought only mingling with the emotional ones pouring down his cheeks.

He felt almost reluctant at the thought of relaying his son's anguish to Sara. If Adam was a mess, it was down to him, Bernard. By contrast, she had such a loving, stable relationship with her own girls. And if he told her what his son had just implied, she would only side with Adam, nag him to do what every bone in his body told Bernard would be an utter disaster. *We can sort it out*, he told himself over and over. *We just need to talk*.

30

That evening Sara was late getting back to the house. Bernard's car was not there and the place, looming sinister against the navy sky, was in darkness. She felt a surge of disappointment. She had not been in touch during the day, still smarting from the row last night and not knowing what to say to him. He had not messaged her, either. But as soon as she got inside, she pulled her phone out. His number went straight to voicemail. So she texted, *Are you on the way?* x

The usual close, padded silence greeted her. The space looked almost ghostly in the moonlight streaming through the windows, the kitchen surfaces gleaming empty, only the faint hint of rosemary on the warm air from the potted plant, standing by the stove, she'd bought the week before. *Where is he?* It was getting late and normally he would have called by now. Unable to settle to anything, she took a bottle of wine from the fridge and poured herself a glass, then stood leaning against the worktop as she sipped, listening for the sound of his car.

The clock ticked on. No other sound disturbed the silence. She checked her phone. Nothing. Rang him again. Voicemail again. Sent another text. A small gnaw of worry began to form in her gut. Knowing the level of guilt and blame that tormented Bernard on an ongoing, visceral level – only hinted at, but so obviously there – she started imagining catastrophic scenarios. In his distracted state, he crashed his car or slipped from the cliff edge on one of his regular walks, strode into the freezing sea. She knew she was being melodramatic, but she had no idea if Bernard was prone to suicidal thoughts.

'This is Bernard Lockmore. Please leave a message after the beep and I'll get back to you,' said the frustrating recording, when she called for the third time. 'It's me, Sara . . . Where are you? Please call me.' Staring at the screen, she willed him to respond. *Is he having a drink with Joe, his phone in his jacket pocket?* He wasn't wedded to his device twenty-four/seven, as she knew well. She thought back to what he'd said about his diary this week. He hadn't mentioned meeting anyone.

Sara nibbled the end of a French loaf with a slick of cream cheese. She felt twitchy in the dark room, jumping at the slightest noise. Even for the cliff house, the air felt unnaturally still and suffocating tonight. *Stop being so stupid, there's no one here*, she told herself, swallowing the last of the snack. In the end, with still no word from Bernard, she trailed up to bed.

Even though she was tired out, sleep wouldn't come. The gnawing in the pit of her stomach about Bernard's whereabouts was sending adrenalin round her body, like a greyhound racing the track. She stared into the darkness and tried to implement a relaxing breath: in for three, out for five. It had worked in the past when she was anxious. Not tonight, though. After only one respiration, her thoughts spun back to Bernard and her heart began to race again.

*

Cold fingers resting fleetingly on her cheek, a voice whispering her name, dragged Sara reluctantly from an exhausted, fathomless sleep. Befuddled, she opened her eyes to find Bernard lying next to her, his face lit by the radiance of the moon framed in the skylight. Its beam sheened his skin blue, his eyes black. He was shivering violently.

'Oh, my God. Where have you been?' she exclaimed, fully awake now. She quickly reached out to him. He was still fully dressed, but his body was icy and stiff. She moved her own until she had wrapped him close in her arms, wincing at the chill through her thin cotton pyjamas. Rocking him, briskly rubbing his back, his head buried in her shoulder, she repeated her question.

'On the beach,' came the muffled reply.

The beach? On a night like this? She shook off the flash of her earlier catastrophizing. Saying nothing, she continued to hold him, waiting for her body heat to warm him through.

'Walking,' he mumbled.

After a long time, the shivering began to subside and she felt him slowly relaxing, the life gradually returning to his frozen limbs. She stroked his forehead, drew her fingers along the broken line of his eyebrow.

His gaze met hers in the moonlight.

'I thought something had happened to you.'

'I'm sorry. Adam called. He was upset. I got distracted.'

'Is he all right?'

'I don't know,' Bernard mumbled. 'Talk about it in the morning.'

A few moments later, she heard his breath begin to

slow, his body giving itself over to sleep. But she lay awake for a long time, unable to let go of all the things she wanted to say to him.

When she jolted awake the next morning, Bernard, unusually, was still in bed. At some time during the night, he must have stripped off his clothes, because he was now naked and sound asleep beside her.

Breakfast in the warm kitchen, after he finally woke, was a quiet affair. Bernard looked wrecked, his eyes hollow, his skin, normally glowing so tanned and healthy, now sallow.

'Why were you on the beach?' Sara asked, raising an eyebrow. 'It was freezing.'

He sipped his coffee. 'I didn't really notice till I got home. I'm glad you were here.'

'So am I. Otherwise you'd probably be dead from hypo-thermia,' she retorted, remembering the state of him and how he'd frightened her.

Bernard reached across the table and took her hand. 'I'm sorry for the way I treated you the other night. You were only trying to help.'

She registered the love she saw so clearly in his eyes through a wave of exhaustion. He let go of her hand and silently busied himself pouring another cup of coffee from the cafetière on the table between them.

'What was Adam saying?'

Bernard seemed to hesitate. 'I think he's worn down and exhausted. He was never very robust, even as a kid . . . Ilsa's tendency to mollycoddle him probably didn't help.'

'Are you worried?'

'What he needs is a proper break.'

'Did he say if he was coming for Christmas?'

He shook his head. 'Clicked off as soon as I pushed him to come home.'

'Oh, Sas. Did you sort it out?' Precious enquired, when Sara told her, later, that she and Bernard had been arguing about his relationship with the twins. But as soon as she began embarking on the details, she was brought up short. *Precious is not allowed to know the real truth*, she remembered.

They were sitting on high stools in the window of a tiny café a street away from their offices, Sara having sent out a distress call for a lunch meeting. The place sold a particularly favourite dish of theirs: mackerel and beetroot salad with slices of homemade spelt toast. But today Sara ordered an energy boosting smoothie – spinach, apple, raspberry, spirulina and kefir: she couldn't face solid food.

The secret was making her tongue-tied in front of her friend: everything she said had to be vetted now. It was the first time in her life that she hadn't shared something so important with Precious and she ached to tell the truth. For a moment she prevaricated. *Can I risk it?* Hearing Bernard's warning in her head, she knew she could not. But she had never in her life lied to Precious. It made her feel even more queasy.

Precious had turned on her stool to look at her. 'Sas? What is it?'

'How do you mean?'

Precious continued to stare at her friend. 'There's something you're not telling me.'

'There isn't,' Sara insisted fiercely. 'I'm just upset because I don't know how to help.'

There was a short silence between the two women.

'I suppose you can't dictate how he deals with his own kids.'

Sara harrumphed. 'I wasn't dictating.'

'Perhaps he thought you were.'

Sara slumped on her stool. 'The trouble is, we don't know each other well enough to have a safe set-to. It didn't feel safe the other night.'

Precious nodded. 'Know what you mean. Sammi and I have an unshakeable system. I shout. He adopts a superior silence. I shout some more and louder. Chinko flounces off in disgust. We huff and puff for the allotted time, then one of us starts to laugh.'

Sara smiled. 'Yeah, me and Pete didn't fight a lot, but I knew when to take his rants seriously. He always called me Mrs Bloody Reasonable.' She felt tears gathering and blinked them away. 'But with Bernard, I just don't know. He said he was sorry and we sort of made up, but he seemed so irritated with me . . . and dismissive, as if my opinion didn't count.' It wasn't just how Bernard had treated her, though, it was that he couldn't be honest with her, which made Sara angry as well as upset. His secret seemed to have more layers than the cliffs his house was built on.

'He's probably blaming himself for the situation with his kids. And that makes him snippy because he doesn't know how to solve it.'

Sara didn't reply. The smoothie was churning uncomfortably in her stomach.

Precious had also fallen into a thoughtful silence. Then she said, 'Just wondering . . . Was either of the twins in the car with Bernard when it crashed? If they were, then is it possible they still have some degree of trauma . . . PTSD? It can have long-term effects if it's not dealt with. Might make them quite unstable.'

Sara jolted, sat up straighter, tried to clear her head from the miasma of a sleepless night. The truth clogged her throat, and she couldn't say another word as she felt a small shiver of fatigue run down her spine. She attempted a nonchalant shrug in reply to Precious's question, but all she was feeling was a quiet desperation to end the lunch and be away from her friend's penetrating gaze. It wasn't so much the worry, if she did tell her friend the truth, that Precious would bruit it across the entire county. It was more that she couldn't face the concerned look on her face, the look that implied Bernard was a bad lot, someone Sara should avoid. She wasn't ready for that.

She forced a smile to her face. 'Anyway, enough of Bernard and his problems. Sorry to whinge on. Are you looking forward to your Christmas in Spain?'

Precious eyed her, a puzzled frown on her face. But she asked no more questions.

Driving back to the cliff house later, Sara felt miserable. For the first time in the twenty years she and Precious had known each other, she sensed a crack opening between herself and her best friend. 'Hiding a truth is the same as lying,' her mother used to say. Today Precious had known, instinctively, that she was concealing something. She was Sara's mainstay, her lifeline, the person to whom, no matter what, she could always turn, in good times and bad. Along with Margaret, she provided the bedrock from which she thrived. *How would she feel if she realized I've been lying to her?* she wondered, suddenly resentful for being put in this position at all.

She also suspected Precious, if she knew the whole truth, might query why Sara persisted in sticking with Bernard. Sara had asked herself the same question. But running beneath the hurt and anger at Bernard's colossal lie, his lack of trust in her, she was aware of a huge thread of sympathy and compassion – alongside her love for him – that kept her by his side.

Bernard and Sara were sitting in the winter sunshine at one of the pine picnic tables behind the mobile food truck next to the beach, cardboard boxes containing their delicious sausage and slaw buns open in front of them. Since the row and its aftermath, both of them had been heads down, working hard, Sara spending a lot of time with Margaret. Not avoiding each other, exactly, but not conceding any gaps during which a serious conversation might pop up. The tension was still there, although both were trying to move past it. But Sara was aware she was missing the spirit of joy and hopefulness from the early days of their relationship.

Christmas was less than a week away now, and there had been no word from Adam and Carrie. They were not coming, that much was clear, and Sara was adjusting to the fact that it would be just the two of them. Which she wouldn't have minded if it hadn't been for the pall the twins' absence cast over the festivities.

'What sort of Christmas did you have when the children were young?' she asked.

Bernard finished his mouthful before replying. 'We celebrated on Christmas Eve, like they do in Finland. Had a big tree, which Ilsa insisted on decorating with real candles that threatened to burn the house down.' He smiled. 'And a goose, lots of presents for the kids. She'd broken off all contact with her family when she was eighteen and she didn't get on with mine. So it was always just us and the twins.'

Sara winced at the sad insularity this implied but didn't comment. 'I've never cooked a goose.'

'Me neither.'

'You had fun, though?'

He gave her a regretful smile. 'Honestly? I think Ilsa found any important family occasion that reminded her of her own upbringing – like Christmas – tricky. She always put a lot of energy into making things perfect for Adam and Carrie on the day, but I knew she was thoroughly relieved when it was all over.' Head bent, he fiddled with the edge of his picnic box. 'I think her childhood with those religious obsessives was pretty grim. She seemed torn between guilt and allowing her true spirit to flourish. Guilt usually won, unfortunately, especially after the twins were born – although she had nothing to blame herself for.'

'Poor woman,' Sara said, with feeling, sensing Bernard's sadness.

'She always seemed to be looking over her shoulder to see who was judging her. I think it terrified her, this imagined retribution for something she hadn't done. Made her ill.'

'How did you cope with that?'

'I didn't really. I didn't know what to do to make her happy.' Looking away towards the shoreline, he added, 'I really loved her. She had a beautiful spirit, but it had been crushed out of her before I knew her, when she was too young to resist. I felt so powerless, not knowing how to help her.'

There was a long silence. Hearing him speak, Sara felt certain the heavy atmosphere in the house, which she still struggled with, was the accumulated weight of all those years of unhappiness. It had seeped into the very walls of the place and taken root. But maybe it wasn't just Ilsa. Maybe it was Bernard's guilt as well.

He turned back to her, forcing a smile. 'You? What did you do?'

'Oh, we had the whole works round at Margaret's when she still had the big house. Me, Pete and the girls and any waif or stray Margaret managed to round up. Sometimes there were twenty of us at the table.' Sara smiled at the recollection. 'Last year Heather did a chicken, but there's no point now Margaret's so ill. Heather's going to her family on Boxing Day and staying for a few days, so I'll stay with Margaret till she gets back.'

'You'll miss not seeing Peggy.'

She nodded. 'It'll be the first time we haven't spent it together.' Each Christmas, as her daughters got older, Sara told herself this would surely be the last. But it was a wrench, nonetheless, when Peggy declared she was off to Berlin.

'Do you mind, Mum?' Peggy had asked. 'I just thought, this year, you'd want to be with Bernard . . .'

'That doesn't mean you can't be here too.'

'I know. But Beng has these people in Berlin – sort of surrogate parents, because his are in St Vincent. And I thought . . .'

'Sounds like fun,' Sara had said gamely. She hadn't met Beng yet, and her daughter was as secretive about him as she was about all her boyfriends. 'Bring him down for a weekend in the New Year,' she'd suggested, and Peggy had agreed she might.

As she'd said goodbye to her daughter, Sara had felt a twinge of sadness that she would never be able to share with Pete a whispered speculation about their girls' liaisons, the relief if the man turned out to have only one head. Sad, too, that, as with Joni's Mason, Pete would never get to meet the man on whom Peggy finally settled.

'So, it looks like it's just us,' Bernard was saying, looking slightly relieved at the prospect. 'To tell you the truth, I'm not a huge fan of Christmas.'

Before she had a chance to reply, Bernard's phone rang. He pulled it from his pocket. 'Sorry, got to take this,' he said, rising from the table and bashing his long legs awkwardly on the bench seat in his hurry to get away. Sara watched him quickly stride off along the roadside. His back was to her, but it was clear from his stance that his body was rigid with tension. She assumed it was one of the twins.

When he eventually returned and plonked himself down, blinking anxiously, his breathing was fast, as if he'd been running. 'Well,' he said, raising his eyebrows and inhaling deeply, 'you're not going to believe this, but that was Carrie.' He still clutched his phone, his expression nonplussed. 'They're both coming. For Christmas.'

'Oh!' Sara exclaimed. 'That's great . . . Isn't it?' she added. Because Bernard's face looked more as if he'd just been delivered news of a death in the family.

He smiled stoically. 'Yes, yes, it is.'

She eyed him. 'Wow . . . What persuaded them, do you think?'

'She didn't say. It was strange, talking to her after all this time. She was really quite friendly.'

Sara was sorry that this should be remarkable for Bernard. 'You're looking uneasy . . .'

'It's just the way she said it. Sounded almost more like a threat than a promise.' He laughed. 'I'm probably just being paranoid.'

'It must be a good sign, that they're coming?'

Bernard reached for her hand. 'I suppose I'm a bit dreading the conversations we need to have. And we must talk. I took your advice and promised Adam we would.'

'Once you're all together, things will probably find a way of sorting themselves out, won't they?' She wanted to reassure him, but she was feeling anxious herself at the prospect.

He nodded. 'I hope they're not all riled up and defensive . . . demanding stuff of me that I can't deliver.' There was a pause, then he added, 'I always seem to disappoint them, Sara.'

Her heart went out to him, thinking of her girls and how lucky she was not to have been faced with the Lockmores' grim set of circumstances.

'I can go to Margaret's if you feel you want to have Carrie and Adam to yourself – I'm going on Boxing Day, anyway, so you'll have time with them then.'

He looked horrified. 'Don't leave me. Please. I really want you there, and I'm longing to introduce you to them.' He gave a mischievous grin. 'Despite all the drama that might entail.'

She clasped her hands, suddenly determined to make

this work for everyone. 'Right. We're on! Better get planning and find a bird from somewhere.'

The days after Carrie's phone call were a swirl of activity in the house on the cliff. From having minimal festive plans – holding off as long as possible, not knowing whom they were catering for – they were suddenly faced with last-minute preparations for a full-blown family celebration. The twins, it had been arranged, were arriving on Christmas Eve, staying until the twenty-seventh. Bernard wanted it all to be perfect.

Sara found she was almost as nervous as he. Carrie sounded fierce and uncompromising: she wasn't sure she would welcome Sara's presence in her father's house. And Adam, well, he seemed like a bit of a lost soul. But all she had to go on were fragments from Bernard and the photos in the album, taken years ago.

She imagined, in her worst moments, a grim scene of mayhem over the goose – the meal descending into shouting, tears, accusations and painful recrimination. However much she told herself – and Bernard – it would all be fine, part of her didn't really believe that was likely. But he had moved things on with his children. He'd got them to come home, however unwillingly, not buried his head and let things slide even further in the wrong direction. She was pleased about that. She just hoped, for everyone's sake, that by the end of their visit, things would be on a more even keel between them all. Something, at least, to build on in the future.

'Can you help?' Bernard called, huffing as he manhandled a huge tree through the front door. Being busy organizing the event had perked him up, the drained look he'd worn so frequently of late replaced by focused intent. She was pretty sure it wouldn't be sustained in the immediate run-up to his children arriving, but there were two days till then and she planned to enjoy them to the full.

'Bloody hell,' she exclaimed, as she hurried over and took the top end of the tree. 'Couldn't you get a bigger one?'

'Only one left,' he gasped, out of breath from exertion.

'How are you going to keep it upright?' Flashes of her family Christmases made her smile wistfully as she remembered the yearly tree wrangles. Pete, in a rare display of stubbornness, insisted on a clapped-out old stand that screwed onto the trunk – never remotely fit for purpose, even new – and tree lights that hailed from the last century and only worked after he'd sat cursing, cross-legged, on the floor for an hour, fiddling painstakingly with each tiny coloured bulb. It was a long-standing family joke: 'Step away from the tree, girls. Dad's doing the lights.' It broke her heart that Bernard did not have the same ease and laughter with his own children.

Now he pulled a face. 'Bucket and stones?'

'Too big.'

'Big bucket and stones?'

She started to laugh. He looked so comical, pine needles in his hair, his arm round the waist of the giant tree as if they'd just got married.

Finally leaning it gingerly against the wall between the windows, Bernard turned and swept her into his arms. 'Thanks for all your help,' he said, then bent to kiss her softly on the lips. 'We haven't done enough of this recently,' he added, smiling as he stroked her hair back from her face.

Which was true, although the previous tension – as they silently contemplated the unease that had burgeoned between them – had been temporarily pushed aside in the whirl of present-buying and goose-sourcing, decorating the house, beating brandy butter and laundering the fragile lace tablecloth that had belonged to Bernard's Scottish mother. Still holding her, he gave a heavy sigh. 'I've got terrible butterflies. Neither of them has been home for well over a year now. I feel I barely know them any more.'

'Things couldn't be worse than they are now, though, eh?'

He didn't answer.

'Come on, let's get this big boy upright,' she said, which made him grin and kiss her again. 'The tree, I mean,' she said.

Sara pulled up on the muddy farm track behind a line of intimidating four-by-fours. A queue of hunched Barboured figures had already formed outside the ramshackle shed where the birds were to be collected. It was the day before Christmas Eve, raining and very cold. Her nerves were shredding as the moment of the twins' arrival got closer.

Lugging the heavy lump of goose in its layers of waxed paper back to the car, she dropped it into the boot and breathed a sigh of relief. Another task ticked off the list. She'd just got back into the car, shivering and damp, when her phone rang.

'How's it going?' Precious's voice demanded. Normally a call from her dear friend was nothing but pleasure.

Today, however, she was reminded that she had to be careful what she said.

'OK, I think.'

'You're on track?'

'Absolutely. We've had quite a fun time getting everything ready.' On a number of occasions, she and Bernard found themselves dissolving into laughter, the festive spirit – although slightly hysterical and crazy – infusing his recent dark mood with a ray of sunlight. For Sara, it felt as if they were inhabiting an alternative universe, where trees were decorated, beloved children came for Christmas, the bird roasted merrily away, love was in the air and all was right with the world. The sky might fall, but not yet. And she'd decided to live in the moment. 'But I'm frankly terrified of his kids.'

'With reason, by the sound of it. Hey, you never know, they may turn out to be all squishy and sweet. There'll be lots of cosy hugs and chocs – you've got chocs, right? – and singing round the tree. It'll be beautiful.'

Sara couldn't help laughing at her friend's Pollyanna-ish version of events. 'Even the goose is making me nervous. It's huge and clammy and uncomfortably goose-like.'

Precious chuckled. 'I'm not keen on trussed-up flesh either. Sammi's cooking paella, thank goodness. It was that or suckling pig and I definitely put my foot down at pig.'

'Give my love to Sammi and all the family. Wish me luck.'

'You'll be fine, darlin',' her friend replied. 'Don't say too much. Let them bash it out between themselves. I know you love the man, and I know you like to sort everyone out . . . but this isn't your problem, remember.'

'Good advice,' she agreed, at the same time knowing that bashing things out wasn't exactly the Lockmores' strongest suit, and also that Precious didn't know the half of it. She had assumed – from what Sara had told her – that they were dealing with a couple of grumpy kids who needed a good kick up the backside.

The house does look gorgeous, Sara thought, on Christmas Eve, as she drew some clingfilm over the hummus she'd made to go with the flatbreads and crudités they were serving, along with an array of other nibbles, instead of a big supper. She and Bernard had had a serious discussion about when to have the goose. She'd thought they should stick to Lockmore tradition and do the big meal on Christmas Eve. But they weren't due to arrive until at least seven, and Bernard insisted they'd be exhausted after such a long drive. He said it was better to do it properly on the day. In the end, Sara had agreed, although she thought Bernard should warn the twins. He'd decided not to, not wanting to open up any avenue of dissent before they arrived. It was just after six, now. Bernard was upstairs, showering. She was glad his kids would be here soon, that the agonizing anticipation would soon be over.

That morning at breakfast, the frenzy of preparations done, Bernard had looked pale and drawn. 'What are you most worried about?' she'd asked him.

Levelling his gaze at her, he'd replied, 'That I won't give them what they want. That I'll make things worse between us. I feel this might be my last chance to retrieve things.' He gave a small laugh. 'You haven't met them, but the twins are a powerful pair – especially when they gang up.'

'They're still your kids, Bernard,' she'd objected. 'Remind yourself of what they were like when they were small. These are the same people, just bigger. You used to hug them, chat to them, play with them. Keep that in mind.'

He looked doubtful. 'I just want to get it right.'

'Don't assume the worst. And *listen*.'

She could see he was about to protest at what might have seemed like a criticism. But he smiled instead. 'Thank God you're here, Sara. I'd be a blithering wreck if I was doing this on my own.'

Now Bernard came downstairs, smart for his children in a white shirt and black jeans, looking scrubbed and expectant. He immediately came over and took her in his arms. 'Love you,' he said, his grey eyes tender. 'Thank you for all your help.' She could feel his body tense as the moment drew near and she hugged him tight, wanting to squeeze his anxiety out of him.

Both jumped as the bell rang. They looked at each other, eyes wide. 'You go,' she said.

32

Carrie came in first, followed closely by her brother, holding the bags. Dressed in an oversized grey jumper, jeans and clumpy black lace-up boots, a mint-green scarf pinning her long white-blonde hair round her neck, she was like a filled-out, robust version of her mother. Just as striking, but strong and healthy – perhaps what Ilsa might have been.

After a brief, almost cursory hug with her father, Carrie turned to Sara, who was hovering in the kitchen area so as not to get in the way of the family greetings. Sara held her breath as their eyes met across the room, dreading seeing resentment flair in Carrie's gaze. The look she received, though, was curious, and there was a smile – albeit a little wary – on the girl's face as she approached and reached out a hand.

'Carrie,' she stated, her handshake firm. 'God, I thought we'd never get here.' Her voice was slightly breathless. 'The traffic was vile. I've been on the road all day.'

'Poor you. Let me get you something to drink. What would you like?' Sara asked, hearing how formal and nervous she sounded.

'Thanks. Water'd be great, for now.'

Bernard's daughter was not quite what Sara had been expecting. She'd envisaged an altogether tougher exterior, someone sharp, a bit hostile, who took no prisoners. But

Carrie appeared to be softer, younger, more charming than he'd described.

She was rescued by Bernard, Adam in tow. 'Sara, this is Adam.'

Goodness, he's so pale, she couldn't help thinking. *Not eating properly, lack of B12, D, iron* . . . He was as tall as his father and with identical light-grey eyes, but he was overly thin and hollow-eyed, his hair the only distinct feature, being dark brown, but cut very short so it was like a shadow above a pale face, which would have been beautiful if it had held any colour, any life.

He resembled his mother too, but in the exact opposite way to his sister. Similar in colouring to Bernard, he'd apparently inherited Ilsa's fragility, the waif-like quality that made her want to scoop him up and nurture him until he was strong again.

Less confident, it seemed, than his sibling, his gaze as he met hers was shy and polite. 'Hi,' was all he said, his hand cold and quickly withdrawn.

They stood about in silence as Sara got water for the twins and put the kettle on – until Bernard took the lead.

'Right,' he said, with forced cheer. 'Time to kick things off. Let's light the candles on the tree.'

The twins glanced at each other, then nodded in unison. This, Bernard had explained to Sara earlier, was a family ritual. One that marked the beginning of the festivities. He held out a box of candles as they gathered round the tree. At first the process was carried out in silence, each of them – Sara busying herself with the tea – twisting the small ivory candles into the metal holders Bernard had secured earlier. Carols from the radio masked the lack of conversation, but Sara couldn't relax. *Say something, someone*, she pleaded silently.

Then Carrie laughed. 'You're tipping the tree, Adam. Don't be so fierce.'

Adam gave her a careless grin. 'It's not my fault. Dad hasn't got a proper stand.'

Sara laughed as she turned to meet Bernard's eye. 'Long story,' Bernard said. 'By the way,' he went on, 'I thought, since you had such a tiring journey and were getting here quite late, we'd do Christmas dinner tomorrow . . . when you've had a chance to recover?'

Sara noticed the twins giving another of their mutual glances, Carrie raising her eyebrow a little, as if to say, *I told you so*. 'OK,' she replied, her voice quiet and noncommittal. Adam just stood there, candle in hand, looking blankly at the tree.

'You don't mind, do you?' Bernard asked anxiously.

Please don't be unkind.

When neither twin said anything more, he went on, 'I know your mum wouldn't approve . . .'

Sara saw Carrie take a long breath. 'Mamma didn't approve of Christmas at all, Dad. So it hardly matters which way we do it now.' Her smile did nothing to soften the edge to her voice.

'She always went to a lot of trouble for us, though.' Adam quickly defended his mother.

'She really did,' Bernard agreed, over-zealously.

'Yeah, but we'd mention Baby Jesus/God/Wise Men on pain of death. And she'd have had the tree out the door on Boxing Day if Dad hadn't stopped her.'

Carrie's remarks had a touch of humour now, which

made Adam smile, at least. Although Bernard looked as if he didn't quite dare. Sara continued to hold her breath.

'Shall we light them?' he asked, handing the cooking matches to Adam, who lit one and passed the box to his sister.

As the tree gradually came to life with the many small candle flames, everyone stood back and stared without speaking. There was something magical and healing about the soft glow, which seemed to fill the room and cut through the tension for a single precious moment.

Sara poured the tea and presented a plate of mince pies, offering it to Carrie, who took one, and Adam, who shook his head with a polite no-thank-you.

'He's gluten free,' Carrie announced.

Bernard frowned, turning to his son. 'Really, Adam? Since when?' He looked irritated.

Adam shuffled, burying his face in his mug of tea. 'Not sure . . . a while now?' He turned to his sister for confirmation, as if she knew better what he ate than he did.

'You do look very thin,' Bernard commented. 'Sara's a nutritionist. You should talk to her about it.'

Sara cringed. *The last thing the poor guy wants*, she thought. *But it explains a lot.* She remembered how stick-thin and enervated Julian Cameron had been on his poor, self-imposed exclusion diet.

Adam, clearly embarrassed, said, 'It's OK, Dad. I'm on top of it. It's nothing serious. I just have to be careful.'

'You should have told me,' Bernard persisted, his tone bordering on peevish. 'We could have got stuff –'

Carrie butted in: 'Leave him, Dad. He's thin because he never eats. It's got sod all to do with gluten.'

Sara detected a hint of scorn on Carrie's part, as if Adam's picky habits irked her. Her brother just shrugged, ignoring them both.

When Adam and Carrie had finished their tea and gone upstairs with the bags, their respective bedroom doors closing behind them, Sara seemed to take the first proper breath since their arrival an hour ago.

Bernard wiped a hand across his forehead, letting out a beleaguered sigh. 'That went well,' he muttered sarcastically.

She went over to him and gave him a long hug. 'It's bound to be a bit tricky when you haven't seen each other in a while.' She laughed. 'They have me to get used to, for a start.' It seemed easier to blame the tension on herself. Although she wasn't sure the twins were really focusing on her. 'We'll get going on the fizz – that'll jolly things along.'

He breathed out slowly, burying his face in her neck, clinging to her. 'Or make things worse.' Raising his face to hers, he added, 'Do you think they still love me, Sara? I can't see it in their eyes, not like I used to.'

She was shocked. 'Don't be ridiculous, Bernard. They're your kids, for goodness' sake.' Although she knew that didn't necessarily mean what it should. She thought briefly of her own father and wondered if Frank had done anything about the house. She'd have to phone in the morning, make her Christmas duty call. *Families, eh?* she thought despairingly.

Carrie appeared downstairs before Adam. She'd stripped off her sweater and boots, rolled her blonde hair into an untidy knot on the top of her head, the white T-shirt she was wearing showing an abstract line drawing of Father Christmas, which made him look decidedly sinister. Seeing Sara's gaze, Carrie pulled out the hem with both hands. 'Like it? Ironic, of course. Neve, this girl I work with, designed a ton of them and got them printed up. Couldn't resist.'

'Not sure I'll be visiting *his* grotto,' Sara commented.

'Yeah, creepy, huh?' Carrie agreed. 'We were lucky. Mamma never let us within a hundred yards of Santa when we were young.'

They stood, the three of them, in anticipatory silence, the champagne flutes lined up on the kitchen table, alongside smoked salmon on squares of brown bread, the hummus, a bowl of quail's eggs with celery salt, sticky cocktail sausages with mustard sauce, a cheese platter surrounded by grapes and crackers, and a pyramid of hot, crispy cheese croquetas with a spicy dip: a Christmas gift from Sammi before he left for Spain.

'What's he doing up there?' Bernard asked, glancing towards the stairs.

His daughter tutted. 'Adam!' Her voice was sharp with irritation.

Sara winced. But Adam's face, appearing over the glass and wood banister on the landing above, was calm and smiling. 'Sorry,' he said, then clattered down the stairs at high speed. 'I'm starving.' He grinned, eyeing the spread hungrily.

I'll feed him up while he's here. Sara felt a strong maternal urge to nurture the boy as Bernard popped the cork and began pouring the champagne.

'Happy Christmas!' Bernard said, as they all chinked glasses.

Sara took a large gulp of champagne, the bubbles going up her nose and threatening to make her sneeze. But she welcomed the alcohol coursing through her system and calming her nerves.

Bernard lifted his glass again and said quietly, 'To Mamma.'

Although Sara, too, raised her glass, she didn't echo Ilsa's name. She wasn't part of this and didn't want to intrude on the family moment.

'Mamma,' the twins said, in unison, looking at each other, not their father.

Bernard moved to his daughter's side and put his free arm tentatively around her shoulders. Carrie didn't shake him off, but neither did she respond beyond a quick raise of her eyebrows in her father's direction.

Conversation, as they sat around the kitchen table, filling their plates with the nibbles, centred on Carrie at first – her love for Liverpool, her crazy boss, her new obsession with climbing, problems with the old Fiat she drove. She was a good raconteur, it turned out, and Sara could tell everyone was relaxing, in light of the delicious spread and expensive wine – of which Bernard kept up a steady flow.

After Sara had handed out the tiramisu she'd whisked up and spooned into individual tumblers, she ventured, 'So tell me about your course, Adam. What stage are you at now?' He had said little so far, except to listen to his sister and barrack her occasionally, laugh at her anecdotes.

He looked at her strangely for a second, as if he thought

she knew something she shouldn't. 'Clinical placements,' he answered. 'I'm starting a community paediatric place-ment in the new year – autism, ADHD, that sort of stuff.' Leaning back in his chair, he rubbed his palm back and forth over his short hair in a distracted way – not unlike Bernard did sometimes, Sara noted. 'It'll be like the real thing soon. Shifts, on-call, the whole nine yards.'

'That's exciting,' she said. 'And maybe a little scary?'

Adam did not look scared at all. 'Yeah . . . I suppose.' Then he sat up straighter and cleared his throat, blinking in his sister's direction. 'The truth is, I'm thinking of quitting.'

The air went still. All Sara heard was the rasp of Ber-nard's intake of breath. Carrie was assiduously licking coffee cream off her spoon.

'*What?*' Bernard gasped out.

Adam levelled his gaze at his father. 'I don't think it's for me, Dad. I've sort of told you that before, but you weren't listening.'

Sara could tell Bernard was panicking. Of all the scen-arios he'd fretted about in the days leading up to his son's arrival, it seemed this was not one of them. 'You can't be serious, Adam,' he said softly, then paused, appearing to fumble for the right words, obviously trying to keep his voice calm. 'You're so nearly there now. I know it's been hugely stressful. But you'd be stark raving mad to give up at the eleventh hour after all the work you've put in.'

Adam reached for his glass again. It was clear, from the hectic flush on his face, that he'd drunk a lot. 'Yeah, well, it's not the eleventh hour, is it? I'm nowhere near finished, Dad. Sure, I get my medical degree next summer, but then there's two years' foundation, and another three at least specializing.' He let out a weary sigh. 'It never ends.'

Carrie put down her spoon. 'He hasn't decided yet . . . have you, Adam?' She spoke lightly, without real conviction, as if she didn't want to have this particular row now.

Her brother seemed in a trance. He didn't reply, just slumped with his elbow on the table and held out his glass for Carrie to refill.

Sara glanced at Bernard. He was rigid with tension, seemingly on the verge of speaking, but continuing to hesitate. She quailed, hoping he wasn't going to sound off at his son.

But he ignored her warning look, his gaze suddenly laser sharp and focused on Adam, as he said, very slowly, 'OK . . . I'm going to ask . . . because I promised we'd open up about it . . . Is the accident – which Sara knows about, by the way – the underlying reason why you're not coping with medical school, Adam?'

Carrie took a quick, anxious breath. 'Here we go.'

'Hold on a minute . . . What did you just say, Dad?' Adam cocked his head to one side sardonically, pretending he hadn't heard. 'Did you say "*underlying*"?' The word rang out like a pistol shot. 'Are you fucking kidding me?' He jumped to his feet, out of breath and clutching his chest. 'You don't get it, do you? There's never been anything *underlying* about the accident,' he panted. 'It's centre stage, lit up like that Christmas tree over there, larger than life . . . The first thing I think about when I open my eyes in the morning, the last before I go to sleep at night and almost every fucking moment in between.'

Into the shocked hush that followed, Sara heard the

scrape of Bernard's chair. He was on his feet and pulling Adam into an embrace. 'Oh, Adam . . . Christ, I'm so sorry, son.'

Adam clung to his father for only a split second. Then he jerked away, his expression incredulous. 'You genuinely didn't think I might be feeling like this?'

Bernard sighed. 'I know you've been upset, obviously. I'm not a fool. But I suppose I hoped . . .'

Sara closed her eyes briefly. She didn't know what to do or say or think, and felt useless – helpless – in the face of Adam's agonizing statement.

Carrie got to her feet as the two men eyed each other in silence. She placed one arm round her father's shoulders, the other round her brother's. Sara watched as gradually Adam and Bernard relaxed, allowed Carrie to hug them. They seemed such a sad, isolated trio, locked in the misery of their collective past. *But at least they're together*, she thought.

After a moment, Bernard cleared his throat. 'We're all exhausted and we've had too much to drink. We need to talk, but let's do it when we can focus properly, OK? Tomorrow? Boxing Day?'

The three were still standing in Carrie's embrace, but it seemed as if the wind had gone out of everyone's sails. Carrie dropped her arms, giving a weary nod. Adam shrugged his assent. He looked too tired to say another word.

'I can't bear it,' Bernard said later, as he and Sara lay in bed. 'I just can't bear it. It's not only medical school, although that's bad enough. It's how he described the torment he feels all the time.'

Hardly daring to breathe — his mood was so fragile, and she felt the wrong word might spark off even greater depths of despair — she cradled him gently in her arms. 'It is heartbreaking.'

'There's so much stuff to process. I don't know where to start.'

'You're talking,' she said. 'Hugging, even. That's huge progress. And, however difficult, it's better out in the open, isn't it?'

'You always put such a positive spin on things, Sara.' He harrumphed. 'So, let me see . . . There's Christmas Day with my turbulent twins to get through. My son's thinking of quitting med school and is an emotional wreck. Everything I've done to protect him from exactly this outcome seems to have turned to dust . . .' He shot her a cynical glance in the half-light, one eyebrow raised. 'And the upside is?'

She couldn't resist his challenge, although this wasn't a game, she was well aware. 'OK . . . The upside is, the twins are here at last, and Adam is saying how he feels so you can help him. And it's Christmas Day tomorrow!'

He shook his head, in mock defeat. But she saw his mouth twitch, before he reached over and switched off the light.

33

Sara woke on Christmas Day to what felt almost like homesickness. She was missing her girls. Everything in recent days had been so much about Bernard's children that she'd barely had room to think of her own. But she also felt a certain relief that neither of her daughters was around to witness the painful ruptures in the Lockmore family, however much she missed them.

As she lay alone in bed now – Bernard having got up at some stage without waking her – she also reminded herself it was her first Christmas with Bernard. A big milestone in their relationship. Christmas meant family and Bernard was now her family. Even the thought was strange: this time last year, she hadn't known he existed. And even now she wasn't sure how well she really knew him. All she knew was that she loved him.

The door opened, interrupting her thoughts. Bernard held a red felt stocking in one hand, a mug of tea in the other. He was grinning. 'Ho, ho, ho! Don't reckon anyone's too old for a Santa gift,' he said, as he handed the stocking to her with a kiss.

She shuffled over so they could sit side by side and began to unwrap her presents: a pretty shell pin tray, a bottle of citrus and amber bath essence, a kitchen timer – because she'd complained about the ear-splitting ring of the current one – and a gorgeous woven bracelet with tiny rose quartz stones that she remembered admiring on one of the stalls in Hastings. That Bernard had bothered to go back and buy it for her almost brought tears to her eyes.

For him, she pulled out a framed picture she'd wrapped a few days ago and slid down beside the bed. It was a print by Paul Klee, an artist she knew he admired. The muted reds, yellows and blues, and flat, two-dimensional box shapes appealed to Sara, too. She'd added a tin of his favourite caramel truffles.

For a long moment, they forgot about the day ahead, just lay in each other's arms, their presents – and the paper and ribbon that had been pulled from them – scattered around their prone figures on the bed. It was a gorgeous start to Christmas, and Sara relished every second.

After Bernard had gone downstairs to prepare breakfast, she sat on the edge of the bed in her pyjamas, phone in hand, steeling herself to do her duty, wanting to get it out of the way before she could enjoy speaking to Margaret and Peggy – her call to Joni would have to wait till after midday. She hoped her father's landline would go to voice-mail and she could leave a jolly Christmas message. But she knew it would not. Unusually, it was not Lois who picked up, but her father. 'Who is it?' His querulous voice sounded expectant.

'Happy Christmas, Frank. It's Sara. Hope you're having a lovely day.' Her delivery was so falsely cheery, it made her cringe.

'Happy Christmas,' he said quickly, as if he were hust-ling the greeting out of the way. 'I need to speak to you, Sara.' There was a muttered exchange, his hand partially over the receiver. When she heard him again, his voice had dropped to a wheezy whisper. 'I don't want Lois hearing, it's none of her business,' he began, with his usual charming regard for his partner. 'But I've spoken to Mervyn, done what you asked. Although I can't for the life of me see why you'd look a gift horse in the mouth like that.'

Resigned, now, to his incomprehension, which said it all, she said quietly, 'Thank you.'

'You'll get nothing,' Frank added, as if he thought she might have misunderstood.

'That's OK.'

There was a long pause. 'My money not good enough for you, is that it?'

'Lois deserves it more,' she said, through gritted teeth, not in the mood for a row.

Frank didn't reply, she heard his chest dragging oxygen into his lungs with considerable effort. Then he said, 'I want to put the record straight before I go.'

Sara waited, suddenly alert.

'I know you blame me, Sara,' he began, 'which is fair enough. But the truth is, your mother didn't want me around.' There was a long pause as he struggled for more breath. 'It had nothing to do with you. You were a sweet little thing, very keen on your daddy, you were.' More rasping filled the airwaves. 'But Gail had got what she wanted from me. She wasn't keen on me hanging about, ruining things.' Frank coughed, got himself under control. 'So I took off. I meant to keep in touch, but I knew you were too small to remember me. There didn't seem much point.'

The speech had obviously exhausted him, because he lapsed into silence.

Sara didn't know what to say. Nothing Frank had revealed surprised or moved her. Maybe her mother had pushed him away. Hardly a valid excuse: he could have fought to see his daughter if he'd really loved her. The odd thing was that Frank had ever known her as a child. No part of her retained a trace-memory of him.

'It's fine,' Sara said dully. 'It doesn't matter any more.'

'I want you to know that I did care about you back then.' His voice tailed off. 'I want you to know that . . .' he repeated softly.

She realized that this was it. This was the sum total of her father's apology. *He's trying*, she told herself. *For the first time in his life, he's trying*. But it felt too little, too late. She couldn't hear the love in his voice, just whiny self-pity.

After she'd spoken a few cheerful words to Lois and clicked off the call, she sat there, in the bedroom, and found herself crying. It seemed so sad. But she was determined: a similar scenario was not going to be played out on Bernard's deathbed, not if she could help it.

The goose lived up to the challenge. A seemingly unending spillage of fat flowed, like a malevolent river, from the massive bird. She had enough in the two Pyrex bowls now, she reckoned, to roast a year's worth of potatoes. By the time the damn thing was resting under foil – at least an hour later than planned – Sara was hot and flustered and promising never to complain about a turkey again.

So far things had seemed more harmonious in the house, the edgy, dangerous atmosphere of the previous evening less pronounced at the breakfast table, the twins clearly more relaxed after a night's sleep in their childhood beds. Carrie had been pleased with the heavy, charcoal-wool cardigan Sara had picked out, Adam less effusive, but clearly touched by the expensive headphones Bernard had chosen.

Sara had spoken to her family: Margaret sounded quite merry and on-the-ball; Peggy said she was missing her but was obviously having fun with her boyfriend; Joni and Mason sent a goofy photo of them both wearing tinselled reindeer ears, hugging and laughing in the sunny pool, with the caption 'It may not look like it, but we're missing you all terribly, and love you so much,' followed by multiple heart emojis. They sounded so normal, so untroubled, compared to the family around her in the cliff house. Speaking to them had wrenched at Sara's heart. She would have done anything, at that moment, to be transported to California with the whole family, including Margaret, Heather and Peggy's mysterious boyfriend, Beng.

Then Bernard had corralled his children for a cliff walk in the windy December sunshine. As he left, he came over to Sara and gave her a self-conscious kiss – aware of them watching – and whispered a quiet 'Love you,' into her hair. It had lifted her heart, brought her back to his side. She realized she'd been inching away to allow the twins room with their father.

The table was a mess of empty bowls, a ravaged Christmas pudding, the debris from pulled crackers, discarded napkins, wine glasses and dripping candles, the strangely pleasant whiff of silver fulminate from the cracker sparks on the air. The goose, for all its resistance, had been sweet and rich, set off to perfection by the sharpness of apple puree and tangy braised red cabbage, although Sara worried her potatoes were a bit too much on the crunchy side. Her perfectionist instincts aside, though, the meal had been a success: Bernard had lit the pudding-brandy to cheers, and there had been much groaning laughter at the cracker jokes.

Sara sat back in her chair. She felt she could now relax a bit. Glancing across at Bernard, she caught his smile and the tiny lift of his eyebrows, as if he, too, felt he could let go and enjoy himself.

Carrie was tipsy, her pale skin flushed, her voice strident as she engaged on various issues with her father. Adam, Sara thought, was perhaps even more inebriated than his sister, although he was the sort of drinker who becomes brooding and mute rather than verbose. But the more wine he knocked back, the more Sara sensed something angry and dark surfacing again, as it had the night before. No reference – as far as she was aware – had been made by anyone during the day to his declared intention to quit medicine. But although his presence had barely impinged during the meal, now she felt him coming to life.

As she got up to make coffee, she saw him pick up one of the cracker slips. 'Listen up, everyone!' Loudly, and with a suitably jokey lilt to his voice, he appeared to be reading from the paper. 'How does a son get his father to really hear what he's saying?'

Sara hovered the spoonful of coffee grounds over the cafetière, hardly daring to move.

Dropping the slip, Adam widened his eyes at Bernard. 'Seriously, Dad. How are things going for you?'

Before Bernard had a chance to respond Adam, tipping back his chair, balancing until the front legs were off the floor, went on, 'You're happy, are you?'

After a long moment, she heard Bernard echo, 'Happy?' his voice tight.

'Yeah, you know. Wake up with a spring in your step, sing on your way to work, sleep with a clear conscience. I'm told it's called happiness, anyway.' Sarcasm dripped from his words, poisoning the air. Sara poured water over the coffee and put Bernard's delicate yellow demitasses with black handles onto the tray containing cream in a jug, coffee spoons and brown sugar cubes. No one was speaking.

Turning, she saw Bernard staring at his son. His cheeks were burning, his mouth pursed.

Adam stared back with a mocking gaze.

'You've had way too much to drink, Adam,' Bernard snapped, sounding for all the world like a stern Victorian pater.

Carrie said, 'It's a fair question, Dad.'

Bernard's head spun round to his daughter, his eyes flashing.

'It's like our lives are just one endless skate across the surface of a frozen lake,' Carrie went on. 'But the water's still churning underneath, Dad. Freezing and totally lethal.'

Bernard sat immobilized by his daughter's words. The silence lengthened, the air around the table jolting. Sara couldn't meet anyone's eye as she laid the tray on the table, squashing cracker debris in the process as nobody attempted to move it. She began pouring coffee into cups, handing them round, silently begging Bernard to listen to his children.

'What do you want me to do about it, Carrie?' Bernard finally found his voice, but although he spoke softly, there was a chill in his tone. 'Short of magicking the whole sorry mess away.'

Neither twin replied, their faces set. It seemed to Sara that they were waiting for some penny to drop, and it wasn't happening.

Adam suddenly got to his feet, shaking his head violently from side to side like a wet dog. 'I told you this wouldn't work,' he said to his sister.

'Dad, *please*.' Carrie frowned at her father. 'Why won't you see? Adam can't go on like this. Neither can I, watching what's happening to my brother. You may be coping fine, but I can assure you, we're totally not.'

'I'm not coping fine,' Bernard growled.

'OK, well, I suppose that's a start,' Adam commented, and abruptly sat down again.

Bernard threw his arms into the air but said nothing. He looked defeated.

'Look, we understand why you did what you did that day. You were saving Adam. Or thought you were ...' Carrie was impassioned now, sparks flying from her pale-blue eyes as she stared at her father. 'What we can't understand is the way you've buried it, Dad, like none of it ever happened. You can see how badly Adam's affected, but you keep brushing him off, telling him it's just stress from the bloody training.' She gulped down more air. 'Feels like you doomed us all to this horrible secret ... then calmly walked away.'

Sara saw Bernard stiffen. *Talk to them*, she begged silently.

For what seemed a long time he did not speak. Sara could feel the battle raging in his head. Then, holding his hands tightly in his lap, he took a deep breath. 'OK . . .' He paused for another drawn-out moment. 'You say you understand why I did what I did that day. But I don't think you fully do.'

Sara saw the twins glance at each other, a small frown forming on Adam's face.

'I don't want to go into long and boring stuff about me and your mum, but a lot of this started long before the accident . . . Two things. First, your mum never thought I'd been a good enough father to you both. She made me promise, only a short time before she died, to take more responsibility when she was gone.' Tears formed in his eyes. 'I did promise, of course, but I didn't take seriously her certainty that she would die. Not then, and not earlier.' He straightened his shoulders and met first Carrie's, then Adam's gaze. 'If I'd got her to hospital sooner, maybe she wouldn't have died.'

Sara felt her breath catch in her throat.

The twins looked shaken by his words. But before they'd had a chance to speak, Bernard went on to explain about shutting himself in his office that day, hearing her cough. His voice was strained, snagging on the words as if they were broken glass.

Silence.

'Mamma coughed all the time, Dad,' Carrie muttered, almost to herself, her expression still blank as she tried to process what her father had said.

Bernard cast a grateful smile at his daughter. 'Anyway,

from the moment your mother died, I was racked with guilt . . . I still am.'

'It wasn't your fault, Dad,' Adam said softly. 'None of us ever quite knew how ill she was.' He sighed. 'She scared me lots of times, then the next minute she'd be totally fine.'

'Thanks, Adam.'

The silence spun out. Sara felt a softening in her breath at the support both children showed for their father. They were obviously much more aware of their mother's idiosyncrasies than Bernard had realized.

'You weren't a bad father,' Carrie asserted quietly. 'Whatever Mamma said.'

Sara saw Bernard's mouth quiver and tears blur his grey eyes again. 'Oh, God, Carrie . . .' He covered his face with his hands for a second, breathing heavily. Sara felt her own eyes mist, and quickly blinked away the tears.

Adam said, 'It was the argument about the ashes that wound us all up that day.'

'I wasn't ready,' Carrie protested. 'You guys seemed so eager to hurl Mamma off into the ocean and I couldn't bear it.'

Bernard, still trying to compose himself, nodded. 'I'm sorry we gave you a hard time, sweetheart. I wasn't ready either. I just thought it was important to get it done.' He gave an uneasy grin. 'Unfinished business, though.'

Sara looked at him. *What does he mean?*

Seeing her puzzled stare, Bernard shifted in his seat. 'We never got around to scattering her, Sara. Ilsa's ashes are still in the cupboard in my office.'

The twins – for whom this was clearly not news – looked uncomfortable.

Sara found she was not surprised that some element of Ilsa was still present in the house. *If I actually believed in ghosts . . .* Although it occurred to her now that the atmosphere in the house since the arrival of the twins had been oddly neutral, the crushing density in the air no longer so apparent. And this at a time when Ilsa could have been more present, rather than less.

Adam was talking, wiping his hands angrily over his eyes. 'I've tried so hard to remember the accident and I just can't. The drive is crystal clear . . .' He reached for his coffee – which must have been stone cold by then – and threw it down his throat in one gulp. 'I put on Arctic Monkeys because I didn't want to talk about Mamma any more. I know it was bright sunshine . . . but then I can't remember a single thing – not the bend, not swerving . . . only the girl on the road. I can only remember the girl.' Swallowing hard, he added softly, 'Maria. We should call her by her name.' He shook his head. 'To this day, I have no idea what I said in the statement I gave the police.'

The tension around the table was still apparent. But there was also a lightening, as if a heavy veil had been lifted just a fraction and cool air allowed in. Sara was aware of a strong desire to get away, step out into the wild cliff wind, shout and scream until she'd sent the pent-up angst she'd carefully contained all day – all week, all month – over the cliffs and into the sea roiling below.

Bernard turned exhausted eyes first on his son, then swung his gaze to include Carrie. 'I'm so sorry,' he said.

There was another long silence.

His daughter laid a gentle hand on his arm. 'The thing is,' she said, 'it's great to be able to open things up like this.

But we're basically stuck in the same place. We have to *do* something, now, Dad. Adam is on his knees.'

Bernard seemed to come out of a trance. 'Do? What can we do?' He looked wary.

'You know what.' His daughter's words were tinged with irritation. 'You and Adam have to go to the police. Tell them what really happened.'

There was a numb silence. Adam snapped upright as if he'd been poked with a stick, his normally tired eyes wide with trepidation. He stared at his sister but said nothing.

'It's the only way we're going to be free of this nightmare,' Carrie added.

Bernard gazed at her with panic in his eyes. 'NO, *no no no*. You don't understand, Carrie. Neither of you understand. "Free" is the last thing we'd be. It'd be a nightmare of police questions, bureaucracy, solicitors, courts . . . And me and Adam could well go to prison. You think it's so simple. Believe me, *it's not.*'

'OK. Maybe it's not simple. But what *you* don't understand, Dad, is that Adam, particularly, is being slowly destroyed by this.'

All the love for her father Sara had sensed in Carrie's voice earlier had been buried by an implacable desire to make Bernard hear.

When he didn't immediately reply, she went on, 'Adam can't tell a *living soul*, not even a best friend, a girlfriend. So he has neither. Imagine what that's like.' She waited, to make sure that that had sunk in, before continuing. She held out her hand to indicate her brother. 'Look at him, Dad! He's skin and bone, knackered . . .' Her eyes welled as she gazed at Adam. 'I honestly don't believe prison – if it even came to that, and I'm sure it won't – could possibly be any worse.'

As the silence spun out, Sara found herself speaking quietly into the Lockmore maelstrom. 'I think Carrie's right.'

She levelled her gaze at Bernard, defiant but trembling. Everyone was staring at her. Bernard looked surprised, then his mouth set, the muscles in his cheek rippling as he clenched his jaw. Carrie also seemed a bit taken aback, but Sara detected a heartbreaking relief and gratitude in her face, too.

'At last,' she said softly.

Bernard's chair scraped violently on the wooden floor as he stood, glowering down at them. 'None of you have the first clue what you're talking about.' Crossing his arms, he went on, 'Adam has his whole life ahead of him. He'd have to give up all hope of being a doctor. He'd find it hard to get any job with a criminal record, even stacking shelves in a supermarket.' He took a breath. 'Maybe you think it'll be all right because nothing outwardly changed for me. OK, I kept working after my conviction . . . But I have my own business.' He took another gulp of air. 'Perjury is seen by the law as worse – oddly enough – than running someone over and killing them. I'm not doing this to Adam. I'm just *not*.'

'I'm right here, Dad,' Adam said. 'Don't talk about me as if I don't have a mind of my own.'

'I wasn't.'

'He's a fully grown man, Dad. He wants to face up to what he did. He *needs* to, regardless of how much we know you sacrificed for him. Don't you? *Don't you?*' she shouted at her brother.

But Adam was holding his hands over his ears, exactly like the child he no longer was. 'Stop it! For fuck's sake, stop it, you two. I can't listen any more.'

Bernard looked as if he'd run out of steam. He slumped as he stood, head bowed.

'Do you want to go to the police, Adam?' Sara asked quietly.

Adam began to cry, angry, despairing sobs that broke her heart. 'Yes . . . *Yes*.'

Sara looked at Bernard, but he wouldn't meet her eye.

'Adam could go on his own,' Carrie pointed out to her father. 'But obviously he doesn't want to do that.' She let out a sigh. 'Look, we know this has serious implications for you, too, Dad. We realize what we're asking.' She threw her arms into the air. 'It's just there doesn't seem to be another way.'

'This is bloody insane,' Bernard muttered fiercely, then turned on his heel and made for the front door, slamming it hard behind him. A moment later they heard the Mercedes' tyres skidding on the gravel and the car roaring away.

34

Carrie turned a stunned expression to Sara. 'What the fuck?'

Adam snorted. 'Like we really expected him to change.'

Sara didn't know what to say. She couldn't defend Bernard's childish actions, although she was tempted to try. But she was not going to be disloyal and talk about him behind his back to his children.

She got up and began to clear away the dinner. Adam and Carrie helped her in silence. They appeared deflated, but also cynically resigned to their father's stance. Which upset Sara. They'd clearly talked about what they would say before the holiday. Planned the whole thing. And Bernard had come so far, to give him his due. But not far enough.

Although it was only eight o'clock, when the clearing up was finished the twins – both still subdued – thanked her politely for the meal and excused themselves, disappearing upstairs to Carrie's room and shutting the door firmly. Sara heard music playing and could only imagine what their conversation was like. She was at a loss. Not in the mood to wait up for Bernard, however – she was too angry with him, leaving them all in the lurch like that – she took herself up to bed, where the paper and presents still strewn on the duvet mocked her with memories of a happier moment.

*

Later, Sara didn't speak as he slid into bed.

'Are you awake?' Bernard's voice came through the darkness.

'Yes.'

He turned on the bedside light and sat up against the pillows, arms crossed. She could tell instantly that he was still angry, too. Slowly she pulled herself into a sitting position. 'What the hell were you thinking? Siding with Carrie like that.'

'I wasn't siding with anyone,' she said. 'I was merely stating my opinion. I've told you before what I think about this.'

'You completely undermined me.'

Reeling from his tone – cold, accusatory – as much as what he was actually saying, Sara glared at him. 'You're blaming me?'

'You had no right.' He cut across her words. 'This is between me and the twins. *My* family. You know how much I've struggled with it all. But then you calmly go and pull the rug out from under my feet.'

She could see he was slightly crazy. His eyes were dark with despair and rage, his body twitching. But she wasn't going to be blamed.

'You changed the whole dynamic by what you said,' he went on. 'Made me the uncaring villain again.'

Putting a firm hand on his arm, she ignored his hysteria. 'But I agree with Carrie. I think she's right.'

He shook her off angrily and was about to speak, but she got in first, her voice rising: 'Something's got to change, Bernard. Carrie sounded afraid for Adam.'

'Christ . . . So now you know more about my son than I do?' His voice was full of contempt.

257

She winced. 'Did you know that was how he was feeling? Has he told you he wants to go to the police before?'

He didn't answer. A quiet fury was coming off him in waves, but he wouldn't be pacified, not by her, anyway. Her instinct was to get out of bed that minute and leave him to his madness. '*My* family', he'd said, and it specifically did not include Sara.

'You forget, they're adults now. It's not only on your shoulders.'

Her words seemed to hang in the air between them. The look he finally turned on her was no longer angry, just lost and full of the most desperate pain.

'None of you fucking realize. I've done it. I've been through the mill of prosecution, the humiliation. To the world, I am a criminal now . . . You have absolutely no idea what that feels like, Sara.'

She couldn't dispute it. 'I know, but –'

'I will not let that happen to my son.' Each word dropped like a lump of lead into the air of the dark bedroom.

'All I understand is that your children are begging you to listen. But instead you walk out like a sulky kid, turn your back on them. Then blame me.'

His rasping intake of breath told her the fury was back. *I'm getting nowhere.* Her presence was serving only to inflame an already inflammatory situation. She got out of bed. Maybe without her there he would be able to talk to the twins more openly.

'Where are you going?' The question was barked out like a checkpoint guard's.

'Lewes.' She had planned to have breakfast with him

and the twins – she wasn't due at Margaret's till eleven. Bernard didn't look at her, didn't respond.

Dressing in the half-light, the bedroom solid with misery, she realized she was shaking. *He'll come to his senses*, she kept telling herself, waiting for him to spring out of bed and wrap her in his arms, tell her how wrong he'd been. But he sat there as if he'd been turned to stone.

Downstairs, she wrote a note to Carrie and Adam: 'I'm sorry I won't have a chance to say goodbye, but I have to get off to my mother-in-law's. I've loved meeting you both. Sara x'. Folding the piece of A4 she'd found on Bernard's desk, she tiptoed upstairs and slid it under Carrie's door.

Then, with a last quick look around, seeing the sad, washed-out aftermath of Christmas in the unlit tree, with the stale scent of goose, the sharpness of alcohol and candle smoke lingering on the air, she quietly opened the front door to the breezy pre-dawn of Boxing Day.

It was still pitch dark, just after five, when she arrived at her house and unpacked the few things she'd brought from Bernard's, then repacked an overnight bag for staying with Margaret. Preparing a soothing mint tea, she tried to make sense of what had just happened. But she was too tired, questions bumping up against each other, wild and incoherent, like teenagers at a rave: *Does Adam understand the implications of a confession? Might Carrie report them herself? How bad is Adam's mental health? Is Bernard right? Was he relieved to see me go?* She remembered the love in his eyes only yesterday as she unwrapped her presents, as he laughed at her horror at the vast quantities of goose fat.

Heard his whispered 'Love you,' as he took the twins for a walk. *It's not about me*, she told herself firmly. But she was not feeling firm. When she tried to stand, her legs were like jelly and she wondered how she would get through the day – and then the ones after that – caring for Margaret.

After a quick embrace, Heather checked Sara over and frowned. 'Everything OK?'

'It's fine, just too much champagne and a bit of a late night.' She summoned her best smile. 'How's Margaret? She sounded jolly when I called yesterday.'

'Yes, she's not been so bad. Still a bit foggy some of the time, but otherwise not much change. The details of her medication are all in the report book. And the timings for when she gets up, et cetera. You know most of it, so you shouldn't have any bother.' Heather handed the exercise book to Sara. She was dressed in a pretty emerald-green top and smart black trousers and Sara could tell she was eager to be off. 'I've done the bed for you,' she added.

'Thanks, you didn't need to. I hope you have a lovely time.'

Heather grinned, her round face lighting up. 'Should be a laugh. My sister's coming with her two this year, so it'll be a full house. Bloody mayhem, I expect.'

'See you Monday, then.'

Earlier, Sara had tried to sleep. But her body had had other ideas. Although she'd lain in her bed for a couple of hours, her muscles had stubbornly refused to give in. Now, as she waved Heather off, exhaustion flooded her bones. Closing the front door and dragging herself along the short corridor to the sitting room, where Margaret was dozing in her chair, she settled quietly on the sofa and closed her eyes. The warmth of the room, the cosy proximity of her surrogate mother, immediately sent her off into a soft, dreamless sleep.

When she opened her eyes later, Margaret was watching her with a fond smile. 'I thought you might sleep the day away, dear.'

Disoriented, Sara pushed herself upright. During her extended nap she must have slumped sideways, because her head was resting on a cushion. 'Gosh, I'm so sorry. What's the time?'

Margaret shrugged. 'I've no idea. You must have been very tired.'

Feeling flustered, Sara rose to her feet and went over to give Margaret a kiss. 'Sorry,' she said again. 'Let me get some tea going.' She hurried out, glancing at the kitchen clock as she turned the tap on to fill the kettle. It read two twenty-five. *I've been asleep for over three hours?* And she'd left her poor mother-in-law without lunch or loo visits or even a cuppa. Ashamed, she went back into the sitting room. 'Are you all right? I feel terrible, I'm supposed to be looking after you and I just crashed out for three hours.'

Margaret laughed. 'No harm done. If I'd needed something, I'd have woken you. I'm not quite incapable yet.'

Relieved and properly awake now, Sara tidied herself in the downstairs toilet. The face gazing back at her was barely familiar. She looked strained, pale, her eyes dull with tiredness and tension, tears hovering just beneath the surface. She wished Precious was not so far away but was then reminded that her friend – through no fault of her own – no longer represented the comfort she once had because she couldn't be completely honest with her. She couldn't afford to break down, though: she had Margaret to think about.

As she waited for the tea to brew, she dug her phone out of her bag, which was lying on the kitchen table. No message from Bernard, which was something of a relief – she wasn't sure how she would handle any contact with him today.

'So tell me about Christmas with your new friend,' Margaret said later. 'Was it lovely?'

Sara had spent the last hour making up for her negligence. She'd given Margaret her pills, taken her to the loo, rubbed her feet – which were freezing – and put an extra pair of bed socks on them, turned up the already high central heating and made her a cheese sandwich and another cup of tea.

'Yes, it was great. I cooked a goose with all the trimmings and we had real candles on the tree because Bernard's wife, who died, came from Finland, and they always do that there. And his twins came, which was wonderful because he hardly ever sees them. Adam is training to be a doctor and Carrie is a fashion designer – or will be soon.' She stopped to draw breath, then felt her chin wobble.

Margaret waited for her to calm down. It was a kind silence, a comforting one.

'I'm sorry,' Sara said, yet again. All she seemed able to do today was apologize.

'Do you want to tell me about it?' the old lady asked.

Sara sighed. 'I'm not allowed to. He made me promise. All I can say is that it's a big lie involving his son.'

Margaret's eyebrow rose. 'You look worried. It's not criminal, is it, dear?'

Sara, struck by how on-the-money her mother-in-law always was, let out a frustrated sigh. 'I seem to have landed myself right in the middle of a massive family problem . . . "Problem" doesn't even begin to describe it. It's a complex nightmare. And it's really affecting my relationship with Bernard.' In that split second, she had a sudden inkling of what Adam, and to a lesser extent Bernard and Carrie, was going through.

'I don't like the sound of this,' Margaret said. 'I hope this chap of yours hasn't hurt someone . . . his son, perhaps?'

Sara flinched. 'No, no,' she said wearily, taking a deep breath. 'He's really a good man, Margaret. He tries so hard to do the right thing. He just never seems to value my opinion. I'm trying to help but he keeps pushing me away.'

There was a short silence. Then Margaret said, 'But you love him, I think.'

Sara was too choked to reply.

Margaret gave a knowing nod. 'That's tricky, then. Because men can be so stubborn.' She gave a discreet yawn. 'The need to be right sometimes blinds them to the truth.'

That sounds spot on, Sara thought grimly.

That night, one ear cocked for Margaret, Sara slept only fitfully. But it wasn't really her mother-in-law who kept her awake. She felt in limbo. Bernard hadn't rung, but then neither had she called him. When she'd left earlier that morning, she'd barely said goodbye to him. And he'd made no move to stop her. *We just need a few days apart*, she told herself.

The twins would still be there. She prayed things had improved between them all in the cool light of day, but she wasn't too hopeful. Bernard's mood last night had been stinking. He didn't appear to be in the frame of mind to take heed, even if his children gave him another chance.

I should ring him, she thought, around midnight, lying in bed, her phone sweaty in her palm. She ached to hear his voice. And she couldn't help but appreciate his dilemma. *Was I too harsh on him?* He was just wound up and lashing out at the only person he could. But the prospect that he might still be angry with her put her off making the call. Instead, she set her phone alarm for seven thirty, so she could get Margaret up, washed and breakfasted on schedule, then closed her eyes, too tired to have even one more thought about Bernard or his unhappy children.

'I've been thinking,' Margaret said, the following morning, as Sara walked her, inch by agonizing inch, on her frame to the sitting room. 'I don't know what's going on with this fellow, but it sounds like he's dragged you into something you're not at all comfortable with.' She lifted her veiny hand from the aluminium frame for a second to push back a wisp of white hair from her forehead and looked up into Sara's face. Her faded blue eyes were full of concern. 'Maybe you should step back, dear, leave him to straighten things out by himself. I don't like the thought that he's involving you in his mess, upsetting you like this.'

That wasn't what Sara wanted to hear. She'd woken

with a small shaft of hope. If he could manage a good chat with Adam and Carrie today, maybe things would feel less fractured between them all ... and therefore between her and Bernard.

She tucked her mother-in-law into her armchair, a rug over her knees: the temperature had dropped overnight and was now hovering around three degrees outside. Sara noticed Margaret's eyelids fluttering, she was on the edge of sleep. 'I've always thought living a lie – if that's what he's doing – kills you on some level.' The words were unambiguous, clear as a bell. They chilled Sara, making her shudder as if a ghost had walked over her grave. *It's as if she knows it all, without being told.* She wanted to say something, to refute her mother-in-law's words. But Margaret's eyes had closed. And what was there to refute? She was right. *Bernard and Adam must go to the police.*

35

Bernard, meanwhile, was drunk. He was at the stage where he automatically reached for another glass, even though it was only midday and he'd only just woken up – still in his clothes, still on the sofa, still clutching his phone to his chest, although no one was calling him. The only way forward seemed to be to drink some more, fry another egg, read some crap in the newspaper – delivered each morning, like some sour reminder of the outside world, the words incomprehensible, swimming before his eyes.

He wasn't a big drinker, normally. But there seemed a surprising comfort in the hazy insouciance it delivered, which helped the days pass without too much coherent thought. In fact, there was relief in letting it all go, in not trying to keep things together a moment longer. It seemed forever, not just five years, that he'd been carrying this tormenting burden, trying to do right by his family. He'd been rubbish at that anyway, even on a good day.

The threat contained in the note the twins had left for him on Boxing Day morning still sat on the coffee-table. An ugly reminder that time was running out. It cut him to the quick that his children had taken off a day early – without even waking him, without saying goodbye. After Sara had left, he'd crashed out, meaning only to doze for an hour or two. But he hadn't woken till gone ten, by which time it was too late.

Aside from hurt at their abrupt departure – for which he realized he was entirely responsible – reading the note itself made him go cold:

Hi, Dad, Sorry to run off like this, but we both decided we couldn't face another conversation/row about everything [Carrie's handwriting told him]. *Adam and I appreciate the chats we did have with you, and the lovely Christmas you and Sara put on. Thanks. But we both feel it's crunch time, now.*

So Adam is planning to go to the police in the New Year. I'll go with him. We can do it from Nottingham. I know this isn't what you wanted, but he feels he has no choice. xxx

He had tried Adam's and Carrie's phones numerous times since. Left desperate voicemails for them to call him back when, inevitably, they didn't pick up – assuming, no doubt, that he would attempt to dissuade them. Then he'd sat with the note in his hand, trying to work out what it would mean if the twins carried out their threat – which he was certain they would. If he didn't go with them, it would look even worse – he was just as culpable as Adam, in a different way. But it would take the burning decision from his hands, he supposed, which might feel almost restful. The twins, however, would shun him forever. He couldn't bear that. *They have no idea what they're getting into . . . They have absolutely no idea.*

His mind was such a mess, it didn't even bother him that Sara wasn't there. Her presence was only a painful reminder of how much he continued to let her, and everyone else, down. It was better this way. They were on different sides of the fence. And it had come between them.

When memories of their time together threatened feeble tears of self-pity, he just reached for another glass of wine. He didn't even ask himself how he would feel if she never came back.

36

While she was caring for her mother-in-law, Sara refused to think about her future with Bernard. *We seem to have reached an impasse*, she thought, as she plodded back along the icy streets to her house after Heather's return. They had not been in touch. Would he even be expecting her back?

But opening her front door, she was greeted by bleak, chilly emptiness. Imagining her life without Bernard, going back to this, the tidy, solitary existence – which had been perfectly acceptable before she'd been reminded of how lovely it was to share your life – was too much for her. In spite of all that had happened over Christmas, she knew, as she stood in the cold, silent kitchen, that she was not yet ready to throw in the towel.

Her mother's mantra, much to young Sara's irritation when faced with a task she was finding difficult, was 'Don't give up, don't give up,' dramatic pause, 'and don't give up again', delivered in a sing-song voice and accompanied by an encouraging kiss.

She knew that if she made herself comfortable now, she might never go back to her new home on the cliff. So, without allowing herself time to think, or settle back into her old home, to put on the heating and do a wash, take some brown bread from the freezer, she quickly gathered up the pile of fliers from the door mat and checked around to make sure nothing had burst or leaked in the sub-zero temperatures. Then she put on her warmest coat and locked the place, inching her way up the hill to where she'd parked the car.

Heading across the frozen, windswept landscape, she almost turned back a number of times. It was horrible negotiating the glassy coast road, and she couldn't imagine what the narrow lanes leading to Bernard's house would be like. *Go home*, she told herself. But then she would be trapped, alone with her moiling thoughts. And that, she decided, was way worse than any snowdrift, any confrontation she might have with Bernard.

The house watched her arrival with its usual lack of enthusiasm. But the Mercedes was there, covered with a thick layer of frozen snow – it was clear he hadn't used it in a while. Sara got out of her car, shivering in the icy needles of sleet, the violent blast that threatened to blow her over. She wondered if he'd heard the car, waited to see if he would open the front door, but nothing moved except the wind.

She felt as if she no longer belonged there. Lifting the heavy iron fish that served as a door knocker, she let it fall. Did it again. On the third knock, she heard socked feet scuffing across the wooden floor inside. There was a pause, then the sound of the locks being pulled and twisted. By the time the door swung open a few inches, she was trembling from the cold . . . and sheer trepidation as to what she might find.

Bernard peered through the gap, like a nervous old man. He hadn't shaved – not since she'd left, by the look of him. His eyes were blank. When he saw her, he almost recoiled. Blinking fast, he muttered, 'Sara.'

It was an acknowledgement rather than a welcome and she might have walked away if she hadn't been so bloody cold. 'Can I come in, please?'

He drew the door wider, allowing her to step into the house. She could see immediately there was a problem. The blinds were down, the house in almost complete darkness apart from the small lamp by the sofa. And everywhere in the half-light were strewn old newspapers, empty wine bottles and lager cans, greasy plates and smeared glasses. Spilt cereal, open milk cartons and used teabags littered the usually pristine surfaces. The mess felt angry, as if he were projecting his rage onto the room. She gaped.

Bernard, behind her, gave a sardonic laugh. 'See me in my true colours.'

She turned, bewildered. Then she noticed his hands were shaking as they covered his face, his body stooped over as if it was suddenly too much effort to stand. She went to him and took him by the shoulders. He smelt rank, of alcohol and old food, musty, greasy, unwashed, but she guided him to the sofa and eased him down. He lay back, eyes closed, breathing heavily.

She sat down opposite him, but he didn't move, didn't open his eyes. He seemed so exhausted she wondered if he'd fallen asleep. 'Bernard?'

Suddenly he sat upright, his gaze on her uncomfortably intense, as if he were trying to fathom her out. 'You don't get it, do you? I'm not the man you think I am, Sara. Hasn't Christmas . . . all my previous lies . . . proved that?'

'Who do I think you are?' Sara spoke calmly, although she was far from feeling it.

His smile was mocking. 'Oh, you know, a standard

271

good guy, no skeletons in the cupboard, someone you can walk off into the sunset with.'

She huffed. 'Don't insult me, Bernard. I know very well who you are.'

'Someone who tries to do the right thing and makes a goddamn mess of it every time?' His eyebrows rose in challenge.

She asked, 'Did you get a chance to have a proper talk with the twins?'

'Ha!' He threw up his hands. 'They were gone by the time I surfaced. Left a day early. Crept out without even saying goodbye. Can you believe that?'

She could, imagining their anger at Bernard's behaviour on Christmas night, the dread of opening up another acrimonious discussion with their father over breakfast. 'I'm sorry.'

'Anyway, Adam is going to the police in the new year. That's the bombshell they dropped in the note they left on the coffee-table.'

Sara wasn't surprised. She felt a small spurt of relief that things were moving on, not stuck in this terrible stalemate. Now it might actually be happening, though, she also felt very anxious about what it could mean for them all. *It's the right thing, isn't it?* 'Have you spoken to them since?'

'Nope. Scared I'll talk them out of it, I assume.'

'So what are you going to do?'

'What choice do I have? I'll go with them, of course.' He looked almost surprised by his own words, as if they'd sprung from his mouth independently.

Sara got to her feet. *At last,* she thought, at the same time aware this was only the beginning. Throughout Bernard's almost comical tirade of bitterness and self-pity, she'd found herself painfully aware of the love she felt for him. It flowed around her heart, her brain, her organs, into all the nooks and crannies in her body. He had lied to her, rejected her, been weak and defiant and self-pitying, a CV from which any sane person would run a mile. But his motives, on all counts, stemmed from a pure – albeit misguided – desire to protect his son. And that, however frustrating, was enough for her.

Feeling a new energy course through her at his decision, she didn't answer him, just turned away, walking briskly over to the kitchen. She pulled out a black bin liner from the cupboard under the sink and shook it open. Then she systematically began collecting the debris: bottles and cans, newspapers and cartons. Bernard, his face showing a tired bewilderment, watched her nervously, as if she were some kind of avenging angel.

She moved on to the glasses, mugs, greasy plates, opening the dishwasher to find all the clean crockery from the Christmas meal – which she and the twins had loaded nearly five days before – still stacked within.

When she eventually finished wiping the surfaces, had wrung out the dishcloth and laid it over the mixer tap – in her own world as she worked, taps on, dishwasher whirring – she turned to find him standing stock still, right behind her. She jumped.

'Sara . . .'

Drying her hands on a tea towel, she glanced up at him quizzically, waiting for him to go on. Her heart was pounding at his closeness, but she refused to show how much he was affecting her.

He pulled the tea towel out of her grasp and slung it on the worktop. Taking her hands firmly in his, he said, 'Sara, listen. This won't work. You and me . . . it's been the best thing in my life . . . But, look at me, I'm a fucking wreck. I've got so much to sort out. And it's not your job to do it for me.' He swallowed hard and shook himself. 'I'm so sorry.' Pulling her into his arms, he held her close for a long, precious moment.

Sara swallowed her own tears: she could be stubborn too. When he finally let her go, she straightened her spine, tossing her head back. She uttered a single word: 'No.' It was not a cry of anguish. Not even an appeal. It was a rock-solid, determined statement of intent.

Bernard, catapulted out of his own misery, echoed, 'No?'

'I'm not leaving you, Bernard,' she said. 'I'm not sorting you out, either, by the way. You're going to stop whining and feeling sorry for yourself and do that yourself.' She took a breath. 'Plus, you're going to follow through with your promise and support the twins.'

A faint look of surprise crossed his face. 'I am?'

Hands on her hips, Sara said, 'Go and have a shower. You stink.'

Later, the house clean and restocked with food, Bernard sweet-smelling in fresh clothes, Sara began to come down from the high that had carried her through the previous hours. Her head ached, her throat was dry with what she feared was the start of a cold, and doubts knocked about like a football in her tired brain. But she told herself she'd made the right decision. *One last chance.*

They sat quietly together on the sofa, each with a glass

of wine, both too tired to speak. The contents of the bowl of crisps she'd put out, the plate of salami – left over from Christmas – had disappeared within seconds. She wondered when he'd last eaten a proper meal.

'You realize it's New Year's Eve tomorrow,' Bernard said.

She frowned. 'I was hoping you hadn't noticed.'

He dropped a kiss to the side of her head. They hadn't kissed properly since she'd been back. But now she felt a sudden frisson. She turned her head. Meeting his grey eyes, the breath caught in her throat. His gaze shot through her, like a hot wind, his mouth touching hers, so gentle, almost trembling.

But even as he kissed her, doubts she could not ignore came crowding back. She wanted to give in to the pleasure of his caresses – to forget for a moment all that had gone before – but she found she could not. She gently pulled back. Would he step up to the plate? How would they all cope with the fallout of a confession? Would Bernard be capable of mending the breach with his children? What would the legal consequences be? Suddenly everything seemed so uncertain, not least where she stood in all this. The twins' deadline was defining. For them and their father, but also for Sara.

37

'Hurry up,' Sara said, taking a sip of her tea. It was nearly ten o'clock on New Year's Eve and they were at the kitchen table, a scuffed, ancient draughts board between them. Both were making a fist of it, going through the motions of a couple enjoying the occasion. But it was clear their hearts weren't in it. Not even the glass of delicious burgundy Bernard had bought for Christmas – until Carrie declared she only drank white and Adam said that red wine gave him blue lips and a headache – seemed to help.

'All very well for you to say,' Bernard muttered, finger pressed to one of his pieces. 'You've won the last two games.'

She'd been taught by her grandfather on those holidays in the tidy Croydon bungalow. By the time she was ten, they would play these draughts matches that went on for hours, each moving their pieces with the speed of light.

Sara had not let Bernard's promise of the day before go idle. During an earlier walk on the cliffs, the wind on the head biting, bringing tears to their eyes, she had stopped and turned to him. 'Have you told them yet?'

He'd shaken his head, but his eyes, which he turned on her, were resolute. 'I don't want to say it in a text or a voicemail, Sara. I thought I'd drive up to Nottingham first thing tomorrow morning, see Adam, talk it all through properly, face to face. See the police up there, if that's what he wants.' His eyes had filled with tears. 'I just want to hug him.'

'What do you think will happen?'

He'd toed the sandy soil with his boot. 'I've no idea.'

'That's your phone,' Sara said, now, hearing the trill from behind them on the coffee-table.

Bernard jumped up. She wondered whether it was one of his children, finally, although it seemed unlikely from their stinging radio silence. Sara had FaceTimed both her daughters earlier. Peggy was back from Berlin, still in the arms of the boyfriend. She was in an unusually dreamy mood. 'I'll call soon for a proper chat,' she'd said, perhaps not comfortable with FaceTime in front of Beng. Joni had been lounging by the pool, drinking an alarmingly neon smoothie through a straw, Mason's handsome face grinning in the background. They'd all seemed so far away, even Peggy. Sara felt as if she was losing touch with her own life, swept up, as she was, in Bernard's. She was so looking forward to her Californian trip and having time to reconnect properly with her eldest.

She swivelled round in her chair and watched as he clicked on the call.

'What? *What?*' His face drained of colour. 'Oh, my God . . . Carrie, sweetheart, slow down, I can't understand what you're saying. Where is he now?' Frowning, he listened for a few moments longer. 'OK, listen, I'm on my way. Meet you there.' He turned wild eyes to Sara. 'Adam's in hospital. They're saying it might have been a suicide attempt.'

Sara shot to her feet, hands pressed to her mouth in horror. 'Is he all right?'

Bernard nodded shakily. 'Luckily, his flatmate came home unexpectedly and found him unconscious, rang the ambulance.'

'Pills?'

Bernard shook his head, baffled. 'No, Carrie said helium. One of those little tank things you use to blow up balloons?'

She frowned. 'They can kill you?'

Ignoring her question, he demanded, 'Where the hell are my car keys?' starting a frantic scrabble in the key tray by the front door, shaking his jacket upside down, tossing cushions into the air.

'I'll drive you.' Sara blew out the candle on the kitchen table, waving her own keys aloft.

For a moment it looked as if he would argue, but his gaze was blank as he followed her, like a child, out of the house and into the cold December night.

Initially, the only voice in the car on the journey north was the mechanical one of Serena-the-satnav: 'At the roundabout, take the second exit and stay on the A21 . . .' As the car sped up the M1, Sara going as fast as she dared – there was no traffic to speak of at this time of night – she heard Bernard's strained voice beside her. 'His decision to go to the police . . .' He turned to her. 'Was it that? He couldn't cope?' He fell silent. 'Surely he didn't mean to do it.'

She didn't know what to say. Adam wasn't a child. He must have been aware of the potential consequences. Glancing sideways at him, she saw his eyes were fixed on the road ahead, his face deathly pale, tinged a sickly orange from the overhead motorway lights. 'This is all my fault,' he said.

By the time they reached the Nottingham turn-off, Sara was wilting and utterly exhausted, her eyes scratchy, her mouth dry, her hands – clinging, white-knuckled, to the wheel – aching in every joint. In their haste, they hadn't brought water or snacks and she was desperately thirsty. Bernard had dozed for a while, for which she was grateful: she had no answers for him.

When they finally stumbled, stiff and cold from the long drive, into the medical centre car park, she breathed a sigh of relief that they'd made it, then steeled herself for what lay ahead.

Carrie stood just inside the entrance to the emergency department, clutching a paper cup of machine coffee and talking earnestly to a plump, stocky man with wiry hot-red hair and pale-rimmed spectacles, dressed in a scruffy mustard sweater. She'd obviously been crying, her cheeks blotchy, her eyes glassy. When she saw her father, she burst into tears again and ran into his arms.

The young man introduced himself to Sara. 'Noah, Adam's flatmate,' he said, shaking her hand firmly.

'You found him?'

He nodded. 'Had a fight with the girlfriend and came home early, thank God.'

It was busy in the unit – New Year's Eve drunks, victims of fights, shouts and loud voices, bewildered people propped on trolleys or wandering around holding bloody wads of tissue to cuts and bruises, some just slumped hopelessly on chairs, others passed out from too much alcohol.

Adam, lying on his back on the cubicle gurney, looked drained of colour, almost transparent, the veins in his forehead pulsing blue, an oxygen mask clamped over his mouth and nose. Sara, standing just outside the open curtain, thought he was asleep. But he opened his grey eyes at the touch of his sister's hand. At first, he seemed not to recognize her, but then he sighed and she saw a solitary tear escape, slowly tracking down towards his ear.

Bernard bent and dropped a kiss on Adam's cheek. 'Hey, we're here, son. It's going to be OK.'

Adam didn't respond, just turned his head away.

Sara was aware of a doctor hovering at her elbow. 'Are you Adam's mother?'

She shook her head, moved so that he could get past. After a quick check of the monitor attached to the grey plastic peg on Adam's finger, he touched Bernard's sleeve. 'A word?'

Leaving Carrie with Adam, Bernard followed the doctor into the corridor, signalling for Sara to come with him.

'You son's going to be all right.' The doctor – over-neat blond hair and cool blue eyes – reassured them. 'His pulse is still a bit high, but his blood pressure's stabilized and his reflexes are good, no neurological damage that we can see. He's been lucky. His friend acted quickly.'

Bernard nodded. 'Has he said anything about how it happened?'

'Noooo.' The word was drawn out. 'But he'd inhaled enough gas to render him unconscious. I'm no psychologist, so I can't comment . . . He'll need to be seen by one of the mental-health team before he can be discharged.'

Bernard's face was still blank with shock. Sara moved a little closer, placing her hand gently on his back.

The doctor was talking again. 'Helium displaces the oxygen we need to breathe,' he said. 'Inhaling gas from a balloon to get a Mickey Mouse voice won't harm you – in most cases – but breathing directly from a tank could cause asphyxiation in a matter of minutes. I imagine a fifth-year medical student – which I gather your son is – would be aware of that.'

Sara saw Bernard take a deep breath. 'So what happens now?'

'He'll stay in overnight and one of my colleagues will assess him in the morning. If they don't feel he's a threat to himself, he can go home.' He paused. 'But I would advise you to keep a good eye on him, make sure he gets the appropriate help. It might be tempting to dismiss this as an unfortunate accident, especially if Adam doesn't want to admit to what he did, but that could be very dangerous.'

Bernard blinked, cleared his throat. 'Thank you,' he said.

The doctor nodded briskly. 'Right, well, they'll be taking him up to the ward in a minute. You should all go and get some sleep.'

'No chance,' Bernard muttered, at the retreating figure. He turned to Sara. 'Oh, my God, I can't believe it. I've gone to such lengths to keep him safe from one disaster, then this happens.' He closed his eyes. 'I didn't see it coming. I should have . . . but I didn't.'

She rubbed his back. 'Let's just get him home tomorrow and go from there.'

'You heard the doctor. Did he really do it deliberately?' he asked softly.

'We should wait, see what Adam says,' she replied diplomatically.

They spent what remained of the night in a nearby Holiday Inn. The room was chilly, Sara and Bernard both wired and overtired. Neither slept.

'Christ, Sara, supposing he'd died?'

She rolled over to face him. Light filtered through the thin blinds. It must be nearly morning. 'He didn't die, Bernard. Listen, you've only ever tried to do what you thought was best for him.' She could tell her words were of no comfort, but she didn't know what else to say.

He closed his eyes and let out a long sigh.

'And you've got the chance now to help him sort himself out.'

Adam looked wan, even paler, if that were possible, than the night before, when they'd picked him up from the medical centre. But at least he had agreed to come home with them for a week or so to recover – a decision his course supervisor had endorsed, so Adam informed them.

'What did the psychiatrist say?' Bernard asked anxiously, as they made their way across the car park. Carrie, who'd stayed with Noah at the flat overnight, had brought a bag with Adam's things and was waiting for them by the Mini.

Adam grunted, gave his sister a cursory hug. He seemed embarrassed.

'Adam?' Bernard pressed. 'How did it go?'

His son held out his hands, palms up, with a cocky grin that rang very false. 'I'm here, aren't I? They wouldn't have let me go if they thought I was some suicidal maniac.'

Nobody laughed.

Carrie hugged him goodbye. 'Call me,' she said, her tone flat. She seemed sullen, almost angry with her brother. Sara couldn't blame her – Adam had frightened them all, however much she must sympathize.

In the car, Adam immediately got out his phone and plugged in his EarPods. He refused to talk on the long journey home, all questions from his father greeted from the back seat with the same dismissive grunts, until Sara put a warning hand on Bernard's thigh, and he stopped trying to get an answer out of his son.

As they sped south, the pent-up air in the car ricocheted with the unsaid until Sara felt her head would burst.

38

Once home, all of them almost comatose with exhaustion, Adam grabbed his bag and went straight up to his room, banging the door shut behind him. Sara and Bernard stood in the kitchen, at a loss. The debris from supper the night before, the draughts board, the half-empty wine bottle, still littered the surfaces, and both began automatically to clear things away. It was supper time, so Bernard rootled around in the freezer and brought out a shepherd's pie.

When the meal was ready, he went to call Adam.

'Don't try to talk to him about it tonight,' Sara warned. 'Leave it till tomorrow.'

Bernard frowned. 'I'm not going to pussy-foot around him, Sara. I can't relax until I know what went on last night. If it was a suicide attempt . . . he's up there, alone in his room. He needs to tell me, once and for all, what happened. So we know where we are.'

'The psych team didn't red flag him . . .'

Bernard harrumphed. 'Adam's smart. He'd know how to pull the wool over their eyes.'

'True, and I understand how worried you are, but wouldn't it be better to have a proper talk in the morning, when we've all had a good night's sleep?'

He turned away. 'Let me deal with this,' he said peremptorily.

Sara winced at his tone. But she didn't challenge him. It had been a terrible twenty-four hours. She waited as he went up and knocked on his son's door, heard a brief exchange, then watched Bernard tread slowly back down the stairs.

'He says he isn't hungry,' he said. 'And he doesn't want to talk.'

Sara went to him and put her arms around him. 'Leave him. He must be feeling fragile and probably not at all well. If he wants something later, he can get it himself.' She kept her tone light, trying to defuse his anxiety.

Bernard's lips pursed. He didn't return her embrace and moved away just fractionally, until she let him go. 'He's not just recovering from a bad hangover, Sara. *This is serious*. I need to know he's safe.'

She was well aware it was serious, but she knew that whatever she said, it would be the wrong thing. So she served the pie and peas, which they picked at in silence, Bernard finishing off the burgundy from the night before in a few swift gulps. She dreaded what tomorrow would bring; Adam's presence upstairs felt looming and huge.

Adam sloped downstairs around eleven the following morning. Bernard had barely slept, as Sara had predicted, and had been fizzing around the house since early light. She'd suggested they go for a walk, but he'd turned her down. She suggested he go to the supermarket. He refused tetchily. 'I want to be here when he wakes up,' he'd said.

Sara handed Adam a cup of coffee as he sat down at the kitchen table. 'Can I make you some porridge, an egg?'

He shook his head. 'I'm OK, thanks.'

Bernard, grasping his own mug in both hands – it was at least his fourth, she calculated – sat down opposite his son. 'Did you sleep?'

Adam nodded. He seemed oddly calm.

'Good. So . . . we need to talk.'

Adam nodded again. Before his father had a chance to go on, he said, 'I'm really sorry for the other night. It was a stupid accident.'

Bernard eyed him. 'What sort of an accident? You must know how dangerous that stuff is.'

Adam shrugged. 'I was . . . you know, wound up, and I'd had a few too many vodkas. There was this balloon filler thing . . . *I* didn't buy it. I think Noah got it for a party we were having tomorrow . . . yesterday now, I suppose. And I don't know . . . I'm not sure what happened . . .' He stopped, biting his lower lip, then reached for the cafetière that Sara had left on the table.

'You really should eat something,' she said, thinking of all that caffeine on an empty stomach, then caught Bernard's frown and said no more.

'So that's it?' Bernard said.

Sighing, Adam replied, 'What can I say, Dad? I did a really stupid thing and worried you all sick. But I wasn't trying to kill myself.' He didn't look his father in the eye as he spoke.

Bernard, maybe wanting to believe him, nodded as if he did. Sara saw his shoulders relax slightly. 'OK, well, if that's what you say happened . . .' He took a sip of coffee. 'Was it the plan to go to the police that wound you up?'

Adam blinked rapidly – he was clearly in a daze – but said nothing.

Bernard went on, 'I'd made the decision to come with you, before all this. We'll go together.'

Adam gave an almost imperceptible nod.

Bernard frowned. 'Did you hear what I just said?'

'That you'll come with me and confess,' Adam said. 'Great,' he added unenthusiastically. Sara thought she detected a hint of sarcasm, too.

'Isn't that what you wanted?'

After a big breath, and sitting up straighter in his chair, Adam said, 'Sorry, Dad, can't seem to focus on anything right now.'

At a loss, Bernard turned his gaze to Sara, but she couldn't help.

Adam got up. 'Think I'll go back to bed for a while.'

When he'd gone, Bernard let out a sigh of frustration.

'It'll take a bit of time for him to recover, Bernard. It's not just the physical thing, it must have been a mental shock to him too, even if it was an accident,' Sara said. She felt so sorry for them both.

'Did you believe him, that he was just mucking about?' Bernard asked, after a moment.

She hesitated. 'No.'

'Me neither.'

During the following days, Adam was like a wraith haunting the house. *Taking over from his mother*, Sara thought, only half in jest. He'd appear unannounced, padding downstairs silently in his bare feet, eat some toast and drink some coffee, then wander back to his room. He didn't go outside, never dressed beyond his joggers and T-shirt. He hardly spoke, politely rebuffing all their attempts to engage.

'I don't know what to do with him, Sara,' Bernard said, when the end of the holidays loomed and they needed to go back to work. This morning they'd left the house for some privacy and were sitting on a bench, wobbly, weather-beaten and surrounded by brambles. It was a horrible day, drizzly and cold, but they didn't notice. Most of their conversations inside were conducted these days in low voices, glancing around, nervous Adam might overhear. *It's like having a fretful baby in the house, who won't sleep*, Sara thought. Except the tension was like a fog that refused to lift. 'He says his course supervisor insists he take a couple of weeks off. But is he really going to go back in this state?'

'What's he said about the police?'

'He wants to go ahead with it as soon as possible.' Bernard's tone was dull with resistance.

He got slowly to his feet, gazing out across the grey expanse of sea. She could see the muscle in his cheek tensing, mouth set. She felt they were in different zones now. He didn't seem really to see her any more. It hurt, but she understood that worry about his son was all-consuming. She just wondered how long it would go on. 'Don't you think he needs professional help, Bernard?' she said, rising too, aware her jeans were damp from the wooden seat.

Bernard didn't reply – she wasn't even sure he had registered her suggestion – as he turned and walked away. She hurried to catch up with him, reaching for his hand. He held hers automatically, but didn't seem conscious of her. After a few moments she eased her hand away.

As they arrived at the house, Bernard stopped short of

the glass doors on the terrace and finally turned to her, pulling her roughly into his arms. 'Oh, God, Sara, I'm so sorry about this. It must be a nightmare for you, getting involved in all my shit. I don't mean to be so snippy with you . . . I love you.' He pulled back, gave her an agonized smile. 'You do know that, don't you?'

Leaning against him with cautious relief, she nodded.

'We mustn't let this thing with Adam come between us.'

Sara felt his genuine desire not to do so. But, in that moment, she knew it already had.

39

Joe, with his robust good humour and American ski tan –
acquired over Christmas spent with Ariel at Lake Placid in
the Adirondacks – was like a blast of fresh air gusting
through the quiet, sealed, strung-out atmosphere of the
cliff house. It was a couple of days before Adam was supposedly returning to Nottingham, barely a fortnight since
the incident with the helium tank. To Sara, who'd watched
father and son skirting round each other, and knew that
nothing had been settled or even discussed, it was out of
the question to let Adam go.

'Bloody hell!' Joe exclaimed, throwing himself down on
one of the sofas and spreading his limbs, waving them
about as if he was trying to create a snow angel. 'I've knackered every fucking muscle in my body on those mountains,
pretending I was twenty-five again. Those trendy try-hards
in their *über*-cool SnowDrifters made me feel like something the cat dragged in. I had to prove them wrong.'

Bernard was laughing, and Sara felt a spurt of pleasure
to see him diverted – for a moment at least. 'Sounds like
you were the try-hard.'

Joe groaned as he accepted the glass of red wine Bernard held out to him. 'I love Americans in general, but that
moneyed New York mob really fancy themselves.' He
lifted his glass to his friend and then to Sara. 'Cheers!
Here's to you both. And here's to being home in one piece.'

As they all took sips from their drinks, Joe asked, sotto voce, obviously having been primed earlier by Bernard, 'Where's the boy?'

'I'll go and tell him you're here,' Sara said, putting her drink down. *Thank goodness for Joe*, she thought, as she climbed the wooden staircase. It would be a relief to have someone else picking up the conversation at supper, and maybe Joe would unlock Adam, where they'd both singularly failed.

'So, are you looking forward to getting back to the grind?' Joe asked Adam, as they ate the spicy lentil and spinach soup, the brown toast and Kentish Blue Adam loved. Conversation so far had been mainly about Joe's time in the States, about Christmas generally, about Carrie – who had, apparently, been in daily phone contact with her brother. Joe hadn't commented on the reason Adam was home, and Adam didn't broach the subject, although he must have known Joe had been told. It was an avoidance that Sara found predictable, but also disconcerting. Not helpful to anyone.

Adam jumped at Joe's question, his head shooting up from his bowl. He stared at him. 'I was totally dreading it,' he said slowly.

Sara frowned as she noted the past tense.

Adam laid his spoon down. Placing his hands flat on the table either side of his empty bowl, he sat poised for a moment, as if preparing to heave himself to his feet. He cleared his throat. Looking only at Joe, he said, 'But I'm not going back.'

'Hallelujah,' Bernard exclaimed, also turning to Joe. 'We've been trying to persuade him it was too soon.'

'No, Dad. I mean I've quit. I emailed the dean and my course supervisor earlier. I'm not going back . . . *ever*. I did warn you.'

There was a stunned silence.

Aiming his remarks at Joe again, ignoring his father, Adam went on, apparently calmly, 'I decided this afternoon, after talking to Carrie. I don't want to be a fucking doctor. I can't hack the endless responsibility, the knife-edge decisions . . .' He was blinking away tears now. 'It's killing me.'

Sara saw his chest heave, maybe with relief that he had finally managed to say it out loud.

'Adam . . .' Bernard had gone pale. 'Son, it's all you've ever wanted, since you were a small kid, to be a doctor.'

Adam shook his head vehemently. 'No, Dad. It's all *Mamma* ever wanted. I never had the breathing space to make my own decision.'

Sara glanced at Bernard. He was leaning back in his chair, poleaxed.

'Is your decision to quit right now tied up with coming clean to the law, Adam?' Joe asked. 'Wouldn't it be better to wait until you know how all that will pan out?'

Adam gave Joe a scathing look, as if he were simple. His voice low and pained, he replied, 'Every *single fucking decision* in my life is tied up with what happened that day, Joe. How could it be otherwise?' He banged his palm on his forehead. 'Maria and I live together in here. She's like my fucking girlfriend . . . except she isn't because I fucking killed her, didn't I?' He closed his eyes, letting out a pained sigh. 'I can't have a real one.'

Bernard groaned, buried his face in his hands. Joe's dark eyes, Sara saw, were filling like her own.

'That's terrible, mate,' Joe said, rising and pulling Adam into his arms, just like Bernard had done on Christmas night. Adam, clasped in the big man's bear hug, looked like a rag doll, his face ashen. 'You need help.'

Letting Adam go, he turned to Bernard. 'I know someone . . .'

Adam seemed to tense at his words, stand up straighter. 'I don't need therapy. I just need to get shot of medicine and make this fucking statement. Then I'll be able to breathe again.' Without another word, Adam turned on his heel and walked off, up the stairs to his room.

There was an uneasy silence in the kitchen. Bernard seemed to Sara to have given up. He just slumped in a heap, staring into space.

'Shall we sit by the fire? I have pudding,' Sara said to Joe.

He smiled, widened his eyes at her, swishing them towards Bernard's bent head. 'Come on,' he said. 'Get up, Bernie. Let's be comfortable and talk this through.'

The table abandoned, they gathered on the sofas around the glowing woodburner. Sara brought out the apple and blackberry crumble, set it on the coffee-table with bowls and spoons, a jug of double cream. It seemed unreasonably *de trop*, under the circumstances, in its warm, juicy unctuousness, and she made no attempt to dole it out.

Joe plonked himself next to his distressed friend, slapping Bernard's thigh encouragingly. 'It'll sort itself out. Adam's standing up for himself, and that's a good sign, no?'

Bernard's look was withering. 'It's an absolute disaster. What the hell is he going to do now?'

Joe sighed. 'Maybe he has a better plan. Maybe, as he says, he'll be freed up, once he's got the past off his chest.

Take off in some new direction.' He smiled at Sara. 'That looks delicious. Can I help myself?'

Bernard turned to him angrily. 'You mean after my son's done time for perverting the course of justice? After he's got himself a criminal record?' He shifted away from his friend, crossing his arms. 'Yeah, we all need a plan like that, Joe.'

His friend, seemingly unfazed by the attack, munched his crumble in silence. 'Moving on, Bernie,' he said. 'At least everyone's moving on.'

40

Things were indeed moving on in the Lockmore house. On Monday morning, after breakfast – it had been decided – Adam and Bernard would go down to Hastings police station together. Carrie had insisted on coming too. She was taking the train down from Liverpool on Sunday. Bernard had also persuaded Naz Kumar on board, the solicitor who had represented him in the original trial and had, until now, been in the dark about Adam's involvement in the accident.

Sara held on as the tension mounted. Not only in the wake of Adam's bombshell – Bernard clearly devastated his son would now never finish his training – but because of the impending visit to the police. Adam was on a mission, and his father put up no further resistance. Bernard, Sara felt, had lost all agency: he was just sleepwalking through the days in a weary haze.

On Sunday night, Bernard and Sara lay sleepless in bed. It was after two. At first, they were both silent, consumed by their thoughts and hoping the other one slept. But, finally, they'd both rolled over onto their backs and begun to talk.

'What do you think the police will do?' Sara asked.

'I talked to Naz. He was obviously stunned that I lied

to him.' Clearing his throat in embarrassment, Bernard went on, 'He said what we already know: perverting the course of justice is very serious. People have been jailed for taking someone else's penalty points, for instance.'

'Does he think they'll charge you both?'

'He says it could go either way. He did wonder if, after all this time, and just when my conviction is a few months off being spent, it would really be in the public interest. But if they choose to make an example of us . . .'

Sara sighed. 'At least it will be done. And at least you and Adam will be on the same page at last.' She turned, moved closer to him. He lifted his arm so she could lay her head on his chest. 'Will Adam feel better, do you think?'

Bernard groaned. 'I'm worried he sees it as a magic bullet: confess and all his stress miraculously disappears. But he still killed Maria Kemp.' There was a long pause. Then he went on, 'I tried so hard to pretend it was me who killed her, Sara, that I almost came to believe I did . . . that Adam had nothing to do with it. Hearing him talk about Maria like he does is so distressing. It brings home the real truth of what he's dealing with.'

As Sara lay there, she had a sudden uncomfortable premonition that the accident's impact was in the ascendency, getting stronger with every passing day. What they'd already experienced was similar to a minor skirmish in the foothills, the real battle still lying ahead on the plain below. She shivered again. However strongly they felt for each other, perhaps Bernard's past would, in the end, prove stronger still.

*

Bernard was smart in a navy suit, white shirt and tie. Adam wore a pair of chinos and his father's tweed jacket, as most of his clothes were still in Nottingham. Carrie, who had arrived late the night before, was insisting on driving them down in Bernard's car and waiting in a nearby café – despite her father telling her they would probably be hours at the station.

Sara cooked a big stack of buckwheat pancakes, with bacon, blueberries and maple syrup, for breakfast, squeezed oranges and made a large pot of coffee. There was an overtly festive atmosphere as they ate, but the humour was black, the banter edgy and slightly desperate. She longed for them to get going.

'Mmm ... thanks, Sara. The prisoner certainly ate a hearty breakfast,' Carrie joked.

Adam, looking awkward in his formal clothes, but stoical, pulled a face at his sister. 'OK for you. You're not the one on the way to the gallows.'

'True, but having my whole family behind bars might be a bit of a challenge, no?' Cassie countered.

'Stop it, you two,' Bernard snapped at them, as if they were five-year-olds. He had eaten barely anything, just downed mug after mug of coffee. The bell rang, making them all jump.

Sara went to the door. It was Mr Kumar. Bernard had asked him to talk things through briefly with Adam – just to make absolutely sure his son understood from a professional what today could mean to his future – and he'd agreed to accompany them both to the station afterwards. Sara liked him immediately. A man in his sixties, bald and plump in a light-grey suit, he was reassuring without being glib, his kind, bespectacled eyes assessing the situation without seeming to judge. But to Sara the morning had the flavour of a family funeral.

'Time to go,' Bernard announced around nine thirty. He came over to Sara, who was by the sink, trying to keep out of everyone's way. 'Thanks for looking after us, sweetheart,' he whispered, with a tender smile. Inhaling sharply, he added, 'I'm shitting myself.'

She gave him a quick hug. 'Loving you all the way,' she said.

When they'd finally gathered up their coats and left, the solicitor following the Lockmores in his cream BMW, she plonked herself down heavily at the kitchen table and laid her head on her folded arms.

41

Sara realized she'd felt almost disengaged while the family ate their breakfast, as if she were the housekeeper, coming and going with more coffee, more pancakes, but not really part of the awful conversation that united the three. It was how she'd been feeling a lot of the time recently: father and son locked in their separate bubble, trying to make sense of each other. She and Bernard hadn't made love since before Christmas. She missed it.

Reaching for her phone, she dialled Precious. She and Sammi had got back from Spain only the day before and Sara felt as if they'd been away a lifetime.

'Oh, my God, Precious!' she exclaimed, when she heard her friend's excited shriek. 'You have no idea how much I've missed you. Did you have a wonderful time?'

'We did – it was heaven to be warm – although Sammi's mum drove me insane. She's never approved of me, obviously, seeing as I'm an unsavoury black person, but as she gets older, she's stopped even pretending. And we always have to stay with *la mamá* over the holidays, of course.'

For a while they chatted about Precious's Christmas, Sara trying to keep a lid on the cauldron bubbling away inside her. In the end she got her turn. 'I've got something to tell you . . . *A lot* to tell you, in fact.'

Precious listened in silence. Then she let out a low whistle. 'Oh my God, Sas. What a nightmare.'

Tears building behind her eyes, Sara said, 'I'm so sorry I wasn't straight with you, Precious. It was hell, not being able to tell you the truth.'

'Hey, don't apologize, sweetheart. I'm proud to have a friend who can keep a secret, even from me.'

She smiled. 'I was so close to telling you, on so many occasions, believe me.'

Precious let out a thoughtful 'Hmm.' Then: 'This is all getting a bit weird, no? First a dead cyclist, then a criminal cover-up, a suicide attempt and now possibly *prison*? You've barely known the guy six months.'

Sara, feeling slightly hysterical at being freed from the shackles of the secret, began to giggle. None of it was remotely funny but letting go of the turmoil of the last weeks, the relief of being onside with her friend again, made her weak. Unable to speak through her laughter, she clutched one hand to her mouth, the other to the mobile as tears streamed down her face.

'Not just one teeny tiny skeleton, then, more like a heaving crowd. What will he come up with next?' Precious said, warming to her theme.

Sara took a breath and tried to control her laughter, feeling suddenly defensive. 'You've met him. He's not even remotely who you're describing.'

'Look, I think Bernard's a good guy, you know I do. I really like him.' Precious paused and Sara waited for the 'but'. 'It's just . . . this seems to be all about him and his family. Where do you fit in?'

Hearing the question, Sara felt a tightening around her heart. The compromise she'd had to make hit home as she insisted to her friend, 'It's wonderful when it's just the two of us.' Although even that wasn't really true any more, Bernard's mood so disconnected from hers.

'You won't get much of that, though, if Adam's given up doctoring. He'll be living with you for a while, won't he? Until he sorts himself out.'

Sara had thought of this. 'I imagine he won't have a choice.'

'But you like him?'

'Yes, we get on OK, I think.' She didn't feel she really knew the man. And the thought of never having Bernard to herself was depressing. What if Adam struggled more rather than less, now he'd lost his life's purpose? Would he be an even bigger worry for Bernard? 'I don't know. I suppose we just have to get over one hurdle at a time.'

'Sorry to be the voice of doom,' Precious said. 'I just worry you're being buffeted about by these crazies with no obvious reward.'

'It's not like that,' Sara said stiffly, knowing it actually was. 'And by the way, thanks, Precious, for being so understanding. It's been driving me nuts, not being able to tell you what's been going on.'

The friends said goodbye, but as Sara clicked off the call, she felt the house close in on her again: the heavy, padded silence, the constant tension, the pressure of all that was wrong with the Lockmores contained within those four walls. As if the house were a malignant guardian desperate to keep hold of its precious wards and their chaos . . . at any cost. She felt like shouting out loud, making it clear that she wasn't daunted, that she wouldn't be run out of the house on the cliff, not against her will.

*

'How did it go? Will they charge you?' she asked, breathless, as she waited for Bernard to speak. It was after one o'clock and she'd been mooching around all morning, unable to settle to anything as she anticipated the verdict.

'They didn't say. It's not up to them, of course. But Naz seemed to think it went as well as could be expected. I'll tell you more when I see you.' He sounded really calm, which surprised her. Then she heard a sharp exhalation. 'To be honest, it was hell. I felt even worse than I did the first time. The cops were polite, but they looked at me with such disdain. Like, what sort of example does this show to a kid?' He sighed. 'I felt so ashamed.'

'I can't even imagine how horrible it must have been,' she replied. 'You've been a long time. I was beginning to worry.'

'Just a lot of sitting about. Then endless questions, on and on – all recorded, of course. It was as if they were trying to catch me out.' He gave a sad laugh. 'They didn't manage to do so last time, of course. But this time was simple: nothing to lie about.' His tone was suddenly light. 'That part was such a relief.'

'How did Adam get on?'

'They interviewed us separately. I haven't had a chance to ask him much, but he seems OK. He and Carrie are on a high now. They want to go for a drink and celebrate . . . if you can call it that.'

'Phew. Well, at least it's done. How are you feeling?'

Bernard let out a small groan. 'I don't know how to describe it, Sara. I'm exchanging one crime for another. I'm not out of the woods by any means. But it's amazing being onside with the twins for the first time in years and years.' She heard him mutter something to someone else. 'Carrie's taking the train back to Liverpool this afternoon, by the way, so after we've had a drink, I'll drop her off. I wanted her to stay longer, but she's got work tomorrow.'

'Give her my love,' Sara said. As she put down her phone, she found she wasn't feeling the same relief she'd detected in Bernard's voice. She'd held on, supported him through the past weeks without focusing on their relationship, because what else would she do? But now the immediate drama was past, she looked to the future with a sense of unease. *What does this all mean for us?*

Adam had a woozy grin on his face when they walked through the door. He didn't look at Sara, just wandered unsteadily around the room, finally throwing himself lengthwise onto the sofa, where he lay, eyes wide open, saying nothing.

'Sorry, he's had a few,' Bernard said, embracing her.

'Didn't the police say anything about what might happen next?'

'Just that we'd be hearing from them in due course. That was after they'd finished giving me the third degree – making me feel like a total villain and a bad father. Most of it was pretty technical: read this, make sure you check it, tell us if anything's incorrect. Sign here. Glad to see the back of us, I expect.'

Sara let out a breath.

'Naz says they'll put it in front of the CPS, but it could be months before we hear anything. He stuck to an optimistic scenario: they let us off because it's not in the public interest to spend money on a couple of remorseful penitents, one of whom has already been punished. But I can't let myself believe he's right.'

Both fell silent. Then Sara said, 'I suppose Maria's family will have to know.'

Bernard nodded.

Hesitating, she ventured, 'Would it help Adam to meet her husband and apologize, now things are out in the open?' It was something she'd been turning over in her head for a while – she'd always believed in truth and reconciliation.

She saw Bernard's eyes widen in horror. 'Are you kidding? *No*. I'd never put him through that.' He shuddered. 'I can't imagine the husband would be up for it, anyway. He must hate me . . . and now us.'

'You should ask Adam, though. It might be something, if the husband was willing . . .'

He pursed his lips as if at something distasteful. 'I'm not going to ask him, Sara. If he wants to, he can say.'

I wish he'd stop treating Adam like a delicate plant, she thought. His son was much stronger than Bernard gave him credit for. *Look how he's bulldozed his incredibly stubborn father into doing his bidding.* But she remembered Bernard mentioning that Ilsa had mollycoddled her son, and Carrie often seemed like an older sister, rather than a twin, the way Adam turned to her for approval and support.

They both stood looking at Adam, who was now curled into a ball, clutching one of his mother's tapestry cushions to his chest, fast asleep.

He gave a tired smile. 'I've held on to this for so long, been so pig-headed about it. Today felt like a bit of an anticlimax.' He rubbed her arm absentmindedly. 'It's been so huge in my mind, I sort of envisaged there'd be more fanfare, more drama, Armageddon, both of us manhandled, hauled roughly away in chains . . . Although being in limbo, perhaps for months on end, feels almost worse.'

'I think it's very brave of you both.'

He gave a sad smile. 'All very well being brave . . . I just wonder what impact this will have on Adam. Joe talked about him maybe having plans for the future up his sleeve, but I can't think what those might be – medicine has been his life. I'm worried he'll just stagnate in the meantime, lose his way. Then it'll be a very long time before he finds it again.'

Sara was worried about that too.

42

'Do you have any washing?' Sara bumped into Adam as she came out of the bedroom with the basket. It was nearly noon and he was dressed in a grubby T-shirt and boxers, obviously having just woken up.

He rubbed his eyes and grunted, 'I'm good,' then pushed past her towards the family bathroom. Like a teenager.

'I've got various things I need to get in Hastings, if you fancy coming with me,' she went on. 'Maybe we could have a coffee in that trendy new café on the hill your dad likes.' She knew she sounded too eager, but it didn't stop her trying.

Adam barely broke shuffle. 'Nah . . .' He didn't even turn to face her before shutting the bathroom door firmly behind him.

She continued downstairs, dumping the basket on the floor in the small utility room by the front door. It was the beginning of February and three weeks since Bernard and Adam had made their statement to the police.

This wasn't the first time Adam had snubbed her. The previous Sunday she'd been making lunch for the three of them. He had strolled into the kitchen and stood watching her put together the couscous she was serving with grilled chicken breasts. His stare was uncomfortable. 'If you don't want this, I can make you a sandwich?' she offered.

Adam turned away, not bothering to reply, and walked upstairs.

While she and Bernard were eating their meal, though, he'd come back down and started rummaging in the fridge, then made himself a sandwich in a marked manner. Sara could have told herself she was overreacting, that his rudeness was merely distraction, if he'd been treating his father in the same way. But he wasn't. He'd basically taken to ignoring her and anything she said – when they were all together at the table, for instance – as if she didn't exist. He would speak to her only when forced, when he knew Bernard was watching, and on the days she was in the cliff house, he hid in his bedroom until he heard his father's voice downstairs. It was as if he was taking his territory back, now he was living there. Sara's fanciful notion was that Ilsa was in league with her son again. She was coaxing Adam, controlling him, as she always had, to reject her.

Now, as she sorted the washing and filled the machine, the worries about Adam's mental health, which had plagued her since the suicide attempt, ran round her head like the clothes in the drum. In the first week following the statement and dropping out of medical school, Adam seemed brighter. At supper he would talk animatedly – his presentation almost too bright and upbeat, as if he were forcing himself – about something he'd read online, or that Carrie had said, or about a friend who was giving him advice about what qualifications he needed to become a professional gamer, which idea had struck horror in Bernard's heart.

'A gamer?' he'd responded, eyes wide with alarm, when

Adam first floated the idea. 'What do you know about that?'

Adam had laughed. 'Well, quite a lot, Dad, you'd be shocked to hear. Misspent hours with Modern Warfare 2, when I should have been learning the bones in the foot, for instance.'

Bernard had not laughed, but Sara couldn't help a smile.

'I can make a ton of money, Dad. It's super-competitive, but I'm good and I love it.'

Bernard had shaken his head in despair. But Sara had thought, *At least Adam has found a direction.*

As the days went on, though, Adam's mood dropped again. In spite of him seeming to settle quietly into day-to-day life at the cliff house – after all, his meals were provided, his washing done, there was a free roof over his head and cash on tap should he need anything – he fell mostly silent, never talking about how he was feeling about anything, how he was coping with the uncertainty of his situation as they waited to hear their fate.

'You don't think you should tackle him again about therapy?' Sara whispered one morning, when she and Bernard were in the kitchen preparing breakfast. 'I know he said no when Joe suggested it, but all that stuff about the accident won't have gone away.'

Bernard put the coffee pot down and took her face in his hands. 'Look, I'm worried too, Sara. But I don't want to nag him at this stage. He's said he doesn't want it and I have to respect that. He can't really move forward yet, anyway, until we get a decision.' He smiled. 'And he is talking to me more . . . Making plans, even if I don't approve of them.' He was waiting for her to agree and she managed a nod. 'Take things slowly, eh?'

Sara wanted to believe Bernard's approach was the right one but expressing her doubts – even articulating Adam's rudeness – felt hard, almost impossible, reluctant as she was to heap more worries on someone who was already buzzing with tension.

'It's going to be good weather this weekend. Shall we all do a walk on Saturday?' she asked, wanting to push away her problem with Adam.

Bernard hesitated, then pulled an apologetic face. 'I was thinking I might go up to town with Adam. Buy him some new clothes, maybe have lunch somewhere nice. We can take the train.'

'OK.' She lowered her face, turning to open the fridge for something she didn't need, so as to hide her disappointment. This was the second weekend she'd been excluded from Bernard and Adam's plans. Last Saturday he'd taken his son walking on the Weald with sandwiches and soup. Then on Sunday they'd gone to see a sci-fi movie in Hastings. She felt his finger under her chin, gently pressing her face upwards.

'You don't mind, do you?'

'Of course not.' She smiled gamely.

'Only I feel when it's just me and him, it's easier for him to open up. I reckon if I keep up lots of father-son stuff and encourage him to talk, we might be able to do without the therapy.'

She couldn't even raise a smile as she tried to tamp down her childish resentment of the boy upstairs, who had caused so much angst for everyone for so long and showed no sign of stopping. She knew she shouldn't feel like this towards Bernard's son, but she couldn't help it, especially with the intensity of father-and-son bonding increasing daily. Often when Sara arrived home, the two would be closeted in Bernard's study, playing backgammon or watching something on his huge desktop computer – she could hear them laughing together. The more she spent time in the same house with Adam, the more it got under her skin. She wasn't sure he actively disliked her, but he clearly didn't want her there, in his house, by his father's side.

Bernard was eyeing her. 'I need to do this, Sara. It won't be long and then he'll be off and doing his own thing again. I feel I owe him this time, after everything he's been through . . .' He smiled. 'And, if I'm honest, I'm enjoying being with him, finding out about things he's never told me before. It's like we're getting to know each other properly for the first time.'

Sara was pleased to hear this; she knew she couldn't fault his mission. But she felt the weight of his words like so many stones in an ever higher wall that was shutting her out, rock by rock. Soon, all she'd be able to see was the top of Bernard's head.

'So how is it going with the loutish stepson?'

Sara laughed. 'Adam's not a lout.' Not wishing to hang around the house with Bernard and Adam in London, she had arranged to meet Precious for lunch at the Lewes house.

'But *there* all the time, nonetheless?'

'I'm trying to be grown up about it,' she replied, giving her friend a brief update on the situation she was dealing with.

'It's sad, Bernard having to struggle so hard to bond with his son,' Precious commented.

'I know. Although I'm hardly the expert on father/child relationships.'

Precious dug her fork into her baked potato, began fluffing up the inside and dolloping crème fraîche on both halves. When she'd finished, she looked up. 'So when the dreaded Frank announced he'd left you his house, didn't you feel anything, like a spurt of affection? Catharsis? Resolution of some sort?'

'No. I'm not even sure I wanted to.'

'Hmm . . . Is your dad religious?'

'Oh, yes. Well, Lois is a fervent Baptist, and they do church every Sunday. And Frank is on the parish council . . . although that's probably because he likes the status and the sound of his own voice.'

'So maybe he's worried about what he'll say to St Peter at the pearly gates?'

'If he was worried about that, disinheriting the woman who's looked after him for fifteen years would hardly score many Brownie points.'

They ate in silence for a moment. 'I know I sound harsh, but I don't like him,' Sara stated. 'Which makes me feel bad. He's my father, for God's sake, however rubbish he's been.'

'I don't like my father much, either. He was always on my case, wanting me to be the perfect daughter. And I've always disappointed him . . . But I sort of love him?'

'Exactly. And, however misguided, I'm sure he loves you, too.'

'No such thing as the perfect father, eh? Or perfect mother, for that matter.'

Sara nodded. 'But when I remember Pete and the girls ... When I look at how Bernard is bending over backwards to accommodate Adam and his problems, and how he caused all this trouble solely in an attempt to do the best by his son, Frank falls so far short as to tip off the scales.'

There was silence, Sara not wanting to talk about her father any more.

'So you're coping OK, up there on the cliff?' Precious asked eventually.

The question caused Sara's eyes to fill with tears. 'Not really. I'm beginning to feel surplus to requirements.'

'Oh, darling.' Precious grabbed her hand. 'Doesn't he see what's happening?'

'All his energy is spent saving his son.'

'I suppose you're a bit stuck until the courts decide.' Precious eyed Sara closely. 'After that, it depends on what you both want, I guess.'

All Sara wanted, she realized, was to stand in the circle of Bernard's arms and shut the world out. She remembered how much she'd longed for him to mend the breach with his two children and gave a wan smile. *Be careful what you wish for.*

43

'I thought it might be a good idea to get away for a long weekend,' Bernard said, a few days after Sara's talk with Precious.

She and Bernard were at the breakfast table, the feeble February sun casting a ghostly beige light across the room. Sara was pleased. She knew where this was coming from. The previous night they'd had a whispered row in the bathroom, neither wanting Adam to hear. It was about a planned trip to the Depot in Lewes. Sara, in an attempt to bond with Adam, had got tickets for a sci-fi film she'd thought he would enjoy, although she wasn't keen on the genre. The plan was for them to have supper first. Sara had taken time to book it. Then, at the last minute, Adam had said he didn't feel like going after all, so Bernard decided not to go either and the tickets were wasted.

'I'm sorry. I know it's annoying,' Bernard had said, 'But I don't want to push him. He's still really fragile.'

Sara hadn't wanted to overreact – it was just a film – but she had a feeling that Adam didn't want to go because she would be there, too.

She'd gone on brushing her teeth, the electric bristles bruising her gums, she was pressing so hard. Bernard had gone on patiently standing there. '*You* could have come, though, couldn't you? You go out to work every day and leave him,' she said, after she'd spat out the toothpaste, wiping her mouth with the back of her hand.

Bernard did not seem abashed by her accusation. 'Look, I'll make it up to you, sweetheart. When this is all over . . .'

A bubble of resentment had filled her chest. But she'd stopped herself from further comment and allowed him to hug her.

Now, she said, 'That would be wonderful . . . Where are you thinking?'

'Well, the closer beaches will still be cold, so a city break perhaps? Prague?'

'I've never been.'

Bernard grinned. 'Shall I investigate, then? We could go crack-of on a Friday and come back late on Sunday night, get in two and a half days?'

'I'd really love that.' The thought of getting away with Bernard was exciting and immediately lifted her spirits.

'It doesn't have to be Prague. It'll be freezing at this time of year, of course. There's Copenhagen – but that'll be cold, too . . . Barcelona?' He held up a finger. 'I know, Lisbon. Now Lisbon is really beautiful.'

'And warmer than Prague or Copenhagen.'

'Right.' He grinned. 'I feel we need a treat.' He reached for her hand. 'You've been amazing, Sara, so patient and kind. I know it hasn't been easy for you.' Getting to his feet, he added, 'This should be fun, the three of us on a jaunt, don't you think? I'll go and consult Adam.'

Sara almost groaned aloud. She'd assumed – foolishly – that the break would be for just the two of them. But she noted the love in Bernard's eyes, heard his attempt to make her happy, and did not carp.

After he had disappeared upstairs, eager to talk to his son about the proposed trip, Sara sat nursing her second cup of coffee. She was disappointed it wouldn't be just her and Bernard, but at least they'd be getting away from the cliff house. *Maybe Adam will feel freer, less irritated with me, in a foreign city*, she thought. *He loves travelling.* She began clearing the table, an incipient smile on her lips. *Lisbon.* It could be a very bonding experience for them all.

When Bernard came back downstairs, Sara was on her laptop at the kitchen table, checking her appointments for the following day. She glanced up, but he was avoiding her eye.

'Is it Lisbon, then?' she asked.

Bernard shifted from one foot to the other, finally pulled a chair out and sat down opposite her, his hands clenched on the table. 'Yeah, I . . . It's tricky . . .'

She smiled. 'Spit it out.'

'Adam doesn't feel up to going away at the moment.'

She frowned. 'OK. Is this about me? Would he want to go if I wasn't coming?' She spoke more forcefully than she'd intended, but Bernard didn't seem surprised by her comment.

'Please don't think he doesn't like you. I know he does.'

She raised one eyebrow, her throat tightening with hurt. '*Did* he say he didn't want me to come, Bernard?'

Almost blushing with confusion, he said, 'Not in so many words. It's more like he's trying to make up for lost dad time. Being a little possessive, I suppose.'

Sara rose to her feet. The question burning on her lips was why couldn't they go away without Adam. It was only for three days. But she knew what his answer would be. She wasn't going to beg.

'Don't be upset.' Bernard's voice was anxious.

As she stood looking down at him, her decision to hold back, to grin and bear it for a while longer, fell at her feet in tatters. 'When you're not here, you realize Adam avoids me, doesn't speak to me? I think he finds it difficult even having me in the house. You must have noticed.' She stopped, not wanting the bitterness to show in her voice.

Bernard got slowly to his feet. 'That's not true, Sara. You're talking nonsense. He knows how much you mean to me.'

She took a deep breath, trying to calm her hurt. 'I understand how momentous this time has been for you both . . .' Tears filled her eyes. 'I don't mean to be childish. It's just sometimes I feel a bit unwelcome.' All she wanted was for Bernard to hurry round the table and hug her. She could almost feel Adam's presence upstairs – *Is he listening to all this? Does he even realize how he makes me feel?*

Bernard did not embrace her. He stood there, the same bewildered expression on his face as before, eyeing her. 'You've got this all wrong.'

'Have I?' Her voice no longer sounded hurt, just small and sad.

Turning on his heel, he said, 'I'm going to get Adam. We have to sort this out.'

'No, no, don't, Bernard. Please, don't.'

He stopped and came over to her but did not touch her. He was like a ball on an elastic band, swinging to her, swinging to Adam, rebounding back to her, pinging off to Adam again. It made her regret her outburst. 'I'm sorry. I shouldn't have said all that,' she muttered, hearing the sulkiness in her voice and feeling ashamed.

He reached out then, his hands resting lightly on her upper arms. The expression in his eyes was pained as he stroked his palms down to her wrists, circling them briefly with his finger and thumb. His hands were warm and she ached to hold him. 'This is difficult for me too.'

They both stood in silence. Sara heard the bathroom door open, Adam's bare feet scuffing down the landing back to his room.

Bernard didn't appear to know what else to say, maybe in his heart of hearts acknowledging the truth. She could almost hear the cogs in his brain batting round and round, as he tried to find a way to please his son and the woman he loved. 'I'm going to talk to Adam,' he said finally. But he didn't move. Levelling his gaze at her, he added, 'I can't choose, Sara. *Please* don't make me choose.' Then he turned and walked up the stairs.

Adam looked tense. Bernard, in the background, was clearly nervous. Sara wished herself anywhere else on earth. She was still smarting from Bernard's last remark and had spent the following twenty minutes trying to work out what it had meant. Or, at least, rejecting what she knew it did mean: *Me or Adam*. It was always going to be his son.

'Dad says you're feeling left out,' he said bluntly, instantly making her feel like a needy fool. Dressed in the usual T-shirt and black tracksuit bottoms, his pale face sharpened by the argument he'd just had with his father, he stood, arms crossed defiantly, waiting for her to speak.

No immediate response came to mind. Unlike Adam, she was upset, rather than hostile, but seeing the anxiety on Bernard's face, she was loath to make things worse.

Standing a little straighter, but shaking inside, she replied softly, 'I know you need time with your dad, Adam. I'm not trying to intrude. If you'd rather the trip was just the two of you, that's fine.'

It looked as if the wind had been taken out of Adam's sails, because his stance sagged. 'It's not important,' he muttered, staring at the floor.

'It is important that we get on,' she said.

Adam raised his eyes. She recognized the same stubbornness she regularly detected in his father's eyes. 'I'm sorry,' he said stonily.

She could tell it almost hurt him to pronounce the two words. If he'd meant what he said, she could have embraced him. Instead, she just nodded and managed a smile. *Where has the other Adam gone?* she wondered, remembering the shy charm he'd shown on Christmas Eve, before his defences were up.

But his intransigence was a tipping point for Sara. She didn't want to fight with Adam. She didn't want to keep pretending to Bernard things were OK or watch him struggling with his son's moods. She was sick of it all. Real life was not her and Bernard wandering around, happily in love. Real life was the accident, the subsequent lies, threat of legal redress, Adam's mental-health issues . . . family breakdown. She could no longer pretend, however much it broke her heart.

After Adam had retreated upstairs, she said, 'You have to get help for him, Bernard. He seems so angry . . . so stuck.' She didn't care any more if he was upset by her interference.

'I've told you, he doesn't want it. And he's over eighteen – I can't force him.' His voice had risen and she sensed his own doubt and frustration. 'I'm truly sorry he's behaving like this – it's probably just misplaced loyalty to his mum.'

Exasperated, but trying to keep her voice even – because she really wanted him to hear – she moved forward and placed her hands on his crossed arms, meeting his eye with as much conviction as she could muster. 'I want the same thing as you, Bernard, for Adam to be healthy and moti-vated again. His problems haven't gone away.' She dropped her arms. '*You can't do this yourself.* You're way too close . . . In fact, you're part of the problem.'

She knew she'd gone too far when he stepped back, his face closing down, like the shutter on a shop. 'Look,' she began again, her tone softer, 'I realize I don't have a voice in this family yet. But Adam tried to kill himself. You're not a professional, Bernard. You don't know how to reach the part of him that did that . . . You're bonding with him, which is great – but it's like Carrie put it at Christmas: skating over a frozen lake.' She stopped, seeing the build-ing indignation in his eyes, but she ploughed on, her voice dropping to scarcely more than a whisper. 'He hasn't even admitted it yet.'

Bernard, when he spoke, sounded as if he was holding himself in very tight. 'I don't need reminding.' The look in his grey eyes was uncompromising and she knew she was wasting her breath. 'I want time with him. Time and a safe space to talk about all the things that are bothering him . . .

with someone who really understands the context of his feelings.'

'But you've had lots of that already. It hasn't changed things,' she persisted stubbornly. 'Whatever you say, Adam isn't better.'

He bit his lip, then said softly, 'Alone. I need time with my son alone.'

44

Taking a moment to understand Bernard's words, Sara spoke as if in a dream. 'You want me to leave?'

He gave a heavy sigh. 'I just think you're right. He's not finding it easy, having you here – for whatever reason. And I know that's wrong. But right now, my only priority has to be seeing him get well.' His tone seemed perfectly reasonable, as if he was reminding her to get loo rolls when she went to the shop.

She was dumbstruck. Clearing her throat from the hurt that was threatening to choke her, she managed to say, 'You're not doing him any favours by being scared of him, you know. By letting him get away with things because you're frightened of what he might do if you don't.'

'I'm not frightened of him.'

She felt the fight go out of her. 'All right,' she said.

The relief she saw wash over his face was like a knife to her guts. But it was immediately followed by a wave of anguish. He came towards her, embraced her. 'I'm so, so sorry. I didn't mean for this to happen. You know I love you, Sara. Please, please understand. It's only for a short time, till I can sort him out.' He was squeezing the life out of her and she fought to get free.

'So, Adam gets his way.' She didn't even try to keep the sarcasm from her voice.

Bernard's expression hardened. 'This is my son's life we're talking about.'

'So persuade him to get professional help, Bernard.' Then she turned on her heel and walked unsteadily towards the stairs.

As she began to pack, shaky now and so angry she wanted to break something, she knew this was the end for her and Bernard. She understood his need to put his son first, of course she did, but nothing would be resolved in a couple of weeks, or even a couple of months. And that wasn't the only factor. Even if Adam got better – which she wasn't confident he would without proper help – and even if the news was good from the courts, Bernard's twistedly indulgent attitude to his son might never change. It was what had got them both into trouble in the first place. Adam might always stand between them.

'Where are you going?' Adam, sitting at the kitchen table with a cup of tea, a mauled packet of Oreos and his iPad, pulled off his headphones as Sara wheeled her case towards the front door.

'I'm going to spend time with my mother-in-law. As you know, she's not well,' Sara said, although she was pretty sure Adam wouldn't be fooled by her excuse. *It doesn't really matter if he is or not*, she thought, as she took down her coat from the hook. *He's got what he thinks he wants*. She hoped Bernard would succeed in helping him, now she was out of the picture . . . but she wasn't holding her breath.

Adam just nodded.

Bernard saw her to the car in silence. As she opened the door, he stayed her hand. 'You're angry, and you have every right to be. I don't even know if this is the right thing. I just have to do what I feel is best . . . give it everything I can.'

Sara listened but could not speak. She pulled away her hand and got into the car. Bernard stood there, looking as lost as she felt, but he did not say another word.

45

Bernard experienced a spike of pure resentment towards his son as the sound of the Mini faded along the twisted clifftop lanes. He turned and walked back into the house, immediately ashamed, knowing it was unfair. It had been his decision to ask her to leave, not his son's. Although now Sara had spelt out Adam's behaviour towards her, Bernard could only see it as ungenerous at best, manipulative at worst. He felt as if there was only room, right now, for one thing in his head: Adam. And when Sara had tried to help – and he did acknowledge it came from a pure desire to help, not interfere – it had felt like a challenge. It was as if she was questioning his ability to be a good father . . . just as Ilsa had done.

'How long is she going for?' Adam asked, when he heard his father return.

'Depends,' Bernard replied tightly. *Her name is Sara*, he silently admonished.

'Is her mother-in-law really ill?'

'Yes, she has been for some time.'

Adam nodded slowly.

'So what do you want to do now?' Bernard said tiredly. 'Is there a film we could watch?' *Does he realize what's just happened? Does he care?* He turned to fill the kettle, for something to do, not because he particularly wanted a cup of tea. What he wanted was Sara.

As he poured water onto the teabag and squelched it with a teaspoon, rendering the liquid an alarming teak colour that he would never drink, he knew his decision just now to ask Sara to leave was probably the worst he'd ever made. For a second he felt the impulse to call her and apologize, ask her to come back. Would she give him a second chance? Or had she already done that with his series of lies and cover-ups? He was shamefaced at the thought of what she'd put up with – so patiently – from him and his family. But he didn't call her, not with his son's precarious mental health a thorn in his heart.

46

Margaret had lost yet more weight. Her tiny frame looked gaunt, almost skeletal, to Sara as she watched her sleep. It was harrowing to see.

Heather, hovering at her elbow, whispered, 'She's not really eating at all now. Not even the smallest teaspoon of soup. She just purses her lips and turns away. I'm not going to force her.'

'No. I wouldn't want you to.'

'She's still taking sips of water, but her organs aren't going to survive long without proper nutrients.'

Sara sighed. 'I'll sit with her for a bit.'

'Cup of tea?'

'Thanks, I'm fine,' she replied, sinking into the armchair by the side of the bed.

She had been home in the Lewes house for a week now. She and Bernard had not talked. She didn't want to ring and have a distracted conversation with Adam listening nearby; Bernard hadn't phoned. However much she rationalized his request that she give them space, and however much she understood his need to help his son, the rejection still hurt. He could insist he loved her till the cows came home but chucking her out of his house – whether for a day or a year or ever – was not what you did to someone you loved. She hated feeling so angry with him, but she couldn't help it.

Margaret opened her eyes. Her gaze settled on Sara's face and initially she frowned as if she couldn't place her. Then she smiled and held out her hand. Sara cradled the cool, featherlight bones in her own. 'How are you feeling?' she asked.

A small shake of the head. 'A bit . . . floaty . . . not quite here most of the time. It's not unpleasant.'

'You're not in any pain?'

Another shake of the head. After a short silence, Margaret said slowly, 'I think it's time for me to go.'

Sara, assuming she was confused, said, 'You don't have to go anywhere, Margaret. You're at home, in your own bed.'

This elicited a smile from her mother-in-law. 'I never gave it much thought till recently . . . but it seems really quite hard to slip away. Harder than I imagined.'

When Sara's face fell, Margaret went on, 'Don't look like that, dear. I've had my time and it's been a good one . . . on the whole.' She cleared her throat. 'You've been such a support to me. So kind. I hope you know how much I appreciate that.' She squeezed Sara's fingers. 'But you must get on now, seize some happiness with your new friend while you can. Pete wants that for you.'

Sara tried to smile. Happiness seemed to be slipping fast through her fingers, but she wasn't going to burden Margaret with her problems. Her mother-in-law had stated her opinion, anyway: 'Leave him alone to sort himself out.' She'd said it often enough in the past, when Pete was being grumpy. For a moment Sara yearned with all her heart to be back in her marriage, have her girls around her, be looking forward to a sprightly Margaret gathering them all in her warm, messy kitchen in the big house, with chicken and mash and the same white china jug filled to the brim with rich, brown, mouth-watering gravy.

Margaret gave a little chuckle. 'I'm afraid I'm too old for a packed church now. All my friends have already shuffled off, thoughtless lot. If you want a show, you'll have to shanghai passers-by off the high street to pad out the pews.'

Thoughts of her mother-in-law's coffin in the church aisle were too much for Sara and she shook her head violently.

'After I'm gone, perhaps you could go on an adventure somewhere, I've left you a little money. You could visit something you've always wanted to see.'

Sara nodded dumbly.

Margaret's voice seemed suddenly weak and far away. The eyes she'd fixed on Sara were still intent but blinking with tiredness. 'You'll be all right without me?'

'I hope so,' Sara said, adding in a whisper, 'I love you very much.' The flutter of a serene smile was the only response she got before her mother-in-law closed her eyes and sank into sleep.

'She seems so sanguine about dying,' Sara commented, accepting the mug of tea held out to her. 'Almost as if she's enjoying the prospect.'

Heather smiled. 'I love her spirit. There's no fear there.'

'She believes she's going to be with Pete and Arthur, of course.'

Both were silent, considering this.

'I don't think it'll be long now,' Heather said gently.

Hearing confirmation of what she already knew, Sara

felt her whole world rock. It was inconceivable that soon this solid anchor of Margaret, Heather, and Pete, in essence, would be gone. Forever. It was always there, always reliably the same, always so loving, so pleased to see her, so interested in her. Somewhere to come back to when other aspects of her life were wobbling. At any time, losing that anchor would have been devastating. But now, with Bernard's rejection burning in her chest, it felt almost unbearable. Tears leaked down her cheeks as Heather's strong arms came round her. For a moment, the two women stood there, swaying silently, as they contemplated their loss.

It was only late afternoon when Sara arrived home. But without giving a moment's thought to the appropriateness of her actions, she did what she hadn't done since she was in her late teens. Retrieving the unopened bottle of vodka – which she'd purchased in the early days of her relationship with Bernard before she knew he didn't much like it – she drank a large measure, neat, with ice, then another, not with ice. It slipped down like a kind friend, as she lay in her velvet armchair, still in her coat. All the pain of the previous weeks began to swim into an amorphous blur, making her cry until her face was tired.

47

The week had been hell without Sara. Bernard was missing her so much, regretting his decision more with every passing day and with all his heart. Every time he thought about her – which was most of the time – he longed to reverse his cavalier decision. But memories of Adam's sulky *froideur* towards Sara stayed his hand. *Just a little bit longer*, he told himself. Sara, however, seemed to be talking to him without his even hearing her voice. The last words she'd spoken rang constantly around his brain in the days following her abrupt departure, like a loud, persistent earworm: *Get professional help*. Now, he picked up his phone.

'Hey.' Adam, sitting on the bed with his laptop propped on his knees, glanced up as his father opened the bedroom door later that day. Closing his screen, he said, 'Ready to go?'

They were off on another of their endless treats – this time a gig in Brighton: a band Adam liked – that served as diversionary tactics, masking the uncomfortable truths that seethed under the floorboards, like a rumbling quake.

Bernard, leaning against the wall, arms crossed, didn't immediately speak as he tried to find the right words. 'We need to talk.'

His son's eyes were immediately wary. 'Is it the CPS?' He got up, as if to ward off the impending discussion.

Bernard shook his head.

'We can do it tomorrow, then, Dad. If we don't leave now, we'll miss the warm-up act – they're supposed to be awesome.'

'If we do, we do. Please . . . sit down, Adam.'

Adam did his usual thing: saying nothing, going very still, watching his father through lowered lids as if he were the enemy. But Bernard wasn't playing that game any more. 'I said, sit down.'

Shrugging, but obviously hearing the tone of his father's voice, Adam reluctantly slumped down onto the black swivel desk chair in the corner, raising his eyebrows with a touch of scorn.

'OK . . . I talked to Joe earlier. He's given me the phone number of a highly respected psychotherapist in Hastings. He's known her for decades.' Bernard delved in his shirt pocket and picked out a folded piece of paper, handing it to his son. 'Here's her number. I want you to give her a call.'

Adam stared at him in silence, making no move to take it. Bernard laid it on his closed laptop.

'You tried to kill yourself, Adam. I'm not qualified . . . You need professional help.'

His words, spoken so quietly, sucked all the air out of the room.

Adam flinched, holding his head in his hands, eyes shut.

Bernard realized he was shaking. In that moment, all the trauma of recent years came back to him, like a violent maelstrom, smacking him in the face, making him physically jolt. As he stared at his son's bent head, it was as if

Adam were the living, breathing manifestation, the person who held all the horror and sadness for the Lockmore family. *Why did I ever think I could unravel this on my own?*

After a stretched-out silence, the room vibrating with his son's distress, Adam lifted his head and gazed at his father, his grey eyes awash with tears that he made no attempt to wipe away. He said nothing. Bernard wanted to speak, to reassure him, tell him that everything would be all right. That he would *make* it all right for his son. But he'd tried that.

Adam inhaled and sat up straighter. In a voice that was surprisingly calm but, oh, so weary, he said, 'I just want it to *stop*, Dad.' He wiped his cheek, his eyes never leaving his father's face. 'Can anyone help me with that?'

Bernard winced at the pain he saw in Adam's eyes. But Adam's question sounded genuine, not cynical or dismissive.

'I think they can,' Bernard replied firmly. 'Realizing you need help is the first step.' He gave his son an encouraging smile. 'I reckon it's worth a try.'

48

Joni's face fell when Sara delivered the news about Margaret, clearly very upset that her beloved grandmother was dying.

As Sara talked, her daughter's eyes filled with tears. 'Oh, God . . . we're so crazy busy, and Mason's buggered the rotor cuff on his left shoulder, so he's in agony and can't lift anything . . . can't even dress himself.' Her face on the screen crumpled. 'But I must come. I want to see Granny.'

'Sweetheart, honestly, I think she might go sooner than that. I'd never tell you not to come if you really want to, but it's a long way and hugely expensive last minute.'

Her daughter's chin wobbled and she didn't speak for a moment as she weighed up her options. With a heavy sigh, she finally said, 'I don't think . . . If it was nearer . . . I can't really leave the gym, not with Mason like he is. I'm the only one in charge.'

She looked so upset. Sara's heart constricted. 'Granny's not worried about dying. It's amazing . . . rather lovely, in fact, if I wasn't so sad.'

'Oh, Mum, I want to give you such a big hug. Is Peggy around? Will you be OK if I'm not there?'

Touched by Joni's concern, Sara assured her she'd be fine. 'Your sister's coming down at the weekend. Precious and Heather are here.' The screen dipped and shook as Joni wiped her eyes. 'I'm afraid this means we'll have to postpone my trip,' Sara added. The fact was, she wasn't sure she could even manage to organize herself onto a train to the airport at the moment, let alone a plane, she was at such sixes and sevens in her head. 'We can rearrange when I know what's happening with Granny.'

After they'd said goodbye, Sara thought about the simple, powerful love the two girls bore Margaret, and she them. She'd been there at every stage of their lives, always a listening ear, a place of safety, a shoulder to cry – or laugh – on. *Parents are seldom perfect*, she remembered Precious's words. *But some grandparents are.* It pained her to think of how selfish and short-sighted Frank had been to miss out on that privilege.

Sara saw Bernard's missed call logged on her voicemail. Even that morning, she would have returned his call. But now she just slung the mobile face down on the kitchen island and went to put the kettle on. As she waited for the water to boil, a small shaft of steel entered her heart. *Such magical months.* But dark too, as she'd watched Bernard disintegrate with the gradual unravelling of his secret. She had wanted to save him. Only it wasn't just him she needed to save – if such a thing were even possible – it was the entire Lockmore family. And that was beyond her.

Enough, she thought. *I've had enough.* The strength of her feelings had to be put to one side. This strange limbo must end. She was always the one to compromise, walk on eggshells, hold her tongue, be ceaselessly understanding . . . in the service of a family in chaos. She would not do it any more. She *could* not. In that moment of decision, she had no notion of what her life would be like going forward. But she would survive. She'd managed worse.

Sara fell asleep in the chair, later, too tired to examine her feelings a second longer, only waking in the small hours to the noise of her phone, leaping and buzzing on the worktop, lighting up the dark kitchen with a warning glow. *Bernard*, she thought, befuddled by sleep and stiff from being scrunched up in the chair. She almost let it ring out. Then suddenly she knew.

'Heather?'

Her voice was soft. 'I went to check on her just now and I'm afraid . . .' She cleared her throat. 'She looks very peaceful.'

'On my way.' Shivering, refusing to think about what Heather had said, she hurried into her coat, pulled on her boots and went out into the freezing February night.

49

Peggy stood in the bedroom doorway as Sara got ready for the funeral. 'You look nice,' she said.

'This was one of your dad's favourites.' She adjusted the shoulders of the navy wool dress. 'I never wear it these days.'

'Do you think they're together, now? Dad and Granny? I like that thought.'

'She certainly believed she would see him again.' As she reached for her hairbrush, the image of the two of them, people she loved with all her heart, together in some ethereal space, momentarily soothed her bruised heart.

'Wish Joni was here. Looks like it's just you and me now, Mum.'

Sara smiled at her daughter. 'It does a bit, doesn't it? Thanks for being here, sweetheart. I couldn't do it without you.'

She was happy to be distracted by the ping from an incoming text. Picking up her phone from where it lay on the duvet, she stared at the screen.

'Who is it?' Peggy asked.

'Bernard . . . he must have seen the notice in the paper.' She tried to ignore the way her breath caught in her throat. *I'm so sorry about Margaret*, the text read. *Hope today isn't too grim. Thinking of you. Please call me. Love you xxx*

She could have killed, in that moment, to feel his arms

around her. But she pushed the thought firmly away, knowing the hug would be festooned with as many complications as corks on a bushman's hat. She didn't have an inch of room in her head to think about it.

Peggy was frowning. 'Didn't you tell him?'

'We haven't spoken in a while.' In fact, it was nearly three weeks, but felt like an eternity.

'So it really is over between you?'

If her daughter had read the text, she might have assumed otherwise. But Sara didn't show it to her. 'We haven't officially ended it . . . but, yes, I'm afraid so.' She turned away from Peggy so she wouldn't ask any more questions, wouldn't see how hard this was for her. His beautiful grey eyes came forcefully to mind, speaking his love for her so clearly. She shook herself. *Not now*, she told herself firmly. Now was Margaret's time.

The packed church – it seemed as if half of Lewes had turned out – made Sara smile through her tears. *You see?* she whispered silently to her mother-in-law. As the vicar droned on, the church reverberated with the love she had felt for Margaret. She clutched Peggy's hand and closed her eyes. *I'm a lucky woman to have had such love in my life.* She felt that comfort now, even in the moment of death, her daughter by her side a reminder that love endures. Pete might be dead, Margaret too, but their love would last forever, a benign force, handed down through the generations, even after there was no one left alive who remembered them.

The rest of the day was spent shaking hands, smiling thanks, exchanging wonderful anecdotes about dear

Margaret with people she mostly couldn't place – but knew she should. Pete's cousin – or was it his second cousin, Sara couldn't remember – hugged her like a long-lost friend, but all she could recall about him was a story Pete had told about when they had both nearly drowned in a rowing boat off the Norfolk coast at the age of twelve. Heather was there, wielding plates of egg sandwiches, often catching her eye over the small crowd crammed into the flat – where Margaret had insisted the wake be held in her detailed instructions for her funeral. Peggy, too, was by her side for much of the day, putting a comforting hand on her back and whispering variations on the theme of 'Who's that lady in the purple coat? She seems to know me.'

The days and weeks that followed were so sad for Sara. She missed Margaret even more than she'd expected. It was as if a rug had been pulled from under her feet. As her mother-in-law's death was not unexpected, a lot of the decisions had already been made, the paperwork ready to be signed off. She seemed to trudge through the time as if through a heavy snowdrift, the grounded part of her dealing mechanically with funeral directors, solicitors, banks and estate agents, the other Sara floating some distance above the ground, lost in the past and remembrance of what Margaret had described so accurately as a 'good life'.

Thoughts of Bernard frequently intruded. But she kept putting off the conversation she knew she should have till after the funeral, after setting probate in train, after emptying the flat, after, after, after . . . He hadn't been in touch since the day they'd buried Margaret; she had not replied to his text. She wondered what he was thinking, whether he was thinking about her, too, how Adam was ... if they'd had any news from the courts. But she felt too battered and sad to deal with anything other than practical matters, which didn't involve her heart.

'That's the last lot.' Heather lugged a bulging bin bag into the hall from Margaret's bedroom. 'I'll drop it off at the recycling on my way home.'

Sara, keys in hand, stood in the passageway, reluctant to say goodbye, to close the door on the empty flat for the final time.

'We'll stay in touch?' she said, embracing Heather.

'Course we will,' Heather said brightly. 'I'll let you know where I'm working next.'

Sara nodded. Margaret had left her carer a generous sum in her will, but Sara knew how hard it would be for Heather to begin again, find another job after the years of looking after her – they had got on so well. As they reached their cars, Sara waiting while she loaded the black bag into her boot, Heather turned to her with a curious smile.

'Can I ask?'

Sara knew what she meant. She shook her head. 'Didn't work out, I'm afraid.'

Heather frowned. 'Shame. You seemed all set.' She gave an encouraging grin. 'Still, better off without him, I imagine.'

Sara fought the tugging wrench Heather's words evoked. 'I probably am.'

50

'I miss Sara so much,' Bernard said to his friend. 'I wish I could find a way to sort things out with her . . . but her mum-in-law died and she hasn't responded to my last couple of attempts to get in touch.'

'Seriously, mate?' Joe gave him an old-fashioned look as they walked along Eastbourne promenade with their morning coffee. He had been in Düsseldorf for a week and they were catching up. 'You think she'll come back after the crap way you treated her?'

Bernard cringed and took a gulp of coffee that burnt the roof of his mouth. 'I know you think it was a dumb decision, but at the time it seemed like the only thing I could do. I was panicking about Adam, as usual, and Sara being there was winding him up.' He took a deep breath. 'But I only intended it to be for a short time, till Adam began to improve.'

As they pulled level with a bench, Joe sat down with a loud groan. 'Bloody back.' He turned to his friend, gave him a wry look. 'Fair enough, but I wouldn't exactly be beating a path to your door if I was Sara and you'd chucked me out like that.'

'OK, OK . . . But she hasn't actually told me it's over,' Bernard pointed out, knowing he was clutching at straws. Sara was such a straightforward woman. If she'd still been thinking the relationship had legs, she'd have called by now, her mother-in-law's death notwithstanding. 'At least Adam's getting his shit together, at last, despite not hearing a peep from the law. He started an online computer course yesterday.'

Joe nodded his approval. 'Did he go and see Janet, in the end?'

Bernard's face cleared. 'Well, I gave him her number after we talked, and he didn't object. But I thought nothing had come of it. Then the other day he waltzed in, cool as a cucumber, and told me he'd just had his first appointment with her.' He grinned. 'I wondered why he'd asked to borrow the car but wouldn't say where he was going.'

'Great!' Joe said, clapping Bernard on the back. 'Let's hope she can get through to him.' Coffees finished, they walked on in silence, the sea at high tide pounding noisily on the shingle to their right. 'He holds things very tight, that son of yours.'

When he got home that evening, the house was in darkness except for the cooker light casting a narrow shaft across the kitchen floor. He didn't see Adam at first and jumped when his son spoke out of the gloom. Turning the lights on, Bernard saw Adam sitting on the sofa, knees drawn up, feet bare.

'You OK?' he asked, going over to him.

'I saw her,' Adam said, not looking at his father. 'Out there. Just outside the window.'

Bernard's heart sank. *Maria again.* But Adam did not seem distressed. In fact, he appeared unusually calm. 'That must have been upsetting.'

His son had a strange smile on his face. 'Mamma . . . I

saw Mamma at the window.' He stopped, glancing up almost sheepishly, maybe waiting for Bernard to scoff.

But Bernard wasn't surprised. He had never actually seen Ilsa since she died, but he'd felt her presence constantly over the years.

He sat down beside his son. 'Were you freaked out?'

'She was just standing there, staring at me, Dad. It was getting dark, and at first I thought I was imagining it.' He turned to his father. 'It wasn't creepy . . . it was sort of . . . comforting.' His eyes filled with tears. 'Do you think she knows I tried to kill myself?'

It was the first time Adam had actually said the words and Bernard held his breath. The sadness of his son's loss, of what he'd been through, broke his heart all over again.

'Do you believe in ghosts . . . in spirits?' his son was asking, wiping his eyes with the back of his hand.

Bernard smiled. 'I didn't, until I met your mum.'

There was a peaceful silence. 'We should scatter her, Dad,' Adam said eventually. 'I think we're holding her back.'

51

Sara watched the first signs of spring gilding the trees with soft green. She saw the vivid yellow of the daffodils, listened to the increased volume of the dawn chorus when she woke in the mornings. Spring was her favourite season. It usually made her heart sing with hope, her step lighter as she went about her day. Not this year, though. Margaret's death had floored her. She still had moments when she forgot her mother-in-law was gone and felt the pangs of loss with renewed pain. She was forcing herself through the motions, keeping to her routine: she knew if she let it slip for one second, everything would fall apart. She saw the daffodils and heard the birds, but they were merely there: they didn't move her.

This Saturday morning, a cold, sunny March day and a month after Margaret's death, Sara left the house early. She felt restless and in need of a bracing walk. She'd asked Precious to come with her, but hadn't expected her friend to agree. Precious saw leaving the shelter of civilization for the nearest hill – knee deep in mud, crying from the wind, heart exploding – as a peculiar way to enjoy yourself.

Sara had been walking for an hour up on the Downs, aiming for Firle Beacon. It was wild, but exactly what she needed. Stopping by a stile, breathless from fighting the wind, she crouched on the muddy bottom step – sheltered by the hedge – and, on impulse, pulled her mobile out of her anorak pocket. She'd had the same intention on a number of occasions since the funeral but had always balked at the last minute, retreating conveniently behind her grief. But yesterday she'd bumped into Joe in the high street.

'Hey, great to see you.' Joe had pulled her into a hug. 'How's it going? I heard about Margaret . . . I'm so sorry.'

They'd talked for a brief while, Sara drumming up an amusing story about the funeral, desperate to stop herself asking the question fizzing on her tongue: *How is Bernard?* But, in the end, she had faltered and fell silent.

'My crazy friend still seems to be nursing the illusion that you might come back one day,' Joe had said, his dark eyes meeting hers directly.

She hadn't answered. Joe seemed to understand. He'd hugged her warmly again in farewell.

The encounter had upset her. She'd tried with all her might to forget the touch of Bernard's lips, the whiff of salt and lavender when she held him, his grey eyes lighting up with laughter. But the various snapshots from their summer together refused to go away. In the cold of early spring, it was impossible to imagine being as hot as they'd felt that night they went down to the sea and swam in the moonlight. But recalling the cool slither of water splashing her nakedness made her jolt with longing. She could still taste the crisp, charred sardines he'd barbecued; the fresh, ripe tomatoes in the salad; the bite of the rosé on her tongue . . .

Joe's message, although not actually stated, had been very clear: *Put the man out of his misery.* She knew it wasn't just for Bernard's sake that she needed to have the conversation. She had walked out that day, and they had not spoken since. Nothing had been discussed. It was almost as if they'd never known each other at all. But he still had her clothes and toiletries at his house, work books. She had his front-door keys . . .

So, taking a deep breath, hunching over, left arm wrapped round her stomach as her gut somersaulted, she pressed on Bernard's number. Words jumbled in her head as to what she would say if he picked up. The wind howled bleakly round her, the sky was suddenly overcast. She jumped when she heard him.

'Sara?' He sounded breathless.

'Hi,' she said, detecting the wobble in her voice.

'How are you?'

Hearing him made her heart feel as if it would burst from her chest. 'OK,' she said. 'It's been busy . . .'

'You must be missing Margaret.'

Sara felt tears choke her. 'How are you?' she managed to ask, ignoring his words.

There was a moment's silence, then Bernard said, 'Yeah, OK . . . although there's still no news.'

'And Adam?'

'He's getting there. Seeing a therapist at last, you'll be glad to hear. And he's started a course in computer something-or-other. To do with gaming.'

She nodded, although he couldn't see her.

'Sara, listen –'

'Don't, Bernard. Please,' she interrupted what she knew would be an apology, aware that the more he talked, the more she would be drawn in.

There was a moment's silence. Then he said, 'Is it really over? Is there no way back for us?'

She didn't reply. She couldn't.

'I haven't called you because I didn't want to intrude after Margaret's death.' There was a pause. 'And because I'm ashamed of how I treated you.' Another pause. 'I'm so sorry.'

Still she said nothing.

'Could we meet up? I really miss you.'

Sara felt an agony of hesitation. 'You've still got a lot on your plate with Adam, Bernard. You should concentrate on that.' She knew she sounded distant, but if she put even an ounce of feeling into her words, she would cry . . . And perhaps capitulate.

Bernard groaned. 'God, Sara, please. Just a coffee . . . half an hour?'

'I can't see you, Bernard.' As she said what she'd planned to say, she felt her body rebel. She began to shake, her heart hammering, her guts churning. It was like it was shouting, 'For God's sake, woman, get to that café. Sit with him, look into his eyes, remember what you mean to each other.' But her pragmatic brain overrode her body, forcing her to remember what it was like in the house on the cliff. Adam was clearly moving forward. But that didn't mean he would welcome her back. And their future still hung in the balance.

She breathed through another loaded silence, then heard Bernard clear his throat.

'The bottom line is . . . you're simply the best thing that's ever happened to me, Sara.'

His dull, defeated acceptance of her decision thudded leaden on her ears. The urge to run to him at that very moment tugged at her like an impatient child. For a split second, she wavered. 'I hope things work out for you and the family, Bernard,' she said, through her tears.

As she clicked off, she heard him calling her name in a long-drawn-out sigh. Still shaking, she realized she hadn't mentioned the stuff she'd left in his house. And neither had he. But she was too distressed to call him back.

52

Adam's request came as a shock to Bernard. He'd seen a change in his son, starting from the time he'd thought he'd seen Ilsa outside the window – which coincided with the start of his sessions with Janet Bairstow. After just a few appointments, it was clear that Adam revered his therapist. He might come home unsettled by the hour with her, but it was obviously helping. Now he was starting to be able to talk to Bernard about the past with a modicum of understanding and perspective.

His son said to him one day, as they were toasting bagels for breakfast, 'Janet thinks it could help to talk to Maria's husband – if he'll let me.' Adam had searched his father's face. 'She says it might be good if you came too. I didn't think you'd want to. I'm going anyway, but I'd rather go with you.' Bernard, in spite of hearing the request like a knife to his throat, had felt he had no choice but to agree.

Is this madness? Bernard wondered, as they approached the house in the Hastings suburb – the appointment negotiated by a police family liaison officer, whom Paul Kemp had insisted need not be present. He was feeling nauseous, the coffee he'd drunk in nervy gulps earlier repeating on him unpleasantly. He glanced across at his son as he drew up in the silent close. It was nearly eleven in the morning and the place was deserted. Adam looked clean and smart and incredibly tense. But there was a light in his eye that Bernard had not seen in a while: determination.

'OK?' Bernard asked, inhaling slowly in an attempt to unknot his stomach. He reached over and gave his son's thigh a comforting nudge.

Adam shot him an apprehensive look, but didn't reply, just undid his seatbelt and opened the car door.

The jolly ding-dong of the doorbell seemed completely at odds with their mission. Bernard thought they probably looked like Jehovah's Witnesses or men from the council to any neighbours twitching their nets. The frosted-glass panels of the door showed a passing shadow, but at first there was no sound from inside. *Maybe he's changed his mind*, Bernard thought – indeed hoped.

Adam glanced at him, whispered, 'Shall I ring again?'

Bernard shook his head. 'He's in there,' he mouthed silently.

Finally, the glass filled with a looming figure and the door was slowly pulled open.

Paul Kemp was in his mid-thirties, tall and thin, with floppy brown hair and pale eyes behind rimless glasses. His expression was hardly welcoming, his mouth a thin line, eyes blinking nervously. 'Come in,' he said, standing back.

As they hovered in silence in the small, featureless hall of the new build – a couple of prints of boats in a harbour, a square mirror in a bobbly, sea-blue glass frame, cream-painted walls – Bernard took control.

Holding out his hand to Paul, he introduced himself, then Adam.

Paul stiffened, his hand barely connecting with Bernard's

before he withdrew it quickly. For Bernard, Paul Kemp was the poster boy for his crime. The living victim. Seeing him in the flesh was strange. He had grown in Bernard's memory all these years, taken on a strength and power that the man in front of them did not possess.

The kitchen, into which Paul herded them, was equally bland, with French windows leading onto a garden that was barely more than a patch of recently sown grass surrounded by a woven-wood fence, looking as raw as the lawn.

Seeing his gaze, Paul said, 'We've only been here a short while.'

Bernard noticed toys in the corner, a child's iPad, a plastic bowl piled with ponytail holders and hairclips on the table. He felt a pang for the motherless child.

'Sit,' Paul said curtly, indicating they should take the other chairs at the round kitchen table. 'I won't offer you tea. This shouldn't take long.'

All the carefully rehearsed speeches Bernard had prepared went clean out of his head. He looked at his son and took a big breath. 'Thank you for seeing us,' he began.

'Yeah, well . . .' Paul didn't finish and Bernard wondered why he had allowed them to come. He didn't have to.

Adam, sitting ramrod straight, began to talk. 'We wanted to come in person, to apologize . . . to let you know how truly sorry we are.' His voice shook slightly as he went on. 'For both the accident, and how we handled it afterwards. What we did was wrong on every level and we've regretted it every single day since.' Another shaky breath. 'Maybe this doesn't help – nothing will bring your wife back – but we wanted to tell you how sorry we both are.'

Adam's speech was clearly practised, and although his voice trembled, he seemed oddly calm. Which was far from how Bernard was feeling.

Paul was staring into space, his hands fiddling with a green felt tip he'd picked up from the table. When he looked up, his eyes were hard. 'If you're looking for forgiveness . . .'

'We're not,' Bernard stated.

Paul turned his gaze to him. 'You're a good liar,' he said sarcastically. 'Although I'm sure you *were* incredibly sorry for what you'd done when you stood up and spouted all that remorse. Must have been a nightmare.' He let out a long breath. 'But imagine what it feels like to be me, OK? A person's wife dying is terrible enough, but then the people responsible concoct a bunch of lies, manipulate the tragedy to suit themselves?' He stared hard at Bernard, making him cringe. 'I thought I knew the truth about how Maria died. It was all I was asking for. But now you and your son, here, have completely changed the story.'

Bernard nodded. 'I understand what you're saying. And you're right. I did a very stupid thing in the heat of the moment. It was absolutely and totally wrong.'

'"Stupid"? It was more than fucking stupid, mate. It was *criminal*.' Paul's tone was no longer restrained. 'Protecting your precious boy here.' He shot a contemptuous glance at Adam. 'So he gets to live his nice, cosy life and takes no fucking responsibility for his recklessness.' He shook his head. 'Maria never got that chance.'

Silence. Bernard was aware of the thrashing in his gut.

Then Adam spoke up again. 'If it's any consolation, it's

been a living hell from the moment I killed her.' Bernard cringed at his blunt choice of words, but his son hadn't finished. 'There is not a single day, hour or minute when I don't relive that terrible image of her lying on the road, not moving.' He cleared his throat. 'I dream about her. I wonder all the time what she would have been doing now, what she would have made of her life. I think of your daughter . . . you.' He stopped, gathered his breath. 'I live, she doesn't. That will haunt me till the day I die.' Adam's eyes misted, but he blinked the tears away. 'There is not even a small part of my life that is "nice" or "cosy", that is not overshadowed by what I did . . .' He shook his head, attempted to speak again, then raised his hand to indicate he had finished.

Paul, barely seeming to have heard Adam, looked straight ahead at the far wall, where children's paintings were Blu-Tacked in messy rows, twisting the pen angrily in his fingers as if he might snap it. *He must be living with someone new and had another child*, Bernard decided, as Paul's daughter had already been four when the accident happened, and these were drawings from a much younger hand.

'*You people*,' Paul started again, his voice rasping. 'You get away with anything because you know the right call to make, know how to manipulate the system. You should both be rotting in jail.'

That might still happen, Bernard thought grimly. Although, as the weeks went on, it began to feel – mistakenly, perhaps – as if the threat were fading. Might not the CPS have jumped on it sooner, if they intended to prosecute? He didn't know. But Paul's anger was escalating. It was time to go. Nothing would be gained by hanging around, waiting for him to punch one of them in the face.

He got up, abruptly. Adam looked momentarily taken aback but followed suit. Addressing Paul, Bernard said, 'Listen, thank you. You did a very generous thing, allowing us to come.'

Paul seemed surprised they were leaving, too. His face still flushed from his outburst, he shot up, then stood there, blinking even faster behind his glasses. He seemed desperate to say something else, but just continued to stare at them in bottled-up silence. Bernard held out his hand. Paul didn't take it this time, his own hands crossed and pressed firmly under each armpit. Bernard could almost see the unspoken words inflating the man in front of him like air in a balloon.

Searching his face, he saw the tears before Paul seemed aware of them himself.

Into the silence, Paul said, his voice choked, 'It was partly my fault.'

Bernard felt Adam start in surprise by his side.

Paul covered his face with his hands, obviously trying to smother his sobs. When he looked up, his expression was pure devastation. 'I lied as well. To the court. I said I hadn't spoken to her since she left to go on the ride.' He sniffed and rubbed his nose with the back of his hand. 'Which was technically true. I didn't *speak* to her because she didn't pick up. But I called her . . . what, ten times? I never mentioned that.'

Bernard frowned, but Paul was still talking. 'We had this row. Just a stupid thing about Becky's pick-ups. But she slammed out the door in a mood. So I called her . . . over and over . . . wanting to make peace.' He stopped again, overcome. 'Her phone was smashed, so I don't know if she was finally going to answer me . . . but I think that's why she stopped. If she hadn't, maybe you wouldn't have hit her. Maybe she'd have been well past the spot by then.' He threw his arms into the air. 'If only I'd waited till she got home instead of nagging her . . . She never knew I was sorry . . . She never knew. You're the one who killed her, of course, but I'll never know if I contributed to her death by calling so persistently.'

The three men seemed set in stone in the chilly, neat kitchen as Paul's words sank in. Bernard understood Paul beating himself up: he'd experienced similar torment himself over Ilsa's death. And, in truth, any accident was a couple of seconds, a couple of feet, a split-second decision from a different outcome. But his son had still swerved onto the wrong side of the road.

Adam moved forward. Bernard thought he might be about to embrace Paul. But he stopped short. Instead, he reached out and grazed the man's sleeve with a sympathetic hand.

Paul saw them into the hall without a word. But this was a very different silence. As he opened the door, Paul picked up his wallet from where it lay on the ledge under the blue-framed mirror. As they watched, he pulled out a dog-eared photograph, gazing at it for a moment before turning it so Adam could see. It was of a pretty brunette with large brown eyes and an engaging smile.

'Maria,' he said simply. 'Please . . . try to remember her like this and not lying dead on that sodding road.'

Bernard had no idea how he got home. They drove in

complete silence, both men knocked for six, holding their breath until they were safely clear of the house. They were in shock. The visit had gone some way, however, towards laying a ghost. Paul, it was clear, had survived, moved on as much as he ever would. He had a new family. He was not the shell of a man Bernard had observed in the courtroom.

'Talk later?' he said to Adam, as they pulled up at the cliff house. 'Think I'll go down to the beach, walk off some of the tension.'

Adam glanced at his father anxiously. 'It was helpful, wasn't it, Dad?'

'For me? Absolutely . . . I was so proud of you in there.'

After a long sigh, his son said quietly, 'It's been the most important day of my life.'

The beach was peopled by windswept dog-owners and their pets, but otherwise empty – no one he had to smile at or to whom he should say hello, thank goodness.

As he crunched across the stones in the soft spring air, he found all thoughts of the morning's visit were driven out, replaced by a vivid, pulsing memory: Sara, naked in his arms in the cold, midnight sea. He physically jerked as he felt again the aching sweetness of her bare skin beneath the waves, so soft and smooth against his fingers. Walking faster, he tried to dispel the image. It would do him no good. That door, as she'd made clear in her phone call, was firmly shut. He had nothing to offer her, anyway.

Bernard walked on, forcing his thoughts – painful as they were – back to Maria's husband. 'You should both be rotting in jail.' The man's words echoed around his mind.

He had never visited a prison. Like many others, he'd seen plenty of grim images on the news or in film and television dramas. He'd tried on a number of occasions to imagine himself locked into a cell, on a rickety metal bunk, with an open toilet, sharing the cramped, probably Victorian space with another convict – who might be at best annoying, at worst violent or nuts – although Naz had said his so-called 'white-collar' crime would probably mean he'd serve any sentence somewhere like Ford open prison in Sussex, with all the suave conmen and money-launderers. Liars, just like him.

Adam always shrugged his shoulders when Bernard brought up court and prison. He didn't seem to care. In his son's mind, it was clear the worst had already happened.

He was tired, he realized, to the very bottom of his soul. It was as if he'd been primed and on the alert for months now – ever since the night Carrie had phoned about Adam. Never quite resting, never completely switching off. Even further back than that, he knew he'd felt no real peace of mind since before Ilsa died. The family secret and subsequent dislocation from the twins had edited, tinged, skewed all his exchanges. Especially with Sara. *Why didn't I come clean with her, right from the start?* It was as if he'd just accepted the lies as part of the fabric of his daily life, like a chronic condition.

But now, in the light of the meeting with Paul Kemp, he felt the faint, unfamiliar stirrings of hope. He was still reeling from it, of course. Even if a ghost had been partially laid, reliving that terrible day in Paul's presence had shaken him, Adam too. But as he stepped over a slimy wooden groin and into a shallow pool of seawater, damp seeping through his trainers to his socks, he was aware that today had been a sort of progress, however small, for them both. They had faced their demons. There was other progress, too. Scattering Ilsa's ashes was now a plan to which both the twins had agreed. Adam was clearly loving his new direction towards gaming. It was only the absence of Sara in his life that left a smarting rupture in his hope.

53

'I'm thinking of going away,' Sara told Peggy over the phone. 'With the money from Granny, I thought maybe I'd take a few months off, go travelling. Margaret suggested I should, before she died. She wanted me to have an adventure, she said.'

Peggy laughed. 'You sound like an excited gap-year student, Mum. What about your clients?'

'I can sort them out . . . leave at the beginning of May, perhaps.'

'Where would you go?'

'Well, I'd start in California with Joni, do the trip I had to cancel because of Granny – be there for her birthday. Then work my way up the coast: Big Sur, Yosemite, San Francisco . . . places I've always wanted to see.' The family had spent their holidays exclusively in Europe when Pete was alive. Places to which they could drive in his van, ignore his phobia of planes.

'On your own? Would that be safe?' Peggy asked, sounding worried.

Sara laughed. 'I won't be visiting crack dens or drug cartels, sweetheart. I think California is pretty tourist-friendly.' It felt a bit scary, travelling without a companion, but also exhilarating – she'd be shaking off all of her responsibilities for what felt like the first time in her life.

'Maybe Joni can come with you.'

'I think she's too busy. Anyway, nothing's set in stone. I'll give it some proper thought and let you know what I decide.'

'Is this trip anything to do with Bernard?' Peggy asked cautiously, after a small silence. 'You wanting to get away?'

Sara could tell that her daughter was curious to hear the details about why they were not together any more. She'd said very little to either Peggy or Joni, let it be assumed it was a mutual parting of the ways. 'Not really. I need a change of scene, I think,' she replied, not entirely untruthfully. 'Do something just for myself. I really miss Granny, but I suppose I do feel a bit freer now I don't have to keep a constant eye.'

'I liked Bernard,' Peggy said wistfully, after a moment, 'I know he had stuff going on, but I thought he was a really great guy.'

'Me too,' Sara said, with a catch in her throat that she quickly cleared. 'Now, tell me what's happening with Beng, I still haven't met the man.'

'Oh, that's over, too. I dumped him last week. Turned out to be a bit of a flake,' declared her daughter, with commendable nonchalance.

Sara listened with one ear as Peggy went on to list all her ex-boyfriend's transgressions.

Her travel idea was just another of her spurts of forced enthusiasm with which she was trying to restart her life. More training, moving house and learning Spanish had all been given the once-over and rejected for lack of even the slightest inclination. Getting far away from Lewes, from her work routine, from friends and all the things that triggered memories of Bernard seemed like the best plan so far. By the time she returned, her mind would have shaken itself free of the recent past. She would be able to start afresh with a clean slate. And maybe with renewed hope, which was sorely missing from her world. Or so she told herself.

After her phone call with Peggy, she didn't allow herself time in which to change her mind. Clicking on Joni's number, she left a message: *Thinking of coming over for a visit sometime early May. Is this a good idea? Talk soon, love you xxx.* Because she knew that once her daughter had her teeth into a plan, there would be no shilly-shallying, no turning back.

Hell, yeah, Mum came back an almost instant reply, the message littered with clapping hands and pumping heart emojis.

Sara's fifty-ninth birthday came and went with a delicious tapas supper Sammi had painstakingly prepared: mouth-wateringly crisp, salty *chipirones*, *patatas bravas* to blow your head off, charred *padrón* peppers, thick slices of herby tortilla, Serrano ham and mixed olives. She drank too much, the evening outwardly lively and fun with her friends, but she couldn't help missing Bernard – knowing how much he would have relished the occasion. She wondered if he even knew it was her birthday. At some point she'd probably told him, as he had her – his, she knew, was in early June. But they had not managed to live through a whole year of birthday celebrations.

Her trip to California was now written in stone: flights booked, car hired, two weeks with Joni on the slate, and various local trips planned. After that it was up to Sara how far and for how long she ventured on her own. Right now, she had butterflies whenever she thought about wrenching herself out of her comfort zone and boarding the plane. But she was also aware of a pleasurable sense of anticipation.

'I'm going up to the cliff house tomorrow,' she told Precious and Sammi, as they sat in the warm April evening, the setting sun filtering through the trees in the nearby gardens. Each had an espresso, while a slab of almond chocolate and a bowl of dusty red grapes were doing the rounds. 'I need to collect the rest of my stuff before I go away.'

Precious frowned. 'Will he be there?'

It was clear from her friends' comments over past weeks that they were in two minds about Bernard. Sammi, with his soft heart, felt, on balance, that Sara should not shut the door on him. Precious worried that if she didn't, she would just be back at square one, overwhelmed by the Lockmore drama again. Sara was pretty sure both saw through her protestations that she was over him.

She shook her head slightly, as if it were not important. His text had been short in response to her asking about the best time to collect her stuff: *I'll be out of the house Thursday and Friday this week x.* Which she took to mean he didn't want to see her. *I don't want to see him, either.* She dreaded the prospect, in fact, knowing it might spark such a longing that she wouldn't be able to hide her feelings. But she also wanted to see him so much she felt as if her skin were being scorched. 'I'm relieved,' she said quickly.

Precious did not speak, but her eyes were kind and quietly sceptical.

'It'd be too awkward,' Sara added, as if her friend had spoken.

'What about Adam?' Precious asked.

She had thought of this, too. 'I've no idea if he's still there. But I assume he'll make himself scarce if he is . . . and he knows I'm coming round.'

Sara could hardly have been more nervous the following day – even compared to the first time she'd come up to the cliff house on the night of the storm. There was no sign of Bernard's Mercedes. She didn't know whether to sigh with relief or cry with disappointment. She reckoned it wouldn't take her long to pack her things – perhaps twenty minutes, at most: she had never moved a huge amount of stuff up to Bernard's. Now that she was there, and on the point of putting her key into the lock, she couldn't wait to be gone again.

The place was its usual silent, cloistered self, a faint smell of toast floating on the still air. She stood by the door and listened. Not a sound. She had knocked on the front door, prior to letting herself in, but no one had answered. Exhaling slowly, she almost tiptoed up the stairs to the bedroom, feeling furtive and uneasy, as if she was an intruder.

Throwing her suitcase from the bottom of the cup-board onto the neatly folded turquoise quilt, she hurried to pack each half, carelessly folding her dresses and sweat-ers and layering them on top of trainers and her red espadrilles. Then she moved into the bathroom, cram-ming her creams and hair products into a washbag too small for the purpose. The faster she worked, the less time there was to be upset by the scent of Bernard's shaving soap, the sight of his toothbrush, his reading glasses lying on the night table beside the bed.

Emerging from the en-suite, her head full of those days when they'd showered together, cuddled and laughed in the darkness, she jumped, heart thumping. Adam stood silently in the doorway.

'God, you gave me a fright,' Sara said, palm to her chest. 'I didn't think anyone was here.'

He shifted on his bare feet. 'Sorry ... I was out walking.'

'I'm just collecting my things. I'm going away,' she said quickly.

He nodded. But he didn't move from the doorway.

Tucking the washbag into the case and closing each side, she barely glanced at him as she asked, 'How are you?'

'I'm ... OK,' he said, a quiet smile lighting up his face in a way she had never seen before. 'Better, anyway.'

'That's good.' She knew she sounded brusque, but she had no desire to get into the politics of Adam's recovery, not again. She flopped one side of the large case over the other and began to labour with the outside zip, pressing down on the bulging canvas and struggling to unite the two. She wished Adam would go away.

Then he was by her side. 'Let me,' he said, bringing his masculine strength to the situation. In his hands, the zip toggle moved effortlessly around the case. 'There,' he said, lifting it to the floor and extending the handle for her.

She smiled up at him. 'Thank you.'

For a second, he hovered. Then he plonked himself

down on the bed. It was clear he wanted to say something. Anxious to go, but curious, she waited, hand on the case handle. It was stuffy in the room, the spring sunshine burning hot through the skylight. She realized she was sweating and thirsty.

'I just wanted to say that I know you did your best . . . with Dad . . . and the whole situation.'

Surprised, she didn't reply.

Adam was looking at his hands, pressed together between his knees. 'For a start, you backed Carrie up . . . That was huge.' Silence fell as he pulled at some loose skin on his index finger. 'And the therapy . . . you were right about that too.'

Giving a small sigh, Sara sat down next to him, not speaking. His words seemed so tenuous, she felt they might evaporate if she interrupted him.

'We went to see Maria's husband the other day. I know you suggested that to Dad, as well.'

'That was brave,' she said, the words scraped almost unwillingly off her tongue. 'How did it go?'

Adam sighed. 'Hellish . . . but ultimately helpful – for all of us, I think.'

'And the therapy?'

He gave a soft laugh. 'Life-changing.'

Wow, Sara thought. *Things really have moved on.*

'No word from the CPS?'

He shook his head. 'It's been so long . . . I try not to think about it.' He pulled a face. 'Impossible, of course.'

How's your dad? The question hung heavy in the quiet room, but she didn't ask it.

'I'm glad you're getting help, Adam.'

364

Finally, he turned and met her eye. His own were painfully similar to Bernard's and she caught her breath. 'I wanted to say . . . we couldn't have done it without you.' His glance shifted as if he were embarrassed. 'Thank you.'

He got up abruptly and walked towards the door. When he reached it, he turned, and added softly, almost as an afterthought, 'I'm sorry I behaved like such an arse, Sara.' Then he was gone.

She heard a door close quietly along the landing as she sat there in stunned silence, trying to unpick what had just happened. Adam seemed like a different man from the one who'd watched her leave that day with barely disguised glee. *How difficult must that have been, just now?* she thought, with respect. *He's come a long way.*

She got up and began to drag her case towards the stairs, suddenly desperate to get away. Letting her guard down, engaging with the problems that had driven her away in the first place, had brought everything back, like the whoosh of an erupting geyser. She wished Adam hadn't spoken to her. His apology was gratifying . . . and moving. She didn't want to be moved.

54

Bernard threw a pizza into the oven. He'd given up cooking, no longer willing to make the effort. All day he'd been on tenterhooks, knowing that Sara would be at the house at some point. The first thing he'd done on arriving home was to go upstairs and check the cupboards. He'd stood contemplating the rattling empty hangers for a long time and wanting to weep.

Earlier, almost as if Sara had prompted it – as she had, unwittingly, so often in the past – he'd rung Naz Kumar, got him to check what was happening with their case. It was over three months now and they'd heard nothing. The call just added to his low mood, reminded him of what was still to come.

Adam sloped downstairs.

'Hey,' Bernard greeted his son, who made a beeline for the fridge and brought out a can of gluten-free beer.

'What's for supper?'

'Pizza . . . again. Did you see Sara?' He hoped, if his son had, that he hadn't been rude to her.

Sitting down at the table and flipping open the tab on his beer with a thumb, Adam nodded slowly. 'Yeah.'

'How was she?'

'Seemed OK.'

Frustrated, Bernard almost snapped, '"OK"? What did she say?'

Adam didn't reply at once as he sipped his beer. Bernard felt his body fizzing with impatience.

'I said I was sorry, Dad. I said I'd been an arse.' He gave him a forlorn smile. 'I thanked her for all the help she'd tried, unsuccessfully, to offer us stubborn Lockmore fucks.'

Bernard let go of the breath held tight in his constricted chest. 'Right . . . That's good . . . And what did she say?'

'Not a lot. Just that she was pleased I'd got help.'

'Did she mention me?' He'd noticed the key he'd given her sitting on the ledge by the front door when he came in, but he'd ignored it. He wasn't sure what he'd expected from her visit. What he'd been hoping for.

Adam shook his head. 'Just packed her things and left.'

Silence fell over the kitchen, both men lost in their own thoughts.

'I'm glad you apologized, Adam.'

Adam chewed his thumbnail. 'She didn't do anything wrong, Dad. We punished her for being the voice of reason . . . for speaking the truth.' He sighed. 'But I just didn't want her around and I was so cruel . . . I'm ashamed of myself.'

The timer pinged. Bernard went to open the oven and take out their supper.

'She said she was going away, Dad.'

Bernard spun round, almost causing the pizza – which looked overcooked and unappetizing now – to slide off the tray. In the past he would have put a salad with it. But tonight he just set it on the table and handed his son the slicing wheel. 'Away? Where to?'

'She didn't say.'

'Maybe she's visiting Joni . . .' Bernard mused, realizing,

after the initial shaft of panic at the thought of her not being there, that it didn't matter one way or the other if she was going for a week or a year. He wouldn't be seeing her anyway.

After a long pause, Adam said, 'Dad . . . do you think you should talk to Sara, try to get her to come back? You two were solid, weren't you? I feel so guilty . . . It was my fault she left.' He rolled the wheel across the pizza without much enthusiasm. 'I know you'll kill me for saying this now, when the damage is already done, but she's nice, a really decent person.'

Bernard gazed out of the window as he waited for Adam to serve himself. It was an unfairly beautiful spring evening – not a breath of wind – and he'd have loved nothing better than to be sitting outside on the terrace with Sara and a glass of good wine. Looking back at his son, he said, 'We still have this problem hanging over our heads. I don't want her to have to deal with that . . . Anyway, I imagine she's moved on.'

55

It was evening, two days before Sara's departure. Precious had come over after work and was now lying on her stomach across the bed while Sara packed, supposedly offering advice on what to take.

Picking up a yellow cardigan from the pile waiting to go into the case, she pulled a face. 'Not sure about this one, darlin'. Is mustard a good look, even in the Californian sun?'

Sara laughed. 'OK, maybe not. I've hardly worn it and there's probably a reason. But I'll need something for the evenings.' She held up a thin blue sweater with three-quarter sleeves, a question in her eyes.

'Yeah, better. Is it cold at night?'

'Cooler, not cold. It should be lovely during the day, Joni says.'

'Wish I was coming with you. We could have had some fun, rocking up the west coast like Thelma and Louise – without the grisly denouement, of course.' She rolled onto her back, still watching Sara. 'Are you really going to go it alone?'

Sara felt suddenly overwhelmed. Clutching the sweater to her chest, she pulled an anxious face. 'I think I am. I don't see myself as the sort of person who does intrepid things, so I am a bit nervous. But I want to do Margaret proud. It's such a privilege, being able to take time off like this.' She smiled. 'I'm going to make the most of it.'

'Oh, sweetheart. I'm so jealous. You'll have a brilliant time. And it'll be good, putting distance between you and any chance of bumping into Bernard.'

Sara gulped.

'Listen, go and be with gorgeous Joni. Have a blast, eat watermelon, get a tan, snog a surfer. Put the last few months behind you.'

Sara tried to connect with Precious's vision. But since seeing Adam she'd felt discombobulated, scratchy, as if she had an actual rash on her body. Being at the cliff house had punched a hole in her albeit flimsy defences. 'I'm not going to forget him, though, am I?'

Her friend sighed impatiently. 'No, obviously not. But things fade with time, you know they do.' Then she sat up straight, her face suddenly questioning as she shot Sara an earnest look. 'You could always phone him before you go, I suppose, get final closure . . .'

'For God's sake, Precious! What are you saying? I'm doing my level best to move on and you're suggesting I *call him*?' Sara flinched. 'Anyway, we have closure.'

Precious calmly raised her eyebrows. 'Keep your wig on. It just seems like the only thing you really want to do.'

56

Bernard saw Naz's name come up on his screen just as he was about to leave for work. He was late, it was after ten, and he had a ton of stuff to do at the office, but he had lain in bed for hours last night, unable to sleep, yet too lethargic to get up and frighten the neighbours with a midnight walk. Then he'd crashed heavily until only half an hour ago. He still felt woozy and sleep-deprived, even with a couple of mugs of strong black coffee inside him. 'Hi, Naz.'

'Good morning, Bernard. Are you driving?'

'Driving? No, why?' His heart began to beat faster. It was impossible to tell from his solicitor's voice whether the news was good or not – Naz always sounded like a slightly formal, benign uncle, even though he was pretty much the same age as Bernard.

'Just thought you might like to swing by the office on your way to work?'

'Oh, my God! You've heard? Tell me now, Naz, for Christ's sake. I can't wait till I get to your bloody office.'

'OK, well, the CPS have finally been in touch, after days of my harassing them –'

'Get on with it.' Bernard was familiar with the phrase, 'your heart's in your mouth', and suddenly he knew where it came from. His was currently choking him.

He heard Naz laugh but did not dare to believe. 'Just had an email from Mr Norris.' His voice took on the nasal tones of a humourless apparatchik as he went on, '"Taking all circumstances of the case into account, and after careful review, this office has decided to terminate all proceedings against Mr Bernard Lockmore and Mr Adam Lockmore on the charge of perverting the course of justice, following the fatal accident on Hunter's Race", et cetera, et cetera.' He took a breath and went on in his normal voice. 'There's more, but that's the important bit. Which means, in plain English, they've dropped the case. No further action will be taken. You're both free men, Bernard. We'll get paper confirmation in due course, with a full note of the reasons for the decision.'

Bernard felt his legs begin to give way under him and staggered across to a kitchen chair. Still clutching the mobile to his ear, he asked, his voice like a weak echo from far away, 'So we're not going to prison?' His question was genuine, but his trembling relief in that moment was not only to do with the spectre of incarceration being dispelled, although that was important, of course. It was the realization that, in a legal sense at least, it was over. The truth was out in the open. There were no secrets to suppress, no more lies to tell, no further hoops to jump through.

Naz was really laughing now. 'No, Bernard. You're not going to prison.'

'Are you absolutely sure, Naz? They got the case number right and everything?'

'One hundred per cent. I'll forward Mr Norris's email so you can see for yourself. Listen, I've got another call coming in, but drop by if you fancy a chat about it all.'

His solicitor clicked off but Bernard continued to stare

at his phone screen, as if he expected it to spring to life again with the single word: 'JOKE'.

Can I believe it? he asked himself. For more than five years, the horror not only of Maria Kemp's death but his subsequent lie – the prospect of being found out – had hung over his head like a fully loaded Messerschmitt bomber. Now the reality refused to sink in, although his whole body was tingling, every nerve end seething, as if his flesh had accepted the truth before his brain was able to. *Adam.*

Rising to his feet with effort, he climbed the stairs to his son's room and banged loudly. When Adam didn't respond, Bernard barged in and shook his sleeping son's shoulder vigorously, eliciting a grumpy growl from the figure on the bed.

'Fuck's sake, Dad.'

'Wake up, Adam, you need to hear this.'

At his father's urgent tone, Adam was immediately alert and wide-eyed. He shot upright in bed. 'What?'

Taking a deep breath, Bernard said, 'They're not going to prosecute.' Then he clasped his hands on top of his head and almost shouted, 'THEY'RE NOT GOING TO PROSECUTE!'

Adam gasped, swung his legs over the side of the bed and sprang to his feet. 'Fuck, Dad . . . Seriously? Neither of us?'

Bernard nodded.

Wrapping his arms around his body, he muttered, 'Oh, my God, oh, my God . . .' his eyes awash with tears. 'I thought this would never happen.' He stared at his father. 'Listen, Maria's still dead and I know I deserved to be punished, but . . .'

Bernard pulled his son into a strong embrace, holding him so tight that Adam laughed and pushed him off, throwing himself back onto the bed. 'Fuck, can't get my head around this . . . So what happens now, Dad?'

'Naz said there'll be a formal letter. I'll go over now and see him, find out more.'

Adam exhaled loudly, spoke quietly: 'I feel so, so, *so* fucking lucky right now.'

That evening, Bernard and Adam both had a stiff whisky in front of them as they sat facing each other on opposite sofas. Bernard, after telling Joe the good news, had met Naz for a relieved coffee in his local café and taken the rest of the day off. He and Adam had gone down to the beach and walked and walked for hours, a lot of it in dazed silence, then come back to a sausage and slaw bun at the Pig.

'How are you feeling?' Bernard asked.

Adam took a long time to reply. 'Mixed, I suppose. It's been such a relief, since going to the police, that it's all out in the open, that I'm not living a lie any more. But there was still the constant anxiety about what it would mean for us both.' He took a breath. 'It feels huge that that's over. Although the guilt doesn't go away, of course.'

'Guilt has been given too much bloody head room in this family. I'm calling time.'

'You weren't the one driving, Dad. I'm not going to prison, but Maria Kemp is still dead. I basically got off scot free.'

Eyeing his son in amazement, Bernard said, 'You really think you haven't been punished, Adam? Hasn't the last five years been a living hell for you?'

Adam shrugged.

'Would prison have made you feel better?'

His son did not reply for a long moment. 'I used to think so. But now I realize it wouldn't have made much difference. I'll never forget that day, even if I was banged up for all eternity. Janet's helped me such a lot, given me some perspective . . . but I know it'll haunt me forever.'

Bernard shuddered at his son's words – the truth they told. He wasn't going to argue. He hoped Adam would find peace one day, come to terms with what had been, after all, a momentary – albeit fatal – lapse of concentration, loss of control. Which could happen to any of us, every single time we get behind the wheel of a car.

57

The evening before Sara left for California, she sat in the garden, eating the remains of some Cheddar on an oat-cake, with a cup of fennel tea and an apple on the table in front of her. The night was warm, almost muggy, and redolent of spring, the wall of her neighbour's house opposite covered in a riot of pale lavender-blue wisteria, her own white lilac bush perfuming the air with its sweet, almost cloying scent. The approach of summer reminded her of the previous year: those halcyon days when she and Bernard first met, when she felt those first stirrings of love. She inhaled sharply, holding her breath, blinking away tears until the spike of pain subsided. *It will be good to get away.*

Everything was done: clients wound down – Julian was now in good health and only came to see her for a top-up session every six weeks – case packed, flight checked in, fridge cleared, rubbish bags taken out to the bins. Her plane didn't leave till five fifteen, arriving in Los Angeles in the evening, and it seemed like an age to wait, although she would have to leave much earlier to get to the airport and plough through security.

A lonely night stretched ahead as she waited to begin a trip that she kept telling herself was supposed to – in some miraculous, arcane fashion she chose not to examine – change her life. Precious's words kept floating back to her . . .

Phone him. She found herself repeating the two words over and over in her mind. However much she stamped on them with the weight of all the solid reasons why it would be a mistake, they kept popping up, like some persistent mantra. She knew she wouldn't call, but she picked up her phone anyway, cradling it in her hand. And jumped as it began to buzz loudly. *Bernard.* She stared for what seemed like an eternity at his name, her breath suddenly suspended.

'Hello?' Her voice, even to herself, sounded faint, hardly above a whisper.

'Hi, Sara.'

Almost unable to hear him through the blood pounding in her ears, she waited.

'Uh, Adam said you were going away soon?'

'Yes, tomorrow. California, to visit Joni. Then I might take off up the coast for a while.'

Her words were mere cyphers, mechanically expelled, the painful subtext roaring beneath.

'Right. Sounds fun.' She heard him inhale sharply. 'OK . . . Listen, I know this isn't really relevant to you any more . . . but I thought you might like to know . . . that the CPS have dropped the case.'

She gasped. 'Oh, Bernard, that's fantastic news. When did you hear?'

'Today, this morning. I still can't really take it in.'

'And Adam?'

'Relieved, obviously, but still plagued with guilt. He says he always will be.'

There was silence. Sara couldn't speak. She was finding it so hard to quell the feelings evoked by the sound of Bernard's voice.

'Anyway, I just rang to tell you.'

'Thank you.'

There was a short silence, during which she was aware of her heart thudding uncomfortably in her chest. She scraped with her nail at a mark on the wooden garden table – it suddenly seemed vitally important she remove it.

'Can I just say something before you go?' she heard Bernard ask. Before she had the chance to stop him, he went on, 'I'm so sorry about all the mistakes I made . . . how badly I treated you, Sara. Adam was right when he said we turned you away because you spoke the truth.'

She swallowed hard, on the verge of tears.

'Have a wonderful trip,' Bernard added softly, when she didn't reply. She noticed the crack in his voice and knew she should say goodbye. The words just wouldn't come. 'Bye, then . . . Take care of yourself,' he said, then clicked off.

She went on clenching the mobile long after Bernard had gone, sitting there, stock still in the dark, silent garden, tears streaming down her face. But her heart did not return to its normal rhythm, her breathing still echoing quick and harsh in her upper chest. She felt like an athlete on the starting blocks before a race, every sinew in her body tensed for an action over which she had no control. As she sat there, she heard an ominous rumble of thunder and raindrops began to plop onto her hair and cheek. She didn't wipe them away, just let the coolness wash over her. As if in a dream, she got up. Most things Sara did in her life were planned, carefully thought through. But not tonight. She picked up her bag and keys, pulled on the first jacket that came to hand – flimsy cotton, no protection against the worsening weather – in a trance, barely aware of what she was doing.

The rain poured onto the windscreen like an emptying bath, the car shook, buffeted by the wind, and the roads were slick with sheets of water being blown hither and yon. It had got to be the worst spring storm she could remember in recent years, and here she was, driving through it – no other nutter on the empty road – urged on by pure instinct to see Bernard face to face one more time before she got on that plane tomorrow.

The outline of the cliff house, backlit by the electric storm, looked like something out of a horror movie as she pulled in beside Bernard's car. Without giving herself time to change her mind, she forced open the Mini's door in the teeth of the wind and fought her way in the pouring rain to the front door. By the time she reached it, water was sluicing off her as if she was standing in the shower.

After what seemed like a lifetime, Bernard opened the door. 'Sara?'

She searched his face, suddenly unsure how welcome this impulsive visit of hers would be. He looked taken aback for a second, then smiled broadly.

'Come in, come in. God, you're soaked. I can't believe you drove through this mayhem.'

He didn't hug her. Nor she him. She pushed her wet hair back from her eyes and peeled off her sodden jacket. 'I hope you don't mind?'

'No, God, no! It's wonderful to see you. I'll get a towel.'

She caught sight of Adam standing in the shadows near the stairs as she waited for Bernard to return and steeled herself. But his 'Hi, Sara' was accompanied by a friendly smile.

She dried her hair as best she could, as they all stood about in awkward silence.

'Listen, I'll leave you two alone . . . Got stuff I need to do for tomorrow,' Adam said, lifting his hand to her with a shy wave. 'Good to see you.'

Sara smiled her acknowledgement. 'Great news about the CPS,' she called after him. She heard his bedroom door shutting firmly.

'Cup of tea? Glass of wine?' Bernard asked. He seemed disoriented, caught off balance by her sudden appearance.

She opted for tea and sat down at the kitchen table while he put the kettle on. Suddenly she felt overcome with embarrassment. 'You must think I'm out of my mind,' she said to Bernard, 'dropping round on a night like this.'

He handed her a mug of tea and chose the chair opposite her. He'd forgotten the milk and had to get up again, retrieve it from the fridge, handing her the plastic bottle in silence. 'I'm glad you did,' he said softly.

She hardly dared meet his eyes for fear of what she would see there . . . what she would reveal in her own. Being with him like this felt so awkward, and so unbearably familiar . . . intimate. 'I don't know why I did,' she said. 'I just got into the car and drove . . .'

He raised an eyebrow. 'Does it matter?'

Tears filled her eyes. 'I'm sorry. This was stupid. I should probably go.'

She shook herself, trying to untangle her thoughts, as a brilliant blade of light split the sky, followed by a heavy thump of thunder growling directly overhead, echoing loudly across the sea into the distance. She shuddered, listening to the wind howling, tearing at the building as if intent on reducing it to a pile of timber and glass.

'You can't go anywhere in this,' Bernard stated, frowning at the din.

Time seemed suspended as the storm raged above them.

Then Bernard began to speak. 'The thought of you going away sent me into a tailspin. Adam kept telling me I should call you. But you were very clear it was over. And I totally understand why. I should never have –'

She put her hand up to interrupt him. 'Let's not.' Her mind was in utter confusion. Part of her wanted to get up and put her arms around him. Part of her wanted to flee – storm or not.

Silence fell again. Head bowed, she heard Bernard's chair scraping as he got to his feet. She looked up. He hesitated, giving her a doubtful grin. 'What do we do now?'

The question made her smile. And the smile turned to a laugh and the laughter turned to tears. And then she was also on her feet and she was taking him in her arms and hugging him, holding him so close that neither could breathe.

For a long time they stood like that. When she drew back, she saw tears in his eyes too.

'I've missed you so much,' he said.

They might have kissed, then, but they did not. Both were being cautious, neither taking anything for granted. As they drew apart, Bernard still held onto her hand. 'Stay until the storm's passed?' he asked.

She nodded, although rain still lashed the windows, the wind battering furiously around the house.

They went over to the sofa and sat side by side in silence. Sara felt all the chaos of the past months, the hurt and confusion, the tension and fear, sitting between them like a physical presence. A presence that had to be acknowledged, finally, had to be aired, like a musty blanket kept too long in a cupboard.

With a deep breath, she began to speak.

It was long into the night, when Sara and Bernard eventually ran out of steam – like the storm outside on the cliff – both of them exhausted. Each had had a chance to express their feelings. There was no blame attached, just a gradual unwinding of all the difficulties that had bedevilled them since the day their relationship had begun.

Lying back on the sofa cushions, Sara let out a sigh. She was almost floating with tiredness and emotion. She looked round at Bernard, a slight frown on her face.

'You know, the house feels different tonight.' She realized she'd sensed it as soon as she walked through the door. Something had lifted. It was as if the storm had mounted a deliberate attack. Invaded the place, dug out the dense, residual sorrow, guilt and fear that had accumulated over long years from all the secret corners and blown it out through the very walls themselves. The house seemed finally to be breathing . . . and at peace.

Bernard nodded slowly. 'Me and the twins scattered Ilsa's ashes last week. Up on the clifftop in the sunlight. It would have been her sixtieth birthday.' He paused. 'It was strange, Sara . . . Her ashes seemed to hover on the breeze for a moment, as if she was saying goodbye to us.' He gave a self-conscious laugh. 'Anyway, it felt good, letting her go. I'd been hanging on to her . . . all that guilt haunting me. I reckon it gave the place a strange atmosphere sometimes.'

'I used to think the house – Ilsa, maybe – was trying to get rid of me,' Sara said, almost embarrassed to admit it.

He laughed. 'Well, maybe she was! I thought I was the only one who felt it.'

There was a long silence.

Is this the end or the beginning? she wondered. Were they wrapping up their past together, readying themselves to move on? Or was there still a chink, a glimmer of something else? She stared at his profile as he sat beside her. Like the house, his whole being seemed quieter, calmer, missing the habitual tension that previously appeared to stalk him.

As if hearing her thoughts, Bernard turned to her and said, his tone uncertain, 'Have I completely wrecked what we had, Sara? Or . . .' He stopped. Then she watched him take a breath and start again, his voice resolute now. 'I know how I feel about you. That hasn't changed.'

It was cool in the room, so late into the wet spring night, and Sara drew her arms around her body. *If it were just about feelings*, she thought, knowing she loved the man sitting quietly beside her. But she also couldn't quite banish the residual wariness that still clung to her, like a stale perfume. Airing stuff was good but, like Adam with Maria, it didn't make it go away.

Bernard was eyeing her now, waiting for her to speak.

'I'm sorry, I don't think I can be clear about anything at the moment,' she said softly.

He nodded, and she sensed a modicum of relief in his expression. Her words, she realized, were not a flat-out rejection. And in that moment, she knew with absolute certainty that she was not rejecting him. Walking away, closing the door, never seeing Bernard again? *No*, her heart pronounced, with an insistence that overrode her aching brain. Although what it would feel like to commit to loving him again – having tried so hard in recent months to root him out of her heart – she was too tired to consider.

'I've been thinking,' Bernard was saying. 'I'd like to rebuild this place, start from scratch. Open it up, introduce more light and air.' He rested his hand gently on hers. He didn't go on, but she heard the unspoken in his silence: *We could build it together, Sara.*

But it felt too soon for them to be making plans. The outpourings from earlier were still raw and undigested. It was an idea she tucked quietly away in her mind, for perusal at another time. She squeezed his hand. 'I should get home.'

She thought he might try and persuade her to stay. But he just nodded.

Sara shivered as they stood outside in the cool dawn, the air washed clean and sparkling from the mayhem of the night before. Bernard put his arms around her.

'Seems like a trick of the light,' he said, his voice hardly above a whisper. 'You come from nowhere, popping up out of the stormy darkness. Now you're disappearing again . . . as if it was all just a lovely mirage.'

She laughed. 'Oh, I'm real enough.'

He exhaled. 'I'll miss you, Sara.'

She met his gaze, lost herself in his beautiful grey eyes. Then she found herself reaching up to kiss him – she just couldn't stop herself. But what started as a brief goodbye kiss lingered, neither drawing back, her eyes closing as she savoured the warmth of his mouth against hers, the tenderness with which he embraced her. It was as if they were kissing for the very first time. *And maybe we are*, she thought. This wasn't the Bernard she had met last summer in the tearoom. And she was not that same woman, laughing about the dentist and munching coffee cake. She hadn't forgotten, though, her initial reaction to him: *He looks nice*, she'd thought. That hadn't changed.

But if Sara sensed the faint glimmerings of something new between them in the kiss – something tempting but still hovering out of reach – it would have to wait. She had a plane to catch, a daughter to visit . . . a stirring adventure to embark upon.

'I'll miss you, too,' she said softly. The second kiss she dropped on Bernard's mouth stretched out, like the last, for a long moment, the touch of his lips reaching into every part of her body. She was saying goodbye, but this also felt like a holding kiss. One she knew she would relive in her months away . . . One she hoped he would remember, too.

Acknowledgements

Clare Bowron and Rebecca Hilsdon for your brilliant editorial input and encouragement.

The wonderfully supportive Maxine Hitchcock, Emma Henderson and all the first-class Penguin Michael Joseph team who pulled the book together.

Hazel Orme – for ironing out my syntax . . . again.

Jonathan Lloyd, my fantastic agent. Lucy Morris and all at Curtis Brown.

My dear family and friends.

Stephen Crocker and Michael Travers for their generosity at a fundraiser for the Sir John Hurt Film Trust. (They won the auction bid to have two characters named in this book and chose their mothers, Heather and Margaret. Their fictional versions have contributed greatly to my story.)

My sincere thanks to you all.

He just wanted a decent book to read ...

Not too much to ask, is it? It was in 1935 when Allen Lane, Managing Director of Bodley Head Publishers, stood on a platform at Exeter railway station looking for something good to read on his journey back to London. His choice was limited to popular magazines and poor-quality paperbacks – the same choice faced every day by the vast majority of readers, few of whom could afford hardbacks. Lane's disappointment and subsequent anger at the range of books generally available led him to found a company – and change the world.

'We believed in the existence in this country of a vast reading public for intelligent books at a low price, and staked everything on it'
Sir Allen Lane, 1902–1970, founder of Penguin Books

The quality paperback had arrived – and not just in bookshops. Lane was adamant that his Penguins should appear in chain stores and tobacconists, and should cost no more than a packet of cigarettes.

Reading habits (and cigarette prices) have changed since 1935, but Penguin still believes in publishing the best books for everybody to enjoy. We still believe that good design costs no more than bad design, and we still believe that quality books published passionately and responsibly make the world a better place.

So wherever you see the little bird – whether it's on a piece of prize-winning literary fiction or a celebrity autobiography, political tour de force or historical masterpiece, a serial-killer thriller, reference book, world classic or a piece of pure escapism – you can bet that it represents the very best that the genre has to offer.

Whatever you like to read – trust Penguin.